Perfecting & Reforming

PERSONAL RELIGION

Linwood Jackson, Jr.

PUBLISHED BY FIDELI PUBLISHING, INC.

ISBN: 978-1-60414-963-0

For information, email the author at
LinwoodJackson@hotmail.com

Published by
Fideli Publishing, Inc.
www.FideliPublishing.com

Contents

Introduction

1. It is terribly important that every one professing to hold some level of faith in the LORD's Christ know Him. It matters not how deep or how superficial that faith or understanding may be, for the counsel is, "Seek ye out of the book of the LORD, and read."[1] If there is a willing mind to feel after heaven's will and understanding, it should be encouraged to think and feel without restriction, and if the heart is touched at the sacrifice of His Christ, then every drive within the human will should be encouraged to bring the heart to fall prostrate before the throne heaven's High Priest for a re-education in personal manners of worship and service. It is alright if one be "so vexed, that he fell sick"[2] "for the excellency of the knowledge of Christ,"[3] for His counsel to such a troubled and trembling soul is, "Blessed are they that mourn: for they shall be comforted,"[4] and, "Blessed are they which do hunger and thirst after righteousness: for they shall be filled."[5]

2. The soul is not to be limited by the heart. The spirit of the mind is not to fall subject to the mind of the heart, becoming servant to the loud, intemperate, and uneducated members of the body. The mind that longs after heaven's Word does desire His understanding from some unnatural happening within the being, for as we are all born without a pure knowledge and experience of right according to the LORD's Standard, we are most naturally born with a conversation "fulfilling the desires of the flesh and of the mind."[6] The one touched by the illustration of the Spirit's sacrifice is brought to respect what they have heard

---

1 Isaiah 34:16
2 2 Samuel 13:2
3 Philippians 3:8
4 Matthew 5:4
5 Matthew 5:6
6 Ephesians 2:3

by "that which is against nature";[7] even as it says, "The Spirit of the LORD began to move him";[8] thus all who are moved by the Spirit are moved to continue "purifying their hearts by faith."[9]

3. "The spirit within me constraineth me,"[10] says the faithful, "for the love of Christ constraineth."[11] This is why Scripture says, "The spirit giveth life,"[12] and, "It is the spirit that quickeneth; the flesh profiteth nothing."[13] For "if ye live after the flesh, ye shall die: but if ye through the Spirit do mortify the deeds of the body, ye shall live."[14]

4. The strange appetite and passions associated with self, whether cultivated or inherited, are to fall under the authority of reason and a sanctified religion. The mind is to govern the heart with its mind and members, and this can only be done through a reformed and regenerated mind educated and corrected by the impression of the Spirit's will and counsel. A flesh-based religion will "glory in appearance, and not in heart."[15] A flesh-based faith born of tradition and superstition surrounded by inward policies and creeds will keep the spirit asleep and the soul temple unclean, for the Spirit has stirred up the mind to move it to reclaim its throne over self, pouring upon the heart a divine influence to cause the spirit to search out the place where that foreign stimulus has fallen out from.

5. "The times of refreshing shall come from the presence of the Lord"[16] when once the spirit should aggravate itself to come to an understanding on the One that it believes is its Savior. To keep the spirit from communicating with the Spirit for recovery of the mental and moral faculties is to embrace a further numbing of already benumbed senses, and to advance in decay those portions of our being that are already

---

7 Romans 1:26
8 Judges 13:25
9 Acts 15:9
10 Job 32:18
11 2 Corinthians 5:14
12 2 Corinthians 3:6
13 John 6:63
14 Romans 8:13
15 2 Corinthians 5:12
16 Acts 3:19

impaired, as the Spirit says, “All they that hate me love death.”[17] When once the heart is set to study after the praise of the LORD’s Faith, when once the spirit has chosen mental taxation and practical application to find out the fact behind His voice, there will be a bestowal of health within the conscience for the purpose of retaining His wisdom, for every word of the LORD is “life unto those that find them, and health to all their flesh.”[18]

6. Health to the flesh is the point of recovering the inward person, for the mind is to house every precept of this LORD’s Spirit “that ye may approve things that are excellent; that ye may be sincere and without offence till the day of Christ. Being filled with the fruits of righteousness.”[19] Herein it should be observed that only “the spirit may be saved in the day of the Lord Jesus.”[20] If the spirit should fail to endure a regeneration and a reformation at this present time, what good will it be to the individual, or to the ones who have failed to learn of and do heaven’s confidence, when all things should be made new and the LORD’s Government reigns throughout the entire earth without dispute? Will a heart and mind now stopped by fear or unbelief find peace in such a Country? Now is the time, if one has in them a longing to abide by His voice, to hear the charge, “Acquaint now thyself with him, and be at peace,”[21] and, “Receive, I pray thee, the law from his mouth, and lay up his words in thine heart.”[22]

7. Says the Spirit, “Forget not my law; but let thine heart keep my commandments.”[23] “Incline thine ear unto wisdom, and apply thine heart to understanding”;[24] “attend unto my wisdom, and bow thine ear to my understanding: that thou mayest regard discretion, and that thy lips may keep knowledge.”[25] “When wisdom entereth into thine heart,

---

17 Proverbs 8:36
18 Proverbs 4:22
19 Philippians 1:10, 11
20 1 Corinthians 5:5
21 Job 22:21
22 Job 22:22
23 Proverbs 3:1
24 Proverbs 2:2
25 Proverbs 5:1, 2

and knowledge is pleasant unto thy soul; discretion shall preserve thee, understanding shall keep thee."[26]

8. From learning of and doing the precepts of the Spirit's Faith, the wisdom and knowledge obtained will provide inward power to decide or act according to one's own judgment. No longer will the heart be a slave to self or the religious world, for the LORD's Word has done exactly what it is ordained to do, that is, "to preach deliverance to the captives, and recovering of sight to the blind, to set at liberty them that are bruised."[27] This is why the Spirit says, "Do not forget my law,"[28] for He has counseled every believer, "If ye love me, keep my commandments."[29] Just as this Christ obeyed every precept of His Father, He has left His assembly with the responsibility to also reverence every word of His LORD and Father, and that acknowledging is through "the washing of water by the word."[30] His Christ did "magnify the law"[31] of His name that we might become cognizant of how He anciently said, "A law shall proceed from me,"[32] for from hearing this law; which law is "the law of the Spirit of life";[33] "we might be made the righteousness of God in him."[34]

9. It is the "law of Christ,"[35] upheld by "the law of the Spirit of life"[36] "by the law of faith,"[37] that gives to the independent and sorrowful soul the disposition, "I applied mine heart to know, and to search, and to seek out wisdom, and the reason of things."[38] The believer is to search for the LORD's knowledge by "the words which the LORD of hosts hath sent in his spirit by the former prophets,"[39] for the hope of His

---

26 Proverbs 2:10, 11
27 Luke 4:18
28 Proverbs 3:1
29 John 14:15
30 Ephesians 5:26
31 Isaiah 42:21
32 Isaiah 51:4
33 Romans 8:2
34 2 Corinthians 5:21
35 Galatians 6:2
36 Romans 8:2
37 Romans 3:27
38 Ecclesiastes 7:25
39 Zechariah 7:12

Spirit, as it relates to every individual case, cannot be succored by men and are not held within any religious tradition. The plea and prayer of the Apostle is, "Be filled with the knowledge of his will in all wisdom and spiritual understanding."[40] The LORD's spiritual kingdom delivers "all spiritual blessings in heavenly places in Christ,"[41] leaving it that an exercised faith is the only prerequisite to receive "showers of blessing"[42] for progressing in "the spirit of wisdom and revelation in the knowledge of him."[43]

10. The human heart is a constricted realm of repetitive obscure intemperance and obsessive impatience. The human heart is base within itself, and when it tries to govern itself to correct itself, its cleanliness is as mud removed from a pool of mud and placed into another mud puddle. The imaginative thoughts of the heart so decay the spirit and thin the moral perception that sincere feeling is repressed, and for fear of warmth to the more nobler and higher faculties of thought and conversation, that which is pure is observed through morbid lenses. It is for this reason that every soul needs health. Every heart needs love that neither self nor another human being can properly address. Every heavenly thing poured out for the revival and reform of our conversation's conscience by God's Man suffering that tree, and was set in place after His ascended to fulfill His new position by His LORD as Son and High Priest, to the end that His intercession may liberate every conversation from the hold so falsely and so strangely placed over the conscience.

11. Let the heart bring its thoughts to the heavenly priesthood of this Christ. Open up its chambers to the Spirit of His mediation for the purpose of receiving right precepts, for the Spirit says, "To him that ordereth his conversation aright will I shew the salvation of God."[44] There is a personal responsibility to let no opportunity pass for intimate communion with the living God, and with His living Christ. How intimate would the LORD have our conversation be? He says, "Behold

40 Colossians 1:9
41 Ephesians 1:3
42 Ezekiel 34:26
43 Ephesians 1:17
44 Psalm 50:23

my hands and my feet, that it is I myself: handle me, and see."[45] The handling of Christ is the work of proving by faith every commandment of His Spirit. For the Spirit's salvation will be given to the one who would consider the saying, "A slothful man hideth his hand in his bosom, and will not so much as bring it to his mouth again."[46] As one subscribes to the counsel, "He that tilleth his land shall be satisfied with bread,"[47] it will be observed that it is "the grace of God that bringeth salvation."[48]

12. "The grace that is in Christ"[49] is "the promise of life which is in Christ,"[50] and this promise of life; His "grace of life";[51] it is "the salvation which is in Christ."[52] This is why it says, "He that hath the Son hath life,"[53] because it is written, "The Spirit is life,"[54] for within "the Spirit of grace"[55] is "the grace of life."[56] The purpose of the power of grace is to strengthen and fortify the human will to act against the mouth of its impure and unsound appetite. For "where sin abounded, grace did much more abound"[57] to strengthen the believer to become "servants of righteousness,"[58] so that they may "become servants to God."[59] As the inwards appropriate to their conversation the end of heaven's will by faith, as they study after and experiment with the cure for their illness, they will be given sound principles of the Spirit's benevolent will, even "the ordinances of justice"[60] in relation to the science of salvation's doctrine, for it says, "Gird up the loins of your mind, be

---

45 Luke 24:39
46 Proverbs 19:24
47 Proverbs 12:11
48 Titus 2:11
49 2 Timothy 2:1
50 2 Timothy 1:1
51 1 Peter 3:7
52 2 Timothy 2:10
53 1 John 5:12
54 Romans 8:10
55 Hebrews 10:29
56 1 Peter 3:7
57 Romans 5:20
58 Romans 6:18
59 Romans 6:22
60 Isaiah 58:2

sober, and hope to the end for the grace that is to be brought unto you at the revelation of Jesus."[61]

13. As we are born with various paralyzing spirits compromising the organs of our conscience, with different plagues of our person, it is the living God's intention to heal the wounds of every heart by their advancing diligence in His Son's heavenly ministry, to the end "that ye should shew forth the praises of him who hath called you out of darkness into his marvellous light."[62] This is why the Apostle wrote, "Through Christ which strengtheneth me,"[63] for he knew that "wisdom strengtheneth the wise."[64] From obeying the Spirit's voice, the wisdom obtained will be as a weapon against the inclination of the heart, even as it says, "Wisdom is a defence."[65] Without cultivating faith to place the virtue of the merits of Christ over the mind of the flesh and spirit, the wisdom and knowledge of the Spirit will not be added to any soul. The reformer, in order to maintain their conversation in right ways, needs to join into the "fellowship of the Spirit"[66] that they may receive health, along with the precepts of truth, to uphold every one of the living God's ten precepts.

14. What the heart is longing for will not be found within itself or in another; "the eye is not satisfied with seeing, nor the ear filled with hearing."[67] The heart will continually exhaust self until it grows tired and without further feeling. The heart is an ignorant organ that is an untrained elected official over the government of the body, and it should not be so. From learning of and doing the wisdom of His Son's mediation, and through the power and wisdom of His Spirit, the spirit of the mind will receive strength to retain and exercise every promise and precept of the LORD His God. As the Spirit's Word is diligently proved with all "patience and comfort of the scriptures,"[68] daily the

---

61 1 Peter 1:13
62 1 Peter 2:9
63 Philippians 4:13
64 Ecclesiastes 7:19
65 Ecclesiastes 7:12
66 Philippians 2:1
67 Ecclesiastes 1:8
68 Romans 15:4

spirit will regain consciousness to fill the soul temple with moral power to regulate the mind and the heart to "sell all that thou hast, and distribute unto the poor."[69]

15. It is time that every believer know the name of the living God's Faith to prove their own heart, for by exercising faith on heaven's will, the countenance will shine bright in health to compel every one within our sphere to take notice of His good intention. For this cause, consider the charge, "Know thou the God of thy father, and serve him with a perfect heart and with a willing mind: for the LORD searcheth all hearts, and understandeth all the imaginations of the thoughts: if thou seek him, he will be found of thee; but if thou forsake him, he will cast thee off for ever."[70]

16. "Ye shall seek me, and find me, when ye shall search for me with all your heart. And I will be found of you, saith the LORD."[71]

---

69 Luke 18:22
70 1 Chronicles 28:9
71 Jeremiah 29:13, 14

1

Practical Living Through Self-Regulation

1. There can be no resemblance of the apostolic Faith if there is no obtaining of that Faith through the Spirit's righteousness. That righteousness of the LORD's Spirit, which is only by faith on His will and commandment, is that "righteousness of the law"[72] fulfilled in us "through faith in his blood,"[73] and that faith must be obtained; not given, not self-willed, not bought, not devised, not of a mock or a counterfeit; and it must be obtained only "through the righteousness of God and our Saviour Jesus Christ,"[74] which in turn is obtained "through the knowledge of God, and of Jesus our Lord."[75]

2. The faith of old is to be like "in a figure transferred"[76] to our conscience that we too may share "the like gift"[77] as them. "We have received a commandment from the Father"[78] to be "partakers of the divine nature"[79] "through the knowledge of him that hath called us,"[80]

72 Romans 8:4
73 Romans 3:25
74 2 Peter 1:1
75 2 Peter 1:2
76 1 Corinthians 4:6
77 Acts 11:17
78 2 John 1:4
79 1 Peter 1:4
80 2 Peter 1:3

yet only when once "having escaped the corruption that is in the world through lust."[81] Heaven's knowledge cannot be experienced if we are yet driven by the same unhealthy spirit of the religious age; that is, "lovers of pleasures more than lovers of God";[82] therefore the gift of the "divine nature" cannot be associated with our conversation because we have not picked up the work of obtaining faith "through the knowledge of God, and of Jesus our Lord."[83]

3. Life eternal is knowledge of the Spirit's Word, and the wisdom of life eternal is "the excellency of the knowledge of Christ Jesus" to alleviate the mind from "sin," which knowledge communicates to the believer, "I have suffered the loss of all things"[84] "that I may know him."[85] "The excellency of knowledge is, that wisdom giveth life,"[86] and seeing as how the "divine nature" is advanced according to "his divine power,"[87] it is that by exercising faith on the name of His Son, we obtain wisdom of faith to appropriate His promises to strengthen life and godliness within our conversation. "Godliness" is contrary to "unrighteousness," and "all unrighteousness is sin."[88] Now, "whatsoever is not of faith is sin,"[89] "and the law is not of faith."[90] The "law" that Paul mentions is the legal religious ordinance of priests and elders. Because "Christ hath redeemed us from the law,"[91] "blotting out the handwriting of ordinances"[92] crafted by *Moses*; whether it be the Moses of that age or any other *Moses* thereafter; "the strength of sin is the law,"[93] and our victory from the uninspired traditions and doctrines of the religious world is through examining and

81 2 Peter 1:4
82 2 Timothy 3:4
83 2 Peter 1:2
84 Philippians 3:8
85 Philippians 3:10
86 Ecclesiastes 7:12
87 2 Peter 1:3
88 1 John 5:17
89 Romans 14:23
90 Galatians 3:12
91 Galatians 3:13
92 Colossians 2:14
93 1 Corinthians 15:56

doing the Word's wisdom, which is why we are counseled, "Be ye transformed by the renewing of your mind."[94]

4. The faith of the Spirit's wisdom is that "like precious faith"[95] transferred to the penitent soul who cares to feel sorrow towards their conversation's face, and that of the entire religious world. Such a faith is obtained, purchased, attained and comprehended, by a thorough and diligent work of obedience and self-renunciation "though sanctification of the Spirit and belief of the truth."[96] The true Christian reformer strives for "the obtaining of the glory of our Lord Jesus Christ"[97] that they may properly love the LORD of His priesthood, "and this is love, that we walk after his commandments."[98] They have believed, and "have obeyed from the heart that form of doctrine"[99] "to obtain salvation by our Lord Jesus Christ"[100] to experience the love of His Father, and "this is the love of God, that we keep his commandments."[101]

5. It is because there is none other way to enter into the reign of grace that it is written, "Give me thine heart, and let thine eyes observe my ways."[102] A decided escape from the spirit of the religious world and into the arms of heaven's High Priest is the work determined for His reformer. God "hath made us accepted in the beloved"[103] because it is written, "Keep through thine own name those whom thou hast given me."[104] From observing the conversation of this Christ to personally live after His example, our heart is to be relinquished to His mediation and resurrected by His Spirit for the purpose of having His name written within our mind. We are to become "the light of the knowledge of the glory of God in the face of Jesus Christ"[105] "who are kept by the power

---

94 Romans 12:2
95 2 Peter 1:1
96 2 Thessalonians 2:13
97 2 Thessalonians 2:14
98 2 John 1:6
99 Romans 6:17
100 1 Thessalonians 5:9
101 1 John 5:3
102 Proverbs 23:26
103 Ephesians 1:6
104 John 17:11
105 2 Corinthians 4:6

of God through faith,"[106] yet only when once there is a desire to first run from "the corruption that is in the world through lust."[107]

6. When one is kept of the Spirit and by His name, they "are dead, and your life is hid with Christ in God."[108] We are not alive to our conversation to live of self, as if our wisdom is complete within self, for "if any man love the world, the love of the Father is not in him."[109] The love of the Father is the love of the Son, and the Son has said, "I have kept my Father's commandments, and abide in his love."[110] If we favor the spirit of the world; which spirit declares, "Men shall be lovers of their own selves;"[111] there will be no natural desire to obtain the love of the Father through the knowledge of His Son's name.

7. It is of a truth that "God was manifest in the flesh"[112] "that the righteousness of the law might be fulfilled in us."[113] For, like as through the first Adam the spirit of man was sacrificed for "philosophy and vain deceit, after the tradition of men, after the rudiments of the world,"[114] so through the last Adam is sacrificed a sober and intelligent conversation created by the Word for every willing spirit to attain to. There is a call to be separate in mind, to be holy in conversation, consecrated in heart and mind to the Word's service internally and without the body, because the Spirit cannot dwell within us otherwise. The wisdom of His Son's mediation is the means to perfect Christlikeness within our conscience, and this perfecting occurring through learning of and appropriating every precious promise of the Spirit's new covenant by faith. Therefore "having these promises, dearly beloved, let us cleanse ourselves from all filthiness of the flesh and spirit, perfecting holiness in the fear of God."[115] Only by redemption's wisdom may we obtain like precious faith with them who are "a witness of the sufferings of

---

106 1 Peter 1:5
107 2 Peter 1:4
108 Colossians 3:3
109 1 John 2:15
110 John 15:10
111 2 Timothy 3:2
112 1 Timothy 3:16
113 Romans 8:4
114 Colossians 2:8
115 2 Corinthians 7:1

Christ,"[116] which is why we is counseled, "Keep my commandments, and live; and my law as the apple of thine eye."[117]

8. The promises of our LORD and Father are given to us for the purpose of cleansing our soul temple. "Thou desirest truth in the inward parts,"[118] it is written, and, "Thy law is the truth,"[119] says Scripture, and in order for us to be acknowledge how it says, "God is with us,"[120] it is that we must learn, "He must increase, but I must decrease."[121] The Spirit's character is to house within the spirit of our mind, and it cannot be done but "through sanctification of the Spirit and belief of the truth."[122] Inwardly we are to be made clean by the divine wisdom of the LORD's Spirit from investigating and doing the sayings of His Christ, to the end the Spirit of grace may have place within our soul temple to help us further cleanse it. Such a course of learning is so crucial to our conversation's development because we are to be "built up a spiritual house"[123] and "polished after the similitude of a palace,"[124] even after "the city of the living God, the heavenly Jerusalem,"[125] "which is the mother of us all."[126]

9. Our soul temple must endure right suffering if it is that we desire to have the character of the living God within the character of our conversation, and if it is that we desire to be found with a conscience in likeness to His Son, reflecting His moral image by our willingness to pick up "the work of faith with power."[127] It is now well with us "if the will of God be so, that ye suffer for well doing"[128] that "the word of Christ dwell in you richly in all wisdom."[129] "Through the knowledge of

---

116 1 Peter 5:1
117 Proverbs 7:2
118 Psalm 51:6
119 Psalm 119:142
120 Isaiah 8:10
121 John 3:30
122 2 Thessalonians 2:13
123 1 Peter 2:5
124 Psalm 144:12
125 Hebrews 12:22
126 Galatians 4:26
127 2 Thessalonians 1:11
128 1 Peter 3:17
129 Colossians 3:16

God, and of Jesus our Lord,"[130] we will obtain wisdom in "all things that pertain unto life and godliness"[131] to maintain abstinence from every legal religious error and hurtful lust. So then "being made free from sin,"[132] we "become servants to God"[133] "unto holiness, and the end everlasting life"[134] "through the knowledge of him that hath called us to glory and virtue."[135]

---

130 2 Peter 1:2
131 2 Peter 1:3
132 Romans 6:22
133 Romans 6:22
134 Romans 6:22
135 2 Peter 1:3

2

As Alive From The Flesh

1. "If any man teach otherwise, and consent not to wholesome words, even the words of our Lord Jesus Christ, and to the doctrine which is according to godliness; he is proud, knowing nothing, but doting about questions and strifes of words, whereof cometh envy, strife, railings, evil surmisings."[136] "But godliness with contentment is great gain."[137]

2. Abstinence in that which is not good for the soul, body or the spirit of the mind, is to lead the one faithful in principle to become the doctrine of the Father and the Son, that is, to become a living testimony of the mystery of godliness, even as it says, "Written not with ink, but with the Spirit of the living God."[138] Without an intelligent effort to cultivate a self-sacrificing spirit to add faith and wisdom to the confidence of our affection; without cultivating "power to forbear working,"[139] relinquishing self for the purpose of "striving according to his working";[140] there will be no personal victories over the flesh's constitution to advance practical godliness in the life. If the professed believer does "consent

---

136 1 Timothy 6:3-4
137 1 Timothy 6:6
138 2 Corinthians 3:3
139 1 Corinthians 9:6
140 Colossians 1:29

not to wholesome words";[141] as it is said, "A wholesome tongue is a tree of life,"[142] which tree of life is that of the Spirit's wisdom, as it again says, "She is a tree of life";[143] it will be impossible to "prosper and be in health,"[144] because "thy soul prospereth"[145] not.

3. That which is to keep us from consuming flesh meats are "wholesome words, even the words of our Lord Jesus Christ":[146] "in whom are hid all the treasures of wisdom and knowledge";[147] of "riches and honour,"[148] "durable riches and righteousness";[149] whose words, when digested, proclaim, "I lead in the way of righteousness."[150] "It is the spirit that quickeneth; the flesh profiteth nothing,"[151] says our High Priest. "The words that I speak unto you, they are spirit, and they are life."[152] The words of this Christ are for regenerating the mind to benevolently care for the heart of the conversation, declaring, "Put a knife to thy throat, if thou be a man given to appetite,"[153] for He has said, "The flesh's rule adds nothing to the conversation."[154] Obedience to the words of Christ are a defense for our "putting off the body of the sins of the flesh,"[155] that of us it may be said, "You hath he quickened."[156]

4. "The temple of God is holy, which temple ye are,"[157] and whereas the flesh profits nothing to the conversation's conscience, the doing of His words are "for our profit, that we might be partakers of his holiness."[158] By learning of and doing His counsel; as He says, "Ye are clean through

---

141 1 Timothy 6:3
142 Proverbs 15:4
143 Proverbs 3:13,18
144 3 John 1:2
145 3 John 1:2
146 1 Timothy 6:3
147 Colossians 2:3
148 Proverbs 8:18
149 Proverbs 8:18
150 Proverbs 8:20
151 John 6:63
152 John 6:63
153 Proverbs 23:2
154 John 6:63
155 Colossians 2:11
156 Ephesians 2:1
157 1 Corinthians 3:17
158 Hebrews 12:10

the word which I have spoken unto you";[159] we are of that Spirit who "hath begotten us again unto a lively hope"[160] if we heed the command, "Set thine heart to understand,"[161] and, "Chasten thyself before thy God,"[162] and, "Consent thou not"[163] "unto thine own understanding."[164] Should we subdue those inclinations and passions that are contrary to edification by applying His counsels within our own experience, we do follow the counsel, "Be renewed in the spirit of your mind."[165] This is why our faith's Counselor says, "The words that I speak are life for the spirit,"[166] even because they are of "the grace of life"[167] to regenerate "the hidden man of the heart,"[168] as it is written, "The fear of the LORD is the beginning of wisdom,"[169] and, "The spirit giveth life."[170]

5. "God hath not called us unto uncleanness, but unto holiness,"[171] therefore it is for you to take on the work of transformation "by the renewing of your mind, that ye may prove what is that good, and acceptable, and perfect, will of God."[172] It is true that the Spirit's will is our sanctification; our complete mental and moral renewal to do every precept of the living God by faith; yet none may know sanctification until "every one of you should know how to possess his vessel in sanctification and honor,"[173] therefore it is said, "Abstain from fornication."[174]

6. An abstemious diet from all hurtful indulgences; concocted both by self and the pen of the religious world; needs to be our first work before we may profess to be commandment keepers. If the will is not

---

159 John 15:3
160 1 Peter 1:3
161 Daniel 10:12
162 Daniel 10:12
163 Proverbs 1:10
164 Proverbs 3:5
165 Ephesians 4:23
166 John 6:63
167 1 Peter 3:7
168 1 Peter 3:4
169 Proverbs 9:10
170 2 Corinthians 3:6
171 1 Thessalonians 4:7
172 Romans 12:2
173 1 Thessalonians 4:4
174 1 Thessalonians 4:3

stirred to prove the LORD's will by personal chastening, if it seems wrong to suffer for the sake of procuring health to the mind that the body may exert a positive influence towards heaven's doctrine, there will be no advancement in virtue, in purity, in modesty, in "uncorruptness, gravity, sincerity, sound speech,"[175] "in behaviour as becometh holiness."[176] The will must be determined to fast from self. When the mind is fixed to subdue natural inclinations by the Spirit's wisdom and power, when within the conscience there is a principle most contrary to that of its natural environment, then it will be known, "We have the mind of Christ."[177]

7. Of David it is said, "David behaved himself wisely in all his ways,"[178] and because of his behavior, "when Saul saw that he behaved himself very wisely, he was afraid of him."[179] Godliness has no argument. A life that reflects the practical application of the words of God will reveal itself through the behavior, through the countenance, and that revelation advanced by heaven's wisdom constraining the heart to subdue self. Such a mind declares, "My heart is not haughty, nor mine eyes lofty: neither do I exercise myself in great matters, or in things too high for me. Surely I have behaved and quieted myself, as a child."[180] This is why our Priest says, "Except ye be converted, and become as little children, ye shall not enter into the kingdom of heaven."[181]

8. The argument for our conversion to the heavenly religion of the Father is our consistent demeanor, and such deportment will prove whether we are of the inherited impaired nature, or are of that born of the Spirit. Before sanctification there comes temperance, and before temperance comes humility, and from humility the soul does become temperate in its profession, advancing godliness without thought of self-willed work. We know that our behavior is of the Spirit because our actions are founded upon His wisdom formed within us from our

---

175 Titus 2:7, 8
176 Titus 2:3
177 1 Corinthians 2:16
178 1 Samuel 18:14
179 1 Samuel 18:15
180 Psalm 131:1, 2
181 Matthew 18:3

handling His name, and we know that His wisdom works in us because we have humbled self to bring self under strict watch of self, to the end that creation's law may advance within our heart, even as it is written, "Not that we are sufficient of ourselves to think any thing as of ourselves; but our sufficiency is of God."[182]

9. It is through "the new man, which after God is created in righteousness and true holiness,"[183] that we are made "a perfect man,"[184] and "perfect, as pertaining to the conscience."[185] For then we dwell in the knowledge of His Christ's name, and in this knowledge is the Word's will and wisdom, and from subduing the conversation to gain knowledge of His doctrine, we are then of the LORD of this Word and Christ, so then as we have cultivated the death of His Man within our flesh that we may obtain life by grace and wisdom, it is that we adopt the principle, "We should not trust in ourselves, but in God which raiseth the dead."[186] "God hath both raised up the Lord, and will also raise up us by his own power,"[187] therefore it said, "Know ye not that your bodies are the members of Christ?"[188]

10. If the power that raised Christ is to yet quicken our flesh's constitution, where then should we fail to become temperate in thought and feeling? "The grace of God which is given you by Jesus Christ"[189] is to advance the gifts of virtue, not to diminish or stall them in their growth. "Many are weak and sickly among you, and many sleep,"[190] because they have not brought the Spirit into the soul temple; they are yet alive within self and satisfied. "If we would judge ourselves"[191] and "be afflicted, and mourn, and weep,"[192] who could deny the working benefit of godliness within us from our strict conversation to know the living God and the

---

182 2 Corinthians 3:5
183 Ephesians 4:24
184 Ephesians 4:13
185 Hebrews 9:9
186 2 Corinthians 1:9
187 1 Corinthians 6:14
188 1 Corinthians 6:15
189 1 Corinthians 1:4
190 1 Corinthians 11:30
191 1 Corinthians 11:31
192 James 4:9

law of His Faith? Yet because we fail to acknowledge and value godliness with patience and temperance, our mind becomes slighted that we may "walk as men."[193]

11. We endorse the lifestyle of man when once a reform on temperance isn't half thought on, or we do count the power of the Godhead as a thing valueless to the perfection of our personal religion when we believe in our own power to reform our flesh. We walk as men, or we war after the spiritual labor of flesh, when depending on carnal forms of existence to swallow up that which is mighty in the living God. Such a conversation is done of them who "having the understanding darkened, being alienated from the life of God through the ignorance that is in them, because of the blindness of their heart,"[194] that they may forward "a shew of wisdom in will worship"[195] "after the commandments and doctrines of men."[196] But the Spirit's reformer is counseled, "Seek those things which are above, where Christ sitteth on the right hand of God."[197]

12. They who profess the *name* of *Christ* do worse than the ignorant by stumbling over the Spirit's plea concerning personal reformation. "If any man defile the temple of God, him shall God destroy,"[198] and this destruction occurring not at an instant. Such a soul endures life in blind corruption, seeing as how they will be given over to "the lusts of their own hearts, to dishonor their own bodies,"[199] even as it says, "God hath given them the spirit of slumber, eyes that they should not see, and ears that they should not hear."[200] It is proof that we do not care to bring the Spirit's mystery into our knowledge by the fact that we do not advancing in the science of His will, to the end we may take right knowledge of our behavior and demeanor. Thus, of the disobedient we read, "God gave them over to a reprobate mind, to do those things which are not convenient,"[201] but for what reason is this fallen upon them? It says,

---

193 1 Corinthians 3:3
194 Ephesians 4:18
195 Colossians 2:23
196 Colossians 2:22
197 Colossians 3:1
198 1 Corinthians 3:17
199 Romans 1:24
200 Romans 11:8
201 Romans 1:28

"Unto them that are defiled and unbelieving is nothing pure; but even their mind and conscience is defiled."[202]

13. Self-sacrifice is purposed that we may bear the undefiled fruit of "the testimony of our conscience."[203] "A sound heart is the life of the flesh,"[204] therefore "he that ruleth his spirit"[205] is in greater health and prosperity "than he that taketh a city."[206] Again, "He that hath no rule over his own spirit is like a city that is broken down, and without walls."[207] Thus, there can be no avoiding the fact! There can be no whole man or woman among us, nor may we consider ourselves rising in health, if there is yet a spirit of intemperance controlling the conversation. "Ye are yet carnal"[208] "and walk as men"[209] when not investing time to perfect that which is dying, for not even God Himself will do any work of reform for us that we must do, and that He has given us power to do.

14. From this mind of death we bear none other spirit than that contentious against the LORD, therefore "there must be also heresies among you,"[210] and there is, "for there is not a just man upon earth, that doeth good, and sinneth not."[211] To never apply the sayings of the Spirit for proper self-instruction will lead to an erroneous "dispensation of the gospel"[212] committed to our understanding from our presumptuous stance against faith's learning. "The truth which is after godliness"[213] is overthrown by selfishness, and such selfishness will encourage a doctrine to compel the heart to endorse "turning the grace of our God into lasciviousness, and denying the only Lord God, and our Lord Jesus Christ."[214] Without surrendering to the Spirit's grace, the heart will create of itself

---

202 Titus 1:15
203 2 Corinthians 1:12
204 Proverbs 14:30
205 Proverbs 16:32
206 Proverbs 16:32
207 Proverbs 25:28
208 1 Corinthians 3:3
209 1 Corinthians 3:3
210 1 Corinthians 11:19
211 Ecclesiastes 7:20
212 1 Corinthians 9:17
213 Titus 1:1
214 Jude 1:4

"damnable heresies,"[215] not realizing that it is "being led away with the error of the wicked."[216]

15. If we would cease walking as men, there must be an effort to restrain that that is not good by the Word's grace and knowledge. "Ye are God's building,"[217] it is said, and, "The temple of God is holy,"[218] therefore it is that His inheritance must "suffer all things, lest we should hinder the gospel of Christ."[219] We will not rest happily in godliness if we do not first pick up the work of edifying the conscience of our conversation, for we are counseled, "Glorify God in your body";[220] whose "bodies are the members of Christ";[221] "and in your spirit, which are God's."[222]

16. "All things are lawful for me, but I will not be brought under the power of any,"[223] says the reformer. For to glorify the Word in my body and in my spirit is to "keep under my body, and bring it into subjection"[224] to His will and counsel, to the end I may eat that which is acceptable only to His Spirit, remaining in His course by the instruction of His throne that I may prosper in health by the regeneration of the spirit of my mind.

---

215 2 Peter 2:1
216 2 Peter 3:17
217 1 Corinthians 3:9
218 1 Corinthians 3:17
219 1 Corinthians 9:12
220 1 Corinthians 6:20
221 1 Corinthians 6:15
222 1 Corinthians 6:20
223 1 Corinthians 6:12
224 1 Corinthians 9:27

3

The Result Of An Abstemious Diet

1. "Dearly beloved, I beseech you as strangers and pilgrims, abstain from fleshly lusts, which war against the soul";[225] "for so is the will of God, that with well doing ye may put to silence the ignorance of foolish men: as free, and not using your liberty for a cloke of maliciousness, but as the servants of God."[226] "Wherefore gird up the loins of your mind, be sober";[227] "as obedient children, not fashioning yourselves according to the former lusts in your ignorance";[228] "for it is better, if the will of God be so, that ye suffer for well doing, than for evil doing."[229] "Wherefore let them that suffer according to the will of God commit the keeping of their souls to him in well doing, as unto a faithful Creator."[230]

2. Abstaining from what provokes the conversation's mind; the flesh's constitution; is a positive witness that we are the servants of the Spirit's confidence, for such a witness is to put to silence spiritual

225 1 Peter 2:11
226 1 Peter 2:15, 16
227 1 Peter 1:13
228 1 Peter 1:14
229 1 Peter 3:17
230 1 Peter 4:19

ignorance within and without the person, even as the LORD's voice is to similarly cause all mouths stop before it. The Ten Commandments were given "that every mouth may be stopped, and all the world may become guilty before God,"[231] therefore it is only fitting that the ones reflecting the character of those commandments should produce the same unspoken effect within their conversation's conscience. For this cause it is written, "Be thou an example of the believers";[232] for it is that the word of God only "effectually worketh also in you that believe";[233] therefore "take heed unto thyself,"[234] "for in doing this thou shalt save thyself, and them that hear thee."[235]

3. It is the Spirit's will that His sons and daughters "for conscience toward God endure grief, suffering wrongfully,"[236] that from patiently enduring affliction through the wisdom of His Spirit, it may be that victory would turn them to delight in fulfilling His will of regeneration over the accomplishment of selfish personal and devotional desire. It is a witness that we are in service to the living God's throne when we overcome the flesh's mind with all of its hereditary weaknesses and cultivated tendencies by a faith exercised in His name. To remain a slave to every unhealthy work of the flesh is proof that His Spirit's righteousness is not within our inward parts, for His character is to cause all mouths to stop, and one, who through instructing self by His Son's name watches their heart, is "a perfect man, and able also to bridle the whole body."[237]

4. A witness to the power of His Son's intercession in the life is the ability to cease self-indulgent appetite and passion, placing them under the rule of reason through grace by faith. A reasonable conversation manifests itself by keeping the tongue with all of its tastes. Therefore "if any man among you seem to be religious, and bridleth not his tongue,

---

231 Romans 3:19
232 1 Timothy 4:12
233 1 Thessalonians 2:13
234 1 Timothy 4:16
235 1 Timothy 4:16
236 1 Peter 2:19
237 James 3:2

but deceiveth his own heart, this man's religion is vain."[238] It is the duty of the reformer to maintain a chaste conversation in heaven's Faith, and an unblemished religion physically and morally through the fact that "he that hath suffered in the flesh hath ceased from sin."[239] Blessed hope! We may indeed cease the flow of sin against the Father's cause within our sin-sick frames if we will choose to do so "through Jesus Christ, to whom be praise and dominion for ever and ever. Amen."[240]

5. "It is better, if the will of God be so, that ye suffer for well doing, than for evil doing. For Christ also hath once suffered for sins";[241] and He "being raised from the dead dieth no more; death hath no more dominion over him. For in that he died, he died unto sin once: but in that he liveth, he liveth unto God"[242] "that he might bring us to God, being put to death in the flesh, but quickened by the Spirit."[243]

6. The work of temptation within our flesh is to bring us in like figure to the death and resurrection of our High Priest, in that we may be touched by His Spirit through the knowledge of His name by a living experience. Just as His Christ did suffer for sin that we may be made the righteousness of God through His name, so we are to suffer for well doing, daily exemplifying that which is just and beating down that which is unjust by experimenting with the Faith of His mediation, to the end we may have a strong foundation in what the will and science of the living God is. The believer, when applying to faith's course, embraces a certain death to self into their conversation, but their mind receives life through exercising faith on the Spirit's voice when depending on the Holy Ghost to regenerate their heart through His grace, working death that they may receive the gift of renewal by the Spirit of grace.

7. Learning of and doing the LORD's Faith will produce a barricade against self-violation, which is why His Son says, "Ye are clean through the word which I have spoken unto you."[244] "As Christ hath

---

238 James 1:26
239 1 Peter 4:1
240 1 Peter 4:11
241 1 Peter 3:17, 18
242 Romans 6:9, 10
243 1 Peter 3:18
244 John 15:3

suffered for us in the flesh, arm yourselves likewise with the same mind,"[245] for he that does suffer according to the Spirit's will ceases from sin against that will because they are operating by His quickening Spirit, even as Christ was quickened by that same Spirit to life from the dead. Therefore we commit the keeping of our souls in faith to His will, believing on the fact that the same power "that raised him up from the dead and gave him glory"[246] would so do the same for us, to the end "that your faith and hope might be in God."[247]

8. The hope of the true Christian is only blessed through personal reformation of the conversation's spirit, and such hope we have of the Spirit because it was first done in His Son for our learning and example. This Christ was raised from the grave by the Spirit of His God to die no more, and just as Christ from the dead had to hear and believe on the working power of the Spirit's voice to raise Him up, so too it is for us to believe on the power of His God to raise us up to die no more in heart or in conscience, in word or in deed. Heaven's will is our complete union to the Father "through sanctification of the Spirit, unto obedience and sprinkling of the blood of Jesus Christ,"[248] that, from "obeying the truth through the Spirit,"[249] we may count the blood of the covenant as the LORD's gift for our rejoicing, "being born again"[250] "by the word of God, which liveth and abideth for ever."[251]

9. It is interesting to note that His word and counsel lives and abides without decomposition, in the same sense that "he that doeth the will of God abideth for ever."[252] Our life and birth in His Son's course of learning is maintained from doing His Spirit's will, which will is that we are regulated by His understanding, which understanding is His truth, which truth is His doctrine and precepts of life and justification. We will abide in His presence; "holy and without blame before

---

245 1 Peter 4:1
246 1 Peter 1:21
247 1 Peter 1:21
248 1 Peter 1:2
249 1 Peter 1:22
250 1 Peter 1:23
251 1 Peter 1:23
252 1 John 2:17

him in love";[253] just as His word abides before Him forever; "hereby we know that he abideth in us, by the Spirit which he hath given us."[254] Because we do His word that the science of His truth may be in us, that wisdom does sanctify our inward parts, proving our birth from the incorruptible seed; working with our conversation's heart by that Spirit; to subdue our conversation by divine power. This is why it says, "Of his own will begat he us with the word of truth."[255]

10. The hope of the faithful soul is the pleasure of blessing the conversation's heart by learning of the character of the Spirit's Son, that by beholding the order of His face, we may welcome the Spirit's of mediation into our conversation's conscience without any hindrance. There is then a reason for temperance reform. From willingly suffering the flesh of our faith to endure self-restriction, we may fulfill the Spirit's will by His quickening Spirit. Abstaining from fleshly lust promotes health towards a godly life, for he or that edifies their faith's confidence will cease sinning against the Word and self. From strict perseverance, it is that we will build faith, wisdom, and confidence in the Spirit's power by doing the will of His wisdom, and such an experience is to help further the accomplishment of "the kindness and love of God our Saviour"[256] within our spirit. It is purposed of the Word that we cultivate principles of self-denial to better hear and cooperate with His voice; that "we eschew evil, and do good";[257] "for this is the will of God, even your sanctification."[258]

11. If it should be said of us, "The very God of peace sanctify you wholly; and I pray your whole spirit and soul and body be preserved blameless,"[259] it must be that we are first willing to exercise discretion over our spirit and soul and body. The reformer has a responsibility to make the heart of their conscience healthy before they may be considered a resting place for the LORD's Spirit, and this is why "Christ

---

253 Ephesians 1:4
254 1 John 3:24
255 James 1:18
256 Titus 3:4
257 1 Peter 3:11
258 1 Thessalonians 4:3
259 1 Thessalonians 5:23

also suffered for us, leaving us an example, that ye should follow his steps."[260] The message of the third angel,[261] which message declares; "Bind up the testimony, seal the law among my disciples,"[262] and again, "Here are they that keep the commandments of God, and the faith of Jesus";[263] cannot be taken into the mind if intemperance reigns within our devotional existence. "Mortality might be swallowed up of life"[264] if we would, through the creative power of grace, "mortify the deeds of the body."[265]

12. "As many as are led by the Spirit of God, they are the sons of God."[266] The Spirit's sons and daughters carry a hope in them that encourages their obedience in the strength of His understanding for a perfect conversation, for we are to be "perfect, as pertaining to the conscience."[267] And this is why "it is written, Be ye holy; for I am holy."[268] When we are not renewing within ourselves the comforts of former spiritual lusts, it is that, through practicing self-denial from applying self to "the knowledge of the Son of God,"[269] we will begin to practice simplicity of faith in all honesty, as it says, "Be ye holy in all manner of conversation."[270] Godliness cannot enter into the sphere of our realm if we are yet intemperate in thought and feeling. When once a restraint is placed on former religious ignorance, it is then that natural piety will flow from our person, for we will have been in that Word by the name of His Son as a "witness of the sufferings of Christ, and also a partaker of the glory."[271]

13. It is a fact that we are to be living testimonies of the Spirit's power after we have experienced the benevolence revealed from His

---

260 1 Peter 2:21
261 Revelation 14:9-11
262 Isaiah 8:16
263 Revelation 14:12
264 2 Corinthians 5:4
265 Romans 8:13
266 Romans 8:14
267 Hebrews 9:9
268 1 Peter 1:16
269 Ephesians 4:13
270 1 Peter 1:15
271 1 Peter 5:1

face. Who is a liar except the one professing service to His face while ruled by the naturally empty mind within the conversation? Who is gone astray by their own heart, except the one not willing to endure love's course because of love? The LORD has returned us to Himself by the Faith of His Son's mediation "according to his abundant mercy";[272] which mercy is of an "abundance of grace";[273] and "hath begotten us again unto a lively hope by the resurrection of Jesus Christ from the dead,"[274] that in us the purpose of His good pleasure would be done, as He says, "I in them, and thou in me, that they may be made perfect."[275] "This is the word which by the gospel is preached unto you,"[276] even "the word of the truth of the gospel,"[277] which gospel is after "the doctrine which is according to godliness."[278]

14. Without an intelligent and diligent work of restraint upon the mental and moral diet, there will be no grace given that we may keep the commandments of our LORD's throne. There will be no mental, moral, physical, or spiritual development within the life and religion, if the two properties of health that flowed from out of the side of God's Man on that tree are counted as filth. For, from Him "came there out blood and water."[279] These came forth from Christ and flowed down His flesh that it may be these two things that bring health to the body of our personal religion. Our effort to reform in every aspect of our devotion is our entrance into the Spirit's presence for the regeneration of our conscience, and from learning of and doing His will and commandment for that regeneration, we will overcome the inherited and self-cultivated meat of our flesh, even as did the Captain of our salvation.

15. The true sheep of the flock will hear the voice of love and will not question duty above love, for when once the heart humbly accepts faith's higher learning, it is that the Spirit "giveth more grace"[280] for

---

272 1 Peter 1:3
273 Romans 5:17
274 1 Peter 1:3
275 John 17:23
276 1 Peter 1:25
277 Colossians 1:5
278 1 Timothy 6:3
279 John 19:34
280 James 4:6

knowledge on how to properly keep and dress the conversation. By bringing the righteousness of God's Son in to the spirit of our mind, it is that through faith on the virtue of the merits of His blood, and through depending on the power of grace to subdue "every high thing that exalteth itself against the knowledge of God"[281] within our heart, we may advance to the call, "Be ye holy in all manner of conversation."[282]

---

281 2 Corinthians 10:5
282 1 Peter 1:15

4

The Meat Of The Body

1. "The light of the body is the eye: if therefore thine eye be single, thy whole body shall be full of light. But if thine eye be evil, thy whole body shall be full of darkness. If therefore the light that is in thee be darkness, how great is that darkness! No man can serve two masters."[283]

2. "I say unto you, Take no thought for your life, what ye shall eat, or what ye shall drink; nor yet for your body, what ye shall put on. Is not the life more than meat, and the body than raiment?"[284] "Therefore take no thought, saying, What shall we eat? or, What shall we drink? or, Wherewithal shall we be clothed?"[285]

3. The light of the body is the eye, or the life of the personal religious conversation is centered within "the eyes of your understanding."[286] It is written, "If thou be a man given to appetite,"[287] "put a knife to thy throat"[288] and "cease from thine own wisdom."[289] Self-sufficiency is the

---

283 Matthew 6:22–24
284 Matthew 6:25
285 Matthew 6:31
286 Ephesians 1:18
287 Proverbs 23:2
288 Proverbs 23:2
289 Proverbs 23:4

diet "of him that hath an evil eye,"[290] whose eyes continually provoke within him the thought, "What shall we eat? or, What shall we drink? or, Wherewithal shall we be clothed?"[291] It is because the soul lacks knowledge of the Spirit's power that such contentions will arise. Gluttony within man results when heaven's wisdom is "counted to him less than nothing, and vanity,"[292] when it is "counted as a strange thing."[293]

4. But the one who acknowledges the voice of the living God to be good; as it says concerning the word "good," "Good to the use of edifying";[294] His character to be excellent and just and admirable to produce in them a bountiful stream of health, it is that through His voice "he is chastened also with pain upon his bed, and the multitude of his bones with strong pain: so that his life abhorreth bread, and his soul dainty meat."[295] "These things worketh God oftentimes with man, to bring back his soul from the pit, to be enlightened with the light of the living."[296]

5. The light of the body is the eye, and it is that we may have our diet of flesh to devour, or we may consume that good Spirit of the Word's Son by learning how to exercise faith on His name. As we take thought of our life or personal religion; which life is a diet comprised of what we are to eat, drink, and wear; it is that we demonstrate a lack of faith and trust in the Spirit of creation. "The lilies of the field,"[297] "they toil not, neither do they spin,"[298] and yet they blossom and flower without their own wisdom. Nature is found subject to the LORD's will, exerting an influence no less nor greater than that which has been put in it, for creation intelligently and diligently follows times and seasons for development, death, and resurrection. Thus, "if God so clothe the

---

290 Proverbs 23:6
291 Matthew 6:31
292 Isaiah 40:17
293 Hosea 8:12
294 Ephesians 4:29
295 Job 33:19,20
296 Job 33:29,30
297 Matthew 6:28
298 Matthew 6:28

grass of the field,"[299] "shall he not much more clothe you, O ye of little faith?"[300]

6. The root of spiritual intemperance lies in the fact that there is no knowledge of heaven's new covenant will to personally exercise faith on it. For the counsel is not heard, "Exercise thyself rather unto godliness. For bodily exercise profiteth little."[301] They of little faith will exercise that which profits little. The word, "bodily" or "body," is here rendered *ptoma*,[302] which means *lifeless* in Greek, therefore the faithless indulge in lifeless religious exercises, while the faithful exert themselves to godliness through that which "is profitable unto all things, having promise of the life that now is, and of that which is to come."[303] Again, the light of the conversation is the eye, and should the mind consume that of the body, it will suffer the fate of the body, as it is written, "Shall of the flesh reap corruption,"[304] yet should we remain single to the diet of life, "Shall of the Spirit reap life everlasting."[305]

7. Through the Spirit of grace we reap life everlasting, or as it is said, "Power everlasting."[306] This "power" is the Spirit's "strength," and it is well to know that "wisdom strengtheneth."[307] Only by the wisdom of our LORD's Spirit may we confidently cease thinking on our life to have the law of the Faith of His Son's mediation transform our conscience. To have "tasted of the heavenly gift, and were made partakers of the Holy Ghost,"[308] requires that we be faithful "partakers of Christ's sufferings," relinquishing self to God by Christ "as unto a faithful Creator."[309] The same everlasting power found in the life of grace is the same wisdom that created all things and keeps all things. This LORD's Word "is before all things, and by him all things

---

299 Matthew 6:30
300 Matthew 6:30
301 1 Timothy 4:7, 8
302 http://1ref.us/h7
303 1 Timothy 4:8
304 Galatians 6:8
305 Galatians 6:8
306 1 Timothy 6:16
307 Ecclesiastes 7:19
308 Hebrews 6:4
309 1 Peter 4:13, 19

consist,"[310] and to have the grace of the Creator within our inwards means to become a subject of His voice for creation, which voice is to transform the body of our confidence into the image of His Son, even as it once transformed an empty earth into a green and living realm.

8. Our LORD's Word and Faith is our Creator, and the power of His voice is most emphatic for the redemption of our the mind and character of our conversation. "If the Son therefore shall make you free, ye shall be free indeed"[311] from "philosophy and vain deceit, after the tradition of men, after the rudiments of the world,"[312] so wherein is there room for doubt? "He that believeth on me,"[313] says our High Priest, "out of his belly shall flow rivers of water."[314] "This spake he of the Spirit which they that believe on him should receive";[315] that is, "that believe on his name";[316] yet if we believe not, if the light of the body is not lightened with the light of the life concerning the gift of grace, it will be as it is written, "Whose God is their belly."[317] "They that are such serve not our Lord Jesus Christ, but their own belly,"[318] "whose glory is in their shame, who mind earthly things."[319]

9. "If therefore the light that is in thee be darkness, how great is that darkness!"[320] A flesh-based diet will lead the LORD's Priest to confess to the impenitent, "Why criest thou for thine affliction? Thy sorrow is incurable for the multitude of thine iniquity: because thy sins were increased, I have done these things unto thee."[321] Therefore "be not deceived; God is not mocked."[322] "The Lord knoweth them that are

---

310 Colossians 1:17
311 John 8:36
312 Colossians 2:8
313 John 7:38
314 John 7:38
315 John 7:39
316 John 1:12
317 Philippians 3:19
318 Romans 16:18
319 Philippians 3:19
320 Matthew 6:23
321 Jeremiah 30:15
322 Galatians 6:7

his"[323] "and who should betray him,"[324] "wherefore be ye not unwise, but understanding what the will of the Lord is."[325]

10. If the light of our body is spiritually sensual, if the eye of our understanding is regulated by flesh meats, our understanding will continually decline until it is said of us, "Her wound is incurable."[326] "Let every one that nameth the name of Christ";[327] that is, that professes the virtue of His name and likeness to His conversation, as it is written, "If we have been planted together in the likeness of his death, we shall be also in the likeness of his resurrection,"[328] that is, "dead indeed unto sin, but alive unto God";[329] "depart from iniquity."[330] No man or woman who remains subject to intemperate devotional indulgences may expect to hear or to comprehend the Spirit's dialect. To the "lovers of their own selves,"[331] and to the "lovers of pleasures more than lovers of God,"[332] our Priest says, "Without me ye can do nothing."[333]

11. Them that reject the work of righteousness to be made "sober, temperate, sound in faith, in charity, in patience,"[334] "in all things shewing thyself a pattern of good works,"[335] such will be "ever learning, and never able to come to the knowledge of the truth."[336] These will never be able to discern the fact of salvation's science, or they, being conscientious and stubborn invalids by depending on that "bondage under the elements of the world,"[337] who enjoy waters that produce both "salt water and fresh,"[338] lack that strength drawing them to accept

---

323 2 Timothy 2:19
324 John 6:64
325 Ephesians 5:17
326 Micah 1:9
327 2 Timothy 2:19
328 Romans 6:5
329 Romans 6:11
330 2 Timothy 2:19
331 2 Timothy 3:2
332 2 Timothy 3:4
333 John 15:5
334 Titus 2:2
335 Titus 2:7
336 2 Timothy 3:7
337 Galatians 4:3
338 James 3:12

a living experience by faith to learn of and do "the acknowledging of the truth which is after godliness."[339] The eye being full of the body finds no place for that light which is to cover and fill the body. As we live "supposing that gain is godliness,"[340] and while professing the *name* of *Christ* through intemperance, it is that we take the name of His LORD in vain, making of none effect the power of His love and voice through our willing rejection of His Spirit's influence over our heart.

12. Such as "profess that they know God; but in works they deny him,"[341] we are counseled, "From such turn away,"[342] and again, "Be not among winebibbers; among riotous eaters of flesh."[343] Then it is fact! The cause for a dead religion, the cause for ignorance putting the heart to sleep, the cause which accepts violating the Spirit's character through popular stubbornness is intemperance, a consumption of an abundance of flesh stimulants, which nonetheless began with one saying, "What shall we eat? or, What shall we drink? or, Wherewithal shall we be clothed?"[344] Faithlessness produces anxiety that leads to self-indulgence, yet who will hear and do the wisdom of soul health, which says "Learn of me,"[345] "and ye shall find rest for your souls."[346]

13. What is the lesson that we must learn in order for our conversation's conscience to have the Word's rest and refreshing? It is written, "Except a corn of wheat fall into the ground and die…it bringeth forth much fruit."[347] Therefore "I say unto you, Take no thought for your life, what ye shall eat, or what ye shall drink; nor yet for your body, what ye shall put on. Is not the life more than meat, and the body than raiment?"[348] "He that loveth his life shall lose it; and he that hateth his life in this world shall keep it unto life eternal";[349] or rather, "life

---

339 Titus 1:1
340 1 Timothy 6:5
341 Titus 1:16
342 2 Timothy 3:5
343 Proverbs 23:20
344 Matthew 6:31
345 Matthew 11:29
346 Matthew 11:29
347 John 12:24
348 Matthew 6:25
349 John 12:25

everlasting,"[350] or "power everlasting";[351] because "that which thou sowest is not quickened, except it die,"[352] and "this is life eternal."[353]

14. If we would relinquish self to the Spirit's will, and with all of self's inherited deficiencies and cultivated habits, if we would die to self and willingly sacrifice the eye of our delectable diet, cultivating self-sacrifice by means of love and faith through fire's learning, we would never fail to come to the knowledge of heaven's divine science. We would never lack the understanding concerning sanctification by the Spirit to render complete obedience to every precept of life and inward health. Through a living experience by faith in the Spirit's wisdom, we would hold fast our life unto, or join beside our efforts of obedience to, the knowledge of the Spirit's grace "till we all come in the unity of the faith, and of the knowledge of the Son of God, unto a perfect man, unto the measure of the stature of the fullness of Christ."[354]

350 1 Timothy 1:16
351 1 Timothy 6:16
352 1 Corinthians 15:36
353 John 17:3
354 Ephesians 4:13

5

The Life Diet

1. It is written, "Labour not for the meat which perisheth, but for that meat which endureth unto everlasting life."[355] "This is the bread which cometh down from heaven, that a man may eat thereof, and not die."[356] "I am the living bread which came down from heaven: if any man eat of this bread, he shall live forever: and the bread that I will give is my flesh, which I will give for the life of the world." "My flesh is meat indeed, and my blood is drink indeed."[357]

2. It is for the believer to stay from that "meat which perisheth,"[358] for "if ye live after the flesh, ye shall die."[359] Should we remain servants of our traditional flesh diet, consumers of generational unrestrained base passions; as it says, "Your vain conversation received by tradition from your fathers";[360] it will be as it is written, "I gave them up unto their own hearts' lust,"[361] "sent leanness into their soul,"[362] "and they

---

355 John 6:27
356 John 6:50
357 John 6:51
358 John 6:27
359 Romans 8:13
360 1 Peter 1:18
361 Psalm 81:12
362 Psalm 106:15

walked in their own counsels."[363] Yet we are counseled, "Labor not for the meat which perisheth,"[364] and, "Seek not after your own heart and your own eyes, after which ye use to go a whoring."[365]

3. For "the wise man's eyes are in his head,"[366] but "Israel would none of me,"[367] says the Spirit. "They hearkened not, nor inclined their ear, but walked in the counsels and in the imagination of their evil heart, and went backward, and not forward."[368]

4. Our High Priest, "having abolished in his flesh the enmity, even the law of commandments contained in ordinances"[369] from every *Moses*; "not only in this world, but also in that which is to come";[370] has set the reformer's diet, and it forsakes all things relating to a course of flesh and blood by the hand of priests and elders. This is why it was necessary for His to suffer the tree, to the end He might, through His spilt blood, accomplish "blotting out the handwriting of ordinances"[371] "ordainined by angels in the hand of a mediator."[372] For this cause, He has said, "He that heareth my word, and believeth on him that sent me, hath everlasting life."[373] And in another place it is said, "As many as received him, to them gave he power to become the sons of God, even to them that believe on his name."[374] "Life" is synonymous with "power." His power is that influence delivered to the reformer for knowledgably governing their conversation. The believer is given His mediation's wisdom for the purpose of regulating and nourishing the spirit of their conscience, to the end every word of His LORD and Father may perfectly penetrate into the entire human core.

---

363 Psalm 81:12
364 John 6:27
365 Numbers 15:39
366 Ecclesiastes 2:14
367 Psalm 81:11
368 Jeremiah 7:24
369 Ephesians 2:15
370 Ephesians 1:21
371 Colossians 3:14
372 Galatians 3:19
373 John 5:24
374 John 1:12

5. "The gift of God is eternal life through Jesus Christ our Lord,"[375] therefore "we have peace with God through our Lord Jesus Christ."[376] "By grace are ye saved through faith,"[377] and this grace being "the exceeding greatness of his power to us-ward who believe,"[378] that we may be "his workmanship, created in Christ Jesus unto good works."[379] There is presently an "abundance of grace"[380] pouring out from the presence our High Priest's office, for "of his fullness have all we received, and grace for grace,"[381] seeing as how "in him dwelleth all the fullness of the Godhead bodily."[382]

6. The entire fullness of the Godhead rests within the heavenly ministry of the LORD's Son, "for it pleased the Father that in him should all fullness dwell."[383] In His Son's name is a never ending supply of life, as He says, "If thou knewest the gift of God,"[384] "he would have given thee living water."[385] This living water is the same as that living bread, for He says, "He that cometh to me shall never hunger; and he that believeth on me shall never thirst."[386] "The gift of God"[387] is indeed "the praise of the glory of his grace,"[388] that mighty power "which he wrought in Christ, when he raised him from the dead,"[389] and it is known that "it is the gift of God,"[390] even "the grace of God"[391] tending to that promised "gift by grace."[392]

---

375 Romans 6:23
376 Romans 5:1
377 Ephesians 2:8
378 Ephesians 1:19
379 Ephesians 2:10
380 Romans 5:17
381 John 1:16
382 Colossians 2:9
383 Colossians 1:19
384 John 4:10
385 John 4:10
386 John 6:35, even as it is written in Isaiah 49:10
387 Ephesians 2:8
388 Ephesians 1:6
389 Ephesians 1:20
390 Ephesians 2:8
391 Romans 5:15
392 Romans 5:15

7. Should we learn of, receive, and do the doctrine of His mediation, engaging the spirit of the mind with the Spirit of His name to actively believe on the will of His name, then within our inward person the Spirit's gift will be "a well of water springing up into everlasting life."[393] Thus, "Except ye eat the flesh of the Son of man, and drink his blood, ye have no life in you,"[394] says our High Priest, or rather we fail to "know him, and the power of his resurrection, and the fellowship of his sufferings, being made conformable unto his death."[395] If we are eating the saying of His ministry, we are assimilating the experience of His conversation within our conscience, yet if we consume the meat that leads to spiritual death, which meat is our own inherited and cultivated traditional theories and suppositions, then we assimilate "death by sin."[396] "Thou art in the gall of bitterness, and in the bond of iniquity,"[397] the Spirit says of us.

8. Continual consumption of flesh ceases the life-current flowing from the Spirit's throne for the heart of conversation, for the Spirit, by His will and understanding, "hath delivered us from the power of darkness, and hath translated us into the kingdom of his dear Son."[398] The reign and kingdom of "the knowledge of his will in all wisdom and spiritual understanding"[399] is that of "the throne of grace,"[400] where our Chief Minister "is gone into heaven, and is on the right hand of God."[401] It is in this Sanctuary where the believer receives a never-ending supply of health for the development of their faith and mind, even "all spiritual blessings in heavenly places in Christ,"[402] to the end that the confidence of His intercession "is made unto us wisdom, and righteousness, and sanctification, and redemption."[403]

---

393 John 4:14
394 John 6:53
395 Philippians 3:10
396 Romans 5:12
397 Acts 8:23
398 Colossians 1:13
399 Colossians 1:9
400 Hebrews 4:16
401 1 Peter 3:22
402 Ephesians 1:3
403 1 Corinthians 1:30

9. "For this is the will of God, even your sanctification, that ye should abstain from fornication."[404] The Spirit's will is only accomplished through abstaining, dieting, and sacrificing self from the religious world for the purpose of "salvation through sanctification of the Spirit and belief of the truth."[405] This is our meat that we may freely consume, even the meat of the Spirit's will found in the knowledge of His Son's name, which meat is digested through a persevering effort to learn of and do the righteousness of heaven's course to more thoughtfully care for the Word, self, and others. Should we eat this meat; the meat of the knowledge of the Spirit's benevolent intention; we would be cultivating right temperance, and we would be consuming His wisdom to grow fond of the jealous love that He has over our soul temple.

10. What is written? "When wisdom entereth into thine heart, and knowledge is pleasant unto thy soul; discretion shall preserve thee, understanding shall keep thee."[406] Should we study after the diet of life for the regeneration of our flesh's constitution, we would greatly advance in temperance reform due to the power of God that is joined to the eating and drinking of His name. King Saul flourished according to the principle, "According to all the desire of thy soul,"[407] yet it is said of David, that he was "in the bundle of life with the LORD."[408] The unhealthy desires of the soul are made to cease when we fully commit self to the instruction of our High Priest's operation, for His course will keep us in the bundle of His life of wisdom and love through showers of blessing "according to the power that worketh in us."[409] The call to consume the Spirit's doctrine is a call that is to cause the believer to exercise intelligent restriction against their heart's members, that their moral recovery would be made sure. "He that eateth me, even he shall live by me,"[410] counsels our Priest. "He that eateth of this bread

---

404 1 Thessalonians 4:3
405 2 Thessalonians 2:13
406 Proverbs 2:10, 11
407 1 Samuel 23:20
408 1 Samuel 25:29
409 Ephesians 3:20
410 John 6:57

shall live for ever"[411] "and shall not come into condemnation."[412] The LORD's wisdom is to educate the struggle between the heart and the mind, and from consuming the doctrine of His Son's experience, we will grow as bold as Job to declare, "My heart shall not reproach me so long as I live."[413]

11. This Christ of the LORD pronounces a fact of heaven-approved and heaven-appointed godliness that we should not ignore. What is "condemned" is "accursed," and, concerning what is accursed, we are counseled, "He that is hanged is accursed of God."[414] As we observe the LORD's Man on the tree, it is well to understand that His flesh is representative of "sin" against His LORD's Faith. Because "the strength of sin is the law,"[415] the flesh of this Christ on the tree illustrates the fact that every handwritten legal religious law and ordinance of priests and elders is become accursed of the Word. When we hear that, as He is nailed on to the tree, "he gave up the ghost,"[416] the illustration presented to us is that the life of traditions and decrees of ministers, being accursed of the Word, is passed away from heaven's new covenant will. Hereafter the only diet that remains for the reformer; seeing as how they are, if sincerely in the LORD's course of learning, "dead with Christ from the rudiments of the world";[417] is Word and the LORD that Word proceeds out from. Our regimen by this Christ is the commandment of His intercession, to the end we may love the LORD of that commandment, "and this is love, that we walk after his commandments."[418]

12. For this cause, should be no intemperate professor of the Father and His Son. "If ye be led of the Spirit"[419] "ye shall not fulfill the lust of the flesh,"[420] which lust is in inventing and subscribing to that

---

411 John 6:58
412 John 5:24
413 Job 27:6
414 Deuteronomy 21:23
415 1 Corinthians 15:56
416 Luke 23:46
417 Colossians 2:20
418 2 John 1:6
419 Galatians 5:18
420 Galatians 5:18

course nailed to the tree. It is apparent that Christ has substituted the diet of the flesh for the diet of the Spirit of life by His sacrifice. A flesh diet will leave us miserable in "death by sin."[421] Instead of feeding on meat that adds health to the soul, because we refuse to acknowledge the laws of health that govern our conversation's conscience, we will die in the corruption of self because we failed to restrain that impaired culture of our nature. The Spirit's will is our sanctification, which will is our revival through learning of and doing every precept of His name, and if the inward desire is not after the work and wisdom of faith that His character may replace that code of stumbling within our heart, our labor is presumptuously accomplished.

13. Christ is for us that High Priest over His LORD's heavenly Sanctuary, "whose house are we, if we hold fast the confidence and the rejoicing of the hope firm unto the end."[422] Our hope and our rejoicing are one, "for our rejoicing is this, the testimony of our conscience,"[423] and that witness maintained through "simplicity and godly sincerity"[424] remaining "fervent in spirit; serving the Lord."[425] Rest is centered within our "joy in the Holy Ghost,"[426] to the end that grace would fashion in us a character that is "sober, just, holy, temperate."[427] The reward of the work of righteousness is a quiet confidence in the gift and presence of the Godhead without a confused heart, for then we begin a "work of faith, and labour of love,"[428] through "patience of hope in our Lord Jesus Christ, in the sight of God and our Father,"[429] "in power, and in the Holy Ghost."[430]

14. It is a fact that the spiritual lusts compromising the constitution of our faith's body will be cancelled through patient and active faith in the virtue of the blood of Christ, for herein is our victory, even our faith

---

421 Romans 5:12
422 Hebrews 3:6
423 2 Corinthians 1:12
424 2 Corinthians 1:12
425 Romans 12:11
426 Romans 14:17
427 Titus 1:8
428 1 Thessalonians 1:3
429 1 Thessalonians 1:3
430 1 Thessalonians 1:5

and hope in the Spirit's promised righteousness within the spirit of our conversation. Should we fail to appropriate the righteousness of Christ for whatever may be our struggle, we do make of none affect the Spirit's offering. "He that believeth not God hath made him a liar,"[431] yet "shall their unbelief make the faith of God without effect?"[432] Heaven's course of learning "is made unto us wisdom,"[433] "and they that are Christ's have crucified the flesh with the affections and lusts."[434]

15. It is because the illustration of God's Man on the tree, and the regenerated from the tree, signifies our removal from the pen of priests and elders to personally examine the Spirit's words, that we are counseled, "Christ being raised from the dead dieth no more; death hath no more dominion over him,"[435] wherefore it is well to remember that "the sting of death is sin; and the strength of sin is the law."[436] The vision given us of God's Man on the tree is that, as He is passed away from the philosophy of the religious world; which philosophy is today "sin," and which "sin" is conversational government by the legal religious bill of flesh; "likewise reckon ye also yourselves to be dead indeed unto sin, but alive unto God through Jesus Christ our Lord."[437] "For ye have not received the spirit of bondage again,"[438] through His name, "for if ye live after the flesh, ye shall die: but if ye through the Spirit do mortify the deeds of the body, ye shall live."[439]

---

431 1 John 5:10
432 Romans 3:3
433 1 Corinthians 1:30
434 Galatians 5:24
435 Romans 6:9
436 1 Corinthians 15:56
437 Romans 6:11
438 Romans 8:15
439 Romans 8:13

6

The Appointed Work Of Reformation

1. Considering the harsh and coarse texture of our nature, it is that through the righteousness of Christ, and by the perfecting grace of His mediation's Spirit, the believer who carries unwavering faith in the virtue of His name may of a truth declare, "I am crucified with Christ: nevertheless I live; yet not I, but Christ liveth in me: and the life which I now live in the flesh I live by the faith of the Son of God, who loved me, and gave himself for me."[440] Herein is the key to temperance, and it is that first we settle the fact, "I am crucified with Christ,"[441] and then it may be that, "Christ liveth in me,"[442] to the end that "in the flesh I live by the faith of the Son of God,"[443] which faith appear by exercising confidence on the fact that He "loved me, and gave himself for me."[444]

2. If the reformer would dare manifest true temperance; true self-restraint against the mind of the flesh for the Spirit's promised benevolence; it is that the conscience must first find itself touched with the

---

440 Galatians 2:20
441 Galatians 2:20
442 Galatians 2:20
443 Galatians 2:20
444 Galatians 2:20

disease of its fleshly condition. If the inward parts are not convinced of the level of ungodliness existing within them, the outward will never be brought to contemplate a reform intelligently devised by reason, but rather the reform will be fulfilled through the imaginations of the heart, falling short of the intended regeneration. Because of self-deception, the experience will never advance nor decline, but will remain in a carnal realm of a settled religious comfort. Should the flesh have no thing to govern it, it will then be the flesh that will govern the inside, and the out, of the human being.

3. Today, it is our responsibility to acknowledge the counsel, "Keep the commandments of God, and the faith of Jesus."[445] This we must do if hopeful to receive an experience "in the kingdom and patience of Jesus Christ."[446] After we add to our faith virtue, and then to virtue knowledge, after we add to our faith the virtue of the blood of Christ through the Spirit's wisdom, we should add patience with physical and spiritual discretion. Without the knowledge of the Spirit's Son regulating our the body of our faith, and without the testimony of the Spirit's love for man before the eyes and placed within the heart by His finger, there will be no mind to watch self, there will be no desire to kill the flesh's constitution to know a more benevolent government. This is why we are counseled, "Put off concerning the former conversation the old man,"[447] and, "Be renewed in the spirit of your mind."[448]

4. Indeed when we do confess, "I am crucified with Christ,"[449] in reality we acknowledge the fact that "if we have been planted together in the likeness of his death, we shall be also in the likeness of his resurrection."[450] Christ has long since died and was "raised again for our justification"[451] to dawn a right conversation before the LORD His Father, and seeing as "if we be dead with Christ,"[452] "knowing that

---

445 Revelation 14:12
446 Revelation 1:9
447 Ephesians 4:22
448 Ephesians 4:23
449 Galatians 2:20
450 Romans 6:5
451 Romans 4:25
452 Romans 6:8

Christ being raised from the dead dieth no more,"[453] "henceforth we should not serve sin,"[454] for it is that "our old man is crucified with him."[455] For this cause "we also should walk in newness of life,"[456] for "if we be dead with Christ, we believe that we should also live with him."[457] Therefore, remembering that "whatsoever is not of faith is sin,"[458] and that "the law is not of faith,"[459] it is that our conversation is passed away from that "sin" abolished by the flesh of God's Man; which "sin" is the legal religious law and ordinance of priests and ministers; when rightly and intelligently acknowledging the name of the living God's Son.

5. As we declare the religion of heaven's assembly, it is that our faith must confess the death of this Christ from our conversation's impaired inherited nature, looking forward to that good nature through His mediation by faith, and believing that it is so true in Him of what hope is to be had by spiritually passing away with Him. Indeed keeping His Father's commandments is the end of His Faith; as it is written, "This is the love of God, that we keep his commandments";[460] yet if our flesh's constitution is not regulated by the law His Faith, which Faith is "the law of the Spirit of life,"[461] even the faith "of the glorious gospel of Christ,"[462] "the word of righteousness,"[463] then our mind will never be brought to make one sacrifice for heaven's Faith. We will never care to live as the LORD's High Priest suggests, for there is no mind of reason behind our faith; a presumptuous will covers our profession.

6. Only the tidings of grace's creative power will cause the heart to give up its confidence to the mind, allowing the reformer to bring every faculty under right reason, relinquishing self to the Spirit after

---

453 Romans 6:9
454 Romans 6:6
455 Romans 6:6
456 Romans 6:4
457 Romans 6:8
458 Romans 14:23
459 Galatians 3:12
460 1 John 5:3
461 Romans 8:2
462 2 Corinthians 4:4
463 Hebrews 5:13

hearing the word of the worth of their soul. After hearing of such a terrible and unfathomable and excellent love as is displayed by the Godhead for unthankful and undeserving man, it will be that the reins of the heart will be willingly consecrated to "the mystery of his will, according to his good pleasure which he hath purposed in himself."[464]

7. As the heart begins to rationalize this LORD's dying to magnify the character of His Father, that it may be made honorable for us to know and love, it is then that perfection is seen not by commandments, not by any human foundational principle of faith, not by any personal doctrine, not by the perception, not by the desire of the imagination, but rather as it is said, "I am crucified with Christ,"[465] and, "I now live in the flesh"[466] "by the faith of the Son of God."[467] The reality of the true reforming Christian now becomes, "If any man will do his will, he shall know of the doctrine,"[468] and, "The law of the Spirit of life in Christ Jesus hath made me free from the law of sin and death."[469]

8. The law of the Spirit's benevolence is the LORD's voice to the soul, and the sound of that voice is, "Behold the Lamb of God, which taketh away the sin of the world."[470] In the "word of the truth of the gospel,"[471] which word emphasizes "the mystery"[472] of "the dispensation of God";[473] which dispensation is that "of the grace of God"[474] administered by His Holy Spirit; it is that through this counsel we are taught, "The mystery of God should be finished."[475] Personal knowledge of the mystery of redemption's science is the end of experimenting with faith on the Spirit's law and judgment, for it is this doctrine that teaches the honest heart of the grace given to keep the LORD's ten

---

464 Ephesians 1:9
465 Galatians 2:20
466 Galatians 2:20
467 Galatians 2:20
468 John 7:17
469 Romans 8:2
470 John 1:29
471 Colossians 1:5
472 Colossians 1:26
473 Colossians 1:25
474 Ephesians 3:2
475 Revelation 10:7

commandments by faith. The mystery of Christlikeness is that which is to be reproduced within our conscience, even as Christ had His Father's name reproduced within His spirit while on earth, for it is said, "God was manifest in the flesh,"[476] and He tells us, "I know him, and keep his saying."[477]

9. "Without controversy great is the mystery of godliness,"[478] for as He ascended up into glory, it is that He brought down "the praise of the glory of His grace."[479] So then "examine yourselves, whether ye be in the faith,"[480] for "where sin abounded, grace did much more abound"[481] that we may be "temperate in all things."[482] As that Faith of Jesus is diligently studied and upheld, it will create in us a cleanliness of heart and mind to lawfully honor the will and course of His mediation. Confidently the believer will say, "I am crucified with Christ: nevertheless I live; yet not I, but Christ liveth in me."[483]

10. Should this law of His mercy fail to enter into the mind of the meat of the desire of our faith's body, there will be no way for the garment of His name to cover our deficient understanding. The soul not touched by the doctrine of their ransom and reconciliation to the Spirit, for whatever reason, will never bring self to refrain from consuming the fleshly diet of the reactionary stimulus of the flesh encouraged by the philosophy of the serpent through impulse. Health reform does not stop at the stomach, nor does it begin there. If the atmosphere of the spirit of the mind is decayed, any outward reform will also resemble that inward death, and that death will be taken for life. Herein is the reason why we are counseled, "The sting of death is sin; and the strength of sin is the law,"[484] to the end we may know the difference between "life" and "death."

---

476 1 Timothy 3:16
477 John 8:55
478 1 Timothy 3:16
479 Ephesians 1:6
480 2 Corinthians 13:5
481 Romans 5:20
482 1 Corinthians 9:25
483 Galatians 2:20
484 1 Corinthians 15:56

11. It is said, "Let not sin reign in your mortal body, that ye should obey it in the lusts thereof."[485] We know that within our mortal bodies are dead inward members; members born of every handwritten baptism of flesh; as it says, "Ye have yielded your members servants to uncleanness and to iniquity unto iniquity";[486] and of these bodily members we read, "The body is dead"[487] and "the end of those things is death."[488] "For if ye live after the flesh, ye shall die: but if ye through the Spirit do mortify the deeds of the body, ye shall live."[489]

12. If in the flesh I live by the Faith of the Son of God; if the knowledge of the Spirit's Son governs my conversation's conscience; then in my flesh I will conquer the members of my flesh and the deeds of those members done unto "sin" and "death." Only by the Faith of this Christ's heavenly ministry may I ever begin the work of temperance, for redemption's plan is founded upon discretion, as it says, "He humbled himself, and became obedient unto death,"[490] and, "Discretion shall preserve thee, understanding shall keep thee."[491] The Spirit's "grace of life"[492] is to work in us the same effect that it wrought in His Son, even humility to the point of self-sacrifice by death for an edifying love. For this cause He said, "Gather my saints together unto me; those that have made a covenant with me by sacrifice."[493]

13. If I live by the faith of the Son of God who loves me, then by the grace of His name and knowledge working within my conscience, and by my cooperation with His Spirit of grace, that which is of the Spirit will conquer and vanquish that which is of my flesh through faith in the power of the voice of His blood. This is a fact of the Faith within the heavenly Sanctuary. Therefore as it was with Him on earth, and it is with Him within the Spirit's heavenly Building, so too is it to be with

485 Romans 6:12
486 Romans 6:19
487 Romans 8:10
488 Romans 6:21
489 Romans 8:13
490 Philippians 2:8
491 Proverbs 2:11
492 1 Peter 3:7
493 Psalm 50:5

the reformer. "God was in Christ,"[494] and by the Word's creative power through grace, "we might be made the righteousness of God in him"[495] to temperately regulate our members to obey His precepts of life, love, and soul liberty, to the end we may know that "God is with us."[496]

---

494 2 Corinthians 5:19
495 2 Corinthians 5:21
496 Isaiah 8:10

7

Godly Living Through The Power Of Wisdom

1. "The fear of the LORD is the beginning of wisdom."[497] "Wisdom is profitable to direct";[498] "the knowledge of the holy is understanding."[499] "I wisdom dwell with prudence,"[500] "I lead in the way of righteousness."[501] "Counsel is mine, and sound wisdom: I am understanding; I have strength."[502] "The LORD giveth wisdom: out of his mouth cometh knowledge and understanding. He layeth up sound wisdom for the righteous."[503]

2. Without receiving Spirit's wisdom, without constructively applying self to the commandment, "Hide my commandments with thee,"[504] and, "Apply thine heart,"[505] we will fail of honoring the other

497 Proverbs 9:10
498 Ecclesiastes 10:10
499 Proverbs 9:10
500 Proverbs 8:12
501 Proverbs 8:20
502 Proverbs 8:14
503 Proverbs 2:6, 7
504 Proverbs 2:1
505 Proverbs 2:2

commandment, "Grow in grace, and in the knowledge of our Lord and Saviour."[506] Wisdom proceeds out of the mouth of the LORD, and this wisdom is His truth, and, "Thy law is the truth,"[507] it is written, and, "The law is light,"[508] it is again said, therefore "a wise man will hear, and will increase learning"[509] from obeying that which comes out from the LORD's Spirit, compelling that one of "the law of the Spirit of life"[510] to consider how that "the words of a wise man's mouth are gracious."[511]

3. Through learning of and doing every word of the living God, the wise "attain unto wise counsels"[512] because they heard and received the commandment, "Keep sound wisdom and discretion,"[513] and, "Discretion shall preserve thee, understanding shall keep thee."[514] Wisdom dwells with prudence and a spirit of learning, wisdom is understanding and carries an abundance of strength to educate the contrary members of our heart, for it is only through wisdom that we may keep self under strict watch to further advance heaven's cause within our soul temple.

4. We are to grow in grace and in the Spirit's knowledge for one reason, and that reason being that the LORD our Father's wisdom is our source of life, and for them who commit their souls to Him, His words are "health to all their flesh."[515] "She is thy life,"[516] says the LORD of His understanding. "Wisdom is the principal thing"[517] because "she shall preserve thee: love her, and she shall keep thee."[518] Only from obeying the instruction of the His Spirit may we come by His grace, which grace is our peace, which peace is the strength found in His knowledge to help us keep our conversation, even as He says,

---

506 2 Peter 3:18
507 Psalm 119:142
508 Proverbs 6:23
509 Proverbs 1:5
510 Romans 8:2
511 Ecclesiastes 10:12
512 Proverbs 1:5
513 Proverbs 3:21
514 Proverbs 2:11
515 Proverbs 4:22
516 Proverbs 4:13
517 Proverbs 4:7
518 Proverbs 4:6

"Take hold of my strength, that he may make peace with me."[519] Again, "My grace is sufficient for thee: for my strength is made perfect in weakness."[520]

5. The thoughts of the LORD concerning us are only fulfilled if we consent to allow our heart to be touched by His divine influence. It is said, "When wisdom entereth into thine heart, and knowledge is pleasant unto thy soul; discretion shall preserve thee, understanding shall keep thee."[521] Wisdom is the means by which every gift of our Father is opened to us, and to attain to such wisdom, it is done as it is said, "Humble thyself,"[522] and, "Be clothed with humility: for God resisteth the proud, and giveth grace to the humble."[523] "He blesseth the habitation of the just"[524] and "giveth grace unto the lowly."[525]

6. "The fear of the LORD is the beginning of wisdom."[526] "The knowledge of the holy is understanding,"[527] "and to depart from evil is understanding."[528]

7. Practically applying the wisdom learned from examining and doing the Spirit's words will lead the believer to end evil's reign within their conversation, for this is the mind of the godly, even regulating self to cease every unprofitable spiritual indulgence by the Spirit's instruction. If we would irrationally work for our own *salvation*, it is said, "Take heed lest he fall,"[529] yet to the one governed by heaven's wisdom, "I can do all things through Christ which strengtheneth me,"[530] they say. The son and daughter of the Spirit's will is to allow His words to reproduce in them an experience bearing fruit of acquired knowledge, therefore it is said, "Teach a just man, and he will increase in learning."[531]

---

519 Isaiah 27:5
520 2 Corinthians 12:9
521 Proverbs 2:10, 11
522 2 Chronicles 34:27
523 1 Peter 5:5
524 Proverbs 3:33
525 Proverbs 3:34
526 Proverbs 9:10
527 Proverbs 9:10
528 Job 28:28
529 1 Corinthians 10:12
530 Philippians 4:13
531 Proverbs 9:9

8. Only from hearing and doing every word that comes out from the LORD's Spirit, only by diligently applying the grace of His Christ's mediation to our weakness that we may have strength, can we overcome the crude tendencies within the body of our faith. "It shall be health to thy navel, and marrow to thy bones,"[532] if we humble ourselves before the Spirit's will and law to search out the depths of the riches of His wisdom that point back to His character. The knowledge of the godly is to depart from evil or dead religious works, for if there is not a desire to restrain self in order to have the reasoning faculties recovered, we do hate the instruction of the LORD, and so it is then written, "All they that hate me love death."[533] Wisdom and discretion, or knowledge and temperance, are to be those things for the reformer to flush the system of religious corruption when once the taste of self-sufficiency is permitted to settle.

9. The desire of the honest soul is to be godly within their devotion to the living God, therefore it is said, "Hear instruction, and be wise, and refuse it not."[534] The instruction of heaven's Faith will war against the nature of a sinful conversation, therefore "neither be weary of his correction,"[535] for He has said, "As many as I love, I rebuke and chasten."[536] We cannot see the Spirit's intention unless we are right in mind and in nature, and in order for Him "to keep you from falling, and to present you faultless before the presence of his glory,"[537] it is that we must first hear the charge, "Cleanse your hands, ye sinners; and purify your hearts, ye double minded."[538] "If I do this thing willingly, I have a reward,"[539] for it is said, "He shall receive the crown of life, which the Lord hath promised to them that love him."[540]

---

532 Proverbs 3:8
533 Proverbs 8:36
534 Proverbs 8:33
535 Proverbs 3:11
536 Revelation 3:19
537 Jude 1:24
538 James 4:8
539 1 Corinthians 9:17
540 James 1:12

10. Thus, "If ye love me, keep my commandments," says our High Priest. "The word which ye hear is not mine, but the Father's."[541] Says the Father, "Shewing mercy unto thousands of them that love me, and keep my commandments."[542]

11. The reward of reform towards temperance is mercy and grace and peace on them that love His name, and we manifest our love by learning how to lawfully keep His counsels. From obeying His voice, wisdom "shall give to thine head an ornament of grace: a crown of glory shall she deliver to thee."[543] Therefore from subjecting our flesh to the Spirit's precepts through His power, and through our own will to learn and do right, it is that we are "a partaker of the glory that shall be revealed"[544] when we do "suffer according to the will of God."[545] As we "let patience have her perfect work,"[546] we "shall receive the crown of life,"[547] even a crown of "the glory of his grace."[548]

12. This is why He has said of His voice, "She is thy life."[549] "By me thy days shall be multiplied,"[550] He says, and again, "Grace and peace be multiplied unto you through the knowledge of God."[551] We inherit the Spirit's knowledge is as we learn of and do His wisdom, and "the knowledge of wisdom"[552] says, "He that diligently seeketh good procureth favour,"[553] and, "The knowledge of the holy is understanding."[554] Self-denial provides the reformer an opportunity to receive "grace and favour"[555] from diligently obeying His voice to gain a quiet and restful spirit.

---

541 John 14:15, 24
542 Exodus 20:6
543 Proverbs 4:9
544 1 Peter 5:1
545 1 Peter 4:19
546 James 1:4
547 James 1:12
548 Ephesians 1:6
549 Proverbs 4:13
550 Proverbs 9:11
551 2 Peter 1:2
552 Proverbs 24:14
553 Proverbs 11:27
554 Proverbs 9:10
555 Esther 2:17

13. Presently "Israel hath cast off the thing that is good."[556] "They sacrifice flesh for the sacrifices of mine offerings, and eat it,"[557] says the Spirit, and this occurs because "Israel hath forgotten his Maker."[558] There is a forgetting of the LORD's Spirit because there is an ignoring of the course to become familiar with the power of the Creator. How may we place faith in that which we refuse to acknowledge? How can we slight the power of the LORD God's grace and expect to serve His Spirit as our Creator? Therefore, "Fear ye not me? saith the LORD."[559] "The fear of the LORD is the beginning of wisdom,"[560] and the reason we lack depth of spiritual intellect is because we refuse to humble self under the instruction of His name. Today the Spirit says of us, "They hated knowledge, and did not choose the fear of the LORD: they would none of my counsel,"[561] and, "Israel would none of me."[562]

14. Ungodliness prevails within our conversation because we have not, in a pure heart and willing mind, sought to bring the Spirit's wisdom into our conscience by a living and active religion. It is that, "being justified freely by his grace through the redemption that is in Christ Jesus,"[563] we have the means for "putting off the body of the sins of the flesh,"[564] seeing as how "he is able even to subdue all things unto himself."[565] Do we believe this fact? The strength of grace is that particular medicine for our flesh's mind, as it says, "Where sin abounded, grace did much more abound."[566] Again, do we believe enough to go forward "rightly dividing the word of truth"?[567]

15. For, "to whom sware he that they should not enter into his rest, but to them that believed not?"[568] It is that rest of the Spirit, or that

---

556 Hosea 8:3
557 Hosea 8:13
558 Hosea 8:14
559 Jeremiah 5:22
560 Proverbs 9:10
561 Proverbs 1:29,30
562 Psalm 81:11
563 Romans 3:24
564 Colossians 2:11
565 Philippians 3:21
566 Romans 5:20
567 2 Timothy 2:15
568 Hebrews 3:18

meditation through which we are edified, which causes us to walk "in the fear of the Lord, and in the comfort of the Holy Ghost."[569] If we do not dwell in "the grace of the Lord Jesus Christ, and the love of God, and the communion of the Holy Ghost,"[570] we cripple our own conscience to believe in the guile of our heart. Yet if we abide by the wisdom of God, if we are in communion with His name by the Spirit of His grace, we may confess, "We have known and believed the love that God hath to us. God is love; and he that dwelleth in love dwelleth in God, and God in him."[571] Again, this "God commendeth his love toward us"[572]that He may personally purge our "conscience from dead works to serve the living God,"[573] even "abundance of grace and of the gift of righteousness."[574]

16. The gift of righteousness is the grace of God through "the righteousness of one,"[575] our High Priest. Yet it is that wisdom declares, "I lead in the way of righteousness."[576] There can be no wisdom obtained without the grace of this Christ's God, and there can be no grace given if not through the righteousness of this Christ's knowledge. There can be no trace of godliness in the life if self is not humbled under His wisdom to produce the grace necessary to order the faculties of reason, for it says, "The knowledge of the holy is understanding."[577]

17. Self's natural conversation must pass away in order to retain the Spirit's wisdom and perfecting grace. For which cause it is written, "I wisdom dwell with prudence"[578] "that thou mayest regard discretion, and that thy lips may keep knowledge."[579] By wisdom our lips are to keep life's right knowledge, or rather it is purposed for wisdom to keep

---

569 Acts 9:31
570 2 Corinthians 13:14
571 1 John 4:16
572 Romans 5:8
573 Hebrews 9:14
574 Romans 5:17
575 Romans 5:18
576 Proverbs 8:20
577 Proverbs 9:10
578 Proverbs 8:12
579 Proverbs 5:2

our "heart with all diligence; for out of it are the issues of life."[580] It is that man is "diseased with an issue of blood,"[581] "a running issue out of his flesh,"[582] yet if we would desire to be "reconciled in the body of his flesh through death,"[583] the LORD our Father "shall also quicken your mortal bodies by His Spirit."[584] This is why we are counseled, "If any man will come after me, let him deny himself, and take up his cross daily, and follow me."[585]

18. He has counseled the faithful soul, saying, "Let thine heart retain my words: keep my commandments, and live."[586] There can be no pure work of revival if there is no determined effort to learn reform. There will be no personal progressive reform if there is not a humbling of the heart to learn how to accept every word of God in its right context, to then do it. The LORD has left us His precepts of justification because "the commandment is a lamp,"[587] yet one will never know the joy of that light if there is yet a set fortified wall to stop His divine influence. To eat purely from the hand of His Spirit, one must exercise personal and devotional self-denial, for how then can His words expect to be magnified within our heart if we yet remain tied to our own? How may we know our Creator as our Maker if we conscientiously reduce ourselves to doubtful feelings and harsh thoughts?

---

580 Proverbs 4:23
581 Matthew 9:20
582 Leviticus 15:2
583 Colossians 1:21,22
584 Romans 8:11
585 Luke 9:23
586 Proverbs 4:4
587 Proverbs 6:23

8

Living By His Mercies

1. "I beseech you therefore, brethren, by the mercies of God, that ye present your bodies a living sacrifice, holy, acceptable unto God, which is your reasonable service."[588]

2. "Your reasonable service,"[589] says Scripture, is the presentation of "your bodies a living sacrifice, holy."[590] No sacrifice, then, can be considered acceptable unto the Spirit's Word unless the conscience within our faith's bodies is holy, or godly; then would our sacrifices be living and not dead. We show blatant disregard for creation's commandment when refusing to apply consciousness to our conscience by grace to form sober patterns of living. We slight the very purpose of the LORD's intention when not regulating our conversation after the confidence that we are persuaded of, and such a profession is an expression of the waywardness of the demeanor, and of the god of the devotion.

---

588 Romans 12:1
589 Romans 12:1
590 Romans 12:1

3. From "having the same conflict which ye saw in me,"[591] says Paul, it is determined for the reformer to "have like precious faith"[592] as the first apostles through self-correction, to the end "your conversation be as it becometh the gospel of Christ,"[593] "as becometh holiness."[594] "The sacrifices of God are a broken spirit,"[595] even the taxation of "the spirit of your mind,"[596] for then may we be "created in righteousness and true holiness."[597] Without yielding the mind to suffer over faith's requirements, should we refuse the counsel, "Work out your own salvation"[598] "by the renewing of your mind,"[599] we will never come to offer those sacrifices necessary for life, which oblations are a proof that our bodies are living and not dead.

4. We are to be created again only as we choose to be born again. The power of the voice of the Creator that formed the earth and all things that are therein; "visible and invisible, whether they be thrones, or dominions, or principalities, or powers";[600] that same power is to consume us "unto all patience and longsuffering with joyfulness"[601] as we are "renewed in knowledge after the image of him."[602] We are made perfect through suffering; as it is said, "In the bitterness of my soul"[603] "is the life of my spirit";[604] and as we join to our re-education "his power to us-ward who believe,"[605] we may grow to maintain a conversation practicing practical godliness.

---

591 Philippians 1:30
592 2 Peter 1:1
593 Philippians 1:27
594 Titus 2:3
595 Psalm 51:17
596 Ephesians 4:23
597 Ephesians 4:24
598 Philippians 2:12
599 Romans 12:2
600 Colossians 1:16
601 Colossians 1:11
602 Colossians 3:10
603 Isaiah 38:15
604 Isaiah 38:16
605 Ephesians 1:19

5. Seeing that we "should be holy and without blemish,"[606] "not having spot, or wrinkle, or any such thing,"[607] it is that we should depend on and study after the wisdom and power of our High Priest's ministry. Paul lets us know how we are to be godly that we may reform our bodies to right life and not death, and he says, "By the mercies of God."[608] Without admitting self to the Spirit's mercies, we will never come to offer those sacrifices that transform the flesh in order to have our feeble offerings mingle with divine righteousness. The flesh cannot please the Spirit's judgment, for the flesh naturally engages the heart with "death," and, again, it is well to remember how it is written, "The sting of death is sin; and the strength of sin is the law."[609] The fleshly conversation, because it is bound to legal religious traditions of priests and ministers, moves the person to fulfill the saying, "They that are such serve not our Lord Jesus Christ, but their own belly,"[610] but concerning the Spirit's steward, they are counseled, "Seek those things which are above, where Christ sitteth on the right hand of God."[611]

6. It is said, Praise Him "ye waters that be above the heavens";[612] "for his mercy is great above the heavens."[613] If every unreasonable diet of the flesh would be made known to us and conquered, the Christian needs to subscribe to that which rests above the heavens that they may hear the LORD's Spirit say, "With great mercies will I gather thee."[614] By the Spirit's mercies; "even the sure mercies of David,"[615] which mercies are, "The covenant of my peace,"[616] says our Priest's LORD; we are to defeat every reckless religious indulgence that leads to a deadening of spiritual and moral perception. Surely this covenant of peace, these sure and great mercies, are nothing but "showers of

606 Ephesians 5:27
607 Ephesians 5:27
608 Romans 12:1
609 1 Corinthians 15:56
610 Romans 16:18
611 Colossians 3:1
612 Psalm 148:4
613 Psalm 108:4
614 Isaiah 54:7
615 Isaiah 55:3
616 Isaiah 54:10

blessing"[617] given to the believer because they have, as it is written, "A covenant with me by sacrifice,"[618] says the Spirit.

7. To offer the spiritual sacrifices of heaven, as they are to be accepted by the LORD and Father of heaven, means to enter into a covenant with His name by sacrifice that we may receive showers of mercy to flavor our experience aright. We cannot sacrifice to the Word any thing acceptable without first sacrificing the spirit of our mind to be made acceptable. Only by the mercies of God can we maintain our bodies as acceptable presents to His name, for it is our Father "who hath blessed us with all spiritual blessings in heavenly places in Christ."[619] If we are not receiving these blessing by His Son's mediation to offer up sacrifices acceptable to Him in the Faith of that mediation, then we are indeed serving another god whom we desire to please. The flesh cannot serve the living God; the Christian should not serve in the confidence of the conversation, but should overcome and refresh the body of their faith by the showers "of the glory of his grace."[620]

8. There is another god striving for the mastery in the one who is stubborn to the requirements of the LORD and Spirit of the Bible. "We see,"[621] say they, "Therefore your sin remaineth,"[622] says our High Priest. There is a terrible curse delivered to the eyes of the one professing faithfulness while denying the power of a right profession, even as it says, "Having a form of godliness, but denying the power thereof."[623] Because "they have chosen their own ways, and their soul delighteth in their abominations,"[624] "I will choose their delusions,"[625] says the Spirit. "When I spake, ye did not hear; but did evil before mine eyes, and did choose that wherein I delighted not,"[626] which is why "they all might be damned who believed not the truth, but had

---

617 Ezekiel 34:26
618 Psalm 50:5
619 Ephesians 1:3
620 Ephesians 1:6
621 John 9:41
622 John 9:41
623 2 Timothy 3:5
624 Isaiah 66:3
625 Isaiah 66:4
626 Isaiah 65:12

pleasure in unrighteousness."[627] Herein it is well to remember that "all unrighteousness is sin,"[628] and that "the strength of sin is the law."[629] That which is "evil" is today that which is understood to be "sin," and "handwriting of ordinances"[630] of priests and elders, due to the passing flesh of God's Man on the tree, is "sin" against heaven's will, and to continue in it is to uphold a conversation of sin and death. Humility to faithfully learn of and do the Spirit's will and judgment is the only means whereby creation's promise may be fulfilled within our conversation's conscience, but if we fail to meditate on His voice, we remain in what separates our heart from His face.

9. No man or woman can claim patience and yet remain intemperate, and there can be none intemperate person professing godliness, for there cannot be two powers striving for the throne of being; we cannot claim faith's course while at the same time claim government by the legal religious bill of flesh. Solomon became a Christian given to willful ignorant indulgence within his conversation, and wrote, "I hated life."[631] We will hate the things of the Spirit should we continue to profess heaven's throne religion without applying to the health of the practice of heaven's High Priest. We cannot have presentable bodies before the living God if not maintaining the soundness of our flesh by His mercies. The heart will fail and the vision will grow dim if we accept to refuse the work of covenanting with the LORD's Spirit by sacrifice – by self-sacrifice and self-discipline.

10. It is that by placing the counsel of Christ's mediation over our troubles, and by applying the grace of God to join with the power of our will to overcome our inherited defects and cultivated tendencies, that we may labor for the saving or delivering of our inward parts "unto all patience and longsuffering with joyfulness."[632] It is said, "The blueness of a wound cleanseth away evil: so do stripes the inward parts

---

627 2 Thessalonians 2:12
628 1 John 5:17
629 1 Corinthians 15:56
630 Colossians 2:14
631 Ecclesiastes 2:17
632 Colossians 1:11

of the belly."[633] The belly needs to be cleansed by soul bitterness that we may have the deficient faculties of our mind renewed by the Holy Ghost, and that cleansing appears by one means, and it says, "Through knowledge shall the just be delivered,"[634] and, "He might sanctify and cleanse it with the washing of water by the word."[635] Should we reject the chastening of the Spirit, should we come to a mountain of impossibility and believe that it cannot be moved, indeed it will not be moved, for we doubt the power to have it moved because we have rejected the experience to grow familiar with that power's wisdom.

11. "The spirit of man,"[636] this is "the candle of the LORD, searching all the inward parts of the belly."[637] The will must be tested and proved "that God may know my integrity."[638] By the mercies of God "the righteous also shall hold on his way, and he that hath clean hands shall be stronger and stronger."[639] Patient perseverance births the wisdom of integrity, and such an individual, who is fond to the challenge of existing by principle within his spirit, will grow stronger and stronger. How and why? It is known, "Thou wilt keep him in perfect peace, whose mind is stayed on thee." "In the LORD Jeho'vah is everlasting strength."[640]

12. If the belly is left void of the Spirit's peace and mercies; the grace and spiritual blessing of wisdom and understanding intended to aid the Christian through every mental and moral struggle; the belly will deplete the life force of the spirit, and there will be a continual relapse into sinful indulgences that will soon take a natural and permanent form. "Being justified by faith, we have peace with God,"[641] and as sharers of "the grace of God,"[642] "being justified by his grace, we should

---

633 Proverbs 20:30
634 Proverbs 11:9
635 Ephesians 5:26
636 Proverbs 20:27
637 Proverbs 20:27
638 Job 31:6
639 Job 17:9
640 Isaiah 26:3,4
641 Romans 5:1
642 Ephesians 3:7

be made heirs according to the hope of eternal life."[643] Therefore "for the hope of Israel I am bound,"[644] which hope is as stated, "If the Spirit that raised up Jesus from the dead dwell in you, he that raised up Christ from the dead shall also quicken your mortal bodies by his Spirit which dwelleth in you."[645]

13. Only by that Spirit which rose up that Christ may we experience the power of a conversation swallowed up in the spiritual newness that is intended for the believer. It is our responsibility to consent to have His Spirit's mind within the spirit of our conversation, for it is not born with us, nor is we our own god. The LORD's Spirit is within our conscience because we have made a choice to do that Spirit's will by faith on the end promised to our heart. We have followed the pattern of Adam, as it says, "He slept,"[646] thereby allowing the Spirit of the Word to work in us because we have fallen asleep to our own wisdom and appetite to "speak the mystery of Christ."[647]

14. "Ye may abound in hope, through the power of the Holy Ghost,"[648] only by the mercies of God. From the grace of God we are to be "full of goodness, filled with knowledge";[649] "filled with the knowledge of his will in all wisdom and spiritual understanding";[650] that we may present ourselves "a living sacrifice"[651] "quickened by the Spirit,"[652] "holy, acceptable unto God."[653] Drunkenness must be checked by the example of the man Daniel who "purposed in his heart that he would not defile himself."[654] "I made a covenant with mine eyes,"[655] the

---

643 Romans 5:15
644 Acts 28:20
645 Romans 8:11
646 Genesis 2:21
647 Colossians 4:3
648 Romans 15:13
649 Romans 15:14
650 Colossians 1:9
651 Romans 12:1
652 1 Peter 3:18
653 Romans 12:1
654 Daniel 1:8
655 Job 31:1

reformer should declare, "that I may know him,"[656] because it is said, "Have made a covenant with me by sacrifice."[657]

15. Without cultivating self-restraint to know the value of heaven's riches, remaining jealous for His attention while patient with self, there will be no level of accepted godliness to advance from the Christian experience into the promised higher learning. We are to be "renewed in knowledge,"[658] which means that we are to not stop correcting self. The Christian must not cease experimenting with trusting the living God's name, to pick up actively believing at a later and more preferable date. We are to be repaired, restored, rehabilitated "after the image of him"[659] now at this present time, and such a work will be relentlessly tiresome and pointless without a full surrendering of the heart to heaven's course. We are to be creatures newly made within our mind to carry out a particularly registered conversation throughout our body, and should there be no mind to cease error that stops pure communication between the Creator and us?

16. Sleep will be given to the eyes of the one who maintains the code of their natural inheritance. Every action begins with our thoughts. From constantly endorsing a thought, the imagination will be carried to the mind that the body may execute it. "The LORD searcheth all hearts, and understandeth all the imaginations of the thoughts,"[660] and if the professor ceases not to kill their heart that His Spirit may find place in it for health, the thoughts will regulate the being, and the mind will become dwarfed and lethargic, not able to understand that the religion of His Christ is after "the acknowledging of the truth which is after godliness."[661] "Godliness" is a conversation without subjection to the legal religious tradition of priests and elders. "Sin," by His Man on the tree, is today recognized by what is nailed to the tree, "even the law of commandments contained in ordinances."[662] It is our responsibility to

---

656 Philippians 3:10
657 Psalm 50:5
658 Colossians 3:10
659 Colossians 3:10
660 1 Chronicles 28:9
661 Titus 1:1
662 Ephesians 2:15

pass away from this error against the living God's name, even as our High Priest "is gone into heaven, and is on the right hand of God."[663]

17. The LORD's intention is to gather "us unto the adoption of children by Jesus Christ"[664] "to the praise of the glory of his grace";[665] which grace in Christ by God "is the earnest of our inheritance"[666] "wherein he hath made us accepted."[667] By the mercies of God we are to have our spirit perfected that we may render acceptable service to His name and cause, and there is no similarity between Him and the religious world. The truth which is after godliness teaches that we cannot serve the living God while breaking His laws of redemption, which laws lead the doer of them to His ten immutable commandments of love, life, and liberty of the heart and mind. Godly living is ordering the life after His every word by grace through faith on the law of soul reconciliation.

18. What then is the counsel of this LORD? "Abstain from fornication";[668] "keep yourselves from idols";[669] "neither shalt thou commit adultery."[670] Idolatry, fornication, adultery, these are all one in the selfsame thing, and to refuse the work of temperance; enduring the painstaking effort to cultivate an abstemious diet from the pen of men in all things, and with a mind to come by knowledge of the Godhead's benevolence; is to reject the will of His Spirit. Obedience to His every precept cannot have place within our conscience if we yet desire to maintain our naturally carnal and decrepit nature, for "the natural man receiveth not the things of the Spirit of God."[671]

19. "Why will ye die, O house of Israel?"[672] It is our "reasonable service"[673] to bear "in the body the dying of the Lord Jesus, that the life

663 1 Peter 3:22
664 Ephesians 1:5
665 Ephesians 1:6
666 Ephesians 1:14
667 Ephesians 1:6
668 1 Thessalonians 4:3
669 1 John 5:20
670 Deuteronomy 5:18
671 1 Corinthians 2:14
672 Ezekiel 18:31
673 Romans 12:1

also of Jesus might be made manifest in our body."[674] Have we forgotten that "as the sufferings of Christ abound in us, so our consolation also aboundeth by Christ"?[675] Should we afflict our souls according to affliction's right commandment, "he shall come unto us as the rain,"[676] and because we do the will of God, "My doctrine shall drop as the rain,"[677] He promises. Therefore "if any man will do his will, he shall know of the doctrine."[678]

20. For the believer, the purpose of the blessings of the new covenant is to come into personal contact with the living God. If we refuse the work of righteousness then we will miss having in us "the doctrine which is according to godliness."[679]

---

674 2 Corinthians 4:10
675 2 Corinthians 1:5
676 Hoses 6:3
677 Deuteronomy 32:2
678 John 7:17
679 1 Timothy 6:3

9

Surrendering To One Diet

1. "The life of the flesh is in the blood,"[680] "it is the life of all flesh."[681] "Abstain from meats offered to idols, and from blood, and from things strangled, and from fornication: from which if ye keep yourselves, ye shall do well."[682] "A sound heart is the life of the flesh."[683] "Abstain from pollutions of idols, and from fornication, and from things strangled, and from blood."[684]

2. There are two types of life that we may apply to the members of our flesh, and they being the life of blood, or that life of a sound heart. Both are the life of the flesh, and we may devour one for life quickened, and the other for the life of death, as it is written, "He that soweth to the flesh shall of the flesh reap corruption,"[685] but "of the Spirit reap life everlasting."[686] For this cause it is said, "Sow to yourselves in

---

680 Leviticus 17:11
681 Leviticus 17:14
682 Acts 15:29
683 Proverbs 14:30
684 Acts 15:29
685 Galatians 6:8
686 Galatians 6:8

righteousness, reap in mercy,"[687] and, "Ye have plowed wickedness, ye have reaped iniquity."[688]

3. There are two dietetic options for the Christian, and one is after "the savour of death unto death; and to the other the savour of life unto life."[689] There is a supply of life for our flesh, or as it says, concerning the definition of "flesh," "My flesh and my heart."[690] There is a confidence found within our heart that will either be a curse or a blessing to us and to others. We may then say, to better understand the counsel given us within the book of Proverbs and Leviticus, "The life of the heart is in the blood," and, "A sound heart is the life of the heart," seeing as how our flesh is in reality stimulated by the defective members within our heart. We may choose proper stimulus for our conversation from regulating the desires of our heart, yet if in every aspect of our existence we refuse to regulate the body of our faith's conscience, we will be left saying, "My heart and my flesh crieth out."[691]

4. We can eat either blood or soundness, and an alcoholic indulgence in both will cause irritability within the mind, compelling the heart to individually alleviate the stress put upon it. It is said, "Abstain from meats offered to idols, and from blood,"[692] for herein is the blood that we can eat which produces an impure current of life, even our flesh meats "after the commandments and doctrines of men"[693] that are our heart idols. "Abstain from pollutions of idols,"[694] it is said, for if we maintain, within our heart, the diet of our flesh's natural meat, we will only be giving birth to an impure spirit within our mind. "Covetousness, which is idolatry,"[695] is the reason why a flood filled the earth in the time of Noah. It is written, "I had not known lust, except the law said, Thou shalt not covet,"[696] for it was because man excessively indulged

---

687 Hosea 10:12
688 Hosea 10:13
689 2 Corinthians 2:16
690 Psalm 73:26
691 Psalm 84:2
692 Acts 15:29
693 Colossians 2:22
694 Acts 15:20
695 Colossians 3:5
696 Romans 7:7

the lust of his flesh, the meat of his conversation, his idolatrous heart, that a flood was deemed necessary to end spiritual and moral pollution.

5. Covetousness is idolatry and it is also lust, and to manage the breath of our life through the meats of our heart is to display the true intention of our person. Who were they that perished in the flood? It is written, "All flesh, wherein is the breath of life,"[697] and again, "All in whose nostrils was the breath of life."[698] Such were they that did "breathe out cruelty"[699] because of their intemperance. Of this land's religious institution, it was said, "As a fountain casteth out her water, so she casteth out her wickedness: violence and spoil is heard in her."[700] Do the scriptures lie? What is the record of Noah's age? "The earth also was corrupt before God, and the earth was filled with violence."[701] In their heart they said, "There is no God,"[702] and this why the LORD said of them, "They are corrupt."[703]

6. It is then a fact, when we eat the blood of violence, which violence is a diet of self-regulation above the living God's precepts; which violence is nailed to the tree; we show our disdain for the Word by stubbornly cherishing our darling idols that should be removed for the good of our conscience. An unhealthy and an unnatural diet is the consumption of the meats of our flesh, which meats are the seeds of covetous practices sown through rebellion against heaven's new covenant will. "Every imagination of the thoughts of his heart was only evil continually,"[704] is what our LORD and Father determined through His investigation of man. Because there was no restraint on passionate inclination, man of old retreated to the doctrine of their mother Eve, who was the mother of all living, even the mother of them born of "the land of the living."[705]

---

697 Genesis 6:17
698 Genesis 7:22
699 Psalm 27:12
700 Jeremiah 6:7
701 Genesis 6:11
702 Psalm 14:1
703 Psalm 14:1
704 Genesis 6:5
705 Psalm 27:13

7. Before we may have the hand of our High Priest deliver us His mediation's Spirit for the purpose of reviving our inwards, whereby we are brought into a confrontation with His face, we are to first pick up self and regulate self by depending on the power and wisdom of His name's grace, that we may know the depth of our condition to grow fond of the Savior of our condition. If freedom is given to the members of the body according the standards of the heart without the living health of the conscience, we will crumble under confusion, we will falsely erect policies to fulfill without having a mind for their necessity. If the Spirit has not brought the mind into poverty by His voice, the flesh will devour its meats to erroneously sustain itself. The heart of the flesh must first feel its woe before it may begin any reform, and then may we afterwards begin to add soundness of life to the constitution of the body of our sin.

8. The mind must retake possession of the body, and this cannot be done but through Spirit's the grace. This is why it is said, "Through the grace of the Lord Jesus Christ we shall be saved."[706] By the creative power of His doctrine we may have the order of our conscience restored to declare, "I delight in the law of God after the inward man."[707] The LORD's grace is for the betterment of our conversation, and the life of our mind is found and maintained from complete obedience to His precepts of liberty and justification, for this is why it is said, "This is the will of God, even your sanctification, that ye should abstain from fornication."[708] Without an effort to cultivate self-denial through grace's redemptive learning, no one will be brought into a living relationship with the living God that He may sanctify their inward parts. We "have made void thy law,"[709] O LORD, from being "given to appetite."[710]

9. A heart given to self is only so endorsed because a removal of the meat of the flesh will cause a breach in the worship of its idol. "Abstain

706 Acts 15:11
707 Romans 7:22
708 1 Thessalonians 4:3
709 Psalm 119:126
710 Proverbs 23:2

from pollutions of idols,"[711] which pollution is "from fornication,"[712] which fornication is "from meats offered to idols, and from blood."[713] The "blood" of men is that life of the flesh leading the individual to maintain the report, "Every imagination of the thoughts of his heart was only evil continually."[714] This life-force carries us back to the doctrine of our inherited nature, "Ye shall be as gods,"[715] therefore as gods we cannot receive the sanctification of the Spirit's Word, seeing as how we are corrupt, violent, covetous, idolatrous, lustful, and given over to freely eat the meat of our flesh, and have found life, as it says, "Thou hast found the life of thine hand."[716]

10. The life of the heart is the blood, and this life is death mistaken for strength to the mind. "Thou mayest not eat the life with the flesh,"[717] it is counseled, and it is so said for the purpose of helping us stay from progressing that nature inherited by self and by men. A diet of blood, a self-prescribed regimen of heart distractions, will keep us in the state that the enemy spirit would have us in. We cannot hear the voice of God when willingly supplying leanness for stability. We cannot retain the sanctifying principles of truth if we are devourers of self. The inward man of the reformer is to house the Law and the Doctrine of Life, and if we are consumers of flesh, we will be destroyed by flesh, and being destroyed by flesh we give ourselves as pawns to the destroyer of all soundness, fulfilling the saying, "They crucify to themselves the Son of God afresh, and put him to an open shame."[718]

11. That which is internal will be manifested outwardly. The character of God is to be engraved "between thine eyes,"[719] for it is in the heart of our mind where the seat of benevolence is to be found. "I will put my law in their inward parts, and write in their hearts,"[720] prom-

711 Acts 15:20
712 Acts 15:20
713 Acts 15:29
714 Genesis 6:5
715 Genesis 3:5
716 Isaiah 57:10
717 Deuteronomy 12:23
718 Hebrews 6:6
719 Exodus 13:16
720 Jeremiah 31:33

ises our LORD, for "it is written in the prophets, And they shall be all taught of God."[721] If that which is internal is of the flesh's rebellion against heaven's will; which "rebellion" is "sin," and "the strength of sin is the law,"[722] which "law" is "the handwriting of ordinances";[723] that diet which is external will also be of the same mind. All that "hath learned of the Father, cometh unto me,"[724] says our High Priest, for it is that only from an encounter with the Father; with the Spirit and His commandments; by relinquishing self to His Faith "after that ye heard the word of truth,"[725] may we honestly begin to reform our conversation from learning of and doing to the words of His Christ.

12. Herein is the reason why our High Priest prays, "Holy Father, keep through thine own name those whom thou hast given me."[726] To learn of the Father is the will of the Father, which will is "salvation through sanctification of the Spirit and belief of the truth."[727] We cannot escape the fact that the religion of God's Christ is the name of the Spirit within the inward parts by way of the gift of grace through a personal reformation in mind and character, therefore to presumptuously uphold the conflict between the flesh and the Spirit is to only kill the force of life from the heart. Therefore "if so be ye have heard him, and have been taught by him, as the truth is in Jesus,"[728] then "you hath he quickened, who were dead in trespasses and sins."[729] The soundness of our flesh is attributed to that which quickens or regenerates the mind, and for our sake it is that the words of this Christ "are life"[730] "that quickeneth."[731]

---

721 John 6:45
722 1 Corinthians 15:56
723 Colossians 2:14
724 John 6:45
725 Ephesians 1:13
726 John 17:11
727 2 Thessalonians 2:13
728 Ephesians 4:21
729 Ephesians 2:1
730 John 6:63
731 John 6:63

13. To have learned of God and to have been taught by Him means to experience the truth as it is in His Son. To experience the character of God as it is in the doctrine of Christ, the believer needs to make an adjustment in diet. If there is consumption of heart meats; whether at regular or irregular intervals; we will be that which we eat. An intelligent faith is developed through consuming the flesh or conversation of the LORD's Christ, not simply receiving His words, but also routinely placing them to supplement the natural inclination to encounter recovery of mind and time. We are to be quickened from death, from numbness within the mental and moral faculties by that manner of devotion for ever nailed to the tree, and an intelligent experience in diligent and watchful obedience by faith in the Spirit's power and wisdom will procure health and blessing to the body and conscience of our conversation.

14. If we are internally digesting the idols of our flesh, then physically we will consume the same diet resulting in the same benumbed leanness pronounced upon them by the sacrificed flesh of the LORD's Man, which is why it says, "For this cause God shall send them strong delusion, that they should believe a lie."[732] We are to be healed from corruption inwardly, which is why, when we admit the Spirit's Faith as personal Savior of the flesh, we commit Him to be governor over our entirely feeble constitution. His authority doesn't stop where we mark it should stop; we are bought with a price, we are all not our own, and should we live as though we are our own, it is not forced upon us to render to the living God what is due. We will suffer the death of Adam because of stubbornness, and will be blessed with confusion until we are consumed of ourselves, not knowing that we are dead within self and are led by "seducing spirits, and doctrines of devils."[733] "Flesh and blood cannot inherit the kingdom of God."[734]

15. May we then have this testimony, "I conferred not with flesh and blood."[735] A sound heart is the life of the flesh of the reforming Christian born of the Spirit by the knowledge and experience of His

---

732 2 Thessalonians 2:11
733 1 Timothy 4:1
734 1 Corinthians 15:50
735 Galatians 1:16

Son's name, for He made "in himself of twain one new man, so making peace."[736] We are yet in flesh and blood and are to be quickened; as it says, "The last Adam was made a quickening spirit";[737] therefore the death of the first Adam is an option, so is the life of the second. Within the will and learning of our High Priest's intercession is the soundness of our conversation, in His name is that right life of our conscience, even as He Himself says, "My flesh is meat indeed, and my blood is drink indeed."[738]

16. "Unto you it is given in the behalf of Christ, not only to believe on him, but also to suffer for his sake":[739] "to be strengthened with might by his Spirit in the inner man: that Christ may dwell in your hearts by faith";[740] "that ye might be filled with the knowledge of his will in all wisdom and spiritual understanding,"[741] "renewed in the spirit of your mind"[742] through "knowledge after the image of him."[743]

---

736 Ephesians 2:15
737 1 Corinthians 15:45
738 John 6:55
739 Philippians 1:29
740 Ephesians 3:16,17
741 Colossians 1:9
742 Ephesians 4:23
743 Colossians 3:10

10

Practical Godliness Made Plain Through Practical Wisdom

1. "The LORD will not suffer the soul of the righteous to famish."[744] "The merciful man doeth good to his own soul."[745] "He that diligently seeketh good procureth favour,"[746] "but he that is cruel troubleth his own flesh."[747] For "the wise in heart will receive commandments";[748] "wise men lay up knowledge";[749] "the mouth of a righteous man is a well of life";[750] "the mouth of the just bringeth forth wisdom."[751] "The labour of the righteous tendeth to life";[752] "the fruit of the righteous is a tree of life";[753] "he is in the way of life that keepeth instruction: but he that refuseth reproof erreth."[754] "Fools die for want of wisdom."[755]

---

744 Proverbs 10:3
745 Proverbs 11:17
746 Proverbs 11:27
747 Proverbs 11:17
748 Proverbs 10:8
749 Proverbs 10:14
750 Proverbs 10:11
751 Proverbs 10:31
752 Proverbs 10:16
753 Proverbs 11:30
754 Proverbs 10:17
755 Proverbs 10:21

2. It is said, "Understanding is a wellspring of life unto him that hath it,"[756] and, "To depart from evil is understanding,"[757] and again, "The knowledge of the holy is understanding."[758] There is spiritual and religious death, and many "are as water spilt on the ground, which cannot be gathered up again,"[759] for a lack of willing obedience towards the Spirit's wisdom, leaving the heart "to do whatsoever thy hand and thy counsel determined before to be done."[760] It is therefore said, "They obeyed not, nor inclined their ear, but walked every one in the imagination of their evil heart."[761]

3. The wisdom of the godly is to depart from their evil heart, for if the voice of the LORD was studiously obeyed, rebellion would not reign within the flesh. "He that refraineth his lips is wise,"[762] says Scripture, "A man of understanding holdeth his peace,"[763] it is written, because "he that trusteth in his riches shall fall"[764] and "he that troubleth his own house shall inherit the wind."[765] We know that we cherish a cruel heart when we trouble our own house, when we indulge the inducement of our flesh without sound reason. The flesh is that which is to receive health; self-development must take place before the living God may trust us beside His Son; and His precepts of liberty are the only health for our soul temple.

4. There is death because there is a lazy disobedience. The wise will receive commandments by way of correction and their knowledge will bear fruit as a tree of life, for wisdom "is a tree of life to them that lay hold upon her."[766] If many would turn from being "lovers of pleasures more than lovers of God,"[767] it is that they must confess in their heart to

---

756 Proverbs 16:22
757 Job 28:28
758 Proverbs 9:10
759 2 Samuel 14:14
760 Acts 4:28
761 Jeremiah 11:8
762 Proverbs 10:19
763 Proverbs 11:12
764 Proverbs 11:28
765 Proverbs 11:129
766 Proverbs 3:18
767 2 Timothy 3:4

the LORD of their High Priest, "What seemeth you best I will do."[768] "He must increase, and I must decrease,"[769] says the lover His Spirit, therefore they are become "a lover of hospitality, a lover of good men, sober, just, holy, temperate."[770] Such as are taught of His Spirit are instructed by Him from lessons which advance the development of His character in them, and as the Christian seeks to depart from what is today "sin" and "evil," remaining diligent to the instruction obtained from thoughtfully depending on the counsel of His mediation, it is then that disobedience is exchanged for reverence towards His name, and purity of heart in respect for the blood of the atonement of their mind.

5. "He that is cruel troubleth his own flesh,"[771] and this is not the lot of the reformer, but rather, "Worship God in the spirit, and rejoice in Christ Jesus, and have no confidence in the flesh,"[772] we are counseled. It is the LORD our Father who "hath made him to be sin for us"[773] "that we might be made the righteousness of God in him,"[774] therefore it is by His wisdom that we are to be made perfect in His doctrine "by the riches of the glory of his inheritance."[775] "The exceeding greatness of his power to us-ward who believe"[776] is found in His saying, "I send the promise of my Father upon you."[777] Indeed "they were filled with the Holy Ghost"[778] "as of fire";[779] "the Spirit gave them utterance";[780] and so too for us, the grace and Spirit of God is given that we may be "enriched by him, in all utterance, and in all knowledge."[781]

6. The flesh is to be conquered by grace through our living faith in the virtue of His blood, to the end that we may gain sound wisdom by

---

768 2 Samuel 18:4
769 John 3:30
770 Titus 1:8,9
771 Proverbs 11:17
772 Philippians 3:3
773 2 Corinthians 5:21
774 2 Corinthians 5:21
775 Ephesians 1:18
776 Ephesians 1:19
777 Luke 24:49
778 Acts 2:4
779 Acts 2:3
780 Acts 2:4
781 2 Corinthians 1:4,5

experience to keep ourselves from ourselves. Without that stream of fire flowing from the throne of grace and into our soul temple, and without admitting that health to the trouble of our heart, there will be no victory gained in His Son's name. It is our assignment to obtain victory of the spirit of the religious world, therefore "let patience have her perfect work,"[782] for "the righteousness of the perfect shall direct his ways."[783] The believer is to be directed by their corrected conscience as they are taught of God, and we know our wisdom is of Him "by the Spirit which he hath given us,"[784] and we know that we are perfected by His Spirit because we trust in His righteousness, even as He says, "Their righteousness is of me, saith the LORD."[785]

7. As we hide self in "the righteousness which is of God by faith,"[786] wisdom will be given to us as we live His charge by His power, which power is the promised inheritance of the believer. "The inheritance of the saints"[787] is given through faith in the merits of the blood of His Christ, wherefore it is said, "In whom also we have obtained an inheritance,"[788] even "that holy Spirit of promise, which is the earnest of our inheritance."[789] Without the promise of life added to the experience, there will be no fruit of life added to the conscience. "Fools die for want of wisdom"[790] because they have given superiority to the idols of the heart to govern the mind, yet "he is in the way of life that keepeth instruction."[791] It is said, "Reproofs of instruction are the way of life,"[792] yet if we are refusing to personally acquaint our conversation with the Creator's wisdom, "All they that hate me love death,"[793] reports His Spirit.

---

782 James 1:4
783 Proverbs 11:5
784 1 John 3:24
785 Isaiah 54:17
786 Philippians 3:9
787 Colossians 1:12
788 Ephesians 1:11
789 Ephesians 1:13
790 Proverbs 10:21
791 Proverbs 10:17
792 Proverbs 6:23
793 Proverbs 8:36

8. "His commandments are not grievous,"[794] for "the law is spiritual"[795] and "it is the spirit that quickeneth; the flesh profiteth nothing."[796] We know if undefiled love is the subject of our heart or if we contain a pure longing for the divine love of God in the soul, "for this is the love of God, that we keep his commandments."[797] "The desire of the righteous is only good,"[798] and only His Spirit's "law is holy, and the commandment holy, and just, and good."[799] The righteous will maintain communion with this Spirit for the purpose of having His name and Word of love within their heart. After they have endured hard chastening to declare within themselves, "I abhor myself, and repent in dust and ashes,"[800] after the recording angel has revealed to the LORD, "He then vexed himself,"[801] the Spirit's Priest declares, "We will come unto him, and make our abode with him."[802]

9. "Understanding is a wellspring of life unto him that hath it"[803] because from obeying the words of His Christ; which words "are spirit, and they are life";[804] the inwards become "a well of water springing up into everlasting life."[805] He or she born of God's Spirit is conceived through learning of and doing His words of mental and moral nourishment, and as "he that is begotten of God keepeth himself,"[806] it is so done because "his seed remaineth in him: and he cannot sin, because he is born of God."[807]

10. We are born of God by experimenting with His wisdom, and the growth of our character and the transformation of our flesh is maintained by the same course. "Every one that doeth righteousness is born

---

794 1 John 5:3
795 Romans 7:14
796 John 6:63
797 1 John 5:3
798 Proverbs 11:23
799 Romans 7:12
800 Job 42:6
801 2 Samuel 12:18
802 John 14:23
803 Proverbs 16:22
804 John 6:63
805 John 4:14
806 1 John 5:18
807 1 John 3:9

of him,"[808] or rather, all that "hear instruction"[809] and "get wisdom, get understanding";[810] all that "criest after knowledge, and liftest up"[811] "for understanding";[812] will obtain wisdom to have continual intercourse with the health of their being. "As the rain cometh down, and the snow from heaven, and returneth not thither, but watereth the earth, and maketh it bring forth and bud,"[813] so too are the Spirit's words to be for our seed of faith. This is that word which "is a discerner of the thoughts and intents of the heart,"[814] to the end that the seed of hope may grow strong through showers of grace as we purify our flesh to bear the fruit and fragrance of righteousness.

11. "Through sanctification of the Sprit and belief of the truth,"[815] we are to have a personal store of knowledge to be as fuel for our faith and for support of one another, even as it says, "Fruit that may abound to your account."[816] The wisdom of life that we are to gain is that which is to turn us from our source of self-sufficiency, and we cannot separate from the lust of our flesh if we are consuming the different dishes of meat found on the table of our heart. Is it a light matter to not consider the need for self-correction by the Spirit's counsel and reproof? Isn't it written, "Reproofs of instruction are the way of life"?[817] The wisdom gained from doing creation's law is to lodge within our spirit; as it says, "Write them upon the table of thine heart";[818] yet wisdom is only gained when we allow the ground of our heart to be given to its owner, killing fear and pride "by patient continuance in well doing,"[819] for it is said, "The patient in spirit is better than the proud in spirit."[820]

---

808 1 John 2:29
809 Proverbs 8:33
810 Proverbs 4:5
811 Proverbs 2:3
812 Proverbs 2:3
813 Isaiah 55:10
814 Hebrews 4:12
815 2 Thessalonians 2:13
816 Philippians 4:17
817 Proverbs 6:23
818 Proverbs 3:3
819 Romans 2:7
820 Ecclesiastes 7:8

12. If the struggling heart would cease early death from unhealthy practices, it would be good to receive the medication that combats trauma to the soul, body, and conscience. There is a need for a personal religion by faith in the righteousness of His Christ, for herein the Christian will receive the LORD's wisdom, and grace through the revelation of His name, to order the spirit of their conversation. A lack of effort to yield self to the influence of His Spirit does show contentment of heart towards that impaired and incontinent nature. We are not made perfect in love, and are not naturally created after the image of love, and through intemperance we slight the work of love. The conversation's conscience is to be renewed in wisdom after the image of Him that ransomed it from the serpent's philosophy; which philosophy is nailed to the tree; and by refusing to allow the instruction of the LORD's grace to do it's perfect work over and within the heart, we are rejecting the authority of His Spirit's commandment over our conscience and His righteousness over our flesh.

13. He that obtains righteousness through His righteousness will be made perfect in love, for the experience will reveal the sure marks of His Son within the conversation. It is wisdom that is to "direct your hearts into the love of God, and into the patient waiting for Christ,"[821] and if it is not the wisdom of the Spirit's Word which does this work within our inwards, "ye receive another spirit,"[822] "another gospel,"[823] "another Jesus."[824]

14. The Christian must submit to the work of obtaining the Spirit's wisdom and grace by faith to sustain themselves for the purpose of benevolent self-management. Then may the believer "lead a quiet and peaceable life in all godliness and honesty,"[825] considering the fact that to grow, I must "be base in mine own sight."[826]

---

821 2 Thessalonians 3:5
822 2 Corinthians 11:4
823 2 Corinthians 11:4
824 2 Corinthians 11:4
825 1 Timothy 2:2
826 2 Samuel 6:22

11

Perfect And Entire, Wanting Nothing

1. "My brethren, count it all joy when ye fall into divers temptations; knowing this, that the trying of your faith worketh patience. But let patience have her perfect work, that ye may be perfect and entire, wanting nothing."[827]

2. The health for the correction of the heart is appropriately derived from the oppressive movements of our environment, whether from the surface of our heart, or from the inevitable or untimed circumstances within our life. Nevertheless, when the Christian allows patience to serve her purpose, when faith is successfully tried by temptation, there is perfection and a certain wholeness added to the individual experience; the mind patiently enduring provocation escapes the trial with better health than when entered into the battle. For this cause, we "shall assure our hearts before him"[828] to "make full proof"[829] of our confidence when we can say, "I have learned by experience."[830]

---

827 James 1:4
828 1 John 3:19
829 2 Timothy 4:5
830 Genesis 30:27

3. Patience is truly made perfect by temptation, for "tribulation worketh patience; and patience, experience,"[831] and yet, "faith worketh patience."[832] It is by faith that pure individual godliness through self-denial is formed, for, he who endeavors to restrain the mouth of their appetite, "the same is a perfect man, and able also to bridle the whole body."[833] Through temperance, the being is exercised to subdue self through faith in the working power of God within the power of the human will, therefore to exercise temperance is to cultivate patience, and to work patience is to exercise faith, for it is that "faith worketh patience."[834]

4. Tribulation pushes for patience and faith works for patience, for when faith enters tribulation then patience is born "that ye may be perfect and entire, wanting nothing."[835] Without allowing faith to enter our trials, we yet bear all things in our own frailty, and the heart given to self will act within itself to produce an end deserving of what was wrought in self. He or she that can keep the mind of their body is one that is perfect because that perfect work of faith has allowed the heart to foster supreme trust in divine power. Growth comes from conflict; character cannot be perfected if there is no anguish of heart. The doing of the Spirit's counsel is committed to the believer to produce "charity out of a pure heart, and of a good conscience, and of faith unfeigned"[836] "that ye may be perfect and entire, wanting nothing."[837]

5. To be found wanting is to exist "through the lusts of the flesh, through much wantonness."[838] Of old it was said, "That which is crooked cannot be made straight: and that which is wanting cannot be numbered."[839] To want is to be crooked, and to be crooked is as it is written, "He hath inclosed my ways,"[840] and, "He hath turned aside my

831 Romans 5:3,4
832 James 1:3
833 James 3:2
834 James 1:3
835 James 1:4
836 1 Timothy 1:5
837 James 1:4
838 2 Peter 2:18
839 Ecclesiastes 1:15
840 Lamentations 3:9

ways."[841] To be wanting is to have the heart turned aside by the lust within the flesh's constitution and enclosed in that deception, for it is said, "A deceived heart hath turned him aside, that he cannot deliver his soul."[842]

6. They who are wanting are those "having eyes full of adultery, and that cannot cease from sin,"[843] counting the word of the LORD unprofitable that says, "Whosoever sinneth hath not seen him, neither known him."[844] It is said, "Whosoever doeth not righteousness is not of God,"[845] and "being filled with all unrighteousness"[846] is no different than being filled with "all ungodliness."[847] The perfect work of patience stops the Christian from holding "the truth in unrighteousness"[848] that they may then cultivate faith through grace to allow self an opportunity to gain knowledge of self, and of the LORD's Word and Faith. The end of patience is godliness, yet the beginning of patience is an experience in temperance that the mind may be renewed from diligently obeying to the precepts of the Spirit's Faith.

7. "That ye may be perfect and entire, wanting nothing,"[849] "let patience have her perfect work."[850] We are to eat "for strength, and not for drunkenness,"[851] and it is that the lusts or enticements of the natural conversation must die for want of the Spirit if "thou mayest prosper and be in health, even as thy soul prospereth."[852] From regulating the diet, the work of patience is to progress us towards godly living, and is to secure in us knowledge of strength for perpetual dependence on our LORD's voice. A living experience by faith through the righteousness of His Christ is to privately prepare the reformer for an active public life with its various circumstances and requirements. If the diet is yet of

---

841 Lamentations 3:11
842 Isaiah 44:20
843 1 Peter 2:14
844 1 John 3:6
845 1 John 3:10
846 Romans 1:29
847 Romans 1:18
848 Romans 1:18
849 James 1:4
850 James 1:4
851 Ecclesiastes 10:20
852 3 John 1:2

flesh then the mind will not be prepared for the restlessness of life, yet from exercise and appropriation of talents and blessings by consistently regulating the mind, and our faith's body by heaven's wisdom, we will prosper outwardly as we have prospered within the inward man.

8. It is that we are to be perfect and entire, whole and sound in mind and in character, when we pick up the effort of watching self by fasting and prayer. This wholeness is as it is said, "The very God of peace sanctify you wholly."[853] Our sanctification is the means for our inward wholeness. Self-regulation with patient diligent obedience to the Spirit's voice is the means for our hearing, receiving, believing, and assimilating the counsel His Son's name within our personal religion. It is said, "Ye have purified your souls in obeying the truth through the Spirit,"[854] for only "through sanctification of the Spirit"[855] may we have the "patience of hope in our Lord Jesus"[856] to keep ourselves. The desire of the mind should be, "Christ in you, the hope of glory,"[857] yet it is that we must first say, "The life which I now live in the flesh I live by the faith of the Son of God."[858]

9. We cannot know the Faith of our High Priest if we are not willing to consent "to speak the mystery of Christ."[859] "The mystery of God should be finished"[860] in His name's reforming believer; therefore "all that will live godly in Christ Jesus shall suffer persecution."[861] If the desire is the mystery of godliness, then we will receive correction "that we might be partakers of his holiness."[862] It cannot be avoided that the work of patience is to move the Christian to live godly according to His definition of godliness, yet the seed of patience is watered by tribulation, and the sun of faith does shine it's beams of strength to help grow the product. Should we care to receive the blessings of the living God,

853 1 Thessalonians 5:23
854 1 Peter 1:22
855 1 Peter 1:2
856 1 Thessalonians 1:3
857 Colossians 1:27
858 Galatians 2:20
859 Colossians 4:3
860 Revelation 10:7
861 2 Timothy 3:12
862 Hebrews 12:10

the hand must take to the plow of temperance, for "the trying of your faith worketh patience,"[863] because "faith without works is dead."[864]

10. Through perplexities and confusions we are to confess, "I have 'obeyed thy voice, and I have put my life in my hand, and have hearkened unto thy words which thou spakest unto me.'"[865] Herein are we counseled, "Refuse not him that speaketh."[866] The patient in faith will receive the crown of life because a still heart is proof of love. Perfection of mind is made through patience in adversity, for this cause we are to remain "rejoicing in hope; patient in tribulation."[867] The hope of patience is the hope of glory, and the end of patience is godliness through an experience that will impress us "to be conformed to the image of his Son."[868] We are delivered snares and provocations that we may grow to remember, "No man should be moved by these afflictions: for yourselves know that we are appointed thereunto."[869] Again, what is written? "All that have a desire to live godly in the full Faith of the Christ and High Priest of the LORD will endure persecution."[870]

11. If we care to have undefiled godliness, it is well to pass away from the idols of our heart to gain a right comprehension of His voice. The mind must willingly unlearn its filth if it would be renewed in newness to carry out newer and higher principles of living. Enduring complexity by faith, and through depending on the course and understanding of His Son's mediation, will settle our hearts in knowledge to regulate temperament. We are to know the Father and the Son from personally learning of their heavenly Order, and as we "suffer according to the will of God,"[871] it is that we are to build up a confident spirit within the house of our character. There can be no perfection of faith if there is not a willingness to humble self, to settle self, that the power of the living LORD God may be embraced to strengthen our weakness.

---

863 James 1:3
864 James 2:26
865 1 Samuel 28:21
866 Hebrews 12:25
867 Romans 12:12
868 Romans 8:29
869 1 Thessalonians 3:3
870 2 Timothy 3:12
871 1 Peter 4:19

12. From bearing long with self, "ye may be perfect and entire,"[872] not desirous of that old spiritual diet, but becoming sound in heaven's new covenant doctrine. Patiently we are made perfect from depending on a diet of "wholesome words,"[873] to the end that we may grow fond of "the doctrine which is according to godliness."[874] As we by close examination take pains to manage our conversation by His counsels, as we place self "in subjection unto the Father of spirits,"[875] it is that we will cease the unstable nature that we have cultivated to "put on the new man, which after God is created in righteousness and true holiness."[876]

13. From allowing self to come into contact with self, it is that through patient obedience to the Spirit's will, we will declare, "I have learned by experience."[877] The trial of our faith is indeed most precious because it is through affliction that we are tested and purged of self and the religious world's sin against the heavenly ministry of His Son. It is said, "The fining pot is for silver, and the furnace for gold,"[878] and the Spirit has said, "Buy of me gold tried in the fire,"[879] therefore "take away the dross from the silver, and there shall come forth a vessel for the finer."[880] If we refuse to experience the fining pot, and then the furnace by faith in His righteousness, where then is there a reason to hold any hope in Him? Isn't it written, "Every one that doeth righteousness is born of him"?[881]

14. Gold tried in the fire is faith and love cultivated through bitter soul anguish at the revelation of self by the revelation of the illustration of God's Man on the tree, and then purged from that tree to become creation's Advocate. This Christ prayed, "I in them, and thou in me, that they may be made perfect in one,"[882] but again, how is it that He

---

872 James 1:4
873 1 Timothy 6:3
874 1 Timothy 6:3
875 Hebrews 12:9
876 Ephesians 4:24
877 Genesis 30:27
878 Proverbs 17:3
879 Revelation 3:18
880 Proverbs 25:4
881 1 John 2:29
882 John 17:23

Himself was made perfect? He has said, "I sanctify myself,"[883] and, "I know him, and keep his saying,"[884] which is why we are counseled, "Sanctify the Lord God in your hearts."[885] It was Christ, who "in the days of his flesh,"[886] "with strong crying and tears"[887] learned "obedience by the things which he suffered,"[888] and herein is the foundation of our education. That we may be joined "to the obtaining of the glory of our Lord,"[889] this Christ suffered the same process of development as His assembly, and it is that through sanctification; a personal experience with the character of His LORD's Spirit that we may render complete obedience to His commandments; the conversation may be perfect and sound in mind, and in every deed, blameless before His throne.

15. "Godliness with contentment is great gain,"[890] and by a patient willingness to settle the heart to consider and comprehend the words of the LORD's Spirit, the understanding of the holy will bless our flesh. Should we allow the development of "the hidden man of the heart, in that which is not corruptible, even the ornament of a meek and quiet spirit, which is in the sight of God of great price,"[891] it is that we will cultivate the principle, "I have learned, in whatsoever state I am, there-with to be content."[892]

16. The beauty of the trial of our faith is without words. The heart desirous to lose self-identification to gain self-identification through the righteousness of Christ is a miracle in and of itself. The work of patience will bear precious fruit that will spring from the scars of the soul, and as self-denial and humility become our education, the spirit of the mind will be revived from the showers of mercy promised for the penitent hearer and doer.

---

883 John 17:19
884 John 8:55
885 1 Peter 3:15
886 Hebrews 5:7
887 Hebrews 5:7
888 Hebrews 5:8
889 1 Thessalonians 2:14
890 1 Timothy 6:6
891 1 Peter 3:4
892 Philippians 4:11

12

Established By Righteousness

1. "But he is a Jew, which is one inwardly; and circumcision is that of the heart, in the spirit."[893] "Circumcise therefore the foreskin of your heart, and be no more stiffnecked."[894] "For thus saith the LORD to the men of Judah and Jerusalem, Break up your fallow ground, and sow not among thorns. Circumcise yourselves to the LORD, and take away the foreskins of your heart, ye men of Judah and inhabitants of Jerusalem."[895] "If thou wilt put away thine abominations out of my sight, then shalt thou not remove":[896] "for as ye have yielded your members servants to uncleanness and to iniquity unto iniquity; even so now yield your members servants to righteousness unto holiness."[897]

2. We are counseled to destroy or blunt the heart, to weaken or impair its vital force, to slow the understanding and perception of our inherited nature, destroying the members of the mind of our flesh by regenerating those same members. The heart is in the spirit; as it says, "The heart, in the spirit";[898] and within the spirit of our mind we are to

---

893 Romans 2:29
894 Deuteronomy 10:16
895 Jeremiah 4:3,4
896 Jeremiah 4:1
897 Romans 6:19
898 Romans 2:29

endure "a grief of mind."[899] As we have by inheritance an innate spirit of corruption; as it is said, "I am carnal, sold under sin";[900] to prevail over that which leaves us baffled within ourselves to declare, "To will is present with me: but how to perform that which is good I find not,"[901] it is that we must be stubborn against the flesh, as it says, "Put off concerning the former conversation."[902]

3. This is the battle of the Christian that will never cease, for as long as we are in this flesh, we are in conflict with our nature. "Circumcise," "break up," "take away," "put away," "yield your members servants,"[903] "break off thy sins by righteousness,"[904] says the Spirit, for this is the lot of His son and daughter, to the end "that every one of you should know how to possess his vessel in sanctification and honour."[905] So then if we would heal our mind, "Break off thy sins by righteousness,"[906] is the counsel, for it is said, "Thou hast loved righteousness, and hated iniquity."[907] His Christ hated iniquity but loved the course of righteousness, therefore it is said, "Thy throne, O God,"[908] is "of righteousness,"[909] and, "Much more doth the ministration of righteousness exceed in glory."[910]

4. It is not in man to break off sin, for transgression is natural and its taste naturally pleasing to the heart. Yet the ministration of the heart is in figure "the ministration of death,"[911] "the ministration of condemnation";[912] as it is said, "What I would, that do I not; but what I hate, that do I";[913] but now as we have yielded self to do His righteous-

---

899 Genesis 26:35
900 Romans 7:14
901 Romans 7:18
902 Ephesians 4:22
903 Romans 6:19
904 Daniel 4:27
905 1 Thessalonians 4:4
906 Daniel 4:27
907 Hebrews 1:9
908 Hebrews 1:8
909 Hebrews 1:8
910 2 Corinthians 3:9
911 2 Corinthians 3:7
912 2 Corinthians 3:9
913 Romans 7:15

ness, the spirit of the mind is profitable under "the ministration of the spirit,"[914] "the ministration of righteousness."[915] Seeing as how we "are built up a spiritual house, an holy priesthood,"[916] it is that as we join self to the throne of righteousness, "grace is poured into thy lips,"[917] for the throne is not only of righteousness, but it is also "the throne of grace."[918]

5. Concerning righteousness we read, "Thy commandments are righteousness,"[919] and, "Thy commandments are truth,"[920] and, "Thy law is the truth."[921] "Righteousness" is the Spirit's course of learning to "purge your conscience from dead works to serve the living God,"[922] which learning advances knowledge on His LORD's ten commandments. Therefore we read, "Grace and truth came by Jesus Christ."[923] For "the LORD will give grace and glory,"[924] even "the glory of his grace"[925] through wisdom that "shall give to thine head an ornament of grace: a crown of glory."[926] The LORD's commandments "lead in the way of righteousness,"[927] and "in this the children of God are manifest, and the children of the devil: whosoever doeth not righteousness is not of God,"[928] but "every one that doeth righteousness is born of him."[929]

6. We are born of His Spirit when His commandment for redemption's creation becomes our own through grace, as it is said, "Our hands have handled."[930] The word of our LORD is living; there is a living and an active power within His grace as it is believed on and properly applied to. It is said, "He hath made the earth by his power, he hath established

---

914 2 Corinthians 3:8
915 2 Corinthians 3:9
916 1 Peter 2:5
917 Psalm 45:2
918 Hebrews 4:16
919 Psalm 119:172
920 Psalm 119:151
921 Psalm 119:142
922 Hebrews 9:14
923 John 1:17
924 Psalm 84:11
925 Ephesians 1:6
926 Proverbs 4:9
927 Proverbs 8:20
928 1 John 3:10
929 1 John 2:29
930 1 John 1:1

the world by wisdom,"[931] again, "When I call unto them, they stand up together."[932] Again it is written, "My grace is sufficient for thee: for my strength is made perfect in weakness,"[933] for grace and strength is "the power of Christ."[934]

7. When "strengthened with all might, according to his glorious power,"[935] it is that we are strengthened with the same power that brought all things to be. For "all things were created by him, and for him,"[936] and we in our minds are to be "renewed in knowledge after the image of him that created."[937] Through grace, man is become the creation of God's Word, for the same power that spoke the worlds into existence, and continues to uphold all things, is that which comes into man by their exercising faith on His voice, as it is said, "By grace are ye saved through faith."[938] Therefore "it is the gift of God"[939] "that we might be made the righteousness of God"[940] in Christ from handling His sayings and precious promises. "Exercise thyself rather unto godliness,"[941] it is said, for if we are cultivating newness of mind, wherein is there a reason for deviating from "the mystery of his will, according to his good pleasure which he hath purposed in himself"?[942]

8. It is said, "Renewed in knowledge,"[943] which means, "Our hands have handled,"[944] and this is the only way that the Christian may gain patient victory over self. The mind must be grieved; the mind must handle every word of God to gain a knowing of the power of that God to continue depending on His name. "Yield your members servants to

---

931 Jeremiah 10:12
932 Isaiah 48:13
933 2 Corinthians 12:9
934 2 Corinthians 12:9
935 Colossians 1:11
936 Colossians 1:16
937 Colossians 3:10
938 Ephesians 2:8
939 Ephesians 2:8
940 2 Corinthians 5:21
941 1 Timothy 4:7
942 Ephesians 1:9
943 Colossians 3:10
944 1 John 1:1

righteousness unto holiness,"[945] it is said, and again, "Exercise thyself rather unto godliness,"[946] for from exercising self in His manner of righteousness we have our end being holy, or godly, therefore we must "have grace, whereby we may serve God acceptably with reverence and godly fear."[947]

9. The throne of grace regulates the course and effect of righteousness, for from doing His righteousness, we receive grace to further our doing, and he that commits himself to this "shall be blessed in his deed."[948] Without applying the wisdom of God; as it says, "Apply thine heart,"[949] and, "Receive my words and hide my commandments,"[950] and, "Keep my commandments, and live; and my law as the apple of thine eye";[951] we will never receive the counsel, "Amend your ways and your doings,"[952] for if "the soul be without knowledge, it is not good."[953]

10. "My people are destroyed for a lack of knowledge,"[954] says the Spirit; even because they have forgotten His character by erring against His name's manner of learning; and when sustaining the mind through natural inclination, it is that intemperance becomes the intellect of the being and the image of the person will be formed out of self. Should the Christian patiently pick up himself or herself, fighting self-indulgence to examine the makeup of their diet, it is then that they will hear, "What fruit had ye then in those things whereof ye are now ashamed?"[955] The name of God is given to the conscience "that every mouth may be stopped, and all the world may become guilty"[956] before the eyes, and should we first surrender the heart to His Spirit, as we learn to handle self by faith in our reconciliation to His benevolence, it is that His voice

---

945 Romans 6:19
946 1 Timothy 4:7
947 Hebrews 12:28
948 James 1:25
949 Proverbs 2:2
950 Proverbs 2:1
951 Proverbs 7:2
952 Jeremiah 7:4
953 Proverbs 19:2
954 Hosea 4:6
955 Romans 6:21
956 Romans 3:19

will bring us into unfamiliar and terrible straits to break the soul so that His precepts may be engraved within it. His wisdom is to stop the mouth of the members of our heart, drawing out shame and guilt, leading us to solemnly remember, as it is understood that we are sinners against heaven's will, "We have an advocate with the Father, Jesus Christ the righteous."[957]

11. Heaven's Faith cannot profit the one not born of that Faith's Spirit and High Priest, for "hereby we do know that we know him, if we keep his commandments."[958] Because there is no natural inclination to honor the LORD with undefiled love and obedience, the Holy Spirit was given of God "in Christ, when he raised him from the dead."[959] Without surrendering to an obedient service by faith in His Spirit's counsel to administer our necessary experience and education, we will forever work a perception of the *character* of *God* into the heart because we have not acknowledged His grace, His power, and His wisdom to work in us. It is the LORD who "gave him";[960] His Christ; "to be the head over all things to the church,"[961] even "the whole family in heaven and earth,"[962] therefore His name is the Savior of our body, and His counsel for the body of the sin of our conversation is, "Break off thy sins by righteousness."[963]

12. Without restraining our heart idols and carefully examining every possible flesh meat of our diet, we will forget the saying, "Ye are not your own."[964] It is a terrible fact that we who profess the name of Christ are not the owners of our body of sin any longer, for "unto GOD the Lord belong the issues of death."[965] This Christ "was delivered for our offences, and was raised again for our justification."[966] Seeing as how we are all naturally born under the curse of sin and sold into religious

---

957 1 John 2:1
958 1 John 2:3
959 Ephesians 1:20
960 Ephesians 1:22
961 Ephesians 1:22
962 Ephesians 3:15
963 Daniel 4:26
964 1 Corinthians 6:19
965 Psalm 68:20
966 Romans 4:25

slavery from birth to the many divisions of our heart, when we learn of and actively believe on His mediation's understanding, the priests of our ministration of death are come to an end by His LORD and Father, who will "quicken your mortal bodies by his Spirit."[967] "In Christ shall all be made alive,"[968] for then "ye have your fruit unto holiness, and the end everlasting life,"[969] and from taking on the new heaven-appointed diet for the spirit of the mind, the diligent restraint put on the old diet will move the reformer to live godly from the nourishment contained in wisdom.

13. Therefore "if ye through the Spirit do mortify the deeds of the body, ye shall live."[970] Practical godliness is to bless our conversation as we hear and do the Spirit's commandments. Our fruit is to be exemplified by works of holiness. Simplicity through godly living by way of familiarity with the precepts of God is the lot of the reforming Christian. Only through His Spirit may we succeed, which to the believer articulates the fact that through, or wound up in His Spirit is our completion through His name and ministry, for "the love of God is shed abroad in our hearts by the Holy Ghost."[971] The heart must endure circumcision if the love of God is to ever come out of it. A restraint on the appetite, on our unhealthy devotional hankerings, is that work of "casting down imaginations, and every high thing that exalteth itself against the knowledge of God, and bringing into captivity every thought to the obedience of Christ."[972]

14. This is the distress of mind that is appointed to the person hopeful to "press toward the mark for the prize of the high calling of God in Christ Jesus."[973] Silencing the imagination of the thoughts of the heart to bring the mind into subjection to heaven's will and course for carrying out that doctrine in the body is the definition of godliness. The health of the mind is in the conviction given by the voice of His Son's

---

967 Romans 8:11
968 1 Corinthians 15:22
969 Romans 6:22
970 Romans 8:13
971 Romans 5:5
972 2 Corinthians 10:5
973 Philippians 3:14

name as administered by His Spirit; as it says, concerning the Spirit, "He will reprove";[974] and the health of the soul is Christ, for "being justified by his blood,"[975] "we shall be saved by His life."[976] The soul is assigned to feel anguish against its conscience by heaven's knowledge within it, and this anguish is managed by the LORD's Spirit, for this is why His Spirit is the Comforter, because when we are convicted of God, "when we are judged, we are chastened of the Lord, that we should not be condemned with the world."[977] Herein is why it is well to know that, "where the Spirit of the Lord is, there is liberty."[978]

15. Howbeit "ye were sometimes darkness, but now are ye light in the Lord: walk as children of light."[979] For "all things that are reproved are made manifest by the light: for whatsoever doth make manifest is light."[980] As children of light born of His Christ's name, it is that we are to declare, "He will bring me forth to the light, and I shall behold his righteousness."[981] Herein can we comprehend how "men loved darkness rather than light, because their deeds were evil."[982] The Spirit's righteousness is that light reproving the conversation of its darling idols, and because there is no honest will to handle the wisdom of His science, "even as they did not like to retain God in their knowledge,"[983] the heart turns the mind from wisdom into the valley of self, delivering the body of our faith "over to a reprobate mind, to do those things which are not convenient."[984]

16. If we would have natural love to obey every word of the living God, then there must be a heart of love determined to act from principle out of love. We are to be made perfect by the impression of His words upon our mind, for "whoso keepeth his word, in him verily the

---

974 John 16:8
975 Romans 5:9
976 Romans 5:10
977 1 Corinthians 11:32
978 2 Corinthians 3:17
979 Ephesians 5:8
980 Ephesians 5:13
981 Micah 7:9
982 John 3:19
983 Romans 1:28
984 Romans 1:28

love of God is perfected."[985] "The end of the commandment is charity out of a pure heart, and of a good conscience, and of faith unfeigned,"[986] and through a self-indulgent spirit the moral intellect is darkened to advance carnal preferences. A heart that lacks moral vitality is that spirit of the world, for the spirit of self-sufficiency keeps its prisoner locked in invisible chains until the being deteriorates under false pressure, causing deterioration to appear as regeneration and that which is reform as distasteful and full of pride. The accepted reproach of the conscience that is in the world is that of a heart of confusion given sway over the body.

17. The wisdom of God is to fashion us "in the likeness of his resurrection,"[987] in that the inwards becomes "alive unto God through Jesus Christ,"[988] and from doing His every word is created "in newness of spirit."[989] In Christ our human familial debilitated nature is consumed "that the body of sin might be destroyed, that henceforth we should not serve sin."[990] As we have been born with an automatic preference for sin against the LORD's name and doctrine, and to accept the violation of our conscience by that falsehood, in Christ "we have obtained an inheritance,"[991] a new inheritance, even the Spirit of truth and of grace, "which is the earnest of our inheritance."[992]

18. The professed believer of the LORD's Faith cannot escape the fact that to serve the living God, the mind must be surrendered to the will and ways of the righteousness of His Son's name. This Christ died and rose "that the righteousness of the law might be fulfilled in us,"[993] and to manifest that righteousness in our personal conversation, it is that one must by righteousness investigate self through His virtue that birth would not be temporary, but most certainly fixed from doing

985 1 John 2:5
986 1 Timothy 1:5
987 Romans 6:5
988 Romans 6:11
989 Romans 7:6
990 Romans 6:6
991 Ephesians 1:11
992 Ephesians 1:14
993 Romans 8:4

righteousness to live every word of His God in right subjection to His Spirit by grace.

19. The commandments of God and the Faith of His Son are the joy and rejoicing of the heart of the true reformer, along with cultivating a reverent culture for the Government of His LORD through soul bitterness. Wisdom and righteousness and grace cannot be separated from the experience, for in them is the health of the soul, and the stability of the flesh.

13

The Essence Of Godly Living

1. "But let it be the hidden man of the heart, in that which is not corruptible, even the ornament of a meek and quiet spirit, which is in the sight of God of great price."[994] "For this cause was the gospel preached also to them that are dead, that they might be judged according to men in the flesh, but live according to God in the spirit."[995]

2. As God's host is kept "according to his abundant mercy,"[996] His servants "shall delight themselves in the abundance of peace,"[997] and as "they which receive abundance of grace and of the gift of righteousness"[998] "continue in faith and charity and holiness with sobriety,"[999] it is purposed, "Walk worthy of God, who hath called you unto his kingdom and glory."[1000] "Therefore being justified by an exercised faith, we have peace with God,"[1001] even abundance of peace and mercy and grace, and as we trust "in the abundance of his

---

994 1 Peter 4:6
995 1 Peter 3:4
996 1 Peter 1:3
997 Psalm 37:11
998 Romans 5:17
999 1 Timothy 2:15
1000 1 Thessalonians 2:12
1001 Romans 5:1

riches,"[1002] even His "durable riches and righteousness"[1003] "in whom are hid all the treasures of wisdom and knowledge,"[1004] we should "be judged according to men in the flesh, but live according to God in the spirit."[1005]

3. When Christ was confronted concerning one caught in the act of adultery, He said, "Ye judge after the flesh,"[1006] or rather, it is said, "Man looketh on the outward appearance."[1007] "But we are sure that the judgment of God is according to truth,"[1008] for it is said, "Thy law is the truth,"[1009] therefore it is written, "As many as have sinned in the law shall be judged by the law."[1010] The one professing godliness is to be "judged according to men in the flesh,"[1011] or rather, as many believe "it strange that ye run not with them to the same excess of riot, speaking evil of you,"[1012] it is the will of God "a man for conscience toward God endure grief, suffering wrongfully."[1013]

4. As excess in appetite removes from the life of the believer, and as showers of health begin to quench intemperance, the heart of the faithful will be tried by their environment that they may learn how to "live according to God in the spirit."[1014] There are two centers of existence, one of the flesh in which spiritual excess is the center of compromise, and one of the spirit, as it is said, "The spirit of your mind."[1015] The will of the flesh is that inherited nature which willfully accepts "lasciviousness, lusts, excess of wine, revelings, banquetings, and abominable idolatries"[1016] as a faithful practice. Such a nature

---

1002 Psalm 52:7
1003 Proverbs 8:18
1004 Colossians 2:3
1005 1 Peter 4:6
1006 John 8:15
1007 1 Samuel 16:7
1008 Romans 2:2
1009 Psalm 119:142
1010 Romans 2:12
1011 1 Peter 4:6
1012 1 Peter 4:4
1013 1 Peter 2:19
1014 1 Peter 4:6
1015 Ephesians 4:23
1016 1 Pete 4:3

delights in "excess of riot,"[1017] for the carnal heart does "count it pleasure to riot in the day time,"[1018] compelling the mind to forget, "She that liveth in pleasure is dead while she liveth."[1019]

5. "For this cause was the gospel preached also to them that are dead,"[1020] "for to be carnally minded is death,"[1021] and such a mind "is not subject to the law of God, neither indeed can be,"[1022] for its eyes are on what is accursed, as it says, "He that is hanged is accursed of God."[1023] The man or woman, who is "elect according to the foreknowledge of God the Father,"[1024] will fall into strange places as their heart is revived "through sanctification of the Spirit."[1025] They, being dead and convicted of their death by the Father; as it is said, "The commandment, which was ordained to life, I found to be unto death";[1026] are to be purified by the criticisms of the ones around them found without the work of "the law of Christ"[1027] in their heart, to the end the believer may further serve the Word in the spirit of their mind. As the Word should "quicken your mortal bodies by his Spirit,"[1028] it is that by conflict our conversation is to turn us to the commandment, "Walk in newness of life."[1029]

6. As the Father of Christ is presently judging His righteous servants by the name and law of His Son's character revealed within their inwards, on this earth it is that, "All that will live godly in Christ Jesus shall suffer persecution."[1030] Godliness is perfected in the heart by wisdom and temperance with patience on the work and effect of righteousness, yet to the one desiring to live godly; in that the benevo-

---

1017 1 Peter 4:4
1018 2 Peter 2:13
1019 1 Timothy 5:6
1020 1 Peter 4:6
1021 Romans 8:6
1022 Romans 8:7
1023 Deuteronomy 21:23
1024 1 Peter 1:2
1025 1 Peter 1:2
1026 Romans 7:10
1027 Galatians 6:2
1028 Romans 8:11
1029 Romans 6:4
1030 2 Timothy 3:12

lent religion of His High Priest is become a personal and devotion fact, both publicly and privately; persecution of heart and mind by His voice is to perfect godliness, and that conversation, as it is found in the spirit of the mind, revealed to the eyes of many.

7. The law of the Spirit's good will is the delight of the godly, and to faithfully study after its accomplishment, according to the counsel of His LORD and Father, is their pleasure. The spirit of such flourishes because they are nourished within "the hidden man of the heart,"[1031] therefore their behavior reflects their inward principle, which principle states, "I delight in the law of God after the inward man."[1032] Such a soul is judged after the flesh by ones within the flesh who have lost themselves to "the vanity of their mind,"[1033] "being alienated from the life of God through the ignorance that is in them, because of the blindness of their heart."[1034] Therefore as the faithful are so ignorantly pressed, they "do well, and suffer for it,"[1035] "rejoicing that they were counted worthy to suffer shame for his name."[1036]

8. For this cause we read, "If ye be reproached for the name of Christ, happy are ye; for the spirit of glory and of God resteth upon you."[1037] The active believer is happy to suffer for the will and doctrine of His name, they inwardly joy in condemnation for His character within their conscience because it is said, "He that keepeth the law, happy is he."[1038] The joy of the true reformer is suffering for the character of God, for in so doing, His precepts are further engraved upon their heart, and as many fail to comprehend the sight of the obedient ones before them; in that "on their part he is evil spoken of, but on your part he is glorified";[1039] the heart of any one beholding such a profession may have a chance to feel for the LORD's cause, thus shaking an honest heart to fall also within the same bond of love as

---

1031 1 Peter 3:4
1032 Romans 7:22
1033 Ephesians 4:17
1034 Ephesians 4:18
1035 1 Peter 2:20
1036 Acts 5:41
1037 1 Peter 4:14
1038 Proverbs 29:18
1039 1 Peter 4:14

them. Godliness requires its subjects to be a "partaker of the afflictions of the gospel";[1040] "even hereunto were ye called."[1041]

9. When "the ornament of a meek and quiet spirit, which is in the sight of God of great price,"[1042] is supported by "an ornament of grace: a crown of glory,"[1043] the Christian will declare, "I press toward the mark,"[1044] rejoicing in "the marks of the Lord Jesus."[1045] Suffering for the name of Christ is avoided by the presumptuous due to the scars over the soul that will be incurred, for they would rather not "suffer persecution for the cross of Christ."[1046] Yet the godly bear an unequalled presence because they "live according to God in the spirit."[1047] The spirit of such is meek and quiet, and though within themselves they confess, "We ourselves also were sometimes foolish, disobedient, deceived, serving divers lusts and pleasures, living in malice and envy, hateful, and hating one another,"[1048] yet they reveal, "I obtained mercy, because I did it ignorantly in unbelief. And the grace of our Lord was exceeding abundant with faith and love."[1049]

10. The deportment of the godly states, "Christ Jesus came into the world to save sinners,"[1050] therefore in warm benevolence they can declare, "I will very gladly spend and be spent for you; though the more abundantly I love you, the less I be loved."[1051] Because they have allowed ill-treatment to further their reformation, because they have endured murder and oppression for the purpose of upholding the commitment of love from where love has been revealed to them, because they have committed "the keeping of their souls to him in well doing, as unto a faithful Creator,"[1052] it is that from experiencing

1040 2 Timothy 1:8
1041 1 Peter 2:21
1042 1 Peter 3:4
1043 Proverbs 4:9
1044 Philippians 3:14
1045 Galatians 6:17
1046 Galatians 6:12
1047 1 Peter 4:6
1048 Titus 3:3
1049 1 Timothy 1:13,14
1050 1 Timothy 1:15
1051 2 Corinthians 12:15
1052 1 Peter 2:19

internal anguish the line is set, "He no longer should live the rest of his time in the flesh to the lusts of men, but to the will of God."[1053]

11. As there is a cause and effect to all things, so too the cause of injustice fulfills the saying, "To the hungry soul every bitter thing is sweet."[1054] The reformer will happily say, "I have suffered the loss of all things, and do count them but dung, that I may win Christ,"[1055] for from the love revealed to them as it is revealed in His Christ, they will have the saying fixed in their heart, "Whom have I in heaven but thee? And there is none upon earth that I desire beside thee."[1056] So then "the righteousness which is of faith speaketh on this wise,"[1057] "I called him alone,"[1058] to the end the heart of the faithful would be revived by showers of blessing, and their mind renewed to carry out in their body a reformation that is to place in them this desire, "I made myself servant unto all."[1059]

12. Torment, whether self-inflicted by examination or stirred up by our external environment, is to expose in us the defects of our conversation's character, and to the LORD is to reveal the true intention of our heart. From enduring privation, from allowing the heart to fall into necessity to restrain the natural impulses to satisfy the thoughts of the flesh, the spirit of the mind will find health and wisdom from self-denial and self-instruction. As the spirit of the mind is proved by circumstance, the mind of love within the sinner will not shun negativity, but will with the grace of God receive rays of blessing for inward cultivation, that in due time the conversation may reflect the religion wrought by faith in the hand of the LORD's Spirit.

13. What is written? "This people draw near me with their mouth, and their lips do honour me, but have removed their heart far from me."[1060] What is the foundation of the religion professing truth and

---

1053 1 Peter 4:2
1054 Proverbs 27:7
1055 Philippians 3:8
1056 Psalm 73:25
1057 Romans 10:6
1058 Isaiah 51:2
1059 1 Corinthians 9:19
1060 Isaiah 29:13

godliness? It is said, "Live according to God in the spirit."[1061] From the spirit of the mind true religion is carried out in the body, and this is why it says, "Be renewed in the spirit of your mind,"[1062] and, "Be ye transformed by the renewing of your mind."[1063] As we are daily renewed in our conversation's conscience, in mind we will become sound and sober, and "in a figure transferred"[1064] the "like precious faith"[1065] of the Family of God, even "the faith in Christ"[1066] concerning "righteousness, temperance, and judgment to come."[1067]

14. The one desirous of His Faith will bring their heart, and the body of their confidence, into subjection that they may know His High Priest and the revelation of His mediation's hope, to honor His name not in word or in form through policy, but as it is said, "In deed and in truth."[1068] We are to "assure our hearts before him,"[1069] to "endure hardness, as a good soldier of Jesus,"[1070] for the end of hardship is godliness, for it is said, "Continue thou in the things which thou hast learned and hast been assured of."[1071] As the heart is assured before His Word and God; confirmed in faith and in truth from a longing for His undivided attention to be perfect even as He is perfect; the religion will fall to the spirit of the mind that wisdom may be added to the frame of faith when doing to His words, thereby assuring our hearts of the living God's power and wisdom defend and encourage.

15. Good works express living virtue, for the religion of this Christ is determined to "purify unto himself a peculiar people, zealous of good works,"[1072] even as it says, "Let every one of us please his neighbour for his good to edification."[1073] Godliness is no haphazard

---

1061 1 Peter 4:6
1062 Ephesians 4:23
1063 Romans 12:2
1064 1 Corinthians 4:6
1065 2 Peter 1:1
1066 Acts 24:24
1067 Acts 24:25
1068 1 John 3:18
1069 1 John 3:19
1070 2 Timothy 2:3
1071 2 Timothy 3:14
1072 Titus 2:15
1073 Romans 15:2

principle, for the pious render service to the Spirit from within the spirit of their mind that His love may then flow out from them. Godly living is reached when we have allowed the foundation of our faith to lead us to claim the virtue of our High Priest's name, to the end we may add wisdom from His wisdom to patiently direct self to rightly live in His presence.

14

According To God In the Spirit

1. Says Scripture, "Live according to God in the spirit,"[1074] or rather, "Be ye transformed by the renewing of your mind, that ye may prove what is that good, and acceptable, and perfect, will of God."[1075] To live according to God in the spirit is to actively function and operate through the transformation had under the course of the Spirit's will. As for the will of God, this is our conscience's purification from learning of and doing to His counsel to keep His commandments, for it is said, "Whoso keepeth his word, in him verily is the love of God perfected."[1076] Seeing as how it is said, "Holy Father, keep through thine own name those whom thou hast given me,"[1077] it serves that the Christian is to keep His Father's name and power with the character and virtue of His Spirit, for which cause it is said, "We do know that we know him, if we keep his commandments."[1078]

2. The will of God is that those professing to believe on His Son's mediation would keep every word of His mouth through the knowledge

---

1074 1 Peter 4:6
1075 Romans 12:2
1076 1 John 2:5
1077 John 17:11
1078 1 John 2:3

of His Son's mediation. His ten commandments are within His truth, and His truth and commandments are synonymous with His word, for which cause it is said, "Sanctify them through thy truth."[1079] The Christian is to be made pure from obeying to the truth or science of His Spirit, and one cannot live pure in Him without any controversy suffered upon the inwards, but to live without controversy is to accept corruption upon the inwards. Therefore we know the liar who says, "I know him," and bears no marks of the fruit of His will for the spirit of the mind, for because they refuse to first say, "I have suffered loss,"[1080] they are not given the privilege of God to "speak the wisdom of God in a mystery."[1081]

3. What is the Spirit's counsel? It says, "Ye say, We see; therefore your sin remaineth."[1082] A willingness to acknowledge the ignorance of the flesh as acceptable knowledge, and without receiving that understanding which comes by humbly examining and doing His will and counsel, is proof that we "believeth not the record that God gave of his Son."[1083] "He that believeth not God hath made him a liar,"[1084] therefore it is easy to believe on the *intelligence* within the members of the heart, for such a confession is proof that value lacks within the mechanism believed to hold depth of reason. For this cause it is said, "If we say we have no sin, we deceive ourselves, and the truth is not in us."[1085]

4. The truth is not within our heat because we have found no reason to submit self to receive an experience to fix our frame, seeing as how we are *pure* within ourselves. The structure of the heart is maintained by "the filth of the flesh,"[1086] for the intelligence that is in the flesh is no greater than that which passes away. But the sons and daughters of God "speak wisdom among them that are perfect: yet not the wisdom of the world, nor of the princes of this world, that come to nought,"[1087] but

---

1079 John 17:17
1080 Philippians 3:8
1081 1 Corinthians 2:7
1082 John 9:41
1083 1 John 5:10
1084 1 John 5:10
1085 1 John 1:8
1086 1 Peter 3:21
1087 1 Corinthians 2:6

rather through that "which the Holy Ghost teacheth."[1088] For while many do not believe on the Spirit's voice for adhering to what is passed away and accursed; even "the handwriting of ordinances";[1089] receiving the spirit of unbelief for truth; as it is said, "The spirit of error"[1090] "because they received not the love of the truth";[1091] they that believe on God and follow after His words are given His "Spirit, which they that believe on him should receive."[1092]

5. What is written? "As many as received him, to them gave he power to become the sons of God, even to them that believe on his name."[1093] To believe on the name of the Son is to believe on the name of the Father, and if we have fellowship with the Holy Ghost, we know that "the love of God is shed abroad in our hearts by the Holy Ghost."[1094] Therefore the liar will claim *Christ* without His LORD and Father, and he or she that claims the Father without His Son's name cannot be cleansed to know the Father, for "the blood of Jesus Christ his Son cleanseth us from all sin"[1095] against His Father's name. "And hereby we know that he abideth in us, by his Spirit which he hath given us,"[1096] therefore "he is an'tichrist, that denieth the Father and the Son."[1097] Herein is why we are counseled, "He that honoureth not the Son honoureth not the Father which hath sent him."[1098]

6. To honor the Son is to believe, "Ye are dead, and your life is hid with Christ in God,"[1099] and, "If we be dead with Christ, we believe we shall also live with him."[1100] "In him we live, and move, and have our being,"[1101] yet it is that He "suffered for sins, the just for the unjust, that he

---

1088 1 Corinthians 2:13
1089 Colossians 2:14
1090 1 John 4:6
1091 2 Thessalonians 2:10
1092 John 7:39
1093 John 1:12
1094 Romans 5:5
1095 1 John 1:7
1096 1 John 3:23
1097 1 John 2:22
1098 John 5:23
1099 Colossians 3:3
1100 Romans 6:8
1101 Acts 17:28

might bring us to God."[1102] The purpose of this Christ's Faith is to purify His faithful "to the uttermost that come unto God by him,"[1103] for He fulfilled the saying, "He will magnify the law and make it honorable,"[1104] to the end that "by one offering he hath perfected for ever them that are sanctified."[1105] The one who comes to Christ is to be brought to God, that is, the one who learns of and executes on His Son's name will receive His Spirit that they may know the character of His LORD and God, as it is said, "I will put my law in their inward parts, and write it in their hearts."[1106]

7. He or she professing submission to His name without receiving His Spirit and power, and without receiving the name of God written in them, fails to honor the living God and that Christ whom He has sent and consecrated. "In fleshly tables of the heart,"[1107] the saying is to be fulfilled within the reformer, "I will put a new spirit within you; and I will take the stony heart out of their flesh, and will give them an heart of flesh."[1108] How will the LORD accomplish this? Through an experience by faith where it is said, "Then shall ye remember your own evil ways, and your doings that were not good, and shall loathe yourselves in your own sight for your iniquities and for your abominations."[1109] From such an experience the Christian is to learn, "Live according to God in the spirit."[1110]

8. The purpose of the Spirit's commandment is to bring to light our personal religious sins and errors "that it might appear sin,"[1111] "that sin by the commandment might become exceeding sinful."[1112] His saying is to bring us to the Word of His intention, or is to cause the reflection of supreme goodness to be brought to our attention that we may actu-

---

1102 1 Peter 3:18
1103 Hebrews 7:25
1104 Isaiah 42:21
1105 Hebrews 10:14
1106 Jeremiah 31:32
1107 2 Corinthians 3:3
1108 Ezekiel 11:19
1109 Ezekiel 36:31
1110 1 Peter 4:6
1111 Romans 7:13
1112 Romans 7:13

ally feel our ignorance to know the inordinate gluttony from which our fever derives, to the end that through pain we should personally know, "We have an advocate with the Father."[1113] "Therefore, brethren, we are debtors, not to the flesh, to live after the flesh."[1114] For the LORD would have "all men to be saved, and to come to the knowledge of the truth,"[1115] even "the acknowledging of the truth which is after godliness"[1116] that teaches, "Live according to God in the spirit."[1117]

9. "To be spiritually minded is life and peace,"[1118] and this is so because "the Spirit is life because of righteousness."[1119] If we have the Spirit of God then we live by "the spirit of truth"[1120] from "the Spirit of truth, which proceedeth from the Father."[1121] We are counseled carry our conversation by the spirit of our mind, or to operate our faith's body from our mind grounded in the truth of God as taught us by the Spirit of truth and righteousness; for this Spirit is to keep us in remembrance of the LORD's will that we may not sin against it. To exist in the spirit is to live by His Spirit according to His will for our mental and moral recovery, fulfilling that which is good and acceptable in His sight that we may learn to be a blessing and not a curse.

10. It is purposed for the reformer to live according to the Word as alive unto the Word, and through the impression of His Spirit by handling His voice. The power of our conversation is derived from His Spirit because His Spirit is of righteousness, which righteousness is the baptism of our conscience. Should our diet fail to revolve around the Spirit's righteousness, then we are malnourished, remaining "by nature the children of wrath,"[1122] "corrupt according to the deceitful lusts."[1123] But rather we are to cultivate the spirit of our mind "which after God is

---

1113 1 John 2:1
1114 Romans 8:12
1115 1 Timothy 2:4
1116 Titus 1:1
1117 1 Peter 4:6
1118 Romans 8:10
1119 1 John 4:6
1120 1 John 4:6
1121 John 15:26
1122 Ephesians 2:3
1123 Ephesians 4:22

created in righteousness and true holiness."[1124] True godliness proceeds from doing the Sprit's Word without any flesh-based mediator, which is why the mind of truth is born after the Word's righteousness, and why it is purposed that our conversation wholeheartedly remain on the Word by a mind only observing truth's science, for it is counseled, "The true worshippers shall worship the Father in spirit and in truth."[1125]

11. Therefore it is a fact "that every one that doeth righteousness is born of Him."[1126] For the Christian is born "by the word of God, which liveth and abideth forever,"[1127] therefore "he that doeth the will of God abideth forever."[1128] To do righteousness is to do His word, and to do His word is to do His will that we may remain in His name and confidence for ever, or that we may retain "length of days, and long life"[1129] for our mind and conversation, for the wisdom of God reports, "By me thy days shall be multiplied, and the years of thy life shall be increased."[1130] "Grace and peace be multiplied unto you through the knowledge of God,"[1131] it is said, for by doing the Spirit's wisdom, we are to receive grace that the spirit of our mind may be furnished to prosper our heart of devotion to serve one another.

12. Whosoever "will do his will, he shall know the doctrine,"[1132] even "the doctrine of God our Saviour."[1133] "God hath not given us the spirit of fear,"[1134] "the spirit of bondage again to fear";[1135] "the bondage of corruption";[1136] "but of power, and of love, and of a sound mind."[1137] The reformer is to live in the sobriety of their mind, for "a sound heart

1124 Ephesians 4:24
1125 John 4:23
1126 1 John 2:29
1127 1 Peter 1:24
1128 1 John 2:17
1129 Proverbs 3:2
1130 Proverbs 9:11
1131 2 Peter 1:2
1132 John 7:7
1133 Titus 2:10
1134 2 Timothy 1:7
1135 Romans 8:15
1136 Romans 8:21
1137 2 Timothy 1:7

is the life of the flesh,"[1138] and that heart and mind cannot be attributed to us unless we desire to "prove what is that good, and acceptable, and perfect, will of God."[1139]

13. It is "God, who quickeneth all things,"[1140] and as Christ was "put to death in the flesh, but quickened by the Spirit,"[1141] "even so we also should walk in newness of life"[1142] "that we should bring forth fruit" "in newness of spirit."[1143] By His Spirit the reformer is to be transformed by the renewing of their mind from "comparing spiritual things with spiritual,"[1144] thereby allowing the heart to search itself through the words of creation to give life and wisdom to the mind for blessing the members of the body. Sin works "in our members to bring forth fruit unto death,"[1145] for such members without the power of grace are yielded to "uncleanness and to iniquity unto iniquity."[1146] Yet by learning of and doing the blood of the LORD's Christ, we are "the servants of righteousness,"[1147] faithful commandment keepers by faith in the righteousness of His name, and "out of a pure heart, and of a good conscience, and of faith unfeigned."[1148]

14. Therefore "live according to God in the spirit,"[1149] for the mind of the believer carries a new breath, decreeing, "Quicken me according to thy word."[1150] His Christ was "put to death in the flesh, but quickened by the Spirit,"[1151] and "if we believe on him that raised up Jesus our Lord from the dead,"[1152] "we shall also live with him"[1153] by "the circumcision

---

1138 Proverbs 14:30
1139 Romans 12:2
1140 1 Timothy 6:13
1141 1 Peter 3:18
1142 Romans 6:4
1143 Romans 7:4,6
1144 1 Corinthians 2:13
1145 Romans 7:5
1146 Romans 6:19
1147 Romans 6:18
1148 1 Timothy 1:5
1149 1 Peter 4:6
1150 Psalm 119:154
1151 1 Peter 3:18
1152 Romans 4:24
1153 Romans 6:8

made without hands, in putting off the body of the sins of the flesh by the circumcision of Christ."[1154] For, "circumcision is that of the heart, in the spirit,"[1155] "and we shall live with him by the power of God."[1156] So then, seeing as how the believer is to be a partaker of that circumcision by an experimental faith on heaven's will, it is that, "Reproach hath broken my heart,"[1157] said Christ, and, "He humbled himself, and became obedient unto death,"[1158] and so too for His hopeful, "We must through much tribulation enter into the kingdom of God."[1159]

15. If we are not willing to be as broken as was our salvation's Captain, to feel such anguish as He felt when on many occasions groaning within His spirit, if we are ashamed of His Faith, "if we deny him, he will also deny us."[1160] To live according to God is to be joined to the conversation of His High Priest, and the life of this Christ was one of discomfort, as testifies the prophet, "A man of sorrows, and acquainted with grief."[1161] He fulfilled the will of His Father that the reformer may "acquaint now thyself with him,"[1162] for it is purposed "that the righteousness of the law might be fulfilled in us,"[1163] therefore a mind of truth, and not of flesh, will allow a furthering of His LORD's benevolent tidings to touch the thoughts and the feelings.

16. Christ was the first to ever experience the living refreshing of the living God, and for us He says, "I will not leave you comfortless."[1164] He was purified from obeying every word of His God, and He says to us, "Ye are clean through the word which I have spoken unto you."[1165] "I sanctify myself,"[1166] He said, but for the Christian it is determined,

---

1154 Colossians 2:11
1155 Romans 2:29
1156 2 Corinthians 13:4
1157 Psalm 69:20
1158 Philippians 2:8
1159 Acts 14:22
1160 2 Timothy 2:13
1161 Isaiah 53:3
1162 Job 22:21
1163 Romans 8:4
1164 John 14:18
1165 John 15:3
1166 John 17:19

"The very God of peace sanctify you."[1167] Therefore as Christ has said, "I came down from heaven, not to do mine own will,"[1168] it is for the Christian to learn of and know, "It is God which worketh in you both to will and to do of his good pleasure."[1169] "His good pleasure which he hath purposed in himself"[1170] is "that we should be holy and without blame before him in love,"[1171] a peculiar group of happy and healthy creatures in Him reflecting the peace from the joy of the anguish of our soul to know Him.

17. As His voice is obeyed, it is that His Spirit will provide the fuel to carry out every one of His words by love. The mind of the reformer cannot exist without the mind of God, and the soul of the living reformer cannot stay within the Word's will and righteousness if not consistently regenerated by His Spirit. "Live according to God in the spirit,"[1172] we are counseled, for as we humbly experience "salvation through sanctification of the Spirit and belief of the truth,"[1173] it is then that we will understand why it says, "Death hath no more dominion over him. For in that he died, he died unto sin once: but in that he liveth, he liveth unto God."[1174]

1167 2 Thessalonians 5:23
1168 John 6:38
1169 Philippians 2:13
1170 Ephcsians 1:9
1171 Ephesians 1:4
1172 1 Peter 4:6
1173 2 Thessalonians 2:13
1174 Romans 6:9,10

15

Shall Live Through Him

1. "Whosoever shall confess that Jesus is the Son of God, God dwelleth in him, and he in God."[1175] "Whosoever is born of God"[1176] "keepeth himself,"[1177] "for his seed remaineth in him."[1178] "The seed is the word of God,"[1179] and "every one that doeth righteousness is born of him"[1180] "and he cannot sin,"[1181] because "God dwelleth in him."[1182]

2. "Every one that doeth righteousness is born of him,"[1183] "for whatsoever is born of God overcometh the world,"[1184] and to overcome the spirit of the world, "the Father sent the Son to be the Saviour of the world."[1185] The Father blessed His Son's name to be that deliverer and healer of "all that is in the world, the lust of the flesh, the lust

---

1175 1 John 4:15
1176 1 John 3:9
1177 1 John 5:18
1178 1 John 3:9
1179 Luke 8:11
1180 1 John 2:29
1181 1 John 3:9
1182 1 John 4:15
1183 1 John 2:29
1184 1 John 5:4
1185 1 John 4:14

of the eyes, and the pride of life."[1186] "Whosoever shall confess that Jesus is the Son of God"[1187] will "live through him"[1188] not "in the flesh to the lusts of men, but to the will of God."[1189] This Christ came to deliver every willing spirit from the taint of "the prince of the power of the air,"[1190] from "the spirit that now worketh,"[1191] even "the spirit of error,"[1192] yet it is said, "Whatsoever is born,"[1193] not, "Whosoever is born," therefore what is born of God, "this is the victory that overcometh the world,"[1194] even that victory which ruins within us "the spirit that now worketh in the children of disobedience."[1195]

3. "Every one that loveth is born of God"[1196] because "God is love,"[1197] and since "Jesus is the Son of God,"[1198] it is plain that the love that is of God is the Son that is of God, for which cause "love is of God,"[1199] and this love displayed by how the LORD "sent his Son to be the propitiation of our sins."[1200] "God commendeth his love toward us, in that, while we were yet sinners, Christ died for us":[1201] therefore "every one that loveth is born of God,"[1202] and this is so because "every one that doeth righteousness is born of him,"[1203] so then the reformer "knoweth God,"[1204] for "we do know that we know him, if we keep his commandments."[1205] Herein is our victory that encourages our

---

1186 1 John 2:16
1187 1 John 4:15
1188 1 John 4:9
1189 1 Peter 4:2
1190 Ephesians 2:2
1191 Ephesians 2:2
1192 1 John 4:6
1193 1 John 5:4
1194 1 John 5:4
1195 Ephesians 2:2
1196 1 John 4:7
1197 1 John 4:8
1198 1 John 5:5
1199 1 John 4:7
1200 1 John 4:10
1201 Romans 5:8
1202 1 John 4:7
1203 1 John 2:29
1204 1 John 4:7
1205 1 John 2:3

conscience and conversation to pass away from the religious world; that spirit of error encouraging "the lust of the flesh, the lust of the eyes, and the pride of life";[1206] even that which is born of the Spirit's Word, for He says, "A law shall proceed from me."[1207]

4. We do know how it is said, "All thy commandments are righteousness,"[1208] therefore it is written, "Every one that doeth righteousness is born of him."[1209] Again, we know that our mind is to be conceived "by the word of God"[1210] "with the washing of the word,"[1211] therefore "whosoever is born of God doth not commit sin; for his seed remaineth in him,"[1212] and this "seed is the word of God."[1213] For which cause it is said, "Whatsoever is born of God overcometh the world,"[1214] and that which is born of God is His doctrine that manifests and ceases sin in the conscience because they exist by the law and commandment of the religious age. The godly confess their loyalty to His Faith by admitting, through their personal religion, that their "mouths must be stopped,"[1215] for the commandments of God are given "that every mouth may be stopped,"[1216] leading the believer to take hold of His Faith to cease the spirit of the world within the heart of their mind, "that the body of sin might be destroyed."[1217]

5. That which ends the spirit of error within "the body of the sin of the flesh"[1218] is "the law of the Spirit of life."[1219] "Our conversation in times past in the lusts of our flesh, fulfilling the desires of the flesh and of the mind,"[1220] end by pure submission to the Savior of

---

1206 1 John 2:16
1207 Isaiah 51:4
1208 Psalm 119:172
1209 1 John 2:29
1210 1 Peter 1:23
1211 Ephesians 5:26
1212 1 John 3:9
1213 Luke 8:11
1214 1 John 5:4
1215 Titus 1:11
1216 Romans 3:19
1217 Romans 6:6
1218 Colossians 2:11
1219 Romans 8:2
1220 Ephesians 2:3

the flesh, "for Christ is the end of the law for righteousness to every one that believeth."[1221] The Spirit's Christ destroyed "sinful flesh, and for sin, condemned sin in the flesh: that the righteousness of the law might be fulfilled in us."[1222] The purpose of the Son is to pronounce the Father, even as He says, "I have declared thy name."[1223] The Law of His LORD's throne; the ten precepts of God revealing His name; are to be kept by faith through His word, His truth, His commandments revolving around the precepts of His name, His righteousness, for it is said of His Son's name, "That we might live through him."[1224]

6. It is said, "He that hath the Son hath life,"[1225] and since "Christ, who is our life,"[1226] became for us "the express image of his person";[1227] the person of the LORD His Father; it is that "whosoever shall confess that Jesus is the Son of God, God dwelleth in him, and he in God."[1228] It is Christ "who of God is made unto us wisdom";[1229] being "the power of God, and the wisdom of God";[1230] for "wisdom giveth life,"[1231] therefore He confessed, "The words that I speak unto you, they are spirit, and they are life."[1232] If the Christian would have an understanding of this Christ's voice, it must be said, "I keep under my body"[1233] "that I may know him,"[1234] for "every one that loveth is born of God, and knoweth God." "Hereby we do know that we know him, if we keep his commandments."[1235]

7. The commandments of God and Faith of His Christ cannot be separated, for the Father sent the knowledge of His Son for that

---

1221 Romans 10:4
1222 Romans 8:4
1223 John 17:26
1224 1 John 4:9
1225 1 John 5:12
1226 Colossians 3:4
1227 Hebrews 1:3
1228 1 John 4:15
1229 1 Corinthians 1:30
1230 1 Corinthians 1:24
1231 Ecclesiastes 7:12
1232 John 6:63
1233 1 Corinthians 9:27
1234 Philippians 3:10
1235 1 John 4:7; 1 John 2:3

wisdom to be the Savior of the religious world. If this knowledge is ordained for the purpose of righteousness in the believer, and if this understanding is our conversation's course of learning; which course is wisdom and grace for the spirit of our mind; it then serves that "the mouth of the just bringeth forth wisdom,"[1236] because "he that speaketh truth sheweth forth righteousness."[1237] We do know how it is said, "Thy law is the truth,"[1238] therefore to confess Christ is "to speak the mystery of Christ,"[1239] "and without controversy great is the mystery of godliness: God was manifest in the flesh,"[1240] therefore of the one found in Christ it will be said, "God dwelleth in him."[1241] So then as truth reveals in the believer a labor expressed by His righteousness, it is that "every one that loveth is born of God."[1242]

8. Godliness is the aim of the faith purposed in Christ. As God was made in the likeness of sinful flesh; as "the Word was made flesh, and dwelt among us";[1243] it is so revealed that the character of God, and the righteousness of His Spirit, dwelt within a naturally erroneous conversation, "and for sin, condemned sin"[1244] that "the mystery of God should be finished"[1245] in them that believe on the science of His name. It is said, "That we might live through him,"[1246] yet only "if so be that we suffer with him."[1247] This is how the conscience is to be made perfect, for "though he were a Son, yet learned he obedience by the things which he suffered."[1248] So then "we know him, if we keep his commandments,"[1249] and we know that we know Him because "the

1236 Proverbs 10:31
1237 Proverbs 12:17
1238 Psalm 119:142
1239 Colossians 4:3
1240 1 Timothy 3:16
1241 1 John 4:15
1242 1 John 4:7
1243 John 1:14
1244 Romans 8:3
1245 Revelation 10:7
1246 1 John 4:9
1247 Romans 8:17
1248 Hebrews 5:8
1249 1 John 2:3

world knoweth us not, because it knew him not."[1250] For this cause, "marvel not, my brethren, if the world hate you."[1251]

9. Of His believers, this Christ declares, "They are not of the world, even as I am not of the world."[1252] "I have chosen you out of the world,"[1253] says the LORD's Christ, therefore "how shall we, that are dead to sin, live any longer therein?"[1254] Christ was given to the world that they who should feel after His God "might live through him,"[1255] that is, might pick up reverence to His LORD and God through a conversation in like fashion to His. And what is it to feel after God? It means to be so bold as to say, "Shew me thy glory."[1256] The spirit learning of and doing the law of His meditation is taken out of the fashions, traditions, and beliefs of the religious world that they may know Him "and the power of his resurrection, and the fellowship of his sufferings, being made conformable unto his death,"[1257] and that living experience through His Son's name, or rather, "Through the faith of Christ, the righteousness which is of God by faith."[1258]

10. Truly "he that hath the Son hath life,"[1259] for the life of man contains thc light of the Spirit's wisdom, which wisdom is His righteousness, which righteousness is born of His will and commandment, and which righteousness is that "law of truth,"[1260] and this truth is necessary in order to explain to the conscience what "the knowledge of sin"[1261] is. Without knowledge of what "sin" is, the heart will naturally keep the mouth of the appetite until the spirit is deadened from being overworked. "Put a knife to thy throat, if thou be a man given

1250 1 John 3:1
1251 1 John 3:13
1252 John 17:16
1253 John 15:19
1254 Romans 6:2
1255 1 John 4:9
1256 Exodus 33:18
1257 Philippians 3:10
1258 Philippians 3:9
1259 1 John 5:12
1260 Malachi 2:6
1261 Romans 3:20

to appetite,"[1262] for "the Spirit is life because of righteousness."[1263] "Hereby know we that we dwell in him, and he in us, because he hath given us of his Spirit,"[1264] and without the Spirit of this LORD, the life of God within His Son's mediation cannot be supplied to our inward parts. The purpose of His Spirit is to convict the heart of sin, to the end that we may "be strengthened with might by his Spirit in the inner man"[1265] to quit what separates our spirit from His Spirit.

11. It is said, "Thou desirest truth in the inward parts: and in the hidden part thou shalt make me to know wisdom."[1266] The Spirit of truth is to nourish "the hidden man of the heart,"[1267] so much so that the Christian confesses: "I delight in the law of God after the inward man,"[1268] and, "The law of the Spirit of life in Christ Jesus hath made me free from the law of sin and death."[1269] Herein the reformer "shall confess that Jesus is the Son of God,"[1270] for "being justified by his blood,"[1271]and "through sanctification of the Spirit"; or as it is said, "Obeying the truth through the Spirit";[1272] His commandments are engraved on the heart from doing the testimony of His name, and wisdom of knowledge added to the spirit of the mind from the victory gained over self from hearing and doing His name.

12. The Christian will have life, wisdom, and understanding, because they abide by the righteousness of His Son to receive grace from His Spirit to perfect right love in them. Love and wisdom are perfected in the soul from learning of and lawfully doing to the Spirit's sayings, and this is sanctification. "The will of God, even your sanctification,"[1273] cannot happen unless "ye should abstain from

---

1262 Proverbs 23:2
1263 Romans 8:10
1264 1 John 4:13
1265 Ephesians 3:16
1266 Psalm 51:6
1267 1 Peter 3:4
1268 Romans 7:22
1269 Romans 8:2
1270 1 John 4:15
1271 Romans 5:9
1272 1 Peter 1:2,22
1273 1 Thessalonians 4:3

fornication."[1274] Fornication is idolatry, and idolatry is that spirit of the world contained in "the lust of the flesh, and the lust of the eyes, and the pride of life."[1275] The spirit of the world cannot comprehend the spirit of truth, therefore it is said, "The world knoweth us not, because it knew him not,"[1276] and, "They that are Christ's have crucified the flesh with the affections and lusts."[1277]

13. "Live according to God in the spirit,"[1278] counsels the Spirit, for then the conversation would "confess that Jesus is the Son of God,"[1279] to the end it would be said, "God dwelleth in him."[1280] The purpose of the Faith of Christ is to give the believer the same edifying love that is within His conversation, and this love cannot be without His Word dwelling within their mind. Christ prays, "I in them, and thou in me, that they may be made perfect,"[1281] for which cause it is said, "Whosoever denieth the Son, the same hath not the Father."[1282] Therefore He says, "Keep through thine own name those whom thou hast given me,"[1283] because the reason for His life, mission, and heavenly ministration, is to perfect man after the name and image of His God, even the character of His own glory as revealed by His precepts of righteousness, that through faith in His sacrifice of reconciliation, many may undergo a process of purification whereby the law of sin and self may be exchanged for the laws and ordinances of truth and justice.

14. Through His righteousness, it is that righteousness is sown, and that which is to be gathered is faith, godly love, and wisdom tried by uncomfortable soul anguish, should we endure. The Christian is to confess that the LORD's Christ is that Son of His Word, and this confession is revealed through a personal and practical religion executing the Faith of His mediation. The conversation is to be the

---

1274 1 Thessalonians 4:3
1275 1 John 2:16
1276 1 John 3:1
1277 Galatians 5:24
1278 1 Peter 4:6
1279 1 John 4:15
1280 1 John 4:15
1281 John 17:23
1282 1 John 2:23
1283 John 17:11

confession of faith, and that faith determined by consistent obedience to His precepts of creation from surrendering the heart to His Spirit. Therefore, "every one that loveth is born of God"[1284] because "every one that doeth righteousness is born of him."[1285] The love of God will be known by them who hear and obey the counsel, "Rise, take up thy bed, and walk."[1286] As the Word dwelt within the spirit of His Christ, so too is the name of the Father to be placed within the mind of the believer by the name of His Son, and then written on the heart and mind by the name of the Spirit, that all may bear the result of the name of the LORD's Faith. "Hereby know we that he abideth in us, by the Spirit which he hath given us."[1287]

15. The reformer is to live according to God in the spirit. The spirit of the mind is to "be renewed in knowledge after the image of him that created him,"[1288] and that knowledge obtained through a personal and experimental religion doing His voice through the wisdom of His Spirit. Should the heart surrender itself, should the love of God be allowed to reach into the chambers of the soul, should the hearer willingly cease activating the stimulus of their old diet to patiently learn of heaven's Pattern of living, the breath of the believer will be revitalized, their moral and intellectual strength will find new life.

16. There is no health for the torn and abused mind outside of the commandments of God, and there will be no healthful advancement in a right conversation without complete surrender to the Savior of the flesh. There will be no acceptance of heaven's will and Faith if the heart refuses to feel conviction of shame and guilt by the Spirit of the living God. The Christian is to confess that they have been with His Son from the fact that they have had their conversation in and with His Father's name, for it is from that intimate relationship that they will joy in His LORD because they have surrendered to the Spirit of His grace.

1284 1 John 4:7
1285 1 John 2:29
1286 John 5:8
1287 1 John 3:24
1288 Colossians 3:10

16

By The Spirit of His Christ

1. "Whosoever believeth that Jesus is the Christ is born of God: and every one that loveth him that begat loveth him also that is begotten of him."[1289] "No man hath seen God at any time; the only begotten Son, which is in the bosom of the Father, he hath declared him."[1290]

2. They that believe on the name of Christ; which name is of God "who hath reconciled us to himself"[1291] "by the death of his Son,"[1292] "by whom we have now received the atonement"[1293] "through faith in his blood";[1294] "to them gave he power to become the sons of God"[1295] that they may "joy in God."[1296] They that examine and do on His Christ's Faith are to be born of His Spirit's Word, and this birth determined by the power given upon pure reception of the virtue of His sacrifice, for then is the believer given wisdom with peace, even praise and reverence of the LORD through "joy in the Holy Ghost."[1297]

1289 1 John 5:1
1290 John 1:18
1291 2 Corinthians 5:18
1292 Romans 5:10
1293 Romans 5:11
1294 Romans 3:25
1295 John 1:12
1296 Romans 5:11
1297 Romans 14:17

3. If the Christian understands that the Word is God, then that Christian is to receive the power of the Holy Ghost "that he might bring us to God."[1298] The ministration of the Son of God is one of reconciliation and restoration to the moral character of His God, therefore the Spirit's Word is "made unto us wisdom, and righteousness, and sanctification, and redemption."[1299] He that first sets himself to believe by faith on the atonement of their spirit to His Spirit for communion; communion that is to have the believer "renewed in knowledge after the image of him";[1300] they will be born of God "not of blood, nor of the will of the flesh, nor of the will of man";[1301] for "flesh and blood cannot inherit the kingdom of God";[1302] but the reformer must "be born of water and of the Spirit,"[1303] that is, "with the washing of water by the word."[1304]

4. Again, that mind "who first trusted in Christ"[1305] is given to the Spirit to be cleansed and sanctified "with the washing of water by the word."[1306] So then what is written? "He that saith he abideth in him ought himself also so to walk, even as he walked."[1307] "This is he that came by water and blood, even Jesus Christ,"[1308] therefore the believer isn't simply born of water "by the washing of regeneration,"[1309] they are also born "with the precious blood of Christ."[1310] For this cause it is said, "That which is born of the Spirit is spirit,"[1311] for by the Spirit's course of learning, the reformer confesses, "I serve with my spirit in the gospel of his Son,"[1312] and because it is the Spirit that advances

1298 1 Peter 3:18
1299 1 Corinthians 1:30
1300 Colossians 3:10
1301 John 1:13
1302 1 Corinthians 15:50
1303 John 3:5
1304 Ephesians 5:26
1305 Ephesians 1:12
1306 Ephesians 5:26
1307 1 John 2:6
1308 1 John 5:6
1309 Titus 3:5
1310 1 Peter 1:19
1311 John 3:6
1312 Romans 1:9

devotion to righteousness by the renewing of the mind, "the fruit of the Spirit is in all goodness and righteousness and truth."[1313]

5. "That the righteousness of the law might be fulfilled in us, who walk not after the flesh, but after the Spirit,"[1314] "the ministration of the spirit,"[1315] "the ministration of righteousness,"[1316] welcomes the believer. "Christ being come an high priest of good things to come, by a greater and more perfect tabernacle,"[1317] "when he had by himself purged our sins, sat down on the right hand of the Majesty on high"[1318] "that we might be made the righteousness of God in him."[1319] The ministration of this Christ is ordained to fulfill the saying, "Bind up the testimony, seal the law among my disciples,"[1320] and as the believer is renewed and purified by doing the word of God by faith in the righteousness of His Christ's counsel, it will be "that every one that doeth righteousness is born of him"[1321] "by the Spirit which he hath given."[1322]

6. "Whosoever believeth that Jesus is the Christ is born of God."[1323] As many stood "looking upon Jesus as he walked,"[1324] it was known that He was Christ from how it was revealed, "Whom thou shalt see the Spirit descending, and remaining on him, the same is he which baptizeth with the Holy Ghost."[1325] Christ walked with, and so lived and worked through the Spirit of His Father, therefore it could be said, "Behold the Lamb of God!"[1326] Therefore the believer is promised, "He shall give you another Comforter, that he may abide with you for ever."[1327] This

1313 Ephesians 5:9
1314 Romans 8:4
1315 2 Corinthians 3:8
1316 2 Corinthians 3:9
1317 Hebrews 9:11
1318 Hebrews 1:3
1319 2 Corinthians 5:21
1320 Isaiah 8:16
1321 1 John 2:29
1322 1 John 3:24
1323 1 John 5:1
1324 John 1:36
1325 John 1:33
1326 John 1:36
1327 John 14:16

is that Comforter "which is the earnest of our inheritance,"[1328] and for this reason "know we that we dwell in him, and he in us, because he hath given us of his Spirit."[1329] As the Spirit remained on His Christ, and this Spirit maintained His walk of love and devotion, so too the reformer is counseled, "Walk in love,"[1330] "because the love of God is shed abroad in our hearts by the Holy Ghost."[1331]

7. If there is a profession of this Christ's confidence, there is a love of the LORD His Father. If there is service to this Christ, and an appreciation for the sacrifice of soul ransom, if the believer declares, "Christ liveth in me,"[1332] it must also be that they are submitted to "the righteousness of God which is by faith of Jesus."[1333] If the believer is without the Father then the profession is formed of an idol, "for they being ignorant of God's righteousness, and going about to establish their own righteousness, have not submitted themselves unto the righteousness of God."[1334] This is why "that which is born after the flesh is flesh,"[1335] "for if ye live after the flesh, ye shall die."[1336]

8. Therefore, "if any man have not the Spirit of Christ, he is none of his." "The Spirit is life because of righteousness,"[1337] "so then they that are in the flesh cannot please God,"[1338] for such a mind "is not subject to the law of God, neither indeed can be."[1339] The Spirit is of truth because its fruit "is in all goodness and righteousness and truth,"[1340] and they who are submitted to Him are submitted to the science of the LORD His father by His Word that they may honor the counsel, "Be ye transformed by the renewing of your mind."[1341] We know that we love

---

1328 Ephesians 1:14
1329 1 John 4:13
1330 Ephesians 5:2
1331 Romans 5:5
1332 Galatians 2:20
1333 Romans 3:22
1334 Romans 10:3
1335 John 3:6
1336 Romans 8:13
1337 Romans 8:10
1338 Romans 8:8
1339 Romans 8:7
1340 Ephesians 5:9
1341 Romans 12:2

the character of God because we uphold faith through the virtue of His Son's character, and from submitting self to the flesh's Deliverer, we know that His character will be engraved in us because we are to be "changed into the same image from glory to glory, even as by the Spirit of the Lord."[1342]

9. It is then a fact that "it is God which worketh in you both to will and to do of his good pleasure."[1343] The course of His blood is "to purge your conscience from dead works to serve the living God"[1344] "to do his will, working in you that which is wellpleasing."[1345] The Spirit's reformer is, by doing the law of His intention, ordained to "keep his commandments, and do those things that are pleasing in his sight,"[1346] and this keeping and doing accomplished by His Spirit resting on and within their conscience, even as it rests within the spirit of His High Priest. His Spirit being ordained of truth is set as an instructor of all righteousness by the true image of righteousness, "because the Spirit is truth,"[1347] and is "even the Spirit of truth."[1348] "Every one that loveth him that begat loveth him also that is begotten of him,"[1349] therefore to love not God is to hate His Son, and to hate His Faith is to despise the image of His Word, for, "whosoever denieth the Son, the same hath not the Father."[1350]

10. They that love God will fall as dead before His glory; they that love His name will accept the education of His glory that they may have that glory within their heart. We know that we do not love the character of God when we stop our heart from processing His manner of love. We know that we do not love His name when we stop our heart from faithfully trusting on the reconciliation of our inward parts to His Spirit. If we love His Son's name, then it must follow that we, by His Spirit's commandment, are perfected into His image, which image is

---

1342 2 Corinthians 3:18
1343 Philippians 2:13
1344 Hebrews 9:14
1345 Hebrews 13:21
1346 1 John 3:22
1347 1 John 5:6
1348 John 15:26
1349 1 John 5:1
1350 1 John 2:23

that of His Father, which image is of that character established on His ten immutable principles of liberty and godly benevolence.

11. If the Christian loves His Faith, they will love His Son's heart and foundation. This Christ Himself says, "I love the Father,"[1351] so then wherefore is the believer justified to exclude the foundation of His profession? "Seeing then that we have a great high priest, that is passed into the heavens, Jesus the Son of God, let us hold fast our profession."[1352] So then hear how He says, "I will declare thy name unto my brethren,"[1353] and, "Whosoever shall do the will of God, the same is my brother, and my sister, and mother."[1354] It is for this reason that it is well to know how it says, "This is the will of God, even your sanctification,"[1355] to the end "the mystery of God, and of the Father, and of Christ,"[1356] would speak by the believer of His Son's name and knowledge, even as He spoke, saying, "I have kept my Father's commandments, and abide in his love."[1357]

12. "If ye keep my commandments, ye shall abide in my love,"[1358] counsels our High Priest. "Whosoever believeth that Jesus is the Christ is born of God: and every one that loveth him that begat loveth him also that is begotten of him. By this we know that we love,"[1359] because "every one that loveth is born of God, and knoweth God."[1360] The Christian is to be born of His Word, alive unto His God, living in the righteousness of His Christ and ordered by every precept of His Spirit's LORD, daily growing up in the knowledge of His Christ's name from learning of and doing those commandments. Herein is the reason why

---

1351 John 14:31
1352 Hebrews 4:14
1353 Hebrews 2:12
1354 Mark 3:34,35
1355 1 Thessalonians 4:3
1356 Colossians 2:2
1357 John 15:10
1358 John 15:10
1359 1 John 5:1,2
1360 1 John 4:7

He says, "He that loveth me not keepeth not my sayings,"[1361] and, "The word which ye hear is not mine, but the Father's which sent me."[1362]

13. Every word of this LORD's Christ is of His Father's character, or else the Spirit lies when saying, "He whom God hath sent speaketh the words of God,"[1363] therefore "whosoever denieth the Son, the same hath not the Father."[1364] For this cause the words of Christ are "spirit, and they are life."[1365] "Every one that loveth him that begat loveth him also that is begotten of him,"[1366] for, He who came out from the Word did speak the doctrine of His LORD's Word, that in the one who should receive His judgment, "to them gave he power to become the sons of God."[1367]

14. "He that hath the Son hath life,"[1368] and this life is for the believer because "he that is begotten of God keepeth himself"[1369] "according to the will of God."[1370] Therefore the doer of heaven's Word will be perfected in love as they "suffer according to the will of God,"[1371] which suffering is as it is said, "Reproached for the name of Christ"[1372] "as ye are partakers of Christ's sufferings."[1373] Such an experience is to create godliness within an erroneous conversation; that is, the mind of Christ engraved within the mind of the conversation;[1374] yet the heart must first accept the counsel, "Every one that loveth him that begat loveth him also that is begotten of him."[1375]

1361 John 14:24
1362 John 14:24
1363 John 3:34
1364 1 John 2:23
1365 John 6:63
1366 1 John 5:1
1367 John 1:12
1368 1 John 5:12
1369 1 John 5:18
1370 1 Peter 4:19
1371 1 Peter 4:19
1372 1 Peter 4:14
1373 1 Peter 4:13
1374 Colossians 1:27
1375 1 John 5:1

17

True Living Devotion

1. It is written, "Live according to God in the spirit,"[1376] or rather, "through the faith of the operation of God,"[1377] keep and honor the commandments of God in the spirit of the mind, because "the spirit giveth life."[1378] For this cause it is said, "Neither in this mountain, nor yet at Jerusalem, worship the Father."[1379] "The true worshippers shall worship the Father in spirit and in truth: for the Father seeketh such to worship him."[1380]

2. The true Christian will neither depend on the structure of a church in the world, nor the imagination of their heart, for learning or praise, for the Spirit's creature says, "We know what we worship,"[1381] and again, "We speak that we do know, and testify that we have seen,"[1382] and again, "That which we have seen and heard declare we unto you."[1383] The spirit of the mind is regenerated only by one means, as it says, "Get wisdom, get understanding,"[1384] and, "Get wisdom:

1376 1 Peter 4:6
1377 Colossians 2:12
1378 2 Corinthians 3:6
1379 John 4:21
1380 John 4:23
1381 John 4:22
1382 John 3:11
1383 1 John 1:3
1384 Proverbs 4:5

and with all thy getting get understanding,"[1385] for it is again said, "We have looked upon, and our hands have handled."[1386] That which is of the spirit is born of an experimental knowledge by faith. Functioning according to God in the spirit would have the believer handling the commandments of God by faith as they practice them within the spirit of the mind, because "God is a Spirit."[1387]

3. It is for this reason that they that honor Him must worship Him in spirit and in truth, renewed after knowledge from circumspectly obeying His science and the precepts of His counsel. "The new man, which is renewed in knowledge,"[1388] excels by handling "the image of him that created him."[1389] There is no newness of mind if there is no personal application of His sayings in the conversation. There is no new heart of love born where there is not an undertaking to remove the old one of corruption. The commandments of God are to be carried out in the flesh by the operation of His Spirit through faith in the grace supplied through His blood. "For by grace are ye saved through faith; and that not of yourselves";[1390] "not of works";[1391] but by believing "on him that justifieth the ungodly,"[1392] "faith is counted for righteousness."[1393]

4. In this righteousness; "the righteousness of God which is by faith of Jesus Christ";[1394] the reformer is to abide by the commandments of God. It is said, "Transformed by the renewing of your mind,"[1395] and this transformation by proving "what is that good, and acceptable, and perfect, will of God."[1396] The spirit is to be renewed by personally handling the precepts of God that wisdom may be added by the

1385 Proverbs 4:7
1386 1 John 1:1
1387 John 4:24
1388 Colossians 3:10
1389 Colossians 3:10
1390 Ephesians 2:8
1391 Ephesians 2:9
1392 Romans 4:5
1393 Romans 4:5
1394 Romans 3:22
1395 Romans 12:2
1396 Romans 12:2

knowledge that is of His Spirit to subdue the members of the body. Scripture says, "Apply thine heart,"[1397] and, "Keep my commandments, and live";[1398] "live according to God in the spirit";[1399] because He has said, "All shall know me."[1400] "Hereby we do know that we know him, if we keep his commandments."[1401]

5. "His commandments are not grievous,"[1402] for the "end of the commandment is charity out of a pure heart,"[1403] and "in this the children of God are manifest, and the children of the devil."[1404] "He that doeth truth cometh to the light, that his deeds may be made manifest";[1405] even "the deeds of the body";[1406] therefore "every one that doeth righteousness is born of him."[1407] "By the law is the knowledge of sin,"[1408] and by coming to the knowledge of God, it is that from patiently handling His precepts, the believer will know truth from error. Redemptions law reveals the knowledge of sin against the living God's name, to the end that, like as this Christ on the tree "abolished in his flesh the enmity, even the law of commandments contained in ordinances";[1409] and "not only in this world, but also in that which is to come";[1410] so also the doer of His mediation's Faith would pass away from that "sin" nailed to the tree to learn godly sorrow and repentance for rightly moving the body to reform.

6. "Every one that doeth evil hateth the light"[1411] "lest his deeds should be reproved,"[1412] for which cause it is said, "He is in the way of

---

1397 Proverbs 2:2
1398 Proverbs 7:2
1399 1 Peter 4:6
1400 Hebrews 8:11
1401 1 John 2:3
1402 1 John 5:3
1403 1 Timothy 1:5
1404 1 John 3:10
1405 John 3:21
1406 Romans 8:13
1407 1 John 2:29
1408 Romans 3:20
1409 Ephesians 2:15
1410 Ephesians 1:21
1411 John 3:20
1412 John 3:20

life that keepeth instruction: but he that refuseth reproof erreth."[1413] Every commandment of God is for the conscience's alleviation, and to suffer executing His word by an experimental faith is to perfect love and wisdom within the conversation. "Whoso keepeth his word, in him verily is the love of God perfected,"[1414] for from sacrificing self, new precepts and ordinances enter into the heart for obedience, and when the storm of trying confusion does pass from the surface of the flesh, the chambers of the mind will be left "perfect and entire, wanting nothing."[1415]

7. In spirit and in truth the worshippers of the Father; they who desire to keep the commandments of God by His own Spirit and wisdom; will serve Him. "He that is dead is freed from sin,"[1416] and by redemption's course that we may, by the grace of His Spirit, have power to live apart from that that held and decapitated us. By diligent practice and effort through His strength, the Christian is to personally know the Spirit's Word from experiencing the Faith of His Son. "All shall know me,"[1417] says the LORD, for all will know the character of God when they submit to the voice of His Son, for He promises, "I will put my law in their inward parts, and write it in their hearts."[1418]

8. The spirit of the mind becomes the new ark for the commandments of God. Adoration, affection, consecration, these are now to be born and expressed from out of the spirit and blessed by His Spirit, to the end that they would be purified by Him to produce honorable works externally. "God is a Spirit,"[1419] says His Son, and through His Faith it is purposed "that the righteousness of the law might be fulfilled in us, who walk not after the flesh, but after the Spirit."[1420] As the new creature is desirous of God; or rather is desirous of the commandments of God that they may be "created in righteousness and true holiness";[1421] so too

1413 Proverbs 10:17
1414 1 John 2:5
1415 James 1:4
1416 Romans 6.7
1417 Hebrews 8:11
1418 Jeremiah 31:33
1419 John 4:24
1420 Romans 8:4
1421 Ephesians 4:24

the keeping and doing of those commandments is after His Spirit. The soul temple is to be "for an habitation of God through the Spirit,"[1422] a temple to keep His counsels in our heart that His Spirit may stir up in us an understanding to efficiently carry them out. For this cause grace is given for the health of our soul temple and for the structure of our character, for "where sin abounded, grace did much more abound."[1423]

9. This praise is "not of blood, nor of the will of the flesh, nor of the will of man,"[1424] "but every one that doeth righteousness is born of him."[1425] To operate by the Word is to allow the Spirit into the heart by the promised blessings given to us by Him. This is why it is well to understand that "it is the spirit that quickeneth; the flesh profiteth nothing."[1426] As the believer faithfully appropriates the grace of God and His righteousness towards their revealed character defects, it is that the spirit will retain knowledge to keep the flesh subdued. Obedience to the words of the LORD will cause a war between the mind and the heart, yet when faithfulness prevails over our inherited unstable nature, the strength, the confidence, and the wisdom learned by doing His wisdom, will turn the Christian to hear, concerning His laws, "Bind them upon thy fingers, write them upon the table of thine heart."[1427]

10. The heart is to be the new table engraved "with the finger of God,"[1428] that is, "with the Spirit of the living God."[1429] Faithful perseverance presents a gift to the believer, even "a well of water springing up into everlasting life."[1430] For this reason it is said, "The righteousness of the perfect shall direct his way,"[1431] and, "Guide thine heart in the way."[1432] From willingly suppressing the flesh through His power,

---

1422 Ephesians 2:22
1423 Romans 5:20
1424 John 1:13
1425 1 John 2:29
1426 John 6:63
1427 Proverbs 7:3
1428 Luke 11:20
1429 2 Corinthians 3:3
1430 John 4:14
1431 Proverbs 11:5
1432 Proverbs 23:19

allowing the spirit to be "renewed in knowledge,"[1433] the Christian will gather a new heart of loyalty and a new mind of understanding. The obedient will arise with a new breath from their experience, and their behavior will confess, "The Spirit of God hath made me, and the breath of the Almighty hath given me life."[1434]

11. "That we might know the things that are freely given to us of God,"[1435] we have received "the spirit which is of God."[1436] "The Spirit searcheth all things, yea, the deep things of God,"[1437] therefore the one born of His Spirit will hear the counsel, "Seekest,"[1438] "searchest,"[1439] "criest,"[1440] "and liftest up thy voice for understanding."[1441] The Spirit of heaven's Faith is not meant for a lazy and cowardice heart, for "slothfulness casteth into a deep sleep; and an idle soul shall suffer hunger."[1442] There will be no soul reformed without physical employment to receive its revival. The renewal of the mind is active, and godly living is expressed outwardly through inward activity completed beforehand. The reformer is "to be strengthened with might by his Spirit in the inner man,"[1443] yet it must first be acknowledged, "Let thine heart retain my words: keep my commandments, and live."[1444]

12. Our conversation is to reveal, "Here are they that keep the commandments of God, and the faith of Jesus."[1445] In spirit and in truth, our service is towards that Faith "set on the right hand of the throne of the Majesty in the heavens,"[1446] which Faith is known of them within "the general assembly and church of the firstborn."[1447] Is

---

1433 Colossians 3:10
1434 Job 33:4
1435 1 Corinthians 2:12
1436 1 Corinthians 2:11
1437 1 Corinthians 2:10
1438 Proverbs 2:4
1439 Proverbs 2:4
1440 Proverbs 2:3
1441 Proverbs 2:3
1442 Proverbs 19:15
1443 Ephesians 3:16
1444 Proverbs 4:4
1445 Revelation 14:12
1446 Hebrews 8:1
1447 Hebrews 12:23

it forgotten that "every one that loveth him that begat loveth him also that is begotten of him"?[1448] What is it that Christ has also said? "Every man therefore that hath heard, and hath learned of the Father, cometh unto me,"[1449] and, "No man can come unto me, except it were given unto him of my Father."[1450]

13. If one with an honest heart desires to become subject to the His intercession's Faith, it is that they must hear, "With the mouth confession is made."[1451] For, "the righteousness which is of faith speaketh on this wise,"[1452] "He that speaketh truth sheweth forth righteousness,"[1453] confessing, "Let my mouth be filled with thy praise and with thy honour."[1454] For this cause the Word's will and commandment is given that "every mouth may be stopped"[1455] who comes to Him by the mediation of His Son, for "whosoever shall confess that Jesus is the Son of God"[1456] "loveth him that begat."[1457]

14. The one who longs after the conversation's Savior will not stop their heart from being taught of the living God, from being regenerated by personal knowledge obtained through soul-aggravation. "Perfect love casteth out fear,"[1458] but "hatred stirreth up strifes,"[1459] and if the believer desires to conquer their unstable nature, then they must hear from the Father, "Ye have not his word abiding in you,"[1460] and, "Ye have not the love of God in you."[1461] Creation's law is given to stop the mouth of our appetite "that sin by the commandment might become exceeding sinful,"[1462] to the end we may faithfully declare, "I exercise

---

1448 1 John 5:1
1449 John 6:45
1450 John 6:65
1451 Romans 10:10
1452 Romans 10:6
1453 Proverbs 12:17
1454 Psalm 71:8
1455 Romans 3:19
1456 1 John 4:15
1457 1 John 5:1
1458 1 John 4:18
1459 Proverbs 10:12
1460 John 5:38
1461 John 5:42
1462 Romans 7:13

myself, to have always a conscience void of offence toward God, and toward men."[1463] This doctrine allows the believer to know that they must pass through an experience with the Father also, for our Priest says, "I am come in my Father's name,"[1464] therefore "he is an'tichrist, that denieth the Father and the Son."[1465]

15. Yet it is said, "He that acknowledgeth the Son hath the Father also,"[1466] because, "Every man therefore that hath heard, and hath learned of the Father, cometh unto me,"[1467] says our Counselor, which is how we come to understand that "Christ is the end of the law for righteousness."[1468] The professor of Christ is not void of the commandments of God, and the one professing the commandments of God is not void of the Faith of the blood of His Son. The reformed mouth of the appetite makes confession that Christ is born of God; that heaven's will and commandment is the Word's instruction; and the one born of God is born of His commandments that stop the mouth of the members of the flesh, therefore the diet of the godly is their confession of faith. Such individuals confess "the Son to be the Savior of the world"[1469] for they adhere to the diet given them, even as it says, "My flesh, which I will give for the life of the world."[1470]

16. The reformer of Christ will not honor His name within himself or herself, but will retreat to His heavenly Sanctuary that the spirit of their mind may find itself edified, for "to be spiritually minded is life and peace."[1471] "The righteousness of the law might be fulfilled in us"[1472] if we can hear how it is written, "The law is spiritual."[1473] The professor of Christ will not be left without an experience whereby His character is written within them, for the believer must have a willing

---

1463 Acts 24:16
1464 John 5:43
1465 1 John 2:22
1466 1 John 2:23
1467 John 6:45
1468 Romans 10:5
1469 1 John 4:14
1470 John 6:51
1471 Romans 8:6
1472 Romans 8:4
1473 Romans 7:14

heart to know God after hearing the word of the ransom of their mind by His sacrifice. The purpose of the voice of Christ is to bring all to His God within the Place of His Spirit, to bring all to keep the commandments that reveal the character of His God through faith in the perfection wrought by His LORD's new covenant. It is for this reason that the Son has said, "I am come in my Father's name,"[1474] and of creation's reformer, "I kept them in thy name."[1475]

17. The professor of Christ will not violate the name of His Father; likewise, the professor will not make void the blood of their purification to retain the name of the Father by the name of the Son. "Of how much sorer punishment, suppose ye, shall be thought worthy, who hath trodden under foot the Son of God, and hath counted the blood of the covenant wherewith he was sanctified, an unholy thing, and hath done despite unto the Spirit of grace?"[1476] The answer is as it is written, "The same shall drink of the wine of the wrath of God."[1477] "For the wrath of God is revealed from heaven against all ungodliness,"[1478] yet if the believer would yield their heart to maintain the provision given them by His Son's mediation, and despite feeling or inclination, it is that their behavior would speak as one "which after God is created in righteousness and true holiness."[1479]

18. It is then a fact that the reforming soul "should walk in newness of life";[1480] or rather, in newness of understanding within the spirit of their conversation; from their desire for birth to God by faithfully taking knowledge of the law of redemption's plan. From committing self to practically apply the words of Christ to the personal religion, and to the lessons learned from the Father through faith on the virtue of His Son's name, it will be "that our old man is crucified with him, that the body of sin might be destroyed, that henceforth we should not

---

1474 John 5:43
1475 John 17:12
1476 Hebrews 10:29
1477 Revelation 14:10
1478 Romans 1:18
1479 Ephesians 4:24
1480 Romans 6:4

serve sin."[1481] Indeed the heart taught of the Spirit cannot sin against His name because within it rests both the Law and Doctrine of His Word arresting their appetite, bringing it under subjection to a tried faith purified by reason and love. The conversation must be renewed in knowledge after the character of this Christ's law that its conscience may appreciate His LORD and Father, for then "if we walk in the light, as he is in the light, we have fellowship one with another."[1482]

19. "He that saith, I know him, and keepeth not his commandments, is a liar, and the truth is not in him. But whoso keepeth his word, in him verily is the love of God perfected: hereby know we that we are in him."[1483] "The true worshippers shall worship the Father in spirit and in truth: for the Father seeketh such to worship him."[1484]

1481 Romans 6:6
1482 1 John 1:7
1483 1 John 2:4,5
1484 John 4:23

18

Renewed In Knowledge

1. "Be renewed in the spirit of your mind";[1485] "put on the new man, which is renewed in knowledge after the image of him that created him";[1486] "the new man, which after God is created in righteousness and true holiness."[1487]

2. The new mind of the heart is to be renewed in knowledge after the image of Him that created him. Who then is the Creator of the new man? It is written, "Ye who sometimes were far off are made nigh by the blood of Christ,"[1488] who made "in himself of twain one new man, so making peace."[1489] The new man is created through the doctrine of the blood of Christ, even as it says, "Of his own will begat he us with the word of truth, that we should be a kind of firstfruits of his creatures."[1490] The reformer is to be renewed after the image of the living God's Son, and it is not said in vain, "Who is the image of the invisible God,"[1491] and, "Who being the brightness of his glory, and

---

1485 Ephesians 4:23
1486 Colossians 3:10
1487 Ephesians 4:24
1488 Ephesians 2:13
1489 Ephesians 2:15
1490 James 1:18
1491 Colossians 1:15

the express image of his person."[1492] It is our assignment to embrace the like passing of this Christ that we may claim His like resurrection, which is why it says, "Renewed in knowledge"[1493] "to be conformed to the image of his Son."[1494]

3. How is the believer to obtain the likeness of Christ? It is said, "Renewed in knowledge,"[1495] and most preferably, "The knowledge of his will in all wisdom and spiritual understanding."[1496] Seeing as how "the law is spiritual,"[1497] and "to be spiritually minded is life and peace,"[1498] there rests "spiritual meat"[1499] for the "spiritual body"[1500] of the believer that without wavering they may declare, "I delight in the law of God after the inward man."[1501] "That was not first which is spiritual, but that which is natural,"[1502] therefore if the believer does long after the Spirit's science, they must settle their natural selves that they may receive that which will perfect both flesh and spirit. For this cause it is said, "Be ye stedfast, unmoveable, always abounding in the work of the Lord,"[1503] for "this is the work of God, that ye believe on him whom he hath sent."[1504]

4. But is "belief" the only requirement? If it was, why then has the LORD instituted an educational process to know Him? If this was so, it would not be said, "Fervent in spirit; serving the Lord."[1505] We are counseled to "live according to God in the spirit,"[1506] earnestly and vehemently serving the Father in that same spirit, for believing is but the first step in order to perform heaven's course for heaven's

---

1492 Hebrews 1:3
1493 Colossians 3:10
1494 Romans 8:29
1495 Colossians 3:10
1496 Colossians 1:9
1497 Romans 7:14
1498 Romans 8:6
1499 1 Corinthians 10:3
1500 1 Corinthians 15:44
1501 Romans 7:22
1502 1 Corinthians 15:46
1503 1 Corinthians 15:48
1504 1 Corinthians 15:58
1505 Romans 12:11
1506 1 Peter 4:6

benevolence. We know how it says, "By every word that proceedeth out of the mouth of the LORD doth man live,"[1507] and, "The LORD giveth wisdom: out of his mouth cometh knowledge and understanding."[1508] The reformer is to order their conversation around that which has come out from the living God, "for whatsoever is born of God overcometh the world,"[1509] therefore it is written, "Two tables of testimony, tables of stone, written with the finger of God."[1510] "The tables were the work of God."[1511] And also He says, "A law shall proceed from me,"[1512] even the Faith of "the law of Christ."[1513]

5. His faithful and to keep His Ten Commandments by actively learning of and believing on that Faith sent and ratified by the blood of His Son, for we read how the Father said, "A law shall proceed from me."[1514] "That was not first which is spiritual, but that which is natural; and afterward that which is spiritual";[1515] for we first see physical tables given to order a temporal structure under a dead covenant, yet now the "fleshy tables of the heart"[1516] are to be "written not with ink, but with the Spirit of the living God,"[1517] that "we shall also bear the image of the heavenly,"[1518] that is, in this application, "the heavenly Jerusalem"[1519] by "Jesus the mediator of the new covenant."[1520] For, "whosoever believeth that Jesus is the Christ is born of God,"[1521] and it is a fact that they are born of the Spirit through His "power to become the sons of God."[1522] From the wisdom given by active faith on the law

---

1507 Deuteronomy 8:3
1508 Proverbs 2:6
1509 1 John 5:4
1510 Exodus 31:18
1511 Exodus 32:16
1512 Isaiah 51:4
1513 Galatians 6:2
1514 Isaiah 51:4
1515 1 Corinthians 15:46
1516 2 Corinthians 3:3
1517 2 Corinthians 3:3
1518 1 Corinthians 15:49
1519 Hebrews 12:22
1520 Hebrews 12:24
1521 1 John 5:1
1522 John 1:12

of His Christ's name and mediation, the reformer will live unto God through His Spirit.

6. They that are of Christ examine His name that they may receive the power of grace to perform heaven's assignment by His Spirit and doctrine. Therefore "if any man have not the Spirit of Christ,"[1523] "even the Spirit of truth, which proceedeth from the Father,"[1524] "he is none of his."[1525] The obedient soul believes on the words of Christ for the purpose of receiving His circumcision to become a son or daughter of the Word, for it was ordained "that we might live through him."[1526] Thus, "Keep my commandments, and live,"[1527] says the Spirit. "Live according to God in the spirit."[1528]

7. The believing reformer is created by the words of His Spirit through faith on the blood of His sacrifice. By His image of a sanctified love that works by faith, the believer is to be renewed in heart and mind, recovered by a personal and experimental knowing of His office and operation. If the Christian would fulfill the Word's right labor, or would faithfully keep and do every commandment of God and of His Son, it is that they must receive His Spirit and cooperate with that Spirit's course of learning, for "the kingdom of God is not in word, but in power"[1529] "and in the Holy Ghost, and in much assurance."[1530] We are to "assure our hearts before him"[1531] "having received the word in much affliction, with joy of the Holy Ghost."[1532]

8. The work of the believer is a "work of righteousness"[1533] whereby the receiver of the Spirit of grace is to be repaired in mind, revived in understanding, by a true and living education with the Spirit's Word to birth a "new man, which after God is created in righteousness and

---

1523 Romans 8:9
1524 John 15:26
1525 Romans 8:9
1526 1 John 4:9
1527 Proverbs 4:4
1528 1 Peter 4:6
1529 1 Corinthians 4:20
1530 1 Thessalonians 1:5
1531 1 John 5:19
1532 1 Thessalonians 1:6
1533 Isaiah 32:17

true holiness."[1534] The new nature given to the believer is one that is in likeness to the character of God, for they are submitted to His counsels and conditions for the reproduction of His mind in them. Every word that comes out from God is knowledge that is to be in the believer wisdom from personal application, from actively executing by faith those commandments. Yet to be an honest son or daughter of His Faith, it is that one must not keep His commandments by the flesh's force through legal religious laws and policies, for the heart must be emptied of self so that His Spirit may reach in to the soul temple to introduce a new and living regimen, even the ordinances of "the living bread which came down from heaven."[1535] This is what it means to possess "a spirit that confesseth that Jesus Christ is come in the flesh."[1536]

9. Concerning bread, we do know that bread is meat. It is said, "All the people came to cause David to eat meat,"[1537] yet David said, "If I taste bread."[1538] For this cause Christ taught, "My flesh is meat indeed."[1539] "I am the bread of life."[1540] "He that eateth me, even he shall live by me."[1541] So then "live according to God in the spirit,"[1542] or, says our High Priest, "Live by my voice according to the Word within the spirit of your mind. Uphold your personal religion by my flesh and blood according to the Word in the spirit. Fulfill and keep the commandments of our LORD and Father in the spirit of your mind by the doctrine of my flesh and my blood." For this cause, "Let your conversation be as it becometh the gospel of Christ"[1543] "that ye might walk worthy of the Lord unto all pleasing."[1544]

1534 Ephesians 4:24
1535 John 6:51
1536 1 John 4:2
1537 2 Samuel 3:35
1538 2 Samuel 3:35
1539 John 6:55
1540 John 6:48
1541 John 6:57
1542 1 Peter 4:6
1543 Philippians 1:27
1544 Colossians 1:10

10. If it is that we must maintain a "good conversation in Christ,"[1545] the counsel must be heard, "Let your conversation be without covetousness."[1546] A covetous spirit is one of error drowned in lust, for we know that no "covetous man, who is an idolater, hath any inheritance in the kingdom of Christ."[1547] There is a heritage of the reformer born of the kingdom of God that they may "be partakers of the inheritance of the saints in light":[1548] one being "that holy Spirit of promise, which is the earnest of our inheritance,"[1549] and the other being reproach for the name of Christ, we being "partakers of Christ's sufferings."[1550] Without surrendering to His Spirit, we are void of His Son's Faith and of that Faith's educating Spirit, and without suffering "according to the will of God,"[1551] we will not be made perfect in Them.

11. A spirit contrary to covetousness is self-sacrifice, and the mind must embrace the pattern of its High Priest's conversation if it would care to maintain a right faith under His wings. Therefore the believer receives the inheritance of them that are in the light, even "the inheritance of the saints in light,"[1552] for only "he that doeth truth cometh to the light."[1553] Therefore, concerning the doer of truth, of righteousness, of the ordinances and statues of justification by faith, "He shall live by me,"[1554] says the Spirit. There can be no progress in the conversation if the body lacks this Christ's righteousness,[1555] for being "reconciled to God by the death of his Son,"[1556] "we shall be saved by his life."[1557] "The righteousness of the law might be fulfilled in us"[1558] only as we surrender to the law of the authority of the blood of Christ to do

1545 1 Peter 3:16
1546 Hebrews 13:5
1547 Ephesians 5:5
1548 Colossians 1:12
1549 Ephesians 1:14
1550 1 Peter 4:13
1551 1 Peter 4:19
1552 Colossians 1:12
1553 John 3:21
1554 John 6:57
1555 Romans 5:18
1556 Romans 5:10
1557 Romans 5:10
1558 Romans 8:4

that which is pleasing in the sight of His God, even "obeying the truth through the Spirit."[1559] "Hereby we do know that we know him, if we keep his commandments."[1560]

12. The Christian is to operate "through the faith of Christ"[1561] to obtain "the righteousness which is of God by faith,"[1562] "that the God of our Lord Jesus Christ, the Father of glory, may give unto you the spirit of wisdom and revelation in the knowledge of him."[1563] The believer is to advance in the rounds of perfection from "understanding what the will of the Lord is,"[1564] and without dispute this is the will of the LORD our Father, that "every one that loveth him that begat loveth him also that is begotten of him."[1565]

13. This is why our High Priest says, "No man cometh unto the Father, but by me."[1566] To retain the name of the Father, it is that the believer must experience the anguish and the rejoicing of His Christ's name. As the Word's faithful "commit the keeping of their souls to him in well doing, as unto a faithful Creator,"[1567] it is not designed that the Christian should expect some magical translation in thought and feeling, for it says, "Be transformed by the renewing of your mind."[1568] Every believer is responsible for his or her own progression. God will not do what He has given man the capability to accomplish. God will not help any one who is not willing to help themselves, therefore "if any of you lack wisdom, let him ask of God"[1569] "in faith, nothing wavering."[1570] The members of the flesh must be sacrificed if there is to be a revival of the spirit of the mind to conquer the benumbed portions

---

1559 1 Peter 1:22
1560 1 John 2:3
1561 Philippians 3:9
1562 Philippians 3:9
1563 Ephesians 1:17
1564 Ephesians 5:17
1565 1 John 5:1
1566 John 14:6
1567 1 Peter 4:19
1568 Romans 12:2
1569 James 1:5
1570 James 1:6

of our heart. We cannot forget that "it is the spirit that quickeneth,"[1571] and the experience of learning how to exercise faith on the sayings of His Christ will add knowledge for right self-government.

1571 John 6:63

19

Conversation With Life And Wisdom

1. It is counseled, "Live according to God in the spirit,"[1572] for the conversation would be of no value if not "in subjection unto the Father of spirits."[1573] "The God of the spirits of all flesh,"[1574] "the Father of lights,"[1575] is needed if we would have "an excellent spirit"[1576] of "light and understanding and excellent wisdom,"[1577] therefore it is said, "Ye have known the Father."[1578] Should we maintain our personal faith with both the Father and the Son, then may it be that "ye are strong,"[1579] "waxed strong in spirit, filled with wisdom,"[1580] because "the word of God abideth in you."[1581] The reformer is to know the Word by His Son's name; they are to have dissolved into the current of their spirit every

1572 1 Peter 4:6
1573 Hebrews 12:9
1574 Numbers 16:22
1575 James 1:17
1576 Daniel 6:3
1577 Daniel 5:14
1578 1 John 2:13
1579 1 John 2:14
1580 Luke 2:40
1581 1 John 2:14

commandment of God "by the spirit of judgment, and by the spirit of burning"[1582] to regulate their conversation. For, "he that is begotten of God keepeth himself,"[1583] because "wisdom is a defence"[1584] to "overcome the wicked one."[1585] This is why it says, "Wisdom giveth life."[1586]

2. Scripture counsels, "Prove what is that good, and acceptable, and perfect, will of God,"[1587] yet how is the Spirit's will to be examined? It is written, "I have proved by wisdom,"[1588] therefore, "I have learned by experience,"[1589] says the doer of creation's science. The Spirit counsels, "Attend unto my wisdom,"[1590] "attend to my words,"[1591] "attend to know understanding,"[1592] "apply thine heart to understanding,"[1593] and "let thine heart retain my words,"[1594] "for the LORD giveth wisdom."[1595] "Out of his mouth cometh knowledge and understanding,"[1596] therefore "the mouth of the just bringeth forth wisdom,"[1597] for they have surrendered to the counsel, "Be renewed in the spirit of your mind"[1598] "in knowledge after the image of him."[1599] For this cause the wisdom and knowledge of the reformer is based upon their willingness to know Him by faith, for it is ordained by the Father that all who profess His Christ's name must declare, "Our hands have handled."[1600]

3. This Christ says, "This is the will of him that sent me, that every one which seeth the Son, and believeth on him, may have everlasting

---

1582 Isaiah 4:4
1583 1 John 5:18
1584 Ecclesiastes 7:12
1585 1 John 5:18
1586 Ecclesiastes 7:12
1587 Romans 12:2
1588 Ecclesiastes 7:23
1589 Genesis 30:27
1590 Proverbs 5:1
1591 Proverbs 4:20
1592 Proverbs 4:1
1593 Proverbs 2:2
1594 Proverbs 4:4
1595 Proverbs 2:6
1596 Proverbs 2:6
1597 Proverbs 10:31
1598 Ephesians 4:23
1599 Colossians 3:10
1600 1 John 1:1

life."[1601] Therefore, "We have seen with our eyes,"[1602] says the reforming Christian, and this is because "the eyes of your understanding being enlightened"[1603] have allowed the mind to retain the sayings and promises of God, "and were persuaded of them, and embraced them,"[1604] and "have received them,"[1605] or "have believed."[1606] It is said, "Let every man be fully persuaded in his own mind,"[1607] for "the wise man's eyes are in his head."[1608] It is said, "Mine eyes,"[1609] that is, "My heart,"[1610] for the heart of man is to be in his head, because "circumcision is that of the heart, in the spirit."[1611] It is well known that "the spirit giveth life,"[1612] and recovery and regulation of the conversation is of the spirit because "wisdom giveth life,"[1613] for as it is said, "A sound heart is the life of the flesh,"[1614] this is the will and word of God through Christ.

4. It is said, "Whoso keepeth his mouth and his tongue keepeth his soul from troubles,"[1615] for "all the labour of man is for his mouth, and yet the appetite is not filled."[1616] Of wisdom it is know, "She is thy life,"[1617] for, concerning the commandments of God, "They are life unto those that find them, and health to all their flesh."[1618] The life of the flesh, or the health of "the body of the sins of the flesh,"[1619] is of "the

1601 John 6:40
1602 1 John 1:1
1603 Ephesians 1:18
1604 Hebrews 11:13
1605 John 17:8
1606 John 17:8
1607 Romans 14:15
1608 Ecclesiastes 2:14
1609 Ecclesiastes 2:10
1610 Ecclesiastes 2:10
1611 Romans 2:29
1612 2 Corinthians 3:6
1613 Ecclesiastes 7:12
1614 Proverbs 14:30
1615 Proverbs 21:23
1616 Ecclesiastes 6:7
1617 Proverbs 4:13
1618 Proverbs 4:22
1619 Colossians 2:11

Father of glory"[1620] to the one "that diligently seeketh,"[1621] searching for knowledge of Him and through Him. From proving the will of the Father, we are to receive "the spirit of wisdom and revelation in the knowledge of him,"[1622] to the end we may keep from "fulfilling the desires of the flesh and of the mind." [1623] "The spirit quickeneth"[1624] because the spirit is life according to obtained wisdom and knowledge, and this quickening is accomplished within the inwards because the organs of the mind exist within and to the Spirit of God, which is why "the Spirit is life because of righteousness."[1625]

5. The spirit gives life because through diligent circumcision by His words, "I may know him,"[1626] and the wisdom gained will fulfill the saying, "Thy foot shall not stumble."[1627] The Christian is to live according to God by wisdom obtained from His wisdom. To the obedient, His precepts are to be "life unto thy soul,"[1628] for it is said, "Without me ye can do nothing."[1629] Wisdom gives life to the spirit of the mind, and the spirit gives life to the conversation because it is now centered on the saying, "The life was manifested."[1630] He that has this Christ's understanding has life and truth; the word of God and His righteousness rests within them because that which they "heard before in the word of the truth of the gospel"[1631] has advanced the fact, "Know that ye have eternal life."[1632]

6. The Christian is to soberly prove the Spirit's will, yet what is His will? His intention is to "make you perfect in every good work."[1633]

1620 Ephesians 1:17
1621 Proverbs 11:27
1622 Ephesians 1:17
1623 Ephesians 2:3
1624 John 6:63
1625 Romans 8:10
1626 Philippians 3:10
1627 Proverbs 3:23
1628 Proverbs 3:22
1629 John 15:5
1630 1 John 1:2
1631 Colossians 1:5
1632 1 John 5:13
1633 Hebrews 13:21

This is why our High Priest, "That they may be one,"[1634] and, "I in them, and thou in me, that they may be made perfect in one."[1635] He said this because the old ministration "could not make him that did the service perfect, as pertaining to the conscience."[1636] The conscience is to be made perfect by housing within it heaven's perfect law of righteousness. The blood of Christ; "the blood of the covenant";[1637] it is to make you perfect, in that His blood is to "purge your conscience from dead works to serve the living God."[1638] Service to God cannot be had if there is no willing submission to be made clean by His blood's course of learning, for it is that after accepting, and by faith, the labor and effect of His righteousness, we are to be brought to His LORD's Spirit for inward regeneration by His Word of creation.

7. It is for this reason that we are counseled to "suffer the word of exhortation"[1639] by the Spirit, to the end we may know "that God hath given to us eternal life,"[1640] for it is written, "Know that ye have eternal life."[1641] The honest Christian will not perish with the spirit and constitution of the religious world, nor with that crucified system and covenant of old, for they know, "The Son of man must be lifted up,"[1642] for "in Christ shall all be made alive."[1643] The knowledge of the LORD's Son is Eternal Life, and the Christian can do no thing to make their conversation perfect in spirit without His name within their conscience; "there is no man that hath power over the spirit to retain the spirit."[1644] When once the will is given over to the Spirit's Eternal Life,

---

1634 John 17:22
1635 John 17:23
1636 Hebrews 9:9
1637 Hebrews 10:29
1638 Hebrews 9:14
1639 Hebrews 13:22
1640 1 John 5:11
1641 1 John 5:13
1642 John 3:14
1643 1 Corinthians 15:22
1644 Ecclesiastes 8:8

the heart will learn that in this Faith is "eternal salvation,"[1645] "eternal redemption,"[1646]"the eternal Spirit,"[1647] and "eternal inheritance."[1648]

8. The Christian surrendered to this Word "through sanctification of the Spirit, unto obedience and sprinkling of the blood of Jesus,"[1649] will hear, "Draw near with a true heart in full assurance of faith."[1650] The Christian is to live according to God in the spirit; obedience to the precepts of God are to be observed in the spirit and not by any act of the conversation; for the spirit is the mind of the conscience, and this mind is to be purged of religious corruption and made clean by faith in the righteousness of the Redeemer's name. Being given the true God and Eternal Life of God by faith, even "the law of the Spirit of life,"[1651] what more can be said, other than "let us cleanse ourselves from all filthiness of the flesh and spirit, perfecting holiness in the fear of God."[1652] With every precious gift and promise of the Word, the believer is to perfect holiness in conversation, godliness in spirit, that the flesh may have peace to execute the vocation entrusted to it.

9. The heart is to be brought under subjection to creation's law that the spirit of the mind may retain "the words of eternal life."[1653] It is that, "according to the eternal purpose of God which he purposed in Christ Jesus";[1654] "by the which will we are sanctified through the offering of the body of Jesus";[1655] we have "boldness and access with confidence by faith of him,"[1656] and through faith in His righteousness, the believer is to be made "holy in all manner of conversation."[1657] The removal of the covering of the heart is ours to do and does not fall on

---

1645 Hebrews 5:9
1646 Hebrews 9:12
1647 Hebrews 9:14
1648 Hebrews 9:15
1649 1 Peter 1:2
1650 Hebrews 10:22
1651 Romans 8:2
1652 2 Corinthians 7:1
1653 John 6:68
1654 Ephesians 3:11
1655 Hebrews 10:10
1656 Ephesians 13:12
1657 1 Peter 1:15

God. The faithful "purifieth himself,"[1658] we are counseled, "even as he is pure."[1659]

10. "Through the righteousness of faith,"[1660] the reformer is to learn of the Father and the Son that "love may abound yet more and more in knowledge and in all judgment."[1661] And herein "is love, that we walk after his commandments";[1662] for His commandments regeneration the mind to embrace cultivating right faith and love; therefore it is said, "Live according to God in the spirit."[1663] The believer who, through heaven's Faith is born of God, will have "no more conscience of sins,"[1664] for they are perfect in heart and in mind, in that they are regulated by the commandments of God and the Faith of His Son. As the believer becomes perfect and entire from being transformed within their mind, the counsel is, "Serve God acceptably with reverence and godly fear."[1665]

11. "The just shall live by faith."[1666] The believer will live by the Faith of their High Priest in the spirit to execute the commandments of His God. The just will live to God, for "the doers of the law"[1667] of redemption, "the doers of the word,"[1668] "the words of eternal life,"[1669] "shall be justified,"[1670] "justified by his grace."[1671] "He that hath the Son hath life,"[1672] and "according to the promise of life which is in Christ,"[1673] according to the pleasure of the Father "which he hath purposed in himself,"[1674] "we should be holy and without blame before

1658 1 John 3:3
1659 1 John 3:3
1660 Romans 4:13
1661 Philippians 1:9
1662 2 John 2:6
1663 1 Peter 4:6
1664 Hebrews 10:2
1665 Hebrews 12:28
1666 Hebrews 10:38
1667 Romans 2:13
1668 James 1:22
1669 John 6:68
1670 Romans 2:13
1671 Titus 3:7
1672 1 John 5:12
1673 2 Timothy 1:1
1674 Ephesians 1:9

him in love,"[1675] and this conversation through the regeneration of the inward person "in knowledge after the image of him."[1676] In the mind of the conversation, the believer is to "serve God acceptably with reverence and godly fear,"[1677] that is, in "a good conscience, in all things willing to live honestly."[1678]

12. "The testimony of our conscience"[1679] is revealed through our "chaste conversation coupled with fear."[1680] The spirit is the true place of worship; it is to be the command center of the heart "to provoke unto love and to good works"[1681] the limbs of the body. The LORD is beyond "faithful that promised"[1682] "to keep you from falling, and to present you faultless before the presence of his glory."[1683] He is that true LORD and Spirit that joys "in bringing many sons unto glory,"[1684] even unto the righteousness of His name. They who are given the Eternal Life of His Spirit, even that Faith born for "eternal salvation"[1685] and "eternal redemption,"[1686] who is of "the eternal Spirit"[1687] possessing the "eternal inheritance,"[1688] and who is made "after the power of an endless life,"[1689] is given every means to experience creation by the Spirit of the living God. It then becomes crucial for us to "have escaped the pollutions of the world through the knowledge of the Lord and Saviour Jesus Christ."[1690]

13. The Word's reformer is to perfect a godly conversation through the Faith of His Son. The justified in spirit excel by exercising faith on

---

1675 Ephesians 1:4
1676 Colossians 3:10
1677 Hebrews 12:28
1678 Hebrews 13:18
1679 2 Corinthians 1:12
1680 1 Peter 3:2
1681 Hebrews 10:24
1682 Hebrews 10:23
1683 Jude 1:24
1684 Hebrews 2:10
1685 Hebrews 5:9
1686 Hebrews 9:12
1687 Hebrews 9:14
1688 Hebrews 9:15
1689 Hebrews 7:16
1690 2 Peter 2:20

His Son's name, and as the conscience is purged of spiritual death from suffering right counsel upon its members, the spirit will retain wisdom and love, for it now possesses that Word who is the true God, and the mediation of His High Priest, who will create them "in truth and love."[1691]

1691 2 John 1:3

20

Serving With Reverence And Godly Fear

1. "I will teach you the fear of the LORD. What man is he that desireth life, and loveth many days, that he may see good? Keep thy tongue from evil, and thy lips from speaking guile. Depart from evil, and do good; seek peace, and pursue it."[1692] "Who is he that will harm you, if ye be followers of that which is good?"[1693]

2. Scripture counsels, "Live according to God in the spirit,"[1694] for "the way which thou shalt go"[1695] is in the fear of the living God, for it is said, "The fear of the LORD prolongeth days."[1696] Should the believer love a long life of mental and moral health; for the Spirit says, "By me thy days shall be multiplied";[1697] the believer of His name must take hold of the counsel, "Forget not my law; but let thine heart keep my commandments,"[1698] because "the fear of the Lord, that is wisdom."[1699]

1692 Psalm 34:14
1693 1 Peter 3:13
1694 1 Peter 4:6
1695 Psalm 32:8
1696 Proverbs 10:27
1697 Proverbs 9:11
1698 Proverbs 3:1
1699 Job 28:28

It is known that reverent obedience is "of the heart, in the spirit,"[1700] for the heart of the believer is to house the precepts of the fear of God for a proper religion, therefore the spirit of the mind is to be the place of wisdom to carry out the commands of that conversation throughout the body.

3. The fear of the LORD adds mental and moral stability to regulate the body. The reformer is counseled, "Sanctify the Lord God in your hearts,"[1701] and, "Serve God acceptably with reverence and godly fear,"[1702] for it is said, "Be ye holy in all manner of conversation,"[1703] "holding faith, and a good conscience."[1704] True worship is obtained from proving His wisdom to obtain governing wisdom; as it says, "That ye may prove,"[1705] and, "Prove your own selves";[1706] for one must strengthen their will to confess, "I applied mine heart to know, and to search, and to seek out wisdom, and the reason of things,"[1707] for the counsel is, "Seek peace, and pursue it."[1708]

4. The body is to be regulated by the mind, yet the flesh without the Spirit's wisdom desires the throne of the heart. A heart that honestly feels after God will desire His wisdom, the life of His name; for His commandments, "they are life unto those that find them";[1709] to correct the error that is in their personal religion, and to make manifest the secret error that is hidden from them. The heart grows in depth and in sincerity by seeking after the LORD's wisdom, by digging through His voice, by experimenting with His counsels through faith in His righteousness, that as the heart becomes circumcised through conflict and mental taxation, the spirit will retain His words to render higher and truer devotion to the intention of His Son's mediation. As the spirit retains His words from humbling self to be brought into a personal

---

1700 Romans 2:29
1701 1 Peter 3:15
1702 Hebrews 12:28
1703 1 Peter 1:15
1704 1 Timothy 1:19
1705 Romans 12:2
1706 2 Corinthians 13:5
1707 Ecclesiastes 7:25
1708 Psalm 34:14
1709 Proverbs 4:22

experience with them, as wisdom is earnestly sought and acted out, so too is peace obtained, for from wisdom the believer obtains "long life, and peace."[1710]

5. It is said, "Seek peace, and pursue it,"[1711] for in "the way of the LORD is strength."[1712] For this cause it is said, "Blessed are the undefiled in the way, who walk in the law of the LORD,"[1713] and, "Blessed are the pure in heart: for they shall see God."[1714] The pure in heart maintain their conversation from their reverence for the person of God and for their fear and respect of His voice. As they excel in wisdom from obedience, they obtain strength to keep the Faith of the Father and His Son. For this cause the Spirit says, "My grace is sufficient,"[1715] and, "My strength is made perfect,"[1716] because without His grace; which is "the exceeding greatness of his power to us-ward who believe";[1717] we will never know that "whosoever believeth that Jesus is the Christ is born of God."[1718] The spirit is purposed to personally cultivate and perfect the entire conversation, and as grace is added to wisdom for regulating the organs of the spirit, guile will pass away from the lips, the heart will become exceeding quiet from its faithful assurance.

6. For this cause it is said, "Keep thy tongue from evil, and thy lips from speaking guile."[1719] The tongue and the lips are one, for it is said, "In the lips of him that hath understanding wisdom is found,"[1720] and, "The wise in heart will receive commandments,"[1721] and, "He that refraineth his lips is wise,"[1722] and again, "The tongue of the just is as choice silver."[1723] The tongue and the lips are synonymous with

---

1710 Proverbs 3:2
1711 Psalm 34:14
1712 Proverbs 10:29
1713 Psalm 119:1
1714 Matthew 5:8
1715 2 Corinthians 12:9
1716 2 Corinthians 12:9
1717 Ephesians 1:19
1718 1 John 5:1
1719 Psalm 34:13
1720 Proverbs 10:13
1721 Proverbs 10:8
1722 Proverbs 10:19
1723 Proverbs 10:20

the heart, which is why Scripture records, "In whose spirit there is no guile."[1724] The lip and "the tongue among our members"[1725] "which are upon the earth";[1726] "the works of the flesh"[1727] manifested by "the deeds of the body";[1728] "the body of the sins of the flesh";[1729] these are to come under strict watch if the believer would see and know God. It is the applied wisdom of God that does quench the desire of the flesh, for wisdom is the beginning of a good conscience towards God and self.

7. The mouth, the lips and the tongue, the spirit and the heart, is to house no thing that will corrupt the good that is to be placed within it by painstaking and diligent obedient effort. The believer should declare, "He hath made my mouth like a sharp sword,"[1730] even like "the sword of the Spirit, which is the word of God."[1731] The spirit is to house the word of God because the mind is to be the center for devotion, love, for order and examination to provoke right actions surrendered to right thoughts and feelings. Herein is how we know that the Spirit's will and law "is a discerner of the thoughts and intents of the heart."[1732]

8. Without possessing that which is born to divide "soul and spirit,"[1733] how may we confess, "The LORD was my stay"?[1734] The heart of the spirit needs to be purified if pure worship and acts of right affection would come from it. His Spirit guards His words, for "it is the Spirit that beareth witness, because the Spirit is truth."[1735] The believer is to possess "the spirit of truth,"[1736] the heart and mouth and mind of righteousness that they may do, and fulfill, righteousness by the Spirit of truth and righteousness. "He that doeth righteousness is

---

1724 Psalm 32:2
1725 James 3:6
1726 Colossians 3:5
1727 Galatians 5:19
1728 Romans 8:13
1729 Colossians 2:11
1730 Isaiah 49:2
1731 Ephesians 6:17
1732 Hebrews 4:12
1733 Hebrews 4:12
1734 Psalm 18:18
1735 1 John 5:6
1736 1 John 3:7

righteous,"[1737] for "the eyes of the LORD are upon the righteous,"[1738] or, "The eye of the LORD is upon them that fear him."[1739] The righteous; they that fear and respect the LORD's Faith, the doers of His righteousness by faith of His righteousness; are preserved in Him as, "The faithful."[1740] "The love of God is shed abroad in our hearts by the Holy Ghost,"[1741] yet the heart must first accept the work to retain the wisdom of God that love may be perfected in spirit, and in truth. This is why His faithful say, "I will meditate in thy precepts, and have respect unto thy ways."[1742]

9. It is known, "Thou wilt keep him in perfect peace, whose mind is stayed on thee,"[1743] therefore it is said, "Let him seek peace, and ensue it."[1744] Should the believer desire the health of their flesh, should they care to see heaven's good intention bless their conversation, and to also know that the character of God and His precepts are "holy, just, and good,"[1745] there must be a longing to serve and wait upon His name in godly fear. To learn of and keep His commandment for creation is to add wisdom to faith, for the process of personal research is progressed through grace, of which will heal the soul of religious error and create new space in the mind to retain knowledge heaven's order. Indeed "I was alive without the law once,"[1746] "but after that the kindness of God our Saviour toward man appeared"[1747] saying, "Reckon ye also yourselves dead indeed unto sin, but alive unto God."[1748] The Christian is to live to the Word by the Word in the spirit through His Spirit's higher learning and not in any "philosophy and vain deceit, after the tradition of men, after the rudiments of the world."[1749]

1737 1 John 3:7
1738 Psalm 34:15
1739 Psalm 33:18
1740 Psalm 31:23
1741 Romans 5:5
1742 Psalm 119:15
1743 Isaiah 26:3
1744 1 Peter 3:11
1745 Romans 7:12
1746 Romans 7:9
1747 Titus 3:4
1748 Romans 6:11
1749 Colossians 2:8

10. "The LORD preserveth the faithful"[1750] and "them that are of a broken heart."[1751] The broken in heart is the contrite in spirit, and this is the mind needed to cultivate the fear of the LORD's Spirit by wisdom with peace. "If thou wilt receive my words, and hide my commandments with thee,"[1752] says His Spirit, "then shalt thou understand the fear of the LORD, and find the knowledge of God."[1753] The Christian is to be renewed in knowledge after the righteousness and praise of the Spirit's will and Word, and this knowledge that renews is gained when obtaining a personal experience with His counsels of recovery out of reverent fear, and in faith of His name. It is written, "He that feareth him, and worketh righteousness is accepted with him,"[1754] for the fear of God and the wisdom of God cannot be separated; from applying to both, the believer harvests a good conscience with genuine faith.

11. To live according to God, to respectfully honor the commandments of God, worship needs to abandon all things tangible to hear the word, "The way of life is above to the wise."[1755] "Our conversation is in heaven"[1756] "where Christ sitteth on the right hand of God,"[1757] "wherefore henceforth know we no man after the flesh."[1758] When the eye of faith is allowed to view where God's Christ resides, the conscience will compel the flesh to fall into subjection to the mind, for every true and honest believer is to be "made sorry after a godly manner."[1759] "Godly sorrow worketh repentance to salvation,"[1760] and such a sorrow is to carry the heart to "serve God acceptably with reverence and godly fear."[1761] Only such service to the Spirit can be acceptable to Him and

---

1750 Psalm 31:23
1751 Psalm 34:18
1752 Proverbs 2:1
1753 Proverbs 2:5
1754 Acts 10:35
1755 Proverbs 15:24
1756 Philippians 3:20
1757 Colossians 3:1
1758 2 Corinthians 5:16
1759 2 Corinthians 7:9
1760 2 Corinthians 7:10
1761 Hebrews 12:28

us because "God loveth a cheerful giver"[1762] and a good conscience that is not forced; no religious policy can encourage "a readiness to will."[1763]

12. Godly fear is built up through godly sorrow, and to possess a spirit filled with the righteousness of God is to allow the spirit to experience and embrace brokenness of heart. The precepts of God contain a love that is elevated beyond finite understanding, yet the Lord has not created us for the purpose of remaining within carnal comprehension. "This is love, that we walk after his commandments,"[1764] that we "walk in truth,"[1765] because the anguish and perplexity of mind to apply and retain His doctrine will perfect acceptable love in the heart. If the soul is willing to break and feel brokenness to retain the word of the Lord to execute it by faith, then "blessed are they which do hunger and thirst after righteousness: for they shall be filled."[1766] All things are become new to the reformer of God hidden in Christ, and for this cause terror is health, bitterness is life, sorrow is joy, because the spirit will know the Lord to properly keep and do those things that please Him.

13. So then what is the purpose of having worship centered in the spirit of the mind? That "we may serve God acceptably with reference and godly fear,"[1767] for without honest fear, what marks the devotion pure? As the believer begins to embrace the work of righteousness that they may know Him, it will be that "God is come to prove you, and that his fear may be before your faces, that ye sin not."[1768]

14. Godly fear is sanctified respect, "choosing rather to suffer affliction"[1769] while "esteeming the reproach of Christ greater riches."[1770] Godly fear is persevering through provocation of the flesh and spirit "as seeing him who is invisible,"[1771] to the end that the soul may have

---

1762 2 Corinthians 9:8
1763 2 Corinthians 8:11
1764 2 John 1:6
1765 3 John 1:4
1766 Matthew 5:6
1767 Hebrews 12:28
1768 Exodus 20:20
1769 Hebrews 11:25
1770 Hebrews 11:26
1771 Hebrews 11:27

"a good conscience"[1772] and "the answer of a good conscience toward God."[1773] For, the fear of the LORD is born within "him that is poor and of a contrite spirit, and trembleth,"[1774] in that the believer would rather die than willingly progress in a thing that will cause separation from His Spirit of life and learning.

15. "I will put my fear in their hearts, that they shall not depart from me,"[1775] says the LORD. Godly fear keeps one from willfully sinning against His name, for godly sincerity has entered the heart. Undefiled obedience is given to God that the conscience may stay on Him and not fall away into negligent religious error, for the fear of the LORD within the spirit is the only way to rightly serve Him. As the Spirit says, "I will put my fear in their hearts,"[1776] it is equally said, "I will put my law in their inward parts, and write it in their hearts."[1777] Because His name, with His precepts and ordinances, has been written within the conscience, the godly cannot sin against the God they joy in struggling to know, for it is sin, and "whatsoever is not of faith is sin,"[1778] and concerning the legal religious laws and traditions of flesh, it says, "The law is not of faith."[1779] This is why "the knowledge of the holy is understanding,"[1780] "and to depart from evil is understanding."[1781]

16. The knowledge of the godly is to restrict self so that an understanding of the LORD's name may be obtained to liberate self. The carnal nature cannot coexist with the divine, and the flesh cannot incorporate the routine of the spirit, for there must be one mind to govern the body. For this cause it is said, "Have grace, whereby we may serve God,"[1782] for without the Spirit's wisdom within our conversation's conscience, we cannot serve him "acceptably with reverence

---

1772 Hebrews 13:18
1773 1 Peter 3:21
1774 Isaiah 66:2
1775 Jeremiah 32:40
1776 Jeremiah 32:40
1777 Jeremiah 31:33
1778 Romans 14:23
1779 Galatians 3:12
1780 Proverbs 9:10
1781 Job 28:28
1782 Hebrews 12:28

and godly fear."[1783] The fear of God, when once entered into the heart, will command the body, "Stand in awe of him,"[1784] and this is that fear which by the strength and grace of the Word will cease sin in the life. When the wisdom of the LORD's Son is accepted, and the work of retaining knowledge is valued, the fear of this LORD will keep the soul from religious error "that we may lead a quiet and peaceable life in all godliness and honesty."[1785]

1783 Hebrews 12:28
1784 Psalm 33:8
1785 1 Timothy 2:2

21

The Devotion Of The Wise

1. "Live according to God in the spirit,"[1786] says Scripture, or rather, "Have your conversation with truth in the spirit," or, "Preserve your conversation with His precepts of life within the mind." Our conversation is our behavior, and our behavior is the address, the demeanor, the management of self in the sight of God and man, to where of us it is said, "Behold, thou art called a Jew."[1787] The one hidden in the Faith of the Spirit's Son is yet a Jew; one that "restest in the law, and makest thy boast of God, and knowest his will, and approvest the things that are more excellent, being instructed out of the law";[1788] and it is that the Jew is to live to God in the spirit of their mind, faithful to His testimony and commandments.

2. It is said, "As many of you as have been baptized into Christ have put on Christ,"[1789] therefore, "We are buried with him by baptism into death."[1790] The believer becomes dead to the spirit of the world by heaven's Faith; "for all that is in the world, the lust of the flesh, and the lust

1786 1 Peter 4:6
1787 Romans 2:17
1788 Romans 2:18
1789 Galatians 3:26
1790 Romans 7:6

of the eyes, and the pride of life"[1791] "is that spirit of an'tichrist."[1792] "He is an'tichrist, that denieth the Father and the Son,"[1793] "but if the Spirit of him that raised up Jesus from the dead dwell in you, he that raised up Christ from the dead shall also quicken your mortal bodies"[1794] to "walk in newness of spirit."[1795] For this cause, "he is Jew."[1796]

3. The believer is to live according to God through the doctrine of His Christ, for all things are "weak through the flesh."[1797] "Thy boast of God"[1798] to "diligently keep the commandments of the LORD your God, and his testimonies, and his statutes, which he hath commanded,"[1799] cannot be done in the flesh; "they that are in the flesh cannot please God";[1800] "but the spirit giveth life."[1801] That manner of worship and service according to the pen of Moses; which devotion is through obeying commandments and traditions for a circumcision and show of devotion; is nailed to the tree, leaving it that "without faith it is impossible to please him."[1802] Because the LORD's Christ, "having abolished in his flesh the enmity, even the law of commandments contained in ordinances,"[1803] "sin" against His LORD's name is become known by the legal religious law of priests and elders; whether in that age or in any other age thereafter. By Him on that tree, we understand that "the strength of sin is the law,"[1804] which is why it is well to know that He suffered "to redeem them that were under the law."[1805] The Christian

---

1791 1 John 2:16
1792 1 John 4:3
1793 1 John 2:22
1794 Romans 8:11
1795 Romans 7:6
1796 Romans 2:29
1797 Romans 8:3
1798 Romans 2:17
1799 Deuteronomy 6:17
1800 Romans 8:8
1801 2 Corinthians 3:6
1802 Hebrews 11:6
1803 Ephesians 2:15
1804 1 Corinthians 15:56
1805 Galatians 4:5

is born under the law of a "vain conversation received by tradition,"[1806] therefore the counsel is, "Be renewed in the spirit of your mind."[1807]

4. "The spirit giveth life,"[1808] or rather, "It is the spirit that quickeneth,"[1809] for it is said, "The grace of our Lord Jesus Christ be with your spirit."[1810] "A shew of wisdom in will worship";[1811] obedience to the legal religious bill; cannot profit the soul of any individual except by gratification of pride through selfish ambition. "He that hath suffered in the flesh hath ceased from sin"[1812] because the weight of violation towards God within the conscience has broken their heart, therefore "whoso keepeth his word, in him verily is the love of God perfected."[1813] As the Christian suffers willing perplexity to know their High Priest, they are to be left "perfect and entire, wanting nothing."[1814] If it is that we reverence the commandments and doctrines of men above that of the living God, we are "sinners" to His Faith. The legal religious law is "sin," and if it is that our conversation is not blessed by His Spirit's voice, it is well to know that "Christ hath redeemed us from the curse of the law, being made a curse for us: for it is written, Cursed is every one that hangeth on a tree."[1815] We need to quit the pen of flesh and commence strengthening our mind if we should hope for the Spirit of His Son to do any thing for our inward person.

5. The spirit secretes "wisdom and revelation in the knowledge of him"[1816] in to our mind by the power of grace when we report, "Therefore is my spirit overwhelmed within me."[1817] The grace of God is given that we may be "enriched by him, in all utterance, and in all knowledge,"[1818] strengthened within the oracles of the Word that

---

1806 1 Peter 1:18
1807 Ephesians 4:23
1808 2 Corinthians 3:6
1809 John 6:63
1810 Galatians 6:18
1811 Colossians 2:23
1812 1 Peter 4:1
1813 2 John 2:5
1814 James 1:4
1815 Galatians 3:13
1816 Ephesians 1:17
1817 Psalm 143:4
1818 1 Corinthians 1:5

we may remain faithful to declare, "I remembered God."[1819] Yet to remember any thing of God, we need help, therefore it is said, "He shall teach you all things, and bring all things to your remembrance."[1820] Without allowing the Holy Ghost in to the soul temple, the spirit will retain no thing to bring the body into subjection. The spirit of the mind our conversation's source of power and wisdom for right government, and the conversation of the godly is to progress renewal of the spirit by the Holy Ghost, that in the body, proper behavior toward God and man would be accomplished in right wisdom and love.

6. It is said, "He that heareth my word, and believeth on him that sent me"[1821] "is passed from death unto life."[1822] "We know that we have passed from death unto life, because we love,"[1823] "and every one that loveth is born of God."[1824] The passage from death to life does not happen at any other time than at the present, and at this time it is ordained "that mortality might be swallowed up of life."[1825] Seeing as how "the spirit giveth life,"[1826] the believer is to "mortify the deeds of the body"[1827] from living faithfully to the precepts of Christ's Faith to receive grace for health to the inward man. Through the virtue of His sayings, the Christian is to pass from death unto life, to be baptized or purified from the deeds of the mind of the flesh to the service of the spirit, therefore it is said, "Lay down our lives for the brethren."[1828]

7. If "all the law is fulfilled in one word, even in this; Thou shalt love thy neighbor as thy self,"[1829] how then may one love according to God if not first willing to live according to God? How can the believer lay down self for another when they have not first sought to lay down themselves to the Spirit's Word? The end of living unto God is that we

---

1819 Psalm 77:3
1820 John 14:26
1821 John 5:24
1822 John 5:24
1823 1 John 3:14
1824 1 John 4:7
1825 2 Corinthians 5:4
1826 2 Corinthians 3:6
1827 Romans 8:13
1828 1 John 3:16
1829 Galatians 5:14

may live for one another, for "that which is abolished"[1830] declares, "By love serve one another,"[1831] and this course of learning is that "law of Christ"[1832] which is to be fulfilled within and by the believer. But "whoso hath this world's good,"[1833] "and shutteth up his bowels of compassion, how dwelleth the love of a God in him?"[1834] Seeing as how "all that is in the world, the lust of the flesh, and the lust of the eyes, and the pride of life,"[1835] it is that "the law is holy, and the commandment holy, and just, and good,"[1836] therefore without that which is good, there can come from no one that great benevolence which is adopted from that good.

8. The Christian is to live according to God within the spirit that "his bowels of compassion from him"[1837] may reveal, "I long after you all in the bowels of Jesus Christ."[1838] For this cause it is said, "Put on therefore, as the elect of God, holy and beloved, bowels of mercies, kindness, humbleness of mind, meekness, longsuffering,"[1839] for this is the law of Christ's name and doctrine, which states, "Every one that loveth is born of God, and knoweth God."[1840] Undefiled love is fulfilled through the bowels of the Spirit's Faith. The one desiring godliness must first live "according to the faith of God's elect,"[1841] which Faith is "the acknowledging of the truth which is after godliness."[1842] Therefore, "he that saith, I know him, and keepeth not his commandments, is a liar, and the truth is not in him."[1843]

9. "Every one that loveth him that begat loveth him also that is begotten of him. By this we know that we love."[1844] It does not say,

---

1830 2 Corinthians 3:13
1831 Galatians 5:13
1832 Galatians 6:2
1833 1 John 3:17
1834 1 John 3:17
1835 1 John 2:16
1836 Romans 7:12
1837 1 John 3:17
1838 Philippians 1:8
1839 Colossians 3:12,13
1840 1 John 4:7
1841 Titus 1:1
1842 Titus 1:1
1843 1 John 2:4
1844 1 John 5:1

"Every one that loveth Him that is begotten, loveth Him that begat," and it is not so written because it says, "No man can come unto me"[1845] unless "he hath learned of the Father."[1846] Love is of God, and the true perception of love is contained in the character of God, therefore the reformer exists according to the revelation of His Christ's name by His Spirit within their spirit in order to love according to that good counsel within their conscience. A dwarfed heart reports, "The good that I would I do not,"[1847] yet the faithful will fight self to "walk in truth."[1848]

10. To walk in the truth is "to lay down our lives,"[1849] to "walk in love, as Christ also hath loved us, and hath given himself."[1850] The spirit of self-sacrificing love quenches the pride of life, or rather, the pride of beautifully adorning the conversation by legal religious laws and traditions. The lust of the flesh and the lust of the eye is broken when "having compassion one of another,"[1851] "speaking the truth in love"[1852] that our conversation may testify, "Thou walkest in the truth."[1853] For, this is the definition of godly affection, "Doest faithfully whatsoever thou doest to the brethren, and to strangers."[1854] Because "every one that doeth righteousness is born of him,"[1855] this expression of benevolence gives "witness of thy charity"[1856] from working with many to reveal to them the name of the Spirit in the face of His Son; "whom if thou bring forward on their journey after a godly sort, thou shalt do well."[1857]

11. It is fair to note that selfless charity is to deliver many "on their journey after a godly sort,"[1858] therefore the beginning of charity is godliness, for none ungodly can safely lead another to become godly

---

1845 John 6:45
1846 John 6:45
1847 Romans 7:19
1848 3 John 1:4
1849 1 John 3:16
1850 Ephesians 5:2
1851 1 Peter 3:8
1852 Ephesians 4:15
1853 3 John 1:3
1854 3 John 1:5
1855 1 John 2:29
1856 3 John 1:6
1857 3 John 1:6
1858 3 John 1:6

within themselves. Today, "ungodliness" is "unrighteousness," and "all unrighteousness is sin."[1859] Because "the strength of sin is the law,"[1860] if it is that we care to bless another, and after heaven's manner of blessing, it is that our mind must first find itself edified away from what "sin" is, which "sin" is "the handwriting of ordinances."[1861] "Love" is edification, wherefore the one "loved" of the living God is counseled, "Let every one of us please his neighbour for his good to edification."[1862] True thoughtful and careful service declares, "I travail in birth again until Christ be formed in you,"[1863] confirming that the love of God is revealed in the sentiment, "I am made all things to all men, that I might by all means save some."[1864]

1859 1 John 5:17
1860 1 Corinthians 15:56
1861 Colossians 2:14
1862 Romans 15:2
1863 Galatians 4:19
1864 1 Corinthians 9:22

22

The Beginning Of
The Creation of God

1. It is said, “Live according to God in the spirit,”[1865] for our agreement with His precepts rest not in unsanctified ambition or passion through any legal ordinance or doctrine, but rather through mental and physical digestion. The LORD has provided us “with all spiritual blessings”[1866] that we may know Him who rests in the second Apartment of the heavenly Temple, for only “the spirit may be saved in the day of the Lord Jesus,”[1867] letting us know that outward forms of sanctity must cease if “we may have confidence, and not be ashamed before him at his coming.”[1868] The spirit of the mind will be taken of the Spirit, therefore every believer of His Christ’s name is commissioned to worship in spirit and in truth “what is good; and what doth the LORD require of thee, but to do justly, and to love mercy, and to walk humbly with thy God?”[1869]

1865 1 Peter 4:6
1866 Ephesians 1:3
1867 1 Corinthians 5:5
1868 1 John 2:28
1869 Micah 6:8

2. Humility without the love of mercy will breed hypocrisy. Our conscience must fall to "the throne of grace, that we may obtain mercy,"[1870] for mercy is the Spirit's grace and wisdom. What is written? "God resisteth the proud, and giveth grace to the humble,"[1871] and, "He giveth grace unto the lowly."[1872] To love the grace of God, the heart must express "love in the Spirit,"[1873] because "the Spirit of grace"[1874] "is the witness of God which he hath testified of his Son."[1875] It is said, "With great power gave the apostles witness of the resurrection,"[1876] even "great grace was upon them all,"[1877] for "they were all filled with the Holy Ghost."[1878] "He that hath the Son hath life,"[1879] and "the Spirit is life"[1880] and "the Spirit is truth,"[1881] therefore without the true witness of the Spirit's Word, none may claim life and power through His Son's heavenly mediation.

3. We know that we are of the LORD's Word because His Spirit is the witness of our earnest belief. The Christian may know that they are of God when their submission to His precepts have fallen out of their doing, for they are actuated by His good Spirit. "He that keepeth his commandments dwelleth in him, and he in him. And hereby we know that he abideth in us, by the Spirit which he hath given us."[1882] If we are of God, we have His Spirit, and we know that we have His Spirit because we progress by Him without any man; "henceforth know we no man after the flesh."[1883] I too confess with the LORD's heavenly host, "When it pleased God, who separated me from my mother's

---

1870 Hebrews 4:16
1871 1 Peter 5:5
1872 Proverbs 3:34
1873 Colossians 1:8
1874 Hebrews 10:29
1875 1 John 5:9
1876 Acts 4:33
1877 Acts 4:33
1878 Acts 4:31
1879 1 John 5:12
1880 Romans 8:10
1881 1 John 5:6
1882 1 John 3:24
1883 2 Corinthians 5:16

womb, and called me by his grace,"[1884] "I conferred not with flesh and blood."[1885] Therefore the Christian must know, "After that ye believed, ye were sealed with that holy Spirit of promise, which is the earnest of our inheritance,"[1886] "and ye need not that any man teach you."[1887] True education is maintained and regulated by the Spirit of the living God through faith in the voice of His Son's name.

4. Without the Spirit of God; without "the anointing which ye have received of him"[1888] "after that ye heard the word of truth"[1889] and "ye believed";[1890] we are nothing. Humility is procured from submitting the mind to the testimony of His accepted sacrifice, for if we are yet without His Spirit, then we are yet without belief in the fact that His Christ has come and conquered in sinful human flesh. "Hereby know we the Spirit of God: every spirit that confesseth that Jesus Christ is come in the flesh is of God."[1891]

5. The mind that bears the testimony of Christ is of the Father and the Son, for the Spirit has been given entrance into the soul temple to rewrite the mind of the conversation. "He that hath the Son hath life,"[1892] yet it is said, "The breath of the Almighty hath given me life."[1893] Again it is said, "Breathed into his nostrils the breath of life,"[1894] for "Adam was made a living soul; the last Adam was made a quickening spirit."[1895] Therefore it was confirmed of Christ, "Quickened by the Spirit,"[1896] and it is for the believer, "Quicken your mortal bodies by his Spirit."[1897] The first man was made a living soul yet the last was made a quickening spirit quickened by the Spirit, and since "it is the spirit that

1884 Galatians 1:15
1885 Galatians 1:16
1886 Ephesians 1:13,14
1887 1 John 2:27
1888 1 John 2:27
1889 Ephesians 1:13
1890 Ephesians 1:13
1891 1 John 4:2
1892 1 John 5:12
1893 Job 33:4
1894 Genesis 2:7
1895 1 Corinthians 15:45
1896 1 Peter 3:18
1897 Romans 8:11

quickeneth,"[1898] the one who carries pure love of the Spirit will bear "the spirit of truth,"[1899] "because the Spirit is truth."[1900]

6. He that has the Son has the breath of life to quicken the flesh's religious constitution, creating that individual as a new Adam within the last Adam. As "God hath given to us eternal life,"[1901] it is that the believer is given the Word's breath to regulate their conversation according to the Word's will and sayings, which breath produces life, "and this life is in his Son."[1902]

7. "He that giveth breath unto the people"[1903] is the same that places their "spirit,"[1904] for it is the same One that "formeth the spirit of man within him,"[1905] "the Father of spirits."[1906] For this cause the Christian must hear "the faithful and true witness, the beginning of the creation of God,"[1907] for they are to be renewed in the spirit of their mind, and that "renewing of the Holy Ghost."[1908] "Christ, who is the faithful witness,"[1909] yet carries "the eternal Spirit"[1910] which "is truth,"[1911] for "it is the Spirit that beareth witness."[1912] "Now the Lord is that Spirit,"[1913] and in Christ is the Spirit of life for the health of the spirit to rule the flesh, "therefore if any man be in Christ, he is a new creature: old things are passed away; behold, all things are become new."[1914]

1898 John 6:63
1899 1 John 4:6
1900 1 John 5:6
1901 1 John 5:11
1902 1 John 5:11
1903 Isaiah 42:5
1904 Isaiah 42:5
1905 Zechariah 12:1
1906 Hebrews 12:9
1907 Revelation 3:14
1908 Titus 3:5
1909 Revelation 1:5
1910 Hebrews 9:14
1911 1 John 2:27
1912 1 John 5:6
1913 2 Corinthians 3:17
1914 2 Corinthians 5:17

8. Again, "He that hath the Son hath life,"[1915] and that life is as Christ says, "I am in the Father, and the Father in me."[1916] "I know that his commandment is life everlasting,"[1917] says our High Priest about His Father's commandment for creation, therefore "he that soweth to the Spirit shall of the Spirit reap life everlasting."[1918] "The Spirit is life because of righteousness,"[1919] "and the life was the light of men";[1920] as it says, "Light is sown for the righteous";[1921] "and this is life eternal,"[1922] "that we may know him that is true."[1923] "Every one that doeth righteousness is born of him,"[1924] for the conscience born of His name perfects the commandment of God by His Spirit. The Spirit is truth and is life because it leads the believer into the Spirit's doctrine, as it says, "Light is sown."[1925] "The true light now shineth"[1926] to the believer that "God is light,"[1927] and the anointing of God "is true, and is no lie,"[1928] for the believer comes by the Word's life through His Spirit, and that life sown for them, and afterwards regulated by them.

9. "If thou wilt enter into life,"[1929] counsels our High Priest, "keep the commandments,"[1930] because life eternal is knowledge obtained "through sanctification of the Spirit and belief of the truth."[1931] "All them which heard the word,"[1932] it is recorded, "the Holy Ghost fell on

1915 1 John 5:12
1916 John 14:11
1917 John 12:50
1918 Galatians 6:8
1919 Romans 8:10
1920 John 1:4
1921 Psalm 97:11
1922 John 17:3
1923 1 John 5:20
1924 1 John 2:29
1925 Psalm 97:11
1926 1 John 2:8
1927 1 John 1:5
1928 1 John 2:27
1929 Matthew 19:17
1930 Matthew 19:17
1931 2 Thessalonians 2:13
1932 Acts 10:44

them,"[1933] "purifying their hearts by faith."[1934] The heart is to be made pure to house the pure words of the Spirit; for "the law is holy, and the commandment holy, and just, and good";[1935] and "except a man be born of water and of the Spirit,"[1936] "he cannot see the kingdom of God."[1937] It is the Spirit that leads us to "know his will, and see that Just One,"[1938] because to see God is to "be filled with the knowledge of his will in all wisdom and spiritual understanding."[1939] Should the one professing Christ desire His prescribed conversation, they cannot come by knowledge without first submitting their heart to be purified, for what is written? "Buy of me,"[1940] says the Spirit.

10. "What man is he that desireth life, and loveth many days, that he may see good?"[1941] For we know that the Spirit's "law is good,"[1942] "and the commandment, which was ordained to life"[1943] is for "a good foundation,"[1944] for "wisdom giveth life to them that have it."[1945] Concerning Stephen, we are told that he was "full of the Holy Ghost and wisdom,"[1946] "a man full of faith and of the Holy Ghost,"[1947] one known by "the wisdom and spirit by which he spake."[1948] The wisdom of God gives life in the same sense that the spirit gives life to the members of the flesh, for wisdom is retained within the spirit of the mind to keep the flesh from trouble, and for this cause it is said, That born of the Spirit is spirit.[1949]

1933 Acts 10:44
1934 Acts 15:8
1935 Romans 7:12
1936 John 3:5
1937 John 3:3
1938 Acts 22:14
1939 Colossians 1:9
1940 Revelation 3:18
1941 Psalm 34:13
1942 Romans 7:16
1943 Romans 7:10
1944 1 Timothy 6:19
1945 Ecclesiastes 7:12
1946 Acts 6:3
1947 Acts 6:5
1948 Acts 6:10
1949 John 3:6

11. Wisdom comes by a living experience by faith in the Spirit of God to retain a pure heart by the knowledge of His Christ, to the end that the spirit may keep that heart pure for God and for man. Without the Holy Ghost, the heart is yet dead, but from the Spirit proceeds health as the believer suffers self to die to gain knowledge of the Word's will, to do that will. As the heart functions without any human effort, as the blood circulates without a thought of circulation, so too the reformer lives through the precepts and the ordinances of the voice of Christ for a perfect conversation, that they may focus on their personal work of knowing the will of God. To subtract the Holy Ghost from faith and wisdom is to subtract Christ from His Father, and if the heart longs to separate the commandments of God from faith in the blood of Christ then they will partake in none of the benefits of His Spirit, for that heart does "glory after the flesh."[1950]

12. It is then a fact, "The Spirit of God hath made me,"[1951] for He is "the beginning of the creation of God."[1952] The new being formed by the knowledge of His Son "after God is created in righteousness and true holiness,"[1953] is created in truth and pure godliness, for "God is faithful";[1954] as it says, "All thy commandments are faithful";[1955] and to dawn the face of our High priest, the heart needs to submit to the Creator of the spirit to be made in His name. He who possesses the virtue of the blood of Christ by faith has life, and this life in Christ is preserved within His Spirit, which Spirit bears witness to our experience, because the Spirit transforms the mind to find harmony with the ten immutable precepts of God. Should one fail to submit their spirit to regeneration through anguish and perplexity of soul, distress of mind and flesh, "let not that man think that he shall receive any thing of the Lord."[1956]

1950 2 Corinthians 12:18
1951 Job 33:4
1952 Revelation 3:14
1953 Ephesians 4:24
1954 1 Corinthians 10:13
1955 Psalm 119:86
1956 James 1:7

13. "Let us have grace, whereby we may serve God acceptably with reverence and godly fear,"[1957] and again, "Let us have grace"[1958] as administered by "the Spirit of grace."[1959] How is it that the Spirit is to be the beginning of the creation of God? It is written, "If we believe on him that raised up Jesus our Lord from the dead."[1960] Who or what is it that raised this Christ from the dead? It is written, "Christ was raised from the dead by the glory of the Father."[1961] And what is the glory of the Father that raised Christ from the dead, which glory is to raise us up also? It is written, "If the Spirit of him that raised up Jesus from the dead dwell in you, he that raised up Christ from the dead shall also quicken your mortal bodies."[1962] Therefore in the Spirit's will and law the believer "should walk in newness of life,"[1963] "should serve in newness of spirit."[1964]

14. The Christian is to live according to God in the spirit of their mind to declare, "With the mind I myself serve the law of God."[1965] The power that is to bring the believer to such single-hearted devotion is that same "power of his resurrection"[1966] by the Spirit of God. The commandments of God are to be kept "through faith in his blood,"[1967] for the believer should "be saved by his life"[1968] through "abundance of grace and of the gift of righteousness."[1969] "Whosoever believeth that Jesus is the Christ,"[1970] or believes in their reconciliation "to God by the death of his Son,"[1971] is immediately transferred into the hand of His Spirit to perfect their conversation by grace. It is the Holy Spirit

---

1957 Hebrews 12:28
1958 Hebrews 12:28
1959 Hebrews 10:29
1960 Romans 4:24
1961 Romans 6:4
1962 Romans 8:11
1963 Romans 6:4
1964 Romans 7:6
1965 Romans 7:25
1966 Philippians 3:10
1967 Romans 3:25
1968 Romans 5:10
1969 Romans 5:17
1970 1 John 5:1
1971 Romans 5:10

that administers "the grace of life,"[1972] which grace is "the gift of righteousness,"[1973] that "we also should walk in newness of life."[1974]

15. So then, "He that hath the Son hath life,"[1975] and "there is therefore now no condemnation to them which are in Christ"[1976] "after the Spirit,"[1977] because "the Spirit is life."[1978] "The Spirit is life because of righteousness;"[1979] even "the righteousness of the law";[1980] for the power in Christ advances "the righteousness of God,"[1981] and if we live through the law of the Faith of His Son, seeing as how it was ordained of the LORD "that we might live through him,"[1982] then "he that believeth on the Son of God hath the witness in himself,"[1983] for "it is the Spirit that beareth witness."[1984] "The Spirit itself beareth witness with our spirit,"[1985] because "God, who quickeneth"[1986] by His Spirit; which "Spirit is life";[1987] breathes wisdom into our spirit for the health of our conscience, and for the order of our faith's constitution, because "the spirit giveth life."[1988]

16. To have Christ is to have the Father and His Spirit, and to live according to His precepts is to abide by "the law of the Spirit of life in Christ."[1989] He has said, "Ye shall be free indeed,"[1990] and the Spirit makes the heart "free from the law of sin and death"[1991] that the

---

1972 1 Peter 3:7
1973 Romans 5:17
1974 Romans 6:4
1975 1 John 5:12
1976 Romans 8:1
1977 Romans 8:4
1978 Romans 8:10
1979 Romans 8:10
1980 Romans 3:22
1981 Philippians 3:9
1982 1 John 4:9
1983 1 John 5:10
1984 1 John 5:6
1985 Romans 8:16
1986 1 Timothy 6:13
1987 Romans 8:10
1988 2 Corinthians 3:6
1989 Romans 8:2
1990 John 8:36
1991 Romans 8:2

Christian may "delight in the law of God after the inward man."[1992] He that is joined to the commandments of God must exist "through the faith of Christ, the righteousness which is of God by faith,"[1993] because the Spirit of God is commissioned to "redeem us from all iniquity, and purify unto himself a peculiar people, zealous of good works."[1994] Therefore the new constitution "after God is created in righteousness and true holiness,"[1995] and it is only so because "the fruit of the Spirit is in all goodness and righteousness and truth."[1996]

1992 Romans 7:22
1993 Philippians 3:9
1994 Titus 2:14
1995 Ephesians 4:24
1996 Ephesians 5:9

23

The True Witness of Godly Living

1. "He that hath the Son hath life,"[1997] "for the life of the flesh is in the blood."[1998] "I have given it upon the altar to make an atonement for your souls,"[1999] says the Spirit, for "the bread that I will give is my flesh, which I will give for the life of the world."[2000] Christ, "that he might sanctify the people with his own blood, suffered without the gate";[2001] that is, "The house of God, and this is the gate of heaven";[2002] that "through the redemption that is in Christ";[2003] that is, "through faith in his blood";[2004] "we have redemption through his blood, even the forgiveness of sins": "for it is the blood that maketh an atonement for the soul."[2005]

1997 1 John 5:12
1998 Leviticus 17:11
1999 Leviticus 17:11
2000 John 6:51
2001 Hebrews 13:12
2002 Genesis 28:17
2003 Romans 3:24
2004 Romans 3:25
2005 Colossians 1:14

2. For this cause "we joy in God through our Lord Jesus Christ, by whom we have now received the atonement."[2006] The soul is to be reconciled to the Father; as it says, "He shall redeem their soul";[2007] for the purpose of cleansing the "conscience from dead works, to serve the living God."[2008] The reformer joys in honoring the ten commandments of God, they keep the name and precepts of God with gladness through the Spirit of the doctrine of His Christ, because it is His Christ who suffered "that he might bring us to God."[2009]

3. Not one honest soul who professes Christ will run from His LORD and God, for "truly our fellowship is with the Father, and with his Son."[2010] The life of Christ is in His blood that He gave for the spirit of the world, "for all that is in the world, the lust of the flesh, and the lust of the eyes, and the pride of life,"[2011] made it necessary for "the Son to be the Saviour of the world."[2012] He is the Savior of that erroneous mind within the religious world, even "the spirit of error,"[2013] "that spirit of an'tichrist, whereof ye have heard."[2014] This spirit is that mind which refuses to confess, withinin its personal religion, "Jesus is come in the flesh."[2015] To refuse the doctrine of the health of Christ is to place no power of life in Him or in the Spirit of His LORD, and as "with the mouth confession is made,"[2016] "whosoever shall confess that Jesus is the Son of God, God dwelleth in him, and he in God."[2017]

4. The mouth is the heart; as it says, "In thy mouth, and in thy heart";[2018] and from "the heart, in the spirit,"[2019] the name and virtue of Christ is to be accepted if one would be preserved, for of "his mercy

---

2006 Romans 5:11
2007 Psalm 72:14
2008 Hebrews 9:14
2009 1 Peter 3:18
2010 1 John 1:3
2011 1 John 2:16
2012 1 John 4:14
2013 1 John 4:6
2014 1 John 4:3
2015 2 John 1:7
2016 Romans 10:10
2017 1 John 4:15
2018 Romans 10:8
2019 Romans 2:29

he saved us, by the washing of regeneration."[2020] When once the spirit faithfully confesses the faith of Christ, the Holy Ghost is then commissioned to convict and to reprove the soul "of sin, and of righteousness, and of judgment."[2021] "It is the spirit that quickeneth"[2022] because "the spirit giveth life,"[2023] "but the Spirit is life,"[2024] "and this life is in His Son."[2025] Therefore "the law of faith"[2026] declares, "We shall be saved by his life,"[2027] and the "law of the Spirit of life"[2028] declares, "They which receive abundance of grace and of the gift of righteousness shall reign in life."[2029]

5. It is His conversation that will recover us, "for the life of the flesh is in the blood."[2030] Only "through the redemption that is in Christ Jesus"[2031] may "the God of peace sanctify you wholly,"[2032] and our deliverance from defiled flesh "through sanctification of the Spirit and belief of the truth."[2033] For this cause it is written, "Sanctify them through thy truth: thy word is truth,"[2034] and that word being "the word of righteousness,"[2035] "the word of truth,"[2036] "the word of God."[2037] Purification appears in the form of mental and spiritual washing and renewing by His Spirit, for we are washed, sanctified, or "justified in the name of the Lord Jesus, and that by the Spirit of our God."[2038]

2020 Titus 3:5
2021 John 16:8
2022 John 6:63
2023 2 Corinthians 3:6
2024 Romans 8:10
2025 1 John 5:11
2026 Romans 3:27
2027 Romans 5:10
2028 Romans 8:2
2029 Romans 5:17
2030 Leviticus 17:11
2031 Romans 3:24
2032 1 Thessalonians 5:23
2033 2 Thessalonians 2:13
2034 John 17:17
2035 Hebrews 5:13
2036 2 Corinthians 6:7
2037 1 John 2:14
2038 1 Corinthians 6:11

6. The believer is to be washed, sanctified, and justified only by the Spirit of God from believing on the name and Faith of His Christ. "The Spirit of truth,"[2039] He "proceedeth from the Father,"[2040] and it is the Spirit that is to engrave within the soul temple the His LORD's precepts that the spirit of the mind may work out what is put in it, to rightly govern the mind of its body. As the Christian learns "love in the Spirit,"[2041] they are "to be strengthened with might by his Spirit in the inner man."[2042] As the believer is "strengthened with all might, according to his glorious power,"[2043] "his power to us-ward who believe";[2044] which "working of his power"[2045] is "the gift of the grace of God";[2046] they are to receive "the grace of life,"[2047] "the gift of righteousness"[2048] "unto justification of life."[2049]

7. It is necessary to remain "looking unto Jesus the author and finisher of our faith,"[2050] for "through the grace of our Lord Jesus Christ we shall be saved."[2051] "Through the faith of Christ, the righteousness which is of God by faith,"[2052] the believer is to be delivered from their members of unrighteousness through the purifying work of the Spirit. By the persuasion of working faith, "The life which I now live in the flesh I live by the faith of the Son of God,"[2053] says the believer. Our life is our conversation, it is "our manner of life, purpose,"[2054] our example "in word, in conversation,"[2055] it is our personal religion. The conversation that we live by, if we profess the name of His Christ, it is

---

2039 John 15:26
2040 John 15:26
2041 Colossians 1:8
2042 Ephesians 3:16
2043 Colossians 1:11
2044 Ephesians 3:7
2045 Ephesians 1:19
2046 Ephesians 3:7
2047 1 Peter 3:7
2048 Romans 5:17
2049 Romans 5:18
2050 Hebrews 12:2
2051 Acts 15:11
2052 Philippians 3:9
2053 Galatians 2:20
2054 2 Timothy 3:10
2055 1 Timothy 4:12

to be ordered according to how it is written, "We might live through him,"[2056] to retain the sentiment, "I serve with my spirit in the gospel of his Son."[2057] All who honestly come to Christ care to know, and to be known of, His Father. All care to be loved in His name and by His confidence from surrendering to the voice of His Son, that by seeing and hearing and handling the love of God by faith, "God hath sent forth the Spirit of his Son into your hearts."[2058]

8. So then as the Spirit is delivered to our mind, we cry, "Father." As the Spirit conforms our mind to fit a higher pattern of existence, "we groan"[2059] "that mortality might be swallowed up of life."[2060] And as "the love of Christ constraineth us,"[2061] it is that we will be "made sorry after a godly manner,"[2062] being "sorrowed to repentance."[2063] Because after that we have sorrowed, being convinced of religious error by His Spirit, we will hear, "Why weepest thou? whom seekest thou?"[2064] Repentance gives birth to an "earnest desire,"[2065] and "mourning"[2066] prepares the way for a "fervent mind."[2067] So then from sorrowing "after a godly sort, what carefulness it wrought in you, yea, what clearing of yourselves, yea, what indignation, yea, what fear, yea, what vehement desire"[2068] to lift up "a readiness to revenge all disobedience."[2069]

9. "Apply thine heart to understanding,"[2070] "seekest her as silver, and searchest for her,"[2071] says the Spirit, because "by the sadness of the countenance the heart is made better."[2072] "Circumcise therefore

---

2056 1 John 4:9
2057 Romans 1:9
2058 Galatians 4:6
2059 2 Corinthians 5:2
2060 2 Corinthians 5:4
2061 2 Corinthians 5:14
2062 2 Corinthians 7:9
2063 2 Corinthians 7:9
2064 John 20:15
2065 2 Corinthians 7:7
2066 2 Corinthians 7:7
2067 2 Corinthians 7:7
2068 2 Corinthians 7:11
2069 2 Corinthians 10:6
2070 Proverbs 2:2
2071 Proverbs 2:4
2072 Ecclesiastes 7:3

the foreskin of your heart,"[2073] says the Spirit, "and circumcision is that of the heart, in the spirit";[2074] "for reproofs of instruction are the way of life,"[2075] and "wisdom is profitable to direct."[2076] "The Holy Ghost"[2077] "shall teach you all things, and bring all things to your remembrance,"[2078] says our High Priest, for the Spirit washes, sanctifies, and justifies, makes right before the Word and His LORD, sealing within the believer "the spirit of wisdom and revelation in"[2079] "understanding what the will of the Lord is."[2080] Without the Instructor of righteousness, the teacher and guide of the reformatory experience, it will not be known, "Through knowledge shall the just be delivered."[2081]

10. "The righteousness of the perfect shall direct his way"[2082] because they have submitted to the work of righteousness, "for the mouth of the just bringeth forth wisdom."[2083] As they "have believed from the heart,"[2084] the believer should receive "also the Holy Ghost, whom God hath given to them that obey him."[2085] It is that as the heart is subdued under the revelation of love delivered to the conscience, the LORD will give "grace to the humble."[2086] His grace is to be the poison of presumptuous sin and personal spiritual error, because "where sin abounded, grace did much more abound."[2087] Through obtained knowledge, the man and woman of God is to be delivered from themselves, for after they confess, "The Lord shall deliver me from every evil work,"[2088] as they "are renewed in knowledge after the image of him that created"[2089]

2073 Deuteronomy 10:16
2074 Romans 2:29
2075 Proverbs 6:23
2076 Ecclesiastes 10:10
2077 John 14:26
2078 John 14:26
2079 Ephesians 1:17
2080 Ephesians 5:17
2081 Proverbs 11:9
2082 Proverbs 11:5
2083 Proverbs 10:31
2084 Romans 6:17
2085 Acts 5:32
2086 James 4:6
2087 Romans 5:20
2088 2 Timothy 4:18
2089 Colossians 3:10

their mind "through the power of the Holy Ghost,"[2090] they are to be "full of goodness, filled with all knowledge, able also to admonish one another,"[2091] "being filled with the fruits of righteousness."[2092]

11. For this reason it is said, "Live according to God in the spirit."[2093] The Christian is to live through the knowledge and experience of the Faith of Jesus "by the power of God"[2094] through the "spirit of faith,"[2095] to the end that "the law of the Spirit of life"[2096] "make you perfect in every good work."[2097] The Christian is to approach the Spirit's Word from first applying self to the righteousness of His Christ, that by faith in that righteousness they may order their body. This is why He counsels, "To him that ordereth his conversation aright will I shew the salvation of God."[2098] The precepts of God are maintained by submitting to all that the blood of Christ claims of itself, for by the law and doctrine of Christ, the believer is to be made after the image of Him to own a purer conversation for the health of their environment.

2090 Romans 15:13
2091 Romans 15:14
2092 Philippians 1:11
2093 1 Peter 4:6
2094 2 Corinthians 13:4
2095 2 Corinthians 4:13
2096 Romans 8:2
2097 Hebrews 13:21
2098 Psalm 50:23

24

The Spirit of His New Creature

1. "Glorify God in your body, and in your spirit, which are God's."[2099] "Know ye not that your body is the temple of the Holy Ghost"?[2100] "Let not sin therefore reign in your mortal body,"[2101] "neither yield ye your members as instruments of unrighteousness unto sin,"[2102] but "present your bodies a living sacrifice, holy, acceptable unto God."[2103]

2. Says Scripture, "Fear God, and give glory to him,"[2104] again, "Who shall not fear thee, O Lord, and glorify thy name?"[2105] The Christian is called to glorify the name or the character of the living LORD God, or to "give honour to him"[2106] in both body and spirit, because "blessed is the man that feareth the LORD, that delighteth greatly in his commandments."[2107] The fear of the LORD; wholehearted and zealous devotion to the commandments of His Spirit; is to fill the members of

---

2099 1 Corinthians 6:20
2100 1 Corinthians 6:19
2101 Romans 6:12
2102 Romans 6:13
2103 Romans 12:1
2104 Revelation 14:7
2105 Revelation 15:4
2106 Revelation 19:7
2107 Psalm 112:1

our body along with the spirit of our mind, because in these two places the Holy Ghost of God should rest. "He that feareth him"[2108] is one that "worketh righteousness,"[2109] and righteousness' course is ordained is to overcome "the body of sin,"[2110] which body is composed of members and fruit regulated by "the law of sin,"[2111] and is also to fill the spirit of the mind, because "it is the spirit that quickeneth"[2112] the conversation to "delight in the law of God."[2113]

3. The LORD has said, "I will give them one heart, and one way, that they may fear me,"[2114] and, "I will put my fear in their hearts, that they shall not depart from me."[2115] To depart from the LORD's name and doctrine would be to follow the pattern, "They have not hearkened to receive instruction. But they set their abominations in the house, which is called by my name."[2116] Therefore "whoso loveth instruction loveth knowledge,"[2117] and since "the fear of the LORD is the beginning of wisdom,"[2118] "the knowledge of wisdom"[2119] reports, "Ye that fear the LORD, trust in the LORD."[2120] To trust in the LORD means to "fear him, and keep his commandments, and obey his voice"[2121] "in singleness of heart,"[2122] because if His Faith is accepted as Savior then "ye are bought with a price,"[2123] even "with the precious blood of Christ"[2124] to "glorify God in your body, and in your spirit."[2125]

2108 Acts 10:35
2109 Acts 10:35
2110 Romans 6:6
2111 Romans 7:25
2112 John 6:63
2113 Romans 7:22
2114 Jeremiah 32:39
2115 Jeremiah 32:40
2116 Jeremiah 32:33,34
2117 Proverbs 12:1
2118 Psalm 111:10
2119 Proverbs 24:14
2120 Psalm 115:11
2121 Deuteronomy 13:4
2122 Colossians 3:22
2123 1 Corinthians 6:20
2124 1 Peter 1:19
2125 1 Corinthians 6:20

4. "Know ye not that your body is the temple of the Holy Ghost which is in you, which ye have of God, and ye are not your own?"[2126] "Know ye not that your bodies are the members of Christ?"[2127] Why then should the believer fulfill the saying, "They set their abominations in the house, which is called by my name"?[2128] If indeed "we are buried with him by baptism into death,"[2129] then truly "unto GOD the Lord belong the issues of death."[2130] "If Christ be in you, the body is dead because of sin,"[2131] and with His name within the mind, "sin shall not have dominion over you"[2132] "if ye be led of the Spirit,"[2133] because we are to be "an habitation of God through the Spirit."[2134] The Spirit is to inhabit the body of death which is set on "fulfilling the desires of the flesh and of the mind,"[2135] and is to wash and regenerate both flesh and mind, body and spirit, conversation and conscience, that we may "offer up spiritual sacrifices, acceptable to God."[2136]

5. The body of our faith and the spirit of our conscience should be one grand member "built up a spiritual house."[2137] Yet says the LORD, "They set their abominations in the house."[2138] If the body and spirit are to be regulated as one functioning entity by the LORD's Spirit, this can only be done as His name is living within that house. Esther did write "in the king's name,"[2139] and did "seal it with the king's ring,"[2140] because when this was accomplished it was known, "May no man reverse."[2141] The name of God is to be sealed within the body and spirit of man only

---

2126 1 Corinthians 6:19
2127 1 Corinthians 6:15
2128 Jeremiah 32:34
2129 Romans 6:4
2130 Psalm 68:20
2131 Romans 8:10
2132 Romans 6:14
2133 Galatians 5:18
2134 Ephesians 2:22
2135 Ephesians 2:3
2136 1 Peter 2:5
2137 1 Peter 2:5
2138 Jeremiah 32:34
2139 Esther 8:8
2140 Esther 8:8
2141 Esther 8:8

by His Spirit, for it is said, "Quicken your mortal bodies by his Spirit."[2142] "The body of the sins of the flesh"[2143] are to be handled through the law of the LORD's Spirit; "through the Spirit do mortify the deeds of the body";[2144] for the body and mind of sin is to be converted for the fear and honor of the LORD's precepts of life and godliness, and not for "the spirit of bondage again to fear."[2145]

6. If indeed our most reasonable service is to present our bodies a living sacrifice to His Spirit, then there should be no form of intemperance and impatience within the soul of the conversation. A living sacrifice becomes living as it is joined to the living health of God, and we do know "the Spirit is life."[2146] If the issues of death; that is, "death by sin";[2147] have passed away from us through the slain flesh of His Christ, there is no doubt that the believer "shall be also in the likeness of his resurrection."[2148] This Christ was "quickened by the Spirit"[2149] and "made a quickening spirit,"[2150] for which cause He says, "That which is born of the Spirit is spirit."[2151] By this Christ Faith, and through His Spirit, our body of members should be "servants to righteousness unto holiness,"[2152] yet this is only possible through purification "of the heart, in the spirit,"[2153] that baptism "with the washing of water by the word."[2154]

7. The believer is purified "through sanctification of the Spirit,"[2155] and that purification is to birth wisdom and knowledge of God gained within the spirit from "obeying the truth through the Spirit."[2156] Our naturally sinful members of the flesh and mind that enjoy "adultery,

---

2142 Romans 8:11
2143 Colossians 2:11
2144 Romans 8:13
2145 Romans 8:15
2146 Romans 8:10
2147 Romans 5:12
2148 Romans 6:5
2149 1 Peter 3:18
2150 1 Corinthians 15:45
2151 John 3:6
2152 Romans 6:19
2153 Romans 2:29
2154 Ephesians 5:26
2155 1 Peter 1:2
2156 1 Peter 1:22

fornication, uncleanness, lasciviousness, idolatry, witchcraft, hatred, variance, emulations, wrath, strife, seditions, heresies,"[2157] are to be recovered through the Spirit to delight in faithfulness, purity, benevolence, honesty, humility with contentment, and godliness with sobriety. "Hereby we know that he abideth in us, by the Spirit which he hath given us";[2158] "for the fruit of the Spirit is in all goodness and righteousness and truth."[2159]

8. The same Spirit that quickened our High Priest is to place within our conscience a reverence to magnify the precepts of His God in every member and faculty of our being. As our members "become servants to God,"[2160] "servants of righteousness";[2161] even as we already know, "All thy commandments are righteousness";[2162] we should develop "fruit unto holiness"[2163] fixed within a new mind of spirit, which spirit "after God is created in righteousness and true holiness."[2164] The LORD's Spirit says, "I will give them one heart and mind to fear Me, that they may never depart from Me, even so will I put My fear in their hearts."[2165] "I will put my law in their inward parts, and write it in their hearts,"[2166] for then would the believer fear and trust Him in right love and faith. The heart and mind of God is to be written and established by "the Spirit of the living God"[2167] within our inward person; there is none other way to be created after His image.

9. "Glorify God in your body, and in your spirit, which are God's,"[2168] "for ye are bought with a price."[2169] The name of God cannot be sealed within the temple of the soul if self is still active. Even of the Gentile

---

2157 Galatians 5:19,20
2158 1 John 3:24
2159 Ephesians 5:9
2160 Romans 6:22
2161 Romans 6:18
2162 Psalm 119:172
2163 Romans 6:22
2164 Ephesians 4:24
2165 Jeremiah 32:39,40
2166 Jeremiah 31:33
2167 2 Corinthians 3:3
2168 1 Corinthians 6:20
2169 1 Corinthians 6:20

enemy of the Jews it is written, "Ha'man refrained himself."[2170] Our bodies of sin are to be quickened now on this earth, for we are, through His Spirit's will and words, to "live soberly, righteously, and godly, in this present world."[2171] For this cause, "our conversation is in heaven"[2172] "to an inheritance incorruptible, and undefiled, and that fadeth not away,"[2173] even "the power of God"[2174] through "that holy Spirit of promise, which is the earnest of our inheritance."[2175] It is Christ "who is gone into heaven, and is at the right hand of God"[2176] "that he might bring us to God,"[2177] for the believer must know why they are counseled, "The grace of our Lord Jesus Christ be with your spirit,"[2178] for "the spirit giveth life."[2179]

10. "This is the promise that he hath promised us, even eternal life,"[2180] for He has said of His Son's mediation, "Thou hast given him power over all flesh, that he should give eternal life."[2181] The knowledge of His heavenly ministry is the Savior of the law of sin that works in the body of our flesh and mind, for it is yet that "as many as received him, to them gave he power to become the sons of God."[2182] Our body and spirit are to be re-educated to maintain active health through labors of good love. The members of our body are to fall subject to a sanctified mind, and it is that the mind is to fall subject to the Spirit's Word, yet the medicine of purification to render every faculty and ambition pure is by the wisdom of His Faith, which is administered by His Spirit's voice exercised by the mind and limbs of the body. "God hath given to us eternal life, and this life is in his Son,"[2183] and seeing as how the Spirit

---

2170 Esther 5:10
2171 Titus 2:12
2172 Philippians 3:20
2173 1 Peter 1:4
2174 1 Peter 1:5
2175 Ephesians 1:13,14
2176 1 Peter 3:22
2177 1 Peter 3:18
2178 Galatians 6:18
2179 2 Corinthians 3:6
2180 1 John 2:25
2181 John 17:2
2182 John 1:12
2183 1 John 5:11

is life, the life of Christ is hidden within the reception of His blood and Spirit, for it is the Spirit that houses "all the fullness of the Godhead"[2184] in His name.

11. "In the light of the king's countenance is life,"[2185] and as our High Priest is "King of righteousness"[2186] and "King of peace,"[2187] "his favour is as a cloud of the latter rain,"[2188] and the one accepted in His name is to have "obtained grace and favour in his sight."[2189] "The riches of the glory"[2190] of God descends as "spiritual blessings,"[2191] and the showers of inheritance are revealed to be "the riches of his grace."[2192] After Christ was risen, "he left not himself without witness";[2193] "whereof the Holy Ghost also is witness for us,"[2194] seeing as how "it is the Spirit that beareth witness";[2195] "in that he did good, and gave us rain from heaven, and fruitful seasons, filling our hearts with food and gladness."[2196] The food of the soul is the life that is in the voice of His Son's operation. The Spirit of life, when once the heart commits to execute the counsels of His voice, is commissioned to "come and rain righteousness"[2197] upon the faith's conscience, for it is said, "I will pour out my spirit unto you."[2198]

12. As the LORD does rain His mind and righteousness on us through His Spirit, it is that He says, "I will make known my words unto you."[2199] "My doctrine shall drop as the rain,"[2200] says our LORD and Father, "for I give you good doctrine, forsake ye not my law."[2201] That

---

2184 Colossians 2:9
2185 Proverbs 16:15
2186 Hebrews 7:2
2187 Hebrews 7:2
2188 Proverbs 16:15
2189 Esther 2:17
2190 Ephesians 1:18
2191 Ephesians 1:3
2192 Ephesians 1:7
2193 Acts 14:17
2194 Hebrews 10:15
2195 1 John 5:6
2196 Acts 14:17
2197 Hosea 10:12
2198 Proverbs 1:23
2199 Proverbs 1:23
2200 Deuteronomy 32:2
2201 Proverbs 4:2

which is to fill our entire being is this LORD's doctrine of creation, which understanding revolves around His throne's ten precepts. That nourishment is to complete in the believer "the doctrine which is according to godliness"[2202] as revealed in "the law of Christ";[2203] teaching the obedient through "the law of the Spirit of life"[2204] by "the truth which is after godliness."[2205] This doctrine bears within it "eternal power"[2206] over the "eternal purpose"[2207] of the LORD's Word "through the eternal Spirit,"[2208] for it is creation's law, and "is the true God, and eternal life."[2209] Within the knowledge of His Son's name and ministry is life because that wisdom is eternal life, and it is currently ordained for "the Son to have life in himself"[2210] that He may give power to such as believe on the virtue of His name and blood, "that believing ye might have life through his name."[2211]

13. The new creature formed by that Faith of this LORD's High Priest will know Him as their Creator. The soul is to "be filled with the knowledge of his will in all wisdom and spiritual understanding,"[2212] and that sufficiency gathered together and distributed by the Spirit of God with all of His fullness. "We shall be saved by his life";[2213] by learning of and doing His conversation; and through "the washing of regeneration, and renewing of the Holy Ghost,"[2214] because through faith in His life-giving and sin-pardoning blood, "of his fulness have all we received, and grace for grace."[2215]

2202 1 Timothy 6:3
2203 Galatians 6:2
2204 Romans 8:2
2205 Titus 1:1
2206 Romans 1:20
2207 Ephesians 3:11
2208 Hebrews 9:14
2209 1 John 5:20
2210 John 5:26
2211 John 20:31
2212 Colossians 1:9
2213 Romans 5:10
2214 Titus 3:5
2215 John 1:16

25

On The Right Hand

1. Says Scripture concerning the LORD's Christ, "After he had by himself purged our sins, sat down on the right hand of the Majesty on high."[2216] Again, "Which of the angels said he at any time, Sit on my right hand, until I make thine enemies thy footstool?"[2217] For "we have such an high priest, who is set on the right hand of the throne of the Majesty in the heavens."[2218]

2. The Spirit is telling us that, after His crucifixion and ascension into the Places of the LORD, His Christ was appointed by His LORD to be seated upon the right hand of the power of His throne. When Christ said, "Hereafter shall ye see the Son of man sitting on the right hand of power,"[2219] what did He mean? Paul's language signifies that there is in fact a throne, or a figurative royal chair by the LORD's throne, which seat had no one to properly fill it on behalf of mankind before His Christ filled it. After God accepted the sacrifice of His Christ, and after He promoted Him as High Priest over His heavenly Sanctuary, to

2216 Hebrews 1:3
2217 Hebrews 1:13
2218 Hebrews 8:1
2219 Matthew 26:64

where Christ "obtained a more excellent name";[2220] even being called, Son and Chief Priest; Christ also picked up the throne that would regulate the new will and covenant of His LORD.

3. It is then natural to question, "If Christ is seated on some thing called, 'The right hand of God,' what then is the right hand of God?" To better understand, to be seated or to be standing is not literally not be found sitting or standing. Christ is settled over, or appointed upon the seat of the right hand of the LORD's Word, and this same right hand is to fulfill the saying that the Father promised Him, "I shall give thee the heathen for thine inheritance."[2221] So what then is He chief priest over in relation to conforming His enemies to become His servants? Moses once said, "Thy right hand, O LORD, is become glorious in power: thy right hand, O LORD, hath dashed in pieces the enemy. And in the greatness of thine excellency thou hast overthrown them that rose up against thee: thou sentest forth thy wrath, which consumed them as stubble."[2222] Herein is observed the Spirit's purpose and intention.

4. When Christ made His first appearance before His Father after He had raised Him from the dead, "unto the Son he saith, Thy throne, O God, is for ever and ever."[2223] "Ask of me, and I shall give thee the heathen for thine inheritance, and the uttermost parts of the earth for thy possession."[2224] The enemies of Christ are them that He recognizes as heathen. These are them "having the understanding darkened, being alienated from the life of God through the ignorance that is in them, because of the blindness of their heart: who being past feeling have given themselves over unto lasciviousness, to work all uncleanness with greediness."[2225] And these are them who LORD counsels on by saying, "The sons of the stranger, that join themselves to the LORD, to serve him, and to love the name of the LORD, to be his servants, every one that keepeth the Sabbath from polluting it, and taketh hold of my

---

2220 Hebrews 1:4
2221 Psalm 2:8
2222 Exodus 15:6,7
2223 Hebrews 1:8
2224 Psalm 2:8
2225 Ephesians 4:18,19

covenant; even them will I bring to my holy mountain, and make them joyful in my house of prayer."[2226]

5. After the Father had said what He had said to His new Prince and High Priest after He had resurrected Him from the dead, Christ responded by saying, "Thou hast made me the head of the heathen: a people whom I have not known shall serve me."[2227] Us alive today who feel after the Christ of God are the heathen and the strangers prophesied to have devout affection for the name and character, the Sabbath and the covenant, of the living LORD God. "You, that were sometime alienated and enemies in your mind by wicked works,"[2228] we are counseled, "hath he";[2229] God the Father; "reconciled in the body of his flesh through death, to present you holy and unblameable and unreproveable in his sight."[2230] It is therefore true that "by one offering he hath perfected for ever them that are sanctified,"[2231] but how does the perfection of God become a living reality? What is the beginning of sanctification after there is adoration in what was heard concerning both the Word and His Christ? The beginning of the Spirit's new creature is found at the right of His LORD, which is His glorious power, that greatness of His excellency, that hand wherein rest wrath and consumption to bring any and all things to stubble.

6. Christ is governor and intercessor over that which fulfills the word, "Who among us shall dwell with the devouring fire? who among us shall dwell with everlasting burnings?"[2232] "They which are called might receive the promise of eternal inheritance,"[2233] which is why we are counseled, "Ye have need of patience, that, after ye have done the will of God, ye might receive the promise."[2234] The will of the Spirit is in fact the covenant of His LORD, and it is the hearing and doing of this present covenant that bestows upon the willing and obedient soul the

---

2226 Isaiah 56:6,7
2227 Psalm 18:43
2228 Colossians 1:21
2229 Colossians 1:21
2230 Colossians 1:22
2231 Hebrews 10:14
2232 Isaiah 33:14
2233 Hebrews 9:15
2234 Hebrews 10:36

blessed promises of that ministry at that right hand of God, even that great fire. This everlasting burning, and this consuming fire that Christ is now Director over, is the Agent that is the only hope of the believer to know both the Word and His Christ. Because this Christ, "through the eternal Spirit offered himself without spot to God,"[2235] "being by the right hand of God exalted, and having received of the Father the promise of the Holy Ghost, he hath shed forth this"[2236] on them that obey the ordinances of His Faith.

7. This throne that Christ is seated upon is "the throne of grace, that we may obtain mercy, and find grace to help in time of need."[2237] His throne is positioned beside the throne of the living God, for it is through the throne and ministration of Christ that every promise of the new covenant will be fulfilled in the one who comes to Him for spiritual recovery and rejuvenation. But how is one supposed to receive the Holy Ghost? Where must one begin in order to receive the only Witness to true and honest conversion? It is counseled, "After ye have done the will of God, ye might receive the promise."[2238] It is the accepting, and the diligent application to the new covenant of the Spirit, that procures the Spirit of God to the inward parts. What then is the new will of God that the believer should study after? Says the LORD, "I will put my laws into their mind, and write them in their hearts: and I will be to them a God, and they shall be to me a people."[2239]

8. The new covenant of God promises "that we might receive the promise of the Spirit through faith."[2240] If our faith is true in the sight of His Word then we will know, "After that ye believed, ye were sealed with that holy Spirit of promise."[2241] When once our love for His Son's name, and our longing for the divine remedy of the Spirit by any means necessary, eclipses our inward fear, the ear of faith will hear, "The anointing which ye have received of him abideth in you, and ye

---

2235 Hebrews 9:14
2236 Acts 2:33
2237 Hebrews 4:16
2238 Hebrews 10:36
2239 Hebrews 8:10
2240 Galatians 3:14
2241 Ephesians 1:13

need not that any man teach you: but as the same anointing teacheth you of all things, and is truth, and is no lie, and even as it hath taught you, ye shall abide in him."[2242] Your honest faith and fervent zeal to overcome the falsehood within you, despite feeling or inclination for consequence, will grab the attention of God Himself, compelling Him to say, "Who is this that engaged his heart to approach unto me?"[2243]

9. God Himself plans to gather the believer to His own name that it may be fulfilled, "I will put my fear in their hearts, that they shall not depart from me."[2244] "By the washing of regeneration, and renewing of the Holy Ghost,"[2245] "through sanctification of the Spirit and belief of the truth,"[2246] the human being is to personally come into contact with the living God to have written, within their conscience, His name by "the Spirit of the living God; not in tables of stone, but in fleshy tables of the heart."[2247] Christ's ministry is joined to the office of "the Spirit of grace,"[2248] for this throne rests by the Place of God to secure within His converted enemies His fear and truth. This is what Christ meant when He said, "Lo, I come to do thy will, O God."[2249]

10. "Grace and truth came by Jesus Christ,"[2250] and because it is known, "Fear God, and keep His commandments,"[2251] and, "The truth is in Jesus,"[2252] and because it says, "Thy law is the truth,"[2253] and, "Thy word is truth,"[2254] the ministration of Christ rests between the commandments of God and the Faith of His name, consolidating both within the heart and mind of the one desirous to win His conversation. The first word of God came directly from God and was written on stone, and the second word of God came directly from God and rested

2242 1 John 2:27
2243 Jeremiah 30:21
2244 Jeremiah 32:40
2245 Titus 3:5
2246 2 Thessalonians 2:13
2247 2 Corinthians 3:3
2248 Hebrews 10:29
2249 Hebrews 10:9
2250 John 1:17
2251 Ecclesiastes 12:12
2252 Ephesians 4:24
2253 Psalm 119:142
2254 John 17:17

within flesh for an everlasting law. It is the Spirit that works to seal within the believer every word of His LORD when once they commit to the hope of the new covenant, which hope is, "I will dwell in them, and walk in them; and I will be their God, and they shall be my people,"[2255] says the LORD. Thus, it cannot be forgotten how it is counseled, "The foundation of God standeth sure, having this seal, The Lord knoweth them that are his."[2256]

11. Them that are the Word's uphold active faith above all things. These are "them that believe to the saving of the soul."[2257] A flesh-based diet will draw its adherent to uphold a faithless conversation. Every thing begins with our faith exercising the organs of its confidence on the name of our High Priest. The soul, who refuses to exercise their faith, cannot receive or achieve the things that God has set in place for them without consistently communing with Him. The old covenant did not openly reserve the privilege for intimately conversing with His Spirit, or of even receiving precious gifts and promises of right and perpetual newness for patient application of what was personally retained from Him. Christ changed and shook every thing in heaven and on earth when He obtained the true throne of the priesthood within the LORD's House in the heavens. From the moment the believer admits the Faith of this Christ's mediation as their personal religion's Savior, they are freely given the same power that overthrew the Egyptians to consume the throne of the natural heart that His name, and the likeness of His conversation, may sit upon it, and that the believer may properly govern self with His counsel as their Head.

2255 2 Corinthians 6:16
2256 2 Timothy 2:19
2257 Hebrews 10:39

26

Remember Now Thy Creator

1. "Remember now thy Creator in the days of thy youth, while the evil days come not, nor the years draw nigh, when thou shalt say, I have no pleasure in them; while the sun, or the light, or the moon, or the stars, be not darkened, nor the clouds return after the rain."[2258]

2. It is the current season to be mindful of our Priest's LORD and God, to "consider the work of God,"[2259] because the season for this appointment will inevitably close. What awaits the professed believer of heaven's doctrine is a time and a day of temporal and spiritual oppression, where "in those days shall men seek death, and shall not find it."[2260] Like the man of the Spirit, many will at this hour exclaim, "Hast thou utterly rejected Judah? hath thy soul lothed Zion? why hast thou smitten us, and there is no healing for us? we looked for peace, and there is no good; and for the time of healing, and behold trouble!"[2261] Such a time fulfills the saying, "I saw under the sun the place of judgment, that wickedness was there; and the place of righteousness, that

---

2258 Ecclesiastes 12:1,2
2259 Ecclesiastes 7:13
2260 Revelation 9:6
2261 Jeremiah 14:19

iniquity was there."[2262] "Behold the tears of such as were oppressed, and they had no comforter; and on the side of their oppressors there was power; but they had no comforter."[2263]

3. If there is no comforter among the oppressed, even though our Priest says, "I will pray the Father, and he shall give you another Comforter, that he may abide with you for ever,"[2264] then it is true that at some point in time, God Himself will remove Himself from His people. For this cause it is written, "Who shall have pity upon thee, O Jerusalem? or who shall bemoan thee? or who shall go aside to ask how thou doest? Thou hast forsaken me, saith the LORD, thou art gone backward: therefore will I stretch out my hand against thee, and destroy thee."[2265] The Spirit of God will in fact be removed from the earth completely; albeit not from His sanctified assembly; and before this should happen, He will remove Himself first from among His openly hypocritical host. When the supposed place of *judgment* joins to the supposed place of *righteousness*, power will be given to that institution to begin a new time of distress against them that are first contrary to the LORD's will and wisdom. While these days continue to brew, and until God has sanctioned this season, "Remember now thy Creator,"[2266] and, "Consider the work of God,"[2267] is the present counsel of His Spirit.

4. Scripture says, "The harp, and the viol, the tabret, and pipe, and wine, are in their feasts: but they regard not the work of the LORD, neither consider the operation of his hands. Therefore my people are gone into captivity, because they have no knowledge: and their honourable men are famished, and their multitude dried up with thirst."[2268]

5. The knowledge of God is concealed within the operation of His hands. The fact and revelation of the Spirit's will for the inward parts is held within the "riches of the full assurance of understanding, to the

---

2262 Ecclesiastes 3:16
2263 Ecclesiastes 4:1
2264 John 14:16
2265 Jeremiah 15:5,6
2266 Ecclesiastes 12:1
2267 Ecclesiastes 7:13
2268 Isaiah 5:12,13

acknowledgement of the mystery of God, and of the Father, and of Christ; in whom are hid all the treasures of wisdom and knowledge."[2269] How may one obtain the wisdom and knowledge of God? How may one even receive the key to unlock the chest of the treasures of understanding for what the will of the LORD is? It is written, "I applied mine heart to know, and to see the business that is done."[2270]

6. The charge to remember the Creator is but advice to "acquaint now thyself with him, and be at peace."[2271] To know that the LORD's Spirit is Creator is but to personally give up the heart to His Son's understanding, "rightly dividing the word of truth."[2272] To know the LORD is to take knowledge of Him by being "transformed by the renewing of your mind, that ye may prove what is that good, and acceptable, and perfect, will of God."[2273] The creation's science is best understood from proving the sayings of His Spirit to know that He is in fact that "God, who quickeneth the dead, and calleth those things which be not as though they were."[2274] It is to reject the way of the majority who ultimately fulfill the saying, "They did not like to retain God in their knowledge."[2275] The Spirit's religion is obtained, retained, sewn within, and inwardly cultivated by the LORD's voice personally, and by His reformer fully cooperating with His Son's course of learning. This is why He says, "If thou criest after knowledge";[2276] "if thou seekest"[2277] "and searchest";[2278] "then shalt thou understand the fear of the LORD, and find the knowledge of God."[2279]

7. Concerning the Spirit's obtained precepts, it is written, "They are life unto those that find them, and health to all their flesh."[2280] Did

---

2269 Colossians 2:2,3
2270 Ecclesiastes 8:16
2271 Job 22:21
2272 2 Timothy 2:15
2273 Romans 12:2
2274 Romans 4:17
2275 Romans 1:28
2276 Proverbs 2:3
2277 Proverbs 2:4
2278 Proverbs 2:4
2279 Proverbs 2:5
2280 Proverbs 4:22

not Christ say, "Except ye eat the flesh of the Son of man, and drink his blood, ye have no life in you"?[2281] It is the Word "that created the heavens, and stretched them out; he that spread forth the earth, and that which cometh out of it; he that giveth breath unto the people upon it, and spirit to them that walk therein."[2282] "Shall we not much rather be in subjection unto the Father of spirits, and live?"[2283] To eat and to drink Christ is better understood as executing the principles of His Faith by an experimental faith, that it may be fulfilled, "If the Spirit of him that raised up Jesus from the dead dwell in you, he that raised up Christ from the dead shall also quicken your mortal bodies by his Spirit."[2284]

8. "The communion of the Holy Ghost,"[2285] joined by the work of proving what "the Holy Ghost teacheth,"[2286] gives to the personal religion a confidence due to the sealing power of the Spirit over the constitution of the mind. "He that soweth to the Spirit shall of the Spirit reap life everlasting,"[2287] and because sowing is but the action of scattering seeds over land, as the seeds of the Spirit are given, it is the duty of the believer to take those seeds and to scatter them over the ground of the heart by the hand of the mind. This is why it is counseled, "The spirit giveth life,"[2288] and, "It is the spirit that quickeneth; the flesh profiteth nothing."[2289] Our LORD counsels, "Let thine heart retain my words: keep my commandments, and live";[2290] this is the only way that the soul may know that He is Creator. For "he is not a God of the dead, but of the living: for all live unto him,"[2291] and all that are alive by Him, and formed of Him to be alive to Him, are to know that "we are his

2281 John 6:53
2282 Isaiah 42:5
2283 Hebrews 12:9
2284 Romans 8:11
2285 2 Corinthians 13:14
2286 1 Corinthians 2.13
2287 Galatians 6:8
2288 2 Corinthians 3:6
2289 John 6:63
2290 Proverbs 4:4
2291 Luke 20:38

workmanship, created in Christ Jesus unto good works, which God hath before ordained that we should walk in them."[2292]

9. The Word's new creation begins as the heart accepts "the word of righteousness"[2293] and "the word of reconciliation."[2294] To be created in Christ Jesus is better understood as being "renewed in knowledge after the image of him."[2295] It is not expected that, after the heart finds joy in what is heard concerning Christ, the heart should then recoil itself to rest under the shadow of a man or a woman. The heart has found joy in Christ's voice because it now recognizes that it can quit trying to be the savior of its body of beliefs, and of its sick members. Thus, when the LORD pours His Spirit out over the soul, and causes that soul to actually hear and to comprehend His voice, the hearer is expected to boldly come before the throne of His Son that it may hear, "Take away the filthy garments"[2296] and "put ye on the Lord Jesus Christ, and make not provision for the flesh, to fulfil the lusts thereof."[2297]

10. As the righteousness of Christ is accepted, examined, and worn, and as self-righteousness now finds itself without a throne, the counsel is to then begin the fight of faith in the righteousness and power of His Spirit. The counsel becomes, "Put off"[2298] "the former conversation"[2299] and "be renewed in the spirit of your mind."[2300] "Put on the new man, which after God is created in righteousness and true holiness."[2301] The mental and the moral faculties are to find themselves repaired as the reformer applies the spiritual truths of God to the personal religion. When the power of the will to know our High Priest's LORD is given sway over superstitious and cultivated fear, the experience attached to purification will allow the believer to hear, "I have caused thine iniquity

2292 Ephesians 2:10
2293 Hebrews 5:13
2294 2 Corinthians 5:19
2295 Colossians 3:10
2296 Zechariah 3:4
2297 Romans 13:14
2298 Ephesians 4:22
2299 Ephesians 4:2
2300 Ephesians 4:23
2301 Ephesians 4:24

to pass from thee."[2302] This Christ "gave himself for us, that he might redeem us from all iniquity, and purify unto himself a peculiar people, zealous of good works,"[2303] but the work of reformation may only begin if the subject is willing to consent to an experience "through sanctification of the Spirit and belief of the truth."[2304]

11. To consider the work of God is to cooperate with the laws of His Son's Faith "through the faith of the operation of God."[2305] Therefore "if a man beget an hundred children, and live many years, so that the days of his years be many, and his soul be not filled with good, and also that he have no burial; I say, that an untimely birth is better than he."[2306] The heart should not be kept from personally experiencing heaven's throne religion, for the end of the Spirit's Faith is "that mortality might be swallowed up of life."[2307] The human being is to be buried while the mind of sin is yet conscious and functioning, and this is the mystery of the work of God. If the former constitution sees no death, if the spirit is not reclaiming the throne of the heart that it may operate the members of the body, then there is an error in the practice. The counsel is, "Worship God in the spirit,"[2308] for although "our outward man perish, yet the inward man is renewed day by day."[2309]

12. This is the work of the LORD's tidings, and the privation caused by the Spirit's abstemious diet, and the reaction felt by the new regimen of God on a daily basis, will wear out the life-force of the individual if there is not a moment of recuperation. It is not just the Faith of His Son that is to be studied and patiently applied to in all simplicity, but it is also the commandments of His God. Therefore concerning the rest for the daily war that is waged against self, we are counseled, "We which have believed do enter into rest."[2310] "There remaineth therefore

---

2302 Zechariah 3:4
2303 Titus 2:14
2304 2 Thessalonians 2:13
2305 Colossians 2:12
2306 Ecclesiastes 6:3
2307 2 Corinthians 5:4
2308 Philippians 3:3
2309 2 Corinthians 4:16
2310 Hebrews 4:3

a rest to the people of God,"[2311] "for he spake in a certain place of the seventh day on this wise, And God did rest the seventh day from all his works."[2312]

13. The battle to sustain the spirit, to apply to the virtue of Christ to retain sustenance for the day, and by that sustenance to beat back the inclinations of the mind of the flesh to exercise the mind of the spirit by the power of His Spirit, this operation wears on the person assigned to this work. The LORD knows that we are human, and that His religion is His own divine appointment obtained only by communion and expression through a faith that works by the love that is had for His name; therefore He did not leave His creation without a day of rest. If any should be willing to hear, "Let them that suffer according to the will of God commit the keeping of their souls to him in well doing, as unto a faithful Creator,"[2313] then if in fact the will of God is being studied and applied to, the rest of the Creator will be the highlight and the praise of the experience.

14. Faith cannot exist temperately and patiently in knowledge without a season of rest. If any should hear and accept the promise, "The very God of peace sanctify you wholly,"[2314] then it must also be heard, "God blessed the seventh day, and sanctified it."[2315] "It is God which worketh in you both to will and to do of his good pleasure,"[2316] and since this is that same "great God that formed all things,"[2317] that same law of sanctification concerning the seventh day belongs to that same God who would sanctify the inward person of man. Because it is "God, who created all things by Jesus Christ,"[2318] must this same Word be denied, who first ordained and rested on the seventh day after creation? It was the Word in the beginning who created all things, and because this same Word, who suffered on the tree within the spirit of

2311 Hebrews 4:9
2312 Hebrews 4:4
2313 1 Peter 4:19
2314 1 Thessalonians 5:23
2315 Genesis 2:3
2316 Philippians 2:13
2317 Proverbs 26:10
2318 Ephesians 3:9

His Christ, is the same One who laid the foundation for the precepts of His Faith at the beginning of the world, every soul now hidden in the second Adam rests under the banner of the Creator's voice.

15. This is the work for the sincere reformer before the LORD begins to handle the hypocrites of His people by the hand of men. The Spirit's rain is falling on souls who will accept the experience attached to faith's higher learning, and for this reason He says, "My doctrine shall drop as the rain."[2319] Again, the LORD promises, "I will pour out my spirit unto you, I will make known my words unto you."[2320] Therefore "according to the power that worketh in us,"[2321] as there is a consistent effort to know the LORD of our High Priest, "the knowledge of his will in all wisdom and spiritual understanding"[2322] will be given that we may further reverence every law of a right nature, which is every law of the LORD His Father.

2319 Deuteronomy 32:2
2320 Proverbs 1:23
2321 Ephesians 3:20
2322 Colossians 1:9

27

The Place Of His Foundation

1. "But Jerusalem which is above is free, which is the mother of us all."[2323]

2. Paul has just taken something that is literal, and has translated it into a context that is new to our understanding. When he says, "Our conversation is in heaven,"[2324] what he is really saying is that our hope is to rests in the Jerusalem of the living God. No longer is the literal Jerusalem relevant for any thing, nor any other of its professed likeness, but the relevance of God is now to be found above, in the mother, or the church, of every believer, "whence also we look for the Saviour."[2325] If in fact the Jerusalem of God is no longer on earth, but is rather in heaven, then there must be a reason why Paul is pointing the believer to that Building in heaven, and not to any Jerusalem on earth.

3. What belonged in Jerusalem that set it apart from all the other places in Israel? God says, "Jerusalem, the city which I have chosen me to put my name there."[2326] "The LORD said to David, and to Solomon his son, In this house, and in Jerusalem, which I have chosen out of all

2323 Galatians 4:26
2324 Philippians 3:20
2325 Philippians 3:20
2326 1 Kings 11:36

tribes of Israel, will I put my name for ever."[2327] The LORD again said, "Since the day that I brought forth my people out of the land of Egypt I chose no city among all the tribes of Israel to build an house in, that my name might be there; neither chose I any man to be a ruler over my people Israel: but I have chosen Jerusalem, that my name might be there; and have chosen David to be over my people Israel."[2328] This is why it says, "In Judah is God known: his name is great in Israel. In Sa'lem (Jerusalem) also is his tabernacle, and his dwelling place in Zion."[2329]

4. Herein we can see why His Christ is likened in Scripture to be that son of David, and why Paul says that in the heavenly Jerusalem we also should expect our Savior to be there, for this Christ has long since fulfilled the saying, "The LORD therefore hath performed his word that he hath spoken: for I am risen up in the room of David my father, and am set on the throne of Israel, as the LORD promised, and have built the house for the name of the LORD God of Israel."[2330] His Christ is that Prince and Governor of this LORD's heavenly Sanctuary, for He is a King or High Priest; a "king," in Scripture's tongue, means "priest" or "ruler" of a church, even as it says, "And hath made us kings and priests,[2331] and, "The chief ruler of the synagogue,"[2332] and, "The chief governor in the house of the LORD."[2333] Herein is why it says, "The LORD hath sworn, and will not repent, Thou art a priest for ever after the order of Melchiz'edek."[2334] This is why Paul likens the LORD's Christ also to Aaron, for He has literally taken the ministration of Aaron to be His own in the LORD's heavenly Temple, sitting in the room or office of Aaron. Therefore "we have such an high priest, who is set on the right hand of the throne of the Majesty in the heavens;

2327 2 Kings 21:7
2328 2 Chronicles 6:5,6
2329 Psalm 76:1,2
2330 2 Chronicles 6:10
2331 Revelation 1:6
2332 Acts 18:17
2333 Jeremiah 20:1
2334 Psalm 110:4

a minister of the sanctuary, and of the true tabernacle, which the Lord pitched, and not man."[2335]

5. The LORD's full religion is no longer on earth and forwarded by a man imbibed with sin's conversation, nor through any institution of any such minister. Paul simply says, "That Jerusalem above the heaven is our mother. Our conversation is above in this Place 'where Christ sitteth on the right hand of God. Set your affection on things above, not on things on the earth.'"[2336] Paul has given this counsel because he knows that if on earth the name of God rested in Jerusalem, so too has God now transferred that same name, and the true ministration of that name, to the true Building of His Spirit by the passing, regenerating, and priestly consecration of His Son, no longer to be where that name rested as only a figurative representation.

6. The LORD told Moses, "According to all that I shew thee, after the pattern of the tabernacle, and the pattern of all the instruments thereof, even so shall ye make it."[2337] Where did the pattern come from? Moses saw in vision the LORD's true House and Structure and simply copied it for the government of Israel on earth. The Israelites, and the theocracy set up by Moses, and the institution cemented by Solomon, was but a figure to represent the Spirit's dispensation to come under the reign of His Christ's mediation. So if the name of God was kept in Jerusalem below the heaven, and in that Place rested the Temple and the ministration of that name, should it now be any different, seeing as how what existed before was but an imperfect fulfillment of what already existed in perfection? If in fact Jerusalem is the City of God, and Christ is the both King and Priest of that Temple of God in the heavens, then this Place is not future, and our entrance into it is not future, but is ever present by our exercised faith. Thus, in present tense, Paul says to every believer, "Ye are come unto mount Si'on, and unto the city of the living God, the heavenly Jerusalem, and to an innumerable company of angels, to the general assembly and church of the firstborn, which are written in heaven."[2338]

2335 Hebrews 8:1,2
2336 Colossians 3:1,2
2337 Exodus 25:9
2338 Hebrews 12:22,23

7. So if the eye of faith is to enter this Place now at this time to trust in its High Priest, upon entering, what is the desire of this Christ for a member of both His LORD's City and Church? And what is it that He is mediator for? Scripture tells us that one of the primary obligations of Christ is "that he might bring us to God."[2339] If in fact the Jerusalem of the Majesty of the heavens now holds His name, then in fact the Priest and King of that Jerusalem wants His citizens to live by the same mind and rule according to the God of that City and Temple, for He is the Minister of the services to that name and Word. So what then is the believer to currently encounter in this Place that reveals the name of God to them? It is written, "Solomon assembled the elders of Israel, and all the heads of the tribes, the chief of the fathers of the children of Israel, unto king Solomon in Jerusalem, that they might bring up the ark of the covenant of the LORD out of the city of David, which is Zion."[2340]

8. Christ is both a symbol of David and Solomon, and as soon as Solomon took the place of his father, the ark of God, symbolizing the complete economy of God, was removed from the city of David to Jerusalem. Likewise when Christ ascended on high to take up His new position beside His LORD's Word, the Father gathered "together in one all things in Christ, both which are in heaven, and which are on earth; even in him."[2341] Thus, when Christ ascended to His Father's throne, that same ark of God followed Him there, and the binding authority of what is contained within that ark becoming the object of respect for every obedient soul through the Faith of His mediation.

9. Every thing done concerning the old ministration of Aaron was done to reconcile what was in the ark of God to the citizen of the Government of God. Christ being now a Son and Minister over the House of God means that He is the means whereby man may commune with God so that now the character of God, as relayed by His Ten Commandments, may be perfectly kept within the personal ark of the soul temple. If this is a lie concerning His Christ, then Paul gives us

2339 1 Peter 3:18
2340 1 Kings 8:1
2341 Ephesians 1:10

false information when he says, "He is able also to save them to the uttermost that come unto God by him, seeing he ever liveth to make intercession for them."[2342] Because every believing soul is to be given into the hands of God that they may consistently reverence the name of His God in all simplicity, and because the Place holding the heavenly Church of His Spirit is to love the name of His LORD, and because the ten immutable precepts therein relay the lovely character that He hopes to engrave within His faithful, then the Sabbath for honoring that name is also known in this Place, even as it was of old.

10. It was known of old "that in Jerusalem is the place where men ought to worship."[2343] Concerning His faithful, the LORD promises, "Even them will I bring to my holy mountain, and make them joyful in my house of prayer."[2344] What is the holy mountain of the LORD? Where is His house of prayer and of thanksgiving? It is written, "And shall worship the LORD in the holy mount at Jerusalem."[2345] This is that Jerusalem that Paul speaks of, for there exists no edifice of God on the earth. In this Place, the heart drawn out to the LORD will find Him, for this is that "church of the living God, the pillar and ground of the truth."[2346] And because it is the pillar and ground of the fact of His Spirit's will and wisdom, which revelation is His mystery within the conscience of a sinful religious conversation, as one enters the gates of His City by faith, they will come across a sign that says, "Thy law is the truth."[2347]

11. "The righteousness of the law might be fulfilled in us"[2348] as our eyes are ever towards His Christ's name and office, and because "the truth is in Jesus,"[2349] or rather, because the laws of the Spirit are in "the law of Christ,"[2350] the law of the Faith of His Christ is an express revelation of the Ten Commandments of His God. As the believer rests

---

2342 Hebrews 7:25
2343 John 4:20
2344 Isaiah 56:7
2345 Isaiah 27:13
2346 1 Timothy 3:15
2347 Psalm 119:142
2348 Romans 8:4
2349 Ephesians 4:21
2350 Galatians 6:2

by faith in the economy of God, they will come to experience the power of the Faith of that God to receive "the sign of circumcision, a seal of the righteousness of the faith."[2351] One cannot abide in the LORD's House without the seal of His Faith's creative power, which is why every member of this assembly of newness within the heavens knows that "God blessed the seventh day."[2352]

12. A woman appreciates, above any gift from her husband, the card that is attached to the gift. Why? Because it expresses, more than any thing, the inward thoughts and feelings; it is a sign, to her senses, of affection and personal value. A gift can be given in any frame of mind, and that same giver of that gift can take back that gift as quickly as he or she gave it. "A gift doth blind the eyes of the wise, and pervert the words of the righteous,"[2353] but an acknowledged sign of true affection "is like apples of gold in pictures of silver."[2354] Such is the seventh-day Sabbath of the living God to the truehearted. Listen to what these confess after entering into the House of this LORD: "He brought me to the banqueting house, and his banner over me was love."[2355] These receive the banner of His Faith as soon as they by faith commence the great work of reformation inside of the Place of reconciliation, but why exactly are is the banner given to them? It says, "Thou hast given a banner to them that fear thee, that it may be displayed because of the truth."[2356]

13. When once the heart personally grows familiar with the power that is filled within the sayings of His Christ, because of that power convincing every foul member of the heart and mind to halt in the presence of the Word, the banner of the LORD will be given as a result of such an executed conversation by faith. The believer will receive the sign of the LORD's benevolent doctrine, and they will remain in that love and bond for ever. This is what it means hearing, "He that dwelleth

2351 Romans 4:11
2352 Genesis 2:3
2353 Deuteronomy 16:19
2354 Proverbs 25:11
2355 Song of Solomon 2:4
2356 Psalm 60:4

in love dwelleth in God, and God in him."[2357] "Hereby know we that we dwell in him, and he in us, because he hath given us of his Spirit,"[2358] and this is why Paul wrote, "The righteousness of the law might be fulfilled in us, who walk not after the flesh, but after the Spirit."[2359] To dwell in God is to "be bound in the bundle of life with the LORD,"[2360] and since "the Spirit is life because of righteousness,"[2361] every one in His Faith will say, "All thy commandments are righteousness,"[2362] and, "We will go into his tabernacles: we will worship at his footstool. Arise, O LORD, into thy rest; thou, and the ark of thy strength."[2363]

14. This is what Paul calls our attention to when he says that the Home and Place for the believer is now above and within the living City of the living God. Every believing soul has a work to accomplish before the ark of God and the Word of that ark, and such a course cannot commence without surrendering the heart to first "consider the Apostle and High Priest of our profession, Christ Jesus."[2364] If there is any Apostle of the LORD to follow, Paul himself has said look nowhere else but to the First Apostle of the Faith that we all share to the living God, who is also our High Priest to that same Majesty. And notice that in the previous paragraph, at the end of the paragraph, the Psalmist says "tabernacles," plural. Christ is now that High Priest who is ministering in "the temple of the tabernacle of the testimony in heaven,"[2365] which is the second tabernacle within the House of God, wherein rests "the ark of the covenant"[2366] that holds "the tables of the covenant."[2367] In this Room, the message of heaven's will and knowledge is clearly pronounced, and it is the joy of every rightly believing and hopeful soul. Herein rests the foundation of every reforming spirit and conversation.

2357 1 John 4:16
2358 1 John 4:13
2359 Romans 8:4
2360 1 Samuel 25:29
2361 Romans 8:10
2362 Psalm 119:172
2363 Psalm 132:7,8
2364 Hebrews 3:1
2365 Revelation 15:5
2366 Hebrews 9:4
2367 Hebrews 9:4

28

Learn To Embrace Reform

1. The first stewards of the LORD's Spirit were perceived by the religious world, and by the ones that claimed heritage from them, as being "unlearned and ignorant men."[2368] The men of heaven's Faith suffered open disrespect to their faces; from the highest hearers to the lowest. Even when told the most foul things concerning themselves and their message, with all sincerity and with all boldness they yet confessed, "I will very gladly spend and be spent for you; though the more abundantly I love you, the less I be loved."[2369] But despite the affection the they gave, their intentions were never fully understood due to the surrounding false *apostles* also preaching in the same churches as them. Paul said of them, "What I do, that I will do, that I may cut off occasion from them which desire occasion; that wherein they glory, they may be found even as we. For such are false apostles, deceitful workers, transforming themselves into the apostles of Christ."[2370]

2. Even in this early season of the Spirit's new dispensation, falsehoods, and the inventors of it, were gaining precedence over the real servants of the living LORD God. These spurious individuals were, of

---

2368 Acts 4:13
2369 2 Corinthians 12:15
2370 2 Corinthians 11:12,13

course, them that had degrees and certifications from men to prove their worth on the subject of *Christ*. The Spirit's first ministers bore no earthy credentials besides the testimony of their conscience and experience, and the result of the working of their testimony in the heart and life of those that heard and accepted it. Desiring to place into the mind of the Corinthians the right proof of the power of the LORD, Paul once wrote, "Do we begin again to commend ourselves? or need we, as some others, epistles of commendation to you, or letters of commendation from you? Ye are our epistle written in our hearts, known and read of all men."[2371]

3. Unlike the credentials of men, the credentials of God are not born for a wall, nor are they placed before one's name. The proof of the Spirit's servant is the fruit that they cultivate, and the healthful benefits that those around them are benefited with from consuming that fruit, "being enriched in every thing to all bountifulness."[2372] Because of this regard for "having men's persons in admiration because of advantage,"[2373] Paul did not hesitate to rebuke the spirit of the Corinthian church. "Ye are not straitened in us, but ye are straitened in your own bowels,"[2374] he wrote. "What communion hath light with darkness? And what concord hath Christ with Be'lial? or what part hath he that believeth with an infidel?"[2375] Paul taught that the aim of these false *teachers* was to "pervert the gospel of Christ."[2376] But they did not openly defame the body heaven's knowledge, for Paul warned that what they teach "is not another"[2377] gospel per se, but rather a distortion of the true, and with the same phrases and characters of Scripture to remove the heart "unto another gospel."[2378] Paul understood their speech to be "Jewish fables, and commandments of men, that turn from the truth."[2379]

2371 2 Corinthians 3:1,2
2372 2 Corinthians 9:11
2373 Jude 1:16
2374 2 Corinthians 6:12
2375 2 Corinthians 6:14,15
2376 Galatians 1:7
2377 Galatians 1:7
2378 Galatians 1:6
2379 Titus 1:14

4. The Gentile churches of Rome were opening their doors to any man or woman with a *Ph.D.* or with a *Masters of Divinity*, or to any one of public philosophical reputation, not knowing that what they were hearing was neither the right fact of the matter, nor any thing that would encourage them to gravitate to the fact behind the science of salvation. This is why Paul wrote to Christian elders and their assemblies, "I am jealous over you with godly jealousy: for I have espoused you to one husband, that I may present you as a chaste virgin to Christ. But I fear, lest by any means, as the serpent beguiled Eve through his subtilty, so your minds should be corrupted from the simplicity that is in Christ."[2380] Paul knew "that because of false brethren unawares brought in,"[2381] that many would "turn away their ears from the truth, and shall be turned unto fables."[2382] He knew that if "certain men crept in unawares, who were before of old ordained to this condemnation, ungodly men,"[2383] should gain the podium of the Christian churches, that corruption against the LORD's name and will would spread, and the saying would again be fulfilled, "Her priests have polluted the sanctuary, they have done violence to the law."[2384]

5. Paul, in all that he assumed would take place, was right in his assumption. So drawn to men of professed *learning*, Paul wrote to the church elders, "Do ye look on things after the outward appearance? If any man trust to himself that he is Christ's, let him of himself think this again, that, as he is Christ's, even so are we Christ's. For though I should boast somewhat more of our authority, which the Lord hath given us for edification, and not for your destruction, I should not be ashamed."[2385] Paul was seeing "them which glory in appearance, and not in heart,"[2386] deeply revered. Eventually he wrote to the elders of the churches, "I write not these things to shame you, but as my beloved sons I warn you. For though ye have ten thousand instructors in Christ,

2380 2 Corinthians 11:2,3
2381 Galatians 2:4
2382 2 Timothy 4:4
2383 Jude 1:4
2384 Zephaniah 3:4
2385 2 Corinthians 10:7,8
2386 2 Corinthians 5:12

yet have ye not many fathers: for in Christ Jesus I have begotten you through the gospel. Wherefore I beseech you, be ye followers of me."[2387] What was the "way" of Paul, if it was not by an army of instructors? He writes, "We have received, not the spirit of the world, but the spirit which is of God; that we might know the things that are freely given to us of God."[2388]

6. Notice the language of Scripture, for if Paul would have said, "Spirit," then that is what he would have said, but rather he says "spirit," that is, "the spirit of your mind."[2389] The one drawn out to God needs no flesh stimulus to hear any thing concerning Him. Paul says that he offered whoever he offered to the Spirit's understanding as a virgin in comprehension, as a heart unsullied by the very special speciously constructed language of the men counted *wise* within the religious world. The spirit of the Spirit, or the mind of God, is a constitution set to search and to dig up all things concerning His name and science. This is why Paul said that he spoke "not in the words which man's wisdom teacheth, but which the Holy Ghost teacheth."[2390] Because "the Spirit searcheth all things, yea, the deep things of God,"[2391] the one drawn out to God will also search after the things of the Word with that same Spirit of the Word. It is not just faith that is needed to understand the LORD's voice, but truly the Agent of true education is the first to be surrendered to. Man can study the things of God all day and every day, yet according to the heart of a man he will discern what he discovers. "What man knoweth the things of a man, save the spirit of man which is in him? even so the things of God knoweth no man, but the Spirit of God."[2392]

7. The way that Paul was, that is the way that he hoped all individuals to be. "I say therefore to the unmarried and widows, It is good for them if they abide even as I,"[2393] he writes. The language is not

---

2387 1 Corinthians 4:14-16
2388 1 Corinthians 2:12
2389 Ephesians 4:23
2390 1 Corinthians 2:13
2391 1 Corinthians 2:10
2392 1 Corinthians 2:11
2393 1 Corinthians 7:8

literal. An unmarried individual is someone without a husband or a wife, and a widow is someone who has lost their spouse by death and has not remarried. A woman or a wife is a symbol of a church, as Paul describes, "Love your wives, even as Christ also loved the church."[2394] A husband fulfills the same reference, in that "the husband is the head of the wife, even as Christ is the head of the church."[2395] If a wife is a church, a husband is the head of a church, her pastor or priest. Thus, we can now see that Paul once had a "wife," for he states, "I am verily a man which am a Jew, born in Tar'sus, a city in Cili'cia, yet brought up in this city at the feet of Gama'liel, and taught according to the perfect manner of the law of the fathers, and was zealous toward God."[2396] And to be more specific, he says, "After the most straitest sect of our religion I lived a Pharisee."[2397]

8. Paul's wife died within him when he allowed the revelation the Spirit's understanding to flourish within His conscience, and he did not afterwards again remarry on earth. What he calls, "The Jews' religion,"[2398] was in reality, "The traditions of my fathers,"[2399] he says. Therefore concerning this new transition in his conversation, he writes, "When it pleased God, who separated me from my mother's womb, and called me by his grace, to reveal his Son in me, that I might preach him among the heathen; immediately I conferred not with flesh and blood: neither went I up to Jerusalem to them which were apostles before me; but I went into Arabia, and returned again unto Damascus."[2400]

9. What is called a "husband" or a "wife" is, in reality, the voice of the preferential religious tradition, or the traditional spiritual upbringing, and this is further called a "mother's womb." Paul, after actually receiving whatever he needed to turn to the LORD in all honesty, actually did just that. He cut out all human interaction for the desire that was in him to know His LORD's will and praise, thus,

---

2394 Ephesians 5:25
2395 Ephesians 5:23
2396 Acts 22:3
2397 Acts 26:5
2398 Galatians 1:13
2399 Galatians 1:14
2400 Galatians 1:15-17

in him the word is fulfilled, "Through desire a man, having separated himself, seeketh and intermeddleth with all wisdom."[2401] He did not go to Jerusalem; a symbol representing the center for religious knowledge, for that is where the church of the Word's first ministers dwelt; but rather he spent time ingratiating himself into the heavenly Culture of the LORD's Son to know Him for his own self. This is why he could say, "Do I now persuade men, or God? or do I seek to please men? for if I yet pleased men, I should not be the servant of Christ. I certify you, brethren, that the gospel which was preached of me is not after man. For I neither received it of man, neither was I taught it, but by the revelation of Jesus Christ."[2402] "All this,"[2403] said Paul, "the LORD made me understand in writing by his hand upon me."[2404]

10. When Paul told the Corinthians to follow him, he was but praying for them to pick up a mind that said, "That I may know him, and the power of his resurrection, and the fellowship of his sufferings, being made conformable unto his death; if by any means I might attain unto the resurrection of the dead."[2405] Paul couldn't understand why hearts turned away from learning of and doing heaven's will to flesh after being moved by the Spirit. This is why he wrote, "Having begun in the Spirit, are ye now made perfect by the flesh?"[2406] He believed, "The love of Christ constraineth us; because we thus judge, that if one died for all, then were all dead."[2407] Real love for the things of God and of His Christ will kill every other thing that does not radiate that love. Because Christ passed away, Paul believed that every other *believer* was also dead to their past substances to know "that they which live should not henceforth live unto themselves, but unto him which died for them, and rose again."[2408] This is why he wrote, "Henceforth know we no man after the flesh,"[2409] because if the love is genuine, and if the

2401 Proverbs 18:1
2402 Galatians 1:10-12
2403 1 Chronicles 28:19
2404 1 Chronicles 28:19
2405 Philippians 3:10,11
2406 Galatians 3:3
2407 2 Corinthians 5:14
2408 2 Corinthians 5:14
2409 2 Corinthians 5:16

heart is calling out to Christ's heavenly intercession, and also accepts that call, the old preferences to know *God*, no matter the weight of their power, will be held in check for the new and better things given by faith's learning. This is why he counsels that, instead of returning to manners of devotion that are lame in and of themselves, "Be ye not unwise, but understanding what the will of the Lord is."[2410]

11. Because the churches still clung to their pagan heritages, and because they adored the laws of men and women who reasoned on the things of *Christ* according to their low perception, these same elders and church members wanted the true stewards of the Word to be like their erroneous favorites. Because they spoke higher of the Spirit, and demanded things of them that inwardly tasked them, and did also cut them in their heart, they spoke against the Spirit's host. At this Paul wrote, "We dare not make ourselves of the number, or compare ourselves with some that commend themselves: but they measuring themselves by themselves, and comparing themselves among themselves, are not wise."[2411] Paul refused to commend "other men's labours"[2412] as if he personally knew those men, or the intention of their work. By his actions, he was trying to establish a principle that taught to work "according to the measure of the rule which God hath distributed"[2413] to know Him. But what measure is this? "Unto every one of us is given grace according to the measure of the gift of Christ,"[2414] he counsels.

12. The measure of God given to every believing soul is the measure of blessing within His Son's name, even "all the fulness of the Godhead bodily."[2415] There literally exists no excuse for faithlessness in any thing. The measure given to us of God is endless, it is infinite, it is boundless, it is inexhaustible, and it is for ever open to be taken and applied to the weaker portions of our heart and mind. Instead of boasting of what was heard or read from men, Paul is saying to purify the tongue with a

---

2410 Ephesians 5.17
2411 2 Corinthians 10:12
2412 2 Corinthians 10:15
2413 2 Corinthians 10:13
2414 Ephesians 4:7
2415 Colossians 2:9

"Thus saith the LORD." His knowledge is filled with every thing our soul needs, and this is why Paul confirms, "Ye are complete in him."[2416]

13. Every one who comes to His Son will be properly clothed and fed. What the soul needs, no man or no institution can give. Flesh foods cannot satisfy the longing of the heart, and if "the soul be without knowledge, it is not good."[2417] The message that Paul was trying to get across to his hearers was that "the time of reformation"[2418] begins when once "the word of reconciliation"[2419] is accepted. This is that reformation of diet that works to check the systems of the body, to the end that the voice of Christ is not only properly discerned, but is also given power to regulate the life.

14. The only way to begin cultivating a culture of diet reform is to learn how to abstain from self's various members, or rather, "Come not at your wives,"[2420] says the Spirit. The LORD is gathering a host to His name that is not only without the mind and dignity of the religious world, but He is constructing an assembly of individuals that long after the Spirit's heritage contained only within the Building of His Presence. Let us then determine to gain entrance into this flock: "These are they which were not defiled with women; for they are virgins. These are they which follow the Lamb whithersoever he goeth. These were redeemed from among men, being the firstfruits unto God and to the Lamb."[2421]

2416 Colossians 2:10
2417 Proverbs 19:2
2418 Hebrews 9:19
2419 2 Corinthians 5:19
2420 Exodus 19:15
2421 Revelation 14:4

29

This Day Of Our Atonement

1. Christ's heavenly administration moves. This is why He says, "My sheep hear my voice, and I know them, and they follow me."[2422] Because Christ is that High Priest over the LORD's House in the heavens, and because He is literally in the Place of His Spirit in "heaven itself, now to appear in the presence of God for us,"[2423] He now literally owns the ministry of that House. If Christ is "the Apostle and High Priest of our profession,"[2424] then one must consider what the governing mind is behind the office of that priesthood. Of old, "Moses was admonished of God when he was about to make the tabernacle: for, See, saith he, that thou make all things according to the pattern shewed to thee."[2425] What Moses saw in vision when beholding the LORD's heavenly order, that image is what he established on earth for God's host, thus creating a figurative ministration from a living reality. But for us at this time, "Christ is not entered into the holy places made with hands, which are the figures of the true; but into heaven itself."[2426]

2422 John 10:27
2423 Hebrews 9:24
2424 Hebrews 3:1
2425 Hebrews 8:5
2426 Hebrews 9:24

2. Because Moses constructed Israel's order according to all that he saw in vision, when Aaron picked up the priesthood to God, he picked up a service of the Temple involving two specific rooms for that service. "There was a tabernacle made; the first, wherein was the candlestick, and the table, and the shewbread; which is called the sanctuary. And after the second veil, the tabernacle which is called the Holiest of all; which had the golden censer, and the ark of the covenant overlaid round about with gold, wherein was the golden pot that had man'na, and Aaron's rod that budded, and the tables of the covenant; and over it the cher'ubims of glory shadowing the mercyseat."[2427]

3. As it was in heaven, so it was on earth, and as it is was with Aaron, so is it now also with His Christ. "The priests went always into the first tabernacle, accomplishing the service of God,"[2428] and when Christ was raised from grave, this is where He spent the first portion of His ministry. In the Holy Place, or rather, in the first room of the Temple, Christ would fulfill the necessary work to be wrought until the time of change should come. "The LORD said unto Moses, Speak unto Aaron thy brother, that he come not at all times into the holy place within the vail before the mercy seat, which is upon the ark,"[2429] for "the way into the holiest of all was not yet made manifest, while as the first tabernacle was yet standing."[2430] Aaron was not supposed to ever go into the second holy place called the Most Holy Place, where the ark sat, at any time throughout the year except on a special day. When this special day should come, then a change in Aaron's ministration would occur.

4. For eight-teen hundred thirteen years, the first phase of Christ's ministration was held within the first Room of the LORD's Temple in heaven.

5. Scripture says, "From the going forth of the commandment to restore and to build Jerusalem unto the Messiah the Prince shall be seven weeks, and threescore and two weeks: the street shall be built again, and the wall, even in troublous times. And after threescore

2427 Hebrews 9:2-5
2428 Hebrews 9:6
2429 Leviticus 16:2
2430 Hebrews 9:8

and two weeks shall Messiah be cut off, but not for himself."[2431] The commandment to restore and to build Jerusalem was secured by Ezra in 457B.C. Because these weeks are better understood to be years, four hundred eighty three years from four hundred fifty-seven B.C. brings us to the baptism of the LORD's Christ, 27A.D. After three and a half years; threescore and two weeks; this same Christ was to fulfill the word, "He was cut off out of the land of the living."[2432] Three and a half years from twenty-seven A.D. brings us to thirty-one A.D., and it is in this year that this Christ was crucified, resurrected, and anointed of the LORD as His High Priest.

6. At this time the Father "raised him from the dead, and set him at his own right hand in the heavenly places."[2433] Scripture says, "Places," plural, because Christ was taken up into His LORD's Temple to receive a new position from Him. It is from this new office that Christ would regulate the two Apartments of the Spirit's Building, or as the LORD says, "My sanctuaries."[2434] This is why it is written, "Unto which of the angels said he at any time, Thou art my Son, this day have I begotten thee? And again, I will be to him a Father, and he shall be to me a Son?"[2435] "The Son, who is consecrated for evermore,"[2436] at His ascension, became "a merciful and faithful high priest in things pertaining to God, to make reconciliation for the sins of the people."[2437]

7. Christ has in fact become that "high priest of good things to come, by a greater and more perfect tabernacle."[2438] What was established under the Mosaic dispensation for Aaron; which in reality was conceived first by that pattern already alive to God; was transferred from earth to heaven in the body of His Christ. What then, to be even more clear, are the "good things" that Christ is now over? We read: "For the law having a shadow of good things to come, and not the very

---

2431 Daniel 9:25,26
2432 Isaiah 53:8
2433 Ephesians 1:20
2434 Leviticus 21:23
2435 Hebrews 1:5
2436 Hebrews 7:28
2437 Hebrews 2:17
2438 Hebrews 9:11

image of the things, can never with those sacrifices which they offered year by year continually make the comers thereunto perfect."[2439] Christ is Priest over that portion of the law of Moses that spoke on perfection. But what is that law? Christ's office is situated under that which contained "the form of knowledge and of the truth in the law."[2440] This "law" Paul further explains: "Perfection were by the Levit'ical priesthood, (for under it the people received the law)."[2441]

8. When Christ says to His Father, "Lo, I come (in the volume of the book it is written of me,) to do thy will,"[2442] He is announcing His position as Mediator and Chief Physician between man and the throne of God for creation within the conscience of the conversation. "Wherefore he is able also to save them to the uttermost that come unto God by him, seeing he ever liveth to make intercession for them."[2443] What is it that He is "saving" His believer from? It is written, "He shall redeem their soul from deceit and violence."[2444] To be "saved" is better understood as undergoing a process of mental and moral reparation, recovery, or regeneration, and this "salvation through sanctification of the Spirit and belief of the truth."[2445] "By the washing of regeneration, and renewing of the Holy Ghost,"[2446] it is ordained by the Word, and through the ministration of His Son, to "make you perfect in every good work to do his will, working in you that which is wellpleasing in his sight, through Jesus Christ."[2447] This process occurs at none other time than at the present, while sin against heaven's Faith and Temple currently devours the heart of the conversation.

9. Because it is the will of the Father that every believing reformer knows His name, being satisfied with the sacrifice of the body of His Son, He anointed His Christ to be creation's High Priest to regulate this plan of redemption. This plan for the recovery of the inward parts

---

2439 Hebrews 10:1
2440 Romans 2:20
2441 Hebrews 7:11
2442 Hebrews 10:7
2443 Hebrews 7:25
2444 Psalm 72:14
2445 2 Thessalonians 2:13
2446 Titus 3:5
2447 Hebrews 13:21

of every willing spirit to live in harmony with His LORD took affect after His coronation in the presence of the Father, which was 31A.D. Aaron's work took place for an entire year within the Holy Place when the economy of God was on earth, but it was always known that "there is a remembrance again made of sins every year."[2448] The remembrance of sin, or the handling of sin, took place once every year, on the tenth day of the seventh month. This second phase concerning the ministration of Aaron took place within the second Room of the Temple in the presence of the ark of God, and was called, "The Day of Atonement."

10. When Paul was alive, he said this about the second phase of Christ's heavenly ministry: "Of which we cannot now speak particularly."[2449] Paul could not speak on what the order surrounding the second spiritual ministration of Christ should be, for he was only alive under the first. Paul had understood that what took place on earth was to be accomplished more perfectly in heaven under the prophesied ministration of Christ. Educated in the manners of the Jews, and perfect in understanding concerning the law of Aaron and his sons, Paul knew what the operation of Christ should be in that first office of ministration. But concerning the second, it was hard to understand. The cleansing of the sanctuary on the Day of Atonement involved the removal of sin. Should Christ then come to the earth and literally remove the sinner and the ungodly? "Our God is a consuming fire,"[2450] warns Paul, so must this Christ; when it comes time to change His administration; literally consume all things contrary to Him and to His LORD? Will His work truly come to an end when His position shifts? "We cannot now speak particularly,"[2451] wrote Paul.

11. He was not alive to speak on the subject, but we today are alive to know the fact of the matter. Christ moving into the second Room would mean a new responsibility for the believer within a new door of hope, and that grand prophecy concerning the beginning of the new movements of Christ began at the mark for the commencement to restore Jerusalem. At the end of the prophecy, His flock would

2448 Hebrews 10:3
2449 Hebrews 9:5
2450 Hebrews 12:29
2451 Hebrews 9:5

again have to follow Him as they before had followed Him into the first section of His Father's Temple. The counsel for this forecasted time was, "Unto two thousand and three hundred days; then shall the sanctuary be cleansed,"[2452] that is, purified.

12. On the matters of prophetic days, the Spirit says, "I have appointed thee each day for a year."[2453] Because the prophecy begins at 457B.C., 2300 years from this time brings us to 1843A.D., and a correct calculation of numbering brings us to 1844A.D. Previous to this date, forty-six years earlier, the LORD told His then disciples, "If therefore thou shalt not watch, I will come on thee as a thief, and thou shalt not know what hour I will come upon thee."[2454] Christ warned His host that He would in fact be coming at another time, and in a manner best described as a "thief." But because this group of people had just come out of a great sleep from under Catholic dominion, they misunderstood the meaning of His words. As time passed, and as many grew unsatisfied that the expectation taught them regarding the second coming of Christ did not happen, and also because of a failed comprehension of the priesthood of Aaron, "while the bridegroom (Christ) tarried, they all slumbered and slept."[2455]

13. At the end of His first administration, the disciples of Christ were expecting Him to literally come to the earth to execute vengeance on those people that they perceived to be without Him, but they were wrong. When describing the nature of His coming, He went on to say, in regard to the obedient soul who should watch for Him, "I will not blot out his name out of the book of life, but I will confess his name before my Father."[2456] The context of His language exposes the fact that the earth did not demand His appointment, but rather His Father. The work of blotting out sin, and the process of confessing persons, is not a work to be done at any other time than in the presence of God directly. When His face does appear the second time, "the Lord

---

2452 Daniel 8:14
2453 Ezekiel 4:6
2454 Revelation 3:3
2455 Matthew 25:5
2456 Revelation 3:5

cometh with ten thousands of his saints, to execute judgment,"[2457] and not to pardon it; therefore this event of His voice coming to execute justice on the ungodly cannot be what He warns of. The event that fulfilled the prophecy in Daniel, and that marked the beginning of the new phase of His ministration at the end of the twenty-three hundred days, was, "The Son of man (Christ) came with the clouds of heaven, and came to the Ancient of days (the LORD His Father)."[2458]

14. The pattern of the Day of Atonement on earth had finally met its accomplishment by the reality established in heaven. The clouds of heaven are but a figurative illustration representing angels. At His ascension, it is written that He "was taken up; and a cloud received him out of their sight. And while they looked stedfastly toward heaven as he went up, behold, two men stood by them in white apparel."[2459] Them that received Him were clothed as the clouds in white apparel. After He was taken from them, the ones who remained with the disciples said to them, "This same Jesus, which is taken up from you into heaven, shall so come in like manner as ye have seen him go into heaven."[2460] This saying was fulfilled at the end of the 2300 years prophesied, from 457B.C. to 1844A.D. Christ had come again to His Father in the presence of His disciples in the clouds of heaven. The prophecy was fulfilled, "The Lord, whom ye seek, shall suddenly come to his temple."[2461] At this time, in 1844A.D., Christ left the first Room of the Temple in the heavens, the Holy Place, and moved into "the Temple of the Tabernacle of the Testimony in heaven,"[2462] fulfilling the word, "The hour of his judgment is come."[2463]

15. Christ's entrance into the Most Holy Place signifies an investigative judgment of the ones therein, and of the ones who were faithfully joined to Him when He ministered in the Holy Place. Just as it took faith to follow Him into the first phase of His high priestly work,

---

2457 Jude 1:14,15
2458 Daniel 7.13
2459 Acts 1:9,10
2460 Acts 1:11
2461 Malachi 3:1
2462 Revelation 15:5
2463 Revelation 14:7

today that same faith is necessary to join Him in the new Place where He is. As Christ stands before the living God, ministering before the ark of God in this second Room, the Father is looking at the individuals within this Room, and at the door of this Room, "counting one by one, to find out the account"[2464] of their reverence towards every word that comes out of His mouth.

16. Because "God judgeth the righteous,"[2465] we can understand that this judgment is not for rebellious or disobedient individuals, but rather, "They shall be mine, saith the LORD of hosts, in that day when I make up my jewels."[2466] There will come a time when Christ literally presents to His Father every mind who has obeyed the process of the divine plan of their purification. "In that time shall the present be brought unto the LORD,"[2467] but for them to be accounted worthy to find themselves in direct vision of the God that they have faithfully served in sinful flesh, they must have had sincerely obliged to the responsibility of the heavenly dispensation of which they lived under. No one could reach God but by His high priest when His theocracy was on the earth, and no one now can think to reach that same God if not by His "high priest over the house of God."[2468]

17. We alive today live under that office of Christ wherein is revealed to us, as it was to John, that "the temple of God was opened in heaven, and there was seen in his temple the ark of his testament."[2469]Every one confessing to be a lover of Christ should be exactly where He is. What friend doesn't know where their friend is? And what particular individual does not know what their favorite star is doing? "Ye are my friends, if ye do whatsoever I command you,"[2470] says our High Priest. Let us then ask Him, "What is some thing You have commanded?" "If any man serve me, let him follow me; and where I am, there shall

---

2464 Ecclesiastes 7:27
2465 Psalm 7:11
2466 Malachi 3:17
2467 Isaiah 18:7
2468 Hebrews 10:21
2469 Revelation 11:19
2470 John 15:14

also my servant be,"[2471] He says. This Christ has spoken, but who will hear? Because there is a judgment passing under His current ministration, which judgment will determine the citizens of the new and eternal Country of His LORD, our High Priest counsels His assembly, "Afflict your souls, and offer an offering made by fire unto the LORD."[2472]

18. Our current Day of Atonement is better understood as the year of the knowledge of cleanliness and renewal. For every one who carries confidence in the virtue of the merits of the sacrifice of Christ, it is a fact that every believing soul is "reconciled" to the Spirit in "the body of his flesh through death."[2473] "God was in Christ, reconciling the world unto himself,"[2474] "that we might be made the righteousness of God"[2475] in that same conversation through our diligent faith in "the word of reconciliation."[2476] If there is acceptance of God's pardoning sacrifice for sin, then there should be a drawing nearer to His name. This is why Paul says: "We also joy in God through our Lord Jesus Christ, by whom we have now received the atonement."[2477]

19. The atonement wrought by Christ to God for us is not that same consensual atonement between the Spirit and the heart. What Christ wrought on the tree opened up the opportunity for the soul to commune with His LORD's Word. The atonement that Christ purchased for every soul is but the key to unlock the door for the person to be fully linked to the Majesty of the heavens. Because we celebrate our victory over sin in His name, that celebration should constrain personal faith to take hold of His virtue and righteousness that the knowledge of His name, or the science of His Spirit's salvation, may be retained and engraved within the walls of the soul temple. The present heavenly dispensation calls for a true education in the things of God from personally encountering those things by experimenting with the sayings of His voice in the life. Our day of atonement is but the season allotted for carefully

2471 John 12:26
2472 Leviticus 23:27
2473 Colossians 1:21,22
2474 2 Corinthians 5:19
2475 2 Corinthians 5:21
2476 2 Corinthians 5:19
2477 Romans 5:11

perceiving, and taking knowledge of, the operation of the hands of God wrought through faith by learning of and doing the doctrine of His Son. This is why Peter says, "Ye have purified your souls in obeying the truth through the Spirit."[2478]

20. The highest education that one can retain is learning how to exercise faith. As the heart receives any thing from the LORD's Word, and regulates what is heard through the power of the will by the power of His Spirit, "the Spirit itself beareth witness with our spirit, that we are the children of God."[2479] A living experience with heaven's mediation by faith to cultivate a personal and lasting religion is the current work for the believer. "It is the Spirit that beareth witness"[2480] that our heart accepts this lot to know the living and true God. Such a work accomplished through faith on the power of the Spirit of God, and through faith on the ordinances of the LORD's wisdom, is to help the reformer joy also in the will of His throne. The hope is that every willing and obedient soul might also joy in God through His Son, that is, the believer also joys in every one of His ten immutable precepts from daily obeying the voice of His Christ through His Spirit's higher education. This is why it says, "Sanctified by God the Father, and preserved in Jesus Christ."[2481]

21. The Spirit's purchased possession is to acknowledge the fact that they are purchased. The One who has purchased them longs to renew the precious treasure that is held under His name, but the treasure must first acknowledge that it is worth nothing in and of itself. Our Purchaser desires to renew what His blood now owns, but nothing can occur until an accepted atonement to God commences with our approaching God to verify the acceptance of that atonement. The current season is one where every heart that is drawn out to heaven's will is to know the LORD for himself or herself, therefore the soul must suffer affliction that a right and acceptable offering may be made

2478 1 Peter 1:22
2479 Romans 8:16
2480 1 John 5:6
2481 Jude 1:1

to Him. Such an offering begins with the charge, "Abstain from fleshly lusts, which war against the soul."[2482]

22. Every one joined to that Christ within the second Room of the LORD's Temple is under "the fast of the seventh"[2483] month, and this fast is not literal, but rather spiritually applied to build up the conversation's frame. The spirit of the mind is to learn to "touch not; taste not; handle not";[2484] any thing concerning "fulfilling the desires of the flesh and of the mind."[2485] Depriving self of every seasoned delight is the right way to obtain a right knowing of the living God's intention. When the members of the heart are become famished, the members of the spirit will rejuvenate to retake the throne of the sensibilities for cultivating sobriety. Our faith is to capture the righteousness of His course that we may execute His counsels, and daily commune with His throne through His Spirit to receive the precious gifts and promises of that Spirit, that we may retain "the faith"[2486] "of the knowledge of the Son of God"[2487] to become "sober, just, holy, temperate."[2488]

23. The current ministration of Christ revolves around independent diet and learning, for the object of heaven's course is to perfect a peculiar assembly that loves every commandment of God above the traditions of men, and of self. Because Christ now mediates within the Most Holy Place, the believer is confronted with three things that the diet of their conversation must not fail to acknowledge: The Word's Spirit over and within the experience; Reverence to the blood of the sacrifice sprinkled on the ark; for it says concerning the high priest and the blood of the sacrifice on this day of atonement, "He shall take of the blood of the bullock, and sprinkle it with his finger upon the mercy seat";[2489] and, The Commandments within the ark.

2482 1 Peter 2:11
2483 Zechariah 8:19
2484 Colossians 2:21
2485 Ephesians 2:3
2486 Ephesians 4:13
2487 Ephesians 4:13
2488 Titus 1:8
2489 Leviticus 16:14

30

The Sign Of Accepted Atonement

1. "And God blessed the seventh day, and sanctified it: because that in it he had rested from all his work which God created and made."[2490]

2. The entrance of Christ into the second Room of His ministration is a sign that the LORD is finalizing His peculiar host. He is beginning to finish the mystery of His name and character within the members of His heavenly congregation, and that mystery is accomplished by what is revealed in the Room of this event. It is for this reason that the peculiar sign of the immutable seventh-day Sabbath shines bright as we enter into the door of this Room.

3. The Spirit's good will is in favor of a new creature and creation. Because the name of the new Adam; the doctrine of His High Priest; regulates the new man; the new mind born through active faith on the voice His Word; and because "all things were made by him"[2491] in the beginning, His seventh-day Sabbath that He ordained at that beginning is for His blessed and regenerated seed for ever. We have entered that second Place of God by faith that we may know Him, and in knowing

2490 Genesis 2:3
2491 John 1:3

Him, to also receive "the sign of circumcision, a seal of the righteousness of the faith."[2492] This is why it says, "Put on the new man, which is renewed in knowledge after the image of him that created him."[2493] By His sacrifice, Christ formed "in himself of twain one new man,"[2494] and because it is "God, who created all things by Jesus Christ,"[2495] that new man formed by the voice of that same LORD, when endeavoring to fully consider the privilege to know and to interact with His Spirit, cannot, and should not exist, without that blessed rest held to the seventh evening and morning of the LORD's Faith.

4. In such a Memorial rests the faith, the virtue, the knowledge, and the temperance of His Son "through mighty signs and wonders, by the power of the Spirit of God."[2496] Is it not written that "through faith we understand that the worlds were framed by the word of God"?[2497] Are not the mental and the moral faculties of man to undergo a transformation "through faith in his blood"?[2498] If this is so, and if we believe that the same power that brought all things to be is now given to create a new heart and mind from out of one void and full of spiritual confusion, then the same principles of creation from the same God of creation apply to the foul human breath, and the same law of the seventh day to the thinking and feeling creature of God also abounds in strength. The science behind "the blessing of the gospel of Christ"[2499] is held within that law pronouncing the authority of the LORD's power, and we have long since entered the season to grow familiar with that power, and the name of the One by whom that power is wonderfully adorned.

5. What jumps out to the reasonable mind is that the seventh-day Sabbath is not connected to any denomination or line of mankind, but rather directly to His Word through a specific line of work. And further, it will be observed that He also Himself refrained Himself from

2492 Romans 4:11
2493 Colossians 3:10
2494 Ephesians 2:15
2495 Ephesians 3:9
2496 Romans 15:19
2497 Hebrews 11:3
2498 Romans 3:25
2499 Romans 15:29

working to embrace this period of quietness, allowing all who should feel after Him to know that He would in fact give no thing that He did not Himself examine. The answer as to why God set apart a holy day for mental and spiritual rejuvenation is given: "Because that in it he had rested from all his work which God created and made."[2500] In setting apart and blessing a day of rest above all other days, the LORD is assuming that His thinking and feeling creation will be joined into the same work as Him. Those who spend six days exerting self under a work of reformation and renovation, regarding the earth and ground of their heart, and concerning the higher atmosphere of that fortress holding their mental faculties as God has commanded, are them that will enjoy this blessed celebration of the living God.

6. Looking at the language of Scripture, it says that God rested from all the work that God created and made. We know that there is more than one God at work in creation from how it is written, "Let us make man in our image."[2501] That word "us" denotes plurality of membership concerning the One speaking. The LORD's Word is Creator, and if His Word is the main figure of creation, this means that it was His Christ's Word that rested on the seventh day from the work that was wrought through Him. Thus we question, "What does it mean that through the LORD created through the Word?" "All things were made by him; and without him was not any thing made that was made."[2502] "By him were all things created, that are in heaven, and that are in earth, visible and invisible, whether they be thrones, or dominions, or principalities, or powers: all things were created by him, and for him: and he is before all things, and by him all things consist."[2503] Because all of this concerning His Word is true, still let us ask, "How is it true?"

7. Stepping aside briefly from the question at hand, Scripture openly confesses every institution related to God as being drawn from and to God through His Christ's name. For example, a principality is a chief head or ruler in a position of government according to order, time, space, or rank. Because His Word is that Creator within the book

2500 Genesis 2:3
2501 Genesis 1:26
2502 John 1:3
2503 Colossians 1:16,17

of Genesis, and because Scripture does not shy away from announcing this, the chief and supreme day of the Sabbath of this same Word is based upon order, time, space, or rank; which was primarily established in the beginning by this same LORD long before man devised his own systems of religion apart from Him, which systems value spurious "days, and months, and times, and years"[2504] contrary to the living God; holds in fact the sole sovereignty of the power of God. Because the seventh-day Sabbath is the second institution blessed by the LORD; the first being marriage; the Sabbath is purposed to draw the heart and mind to the remembrance of that Creator who, in the beginning, fully refreshed the earth, and who later in the line of His existence within the spirit of His Christ, "being found in fashion as a man, he humbled himself, and became obedient unto death, even the death of the cross."[2505]

8. The seventh day that God set apart is for ever a Memorial of the work that commenced in heaven by His Christ on the tree, and of the work that commences within the conscience when what was set in motion by that event is personally accepted. The seventh-day Sabbath is in fact a law of the LORD's Government, and to reject this commandment is to join thc class of "them that walk after the flesh in the lust of uncleanness, and despise government. Presumptuous are they, self-willed, they are not afraid to speak evil of dignities."[2506] Of such individuals, Our Priest says, "Those mine enemies, which would not that I should reign over them."[2507] The acknowledging of His seventh-day Sabbath is a sign of the fact that the reconciliation wrought by Christ rules over the heart and mind. To reject the work of pressing the heart to obtain an education on the blessed evening and morning that God set apart, only to pick up another spurious day of rest, is to inevitably fulfill the word, "Thine enemies take thy name in vain."[2508] To take Christ's name or character in vain, is to ascribe falsehood to His Faith where no error against His LORD exists. There is no error in heaven's will and doctrine, and to observe a false day of rest contrary to what

2504 Galatians 4:10
2505 Philippians 2:8
2506 2 Peter 2:10
2507 Luke 19:27
2508 Psalm 139:20

He has established in the beginning, and to ascribe His *name* for its authenticity, is to expose, that from within the heart, there is unquestionable belief that such a Christ and doctrine is full of error. We are in fact haters of His Word and know Him not.

9. Nevertheless, the fact of God is given to the one who should follow the principles of knowledge constructed throughout the creation of the world. All things were created by the Word because "in him was life."[2509] What does this mean? "The Spirit is life,"[2510] therefore even in the beginning of the world "God was in Christ, reconciling the world unto himself."[2511] His Word uttered the voice of creation, but it was the power of His Spirit that sealed all things as they were spoken. This is why it says, "The counsel of the LORD standeth for ever, the thoughts of his heart to all generations."[2512] Every thing spoken by God before, during, and after creation is an express revelation of His mind. Who dare violate His immutable counsel? Who dare join into the class of them that "changed the truth of God into a lie"?[2513] This is why it says, "Whatsoever God doeth, it shall be for ever: nothing can be put to it, nor any thing taken from it: and God doeth it, that men should fear before him."[2514] Is it not time that every believer is found outside of the category of him or her that "hated knowledge, and did not choose the fear of the LORD"?[2515]

10. The Spirit looks forward to every seventh day of every week with His host. Because His Word created the world, this day is an open confession that "we are his workmanship, created in Christ Jesus."[2516] This is why it says, "Thou hast given a banner to them that fear thee, that it may be displayed because of the truth."[2517] If one is created by that same Creator in the beginning, then they are being developed by the same life that existed before and after the world. Therefore being

---

2509 John 1:4
2510 Romans 8:10
2511 2 Corinthians 5:19
2512 Psalm 33:11
2513 Romans 1:25
2514 Ecclesiastes 3:14
2515 Proverbs 1:29
2516 Ephesians 2:10
2517 Psalm 60:4

the work of creation, the blessed refreshing of creation is known also to that individual. It is for this reason that it is written, "Be renewed in the spirit of your mind,"[2518] and, "Put on the new man, which after God is created in righteousness and true holiness."[2519]

11. "The last Adam was made a quickening spirit,"[2520] and because this Adam is His Christ, He was made, or conformed, to exist by the spirit of His mind to God while existing in sinful flesh, as opposed to a life bound to the mind of the flesh, as found in the first Adam. The Spirit's Faith is after a second creation, and that creation by the Spirit of God from learning of and doing the voice of His Christ, even like as the first creation did obey the voice of God. In the beginning, the Spirit spoke the word for the earth to hear and do, and today He says, "Be ye transformed by the renewing of your mind, that ye may prove what is that good, and acceptable, and perfect, will of God."[2521] The renewing of the spirit of the mind is exemplified from the obedience displayed by the visible and invisible materials of creation to form a reality. The earth did not have to welcome the voice of the Creator, nature could have rejected the creative power of the LORD's commandment, but every thing obeyed. The mind drawn out to His Christ's Faith is to hear, "Come and see,"[2522] and, "Behold my hands and my feet, that it is I myself: handle me, and see."[2523] From obeying creation's charge; which charge is "the law of the Spirit of life";[2524] a right understanding of the Spirit's mind will be given so that a new creature may come to exist within the soul temple.

12. This work of creation is the plan of redemption for the regeneration and reformation of the conversation's conscience. Just as the earth cooperated with the resources of God, every reforming soul is to encounter "salvation through sanctification of the Spirit and belief of

2518 Ephesians 4:23
2519 Ephesians 4:24
2520 1 Corinthians 15:45
2521 Romans 12:2
2522 John 1:39
2523 Luke 24:39
2524 Romans 8:2

the truth."[2525] Under the work of reformation, the heart will transform from a void and darkened plain of nothingness, to a green a fertile land producing the fruit of the Spirit. And because God rested from the work that God created and made, the example is set forth for the reformer to also rest from the work that God is inwardly creating and making in them. Cooperating with the laws and ordinances of the voice of Christ, and allowing that education to fall into the hands of the Spirit that those charges may find their proper place within the mind, and then taking what is written on the heart by the finger of God to be exercised by the limbs of the body through faith, demands a rest. All things wrought concerning the new nature of His believer is fashioned by human cooperation with that conversation pronounced by His Son's name and office. The LORD framed all things in creation to provide evidence for the continual newness to be developed within His Adam. He therefore saw fit to ordain a time of environmental quietness for him to cease plowing the field of his heart, and to receive the special blessing that He placed within the seventh day for the aggravating labor of the six pervious days.

13. The word "day," as it is used when speaking of the Day of Atonement, is better understood to mean "light," as it says, "Ye are all the children of light, and the children of the day."[2526] We today live under the dispensation of Christ's name under the spiritual Day of Atonement, or the day of the light of expiation from the inward parts. This current season is for personally examining "the light of the knowledge of the glory of God in the face of Jesus Christ."[2527] Every believer is to perceive the LORD's Son for their own self, every heart is to examine the internal operation of the hands of God, every soul is to suffer hardship to personally experience the revelation of the science of the Faith of His Spirit. The experience of accepting the will of the atonement ratified by the blood of Christ on the tree is to compel the tongue to utter, "Create in me a clean heart, O God; and renew a right spirit within me."[2528] The face of Jesus is better

---

2525 2 Thessalonians 2:13
2526 1 Thessalonians 5:5
2527 2 Corinthians 4:6
2528 Psalm 51:10

understood to be the heart of the Spirit's good intention. As obedience to the law of the voice of the Son of God ensues, the light of the knowledge of the work of the Spirit within the inwards parts is to be known.

14. It is written, "I am not ashamed of the gospel of Christ: for it is the power of God unto salvation."[2529] The Faith of Christ is the power of God to the saving and reparation of the benumbed mental and moral faculties of the conversation's heart. "Therein is the righteousness of God revealed,"[2530] that is, in the law of Christ, the equity and the rectitude of God is revealed and openly displayed. Because man destroyed himself, and in turn separated himself from not only properly obtaining the LORD's mind, but also joying in His Spirit and the work to know Him, God did not hold this against him. "When the fulness of the time was come, God sent forth his Son, made of a woman, made under the law, to redeem"[2531] "and deliver them who through fear of death were all their lifetime subject to bondage."[2532] Herein the righteousness of God is seen. "Herein is love, not that we loved God, but that he loved us, and sent his Son to be the propitiation for our sins,"[2533] because "the strength of sin is the law"[2534] and "handwriting of ordinances."[2535]

15. Our Father's plan to accomplish the recovery of the conversation is held within the experience of His Word's will and wisdom "by the power of the Spirit of God."[2536] This is why every believer is counseled, "If the Spirit of him that raised up Jesus from the dead dwell in you, he that raised up Christ from the dead shall also quicken your mortal bodies by his Spirit that dwelleth in you."[2537] The language of Paul is not future tense, neither is it past, but ever falls within the realm of the present. The light of the knowledge of the glory of God is the understanding, and the experience, concerning the recovery of the

---

2529 Romans 1:16
2530 Romans 1:17
2531 Galatians 4:4,5
2532 Hebrews 2:15
2533 1 John 4:10
2534 1 Corinthians 15:56
2535 Colossians 2:14
2536 Romans 15:19
2537 Romans 8:11

mind through the Spirit of God. God gives the gift of His Spirit to every believing spirit for regeneration when once faith on the illustration of His sacrificed Christ is had. For this cause, "I may know him"[2538] only "by the washing of regeneration, and renewing of the Holy Ghost."[2539] This is the science of the righteousness of God concerning man. "Christ was raised up from the dead by the glory of the Father,"[2540] and that glory that raised Him up was the Spirit of His Father, and through this same Spirit "we shall be also in the likeness of his resurrection."[2541]

16. If one desires to cooperate with both the voice of Christ and the Spirit of His God to be a new creature formed by the confidence of His mediation, the word cannot be ignored, "God blessed the seventh day, and sanctified it: because that in it he had rested from all his work which God created and made."[2542] For the new creature of God, the seventh day is a witness concerning the consensual relationship between the Spirit of God and the spirit of His creation. If one should say, "The Spirit of God hath made me,"[2543] they are but confessing to the object of His Son's Faith. Creation is by the Spirit of God from doing His will and commandment for creation, and this is why it says, "Ye have purified your souls in obeying the truth through the Spirit."[2544]

17. "This is the will of God, even your sanctification."[2545] Should the soul under sanctification be without that Sabbath sanctified of the living God? The reformer is to know the light, or the experiential knowledge pertaining to the restitution of the heart and mind to His Word. This is the current assignment for the one joined to the throne of God and of Christ, and because this work is one counseling, "Abstain from fornication,"[2546] the weariness of this lot elevates the blessed day of rest pronounced for His creation.

2538 Philippians 3:10
2539 Titus 3:5
2540 Romans 6:4
2541 Romans 6:5
2542 Genesis 2:3
2543 Job 33:4
2544 1 Peter 1:22
2545 1 Thessalonians 4:3
2546 1 Thessalonians 4:3

31

The Appropriate Fast

1. "Blow the trumpet in Zion, sanctify a fast, call a solemn assembly: gather the people, sanctify the congregation, assemble the elders, gather the children, and those that suck the breasts: let the bridegroom go forth of his chamber, and the bride out of her closet. Let the priests, the ministers of the LORD, weep between the porch and the altar, and let them say, Spare thy people, O LORD, and give not thine heritage to reproach, that the heathen should rule over them: wherefore should they say among the people, Where is their God?"[2547]

2. "The sound of the trumpet"[2548] is in reality an "alarm of war."[2549] There is only one war that the Spirit's faithful must consider. When it begins, the cry will go forth, "They have made void thy law."[2550] Them called "the heathen," are described as, "The heathen that have not known thee,"[2551] and, "The kingdoms that have not called upon thy name,"[2552] who "have said, Come, and let us cut them off from being a

2547 Joel 2:15-17
2548 Jeremiah 4:19
2549 Jeremiah 4:19
2550 Psalm 119:126
2551 Psalm 79:6
2552 Psalm 79:6

nation; that the name of Israel may be no more in remembrance."[2553] At this time when "the heathen rage,"[2554] it is fulfilled, "The nations were angry,"[2555] for "the kings of the earth set themselves, and the rulers take counsel together, against the LORD, and against his anointed, saying, Let us break their bands asunder, and cast away their cords from us."[2556] The members of the Church of God in that Si'on of the heavens, the seed of His High Priest who bear His name and character, will be cruelly handled. But before these things occur, the counsel is given to learn of, and to execute, the present fast of the living God.

3. The heathen hate the Spirit's Israel, and it is not so much that they hate them, but they hate their remembrance, their token, their memorial. They would love Israel if they were not constantly reminded that their heritage is not found among them. This is that Israel confessing before their LORD, "The desire of our soul is to thy name, and to the remembrance of thee."[2557] The remembrance of the living God is the sign of the power of His name, and these that are hated for loving the LORD cannot be hid, for they have the "Father's name written in their foreheads."[2558] The forehead is better understood as that place between the eyes wherein the mind sits. The name of God is engraved within the mind of his son, "for his seed remaineth in him: and he cannot sin, because he is born of God."[2559] It is sin to violate the name and character of God, and because these have been in the presence of God, all that observe them know "that they had been with Jesus."[2560] Being with His Faith, they are beneficiaries of His Son's intercession, and being beneficiaries, they are witnesses of His name's power.

4. Because these have encountered the Spirit's wisdom, and have lived in that power to learn how to properly exercise that power, they ascribe glory to the God of all power. They confess, "Ah Lord GOD!

2553 Psalm 83:4
2554 Psalm 2:2
2555 Revelation 11:18
2556 Psalm 2:2,3
2557 Isaiah 26:8
2558 Revelation 14:1
2559 1 John 3:9
2560 Acts 4:13

behold, thou hast made the heaven and the earth by thy great power and stretched out arm, and there is nothing too hard for thee."[2561] What is that work connected to the creative power of God that is perceived to be too hard for Him to accomplish? It is written, "He might redeem us from all iniquity, and purify unto himself a peculiar people, zealous of good works."[2562] Because His faithful have diligently applied themselves to that "word of reconciliation,"[2563] and accepting the fact of their atonement to God by Christ, they have allocated that power to the more feeble portions of their constitution to "grow up as calves of the stall."[2564] Being convinced that the same power that brought all things to be; which power yet maintains all things originally created by it; has effectively worked within their heart, they are then blessed of God to have "received the sign of circumcision, a seal of the righteousness of the faith."[2565]

5. The remembrance of the ones bearing the work and character of God is in fact His seventh-day Sabbath. The heathen are them that magnify "the chariots of the sun."[2566] Their priests are them that have "burned incense unto Ba'al (the god of the sun), to the sun (on the day of the sun, which day we today call Sunday), and to the moon, and to the planets, and to all the host of heaven."[2567] The institution of the seventh-day Sabbath aggravates contrary individuals because they are not familiar with the power of the fullness of the living God. Authenticity of religion, to them that do not know creation's law, is rather exemplified through "the commandments and doctrines of men."[2568] Because the congregation of God and of His Christ will not violate the name of God for the vanities of priests and elders, seeing as how His name is intertwined with their religious experience, they will hurt the host of God. This oppression will grow worse and worse as the level

---

2561 Jeremiah 32:17
2562 Titus 2:13
2563 2 Corinthians 5:19
2564 Malachi 4:2
2565 Romans 4:11
2566 2 Kings 23:11
2567 2 Kings 23:5
2568 Colossians 2:22

of the perceived disrespect to their god heightens. Nevertheless, "they that understand among the people shall instruct many: yet they shall fall by the sword, and by flame, by captivity, and by spoil, many days."[2569]

6. Before these things against the peculiar nationality of the living God should begin, the heart drawn out to His Word is counseled to pick up the right fast of His knowledge. The knowledge of this fast, and the execution of it, is required today. We know that today is the day for this fast to commence from how it is written, "Let the bridegroom go forth of his chamber, and the bride out of her closet."[2570] John once said, "I am not the Christ."[2571] "He that hath the bride is the bridegroom."[2572] The LORD's High Priest is the bridegroom. A chamber is a symbol of a closet, and a closet is a room behind a door, or in times of old, behind a veil. Therefore, concerning this Christ, we know that He "entereth into that within the veil."[2573] The Temple of God has two veils, or doors. One to enter in order to stand in the Holy Place, or in the first Room of the House of God, "and after the second veil, the tabernacle which is called the Holiest of all."[2574] When Christ should exit His first chamber, going forth of the first veil, a fast that promotes sanctification according to the commandment of God should commence.

7. Being resurrected from the grave and ascending up to God, He entered into the first veil of the Temple of God in the heavens "accomplishing the service of God."[2575] But the time would come when He would have to leave His chamber to go out and meet with His bride. Thus, when Christ left the first Room of His ministration, the saying was fulfilled: "The Son of man came with the clouds of heaven, and came to the Ancient of days, and they brought him near before him. And there was given him dominion, and glory, and a kingdom."[2576] What we have before us is a marriage. "The bride, the Lamb's wife,"[2577] is "that great

---

2569 Daniel 11:33
2570 Joel 2:16
2571 John 1:20
2572 John 3:28,29
2573 Hebrews 6:19
2574 Hebrews 9:3
2575 Hebrews 9:6
2576 Daniel 7:13,14
2577 Revelation 21:9

city, the holy Jerusalem."[2578] When Scripture says, "Behold, the bridegroom cometh,"[2579] it is but pronouncing a call for every willing soul to join "with him to the marriage."[2580] Today, the Spirit's call is, "Come unto the marriage."[2581]

8. Because a bride is not the guest of her own wedding, the people of God are not His bride, but are guests in the room of the wedding. The wedding room is that Room where the bridegroom now finds Himself before His Father, even in the Most Holy Place. The bride given Him is the entire portion of His dominion in God, which is why the eye of faith should be exercised to discern the Place of God, and the Church therein. It is for this reason that the fast of the solemn assembly called at the time Christ exits His first chamber, to enter into the second to stand before the Father, who is making up the guest list of both the marriage and the marriage supper, begins at that time which anciently said, "There shall be a day of atonement: it shall be an holy convocation unto you."[2582]

9. For us alive today, our High Priest counsels, "Let your loins be girded about, and your lights burning; and ye yourselves like unto men that wait for their lord, when he will return from the wedding; that when he cometh and knocketh, they may open unto him immediately. Blessed are those servants, whom the lord when he cometh shall find watching: verily I say unto you, that he shall gird himself, and make them to sit down to meat, and will come forth and serve them."[2583]

10. The coming of this Faith in the glory of His Father is His return from the wedding. From the time He entered into the second Room of His ministration; 1844A.D.; until He leaves that Room, His faithful son and daughter is to be there with Him. The counsel concerning the work to be done by the believer while they wait for Him is, "Know him, and the power of his resurrection, and the fellowship of his sufferings,

---

2578 Revelation 21:10
2579 Matthew 25:6
2580 Matthew 25:10
2581 Matthew 22:4
2582 Leviticus 23:27
2583 Luke 12:35-37

being made conformable unto his death."[2584] "Is not this the fast that I have chosen?"[2585] says the Spirit, "to loose the bands of wickedness, to undo the heavy burdens, and to let the oppressed go free, and that ye break every yoke?"[2586] "Is it not to deal thy bread to the hungry, and that thou bring the poor that are cast out to thy house? when thou seest the naked, that thou clothe him; and that thou hide not thyself from thine own flesh? Then shall thy light break forth as the morning, and thine health shall spring forth."[2587]

11. The Spirit's fast is not literal; "the law is spiritual."[2588] The call to afflict the soul, and to make an offering by fire, is better understood as fulfilling the commandment, "Cleanse your hands, ye sinners; and purify your hearts, ye double minded. Be afflicted, and mourn, and weep: let your laughter be turned to mourning, and your joy to heaviness. Humble yourselves in the sight of the Lord, and he shall lift you up."[2589] Because it is promised that Christ "shall baptize you with the Holy Ghost and with fire"[2590] "according to your faith,"[2591] the commandment is designed for one to familiarize himself or herself with God through His Spirit "to offer up spiritual sacrifices, acceptable to God by Jesus Christ."[2592] Such a work commences when the mind is afflicted, or when faith has a mind to tell the heart, "Refrain thyself."[2593] When once self-development begins under the Word's regulating wisdom, the spirit will accept the commandment, "Whosoever will come after me, let him deny himself, and take up his cross, and follow me."[2594]

12. A reform on diet is that present work to seal the knowledge of regeneration within the heart and mind. This current day of our atonement is but a season to grow familiar with the light of the science of

---

2584 Philippians 3:10
2585 Isaiah 58:6
2586 Isaiah 58:6
2587 Isaiah 58:7,8
2588 Romans 7:14
2589 James 4:8-10
2590 Luke 3:16
2591 Matthew 9:29
2592 1 Peter 2:5
2593 Isaiah 64:12
2594 Mark 8:34

God's redemption from "rightly dividing the word of truth."[2595] An intimate and personal knowing of the Word is to commence within the one who accepts their atonement to His Spirit through the blood of His Son. This understanding "is not in word, but in power."[2596] "Not in the words which man's wisdom teacheth, but which the Holy Ghost teacheth"[2597] "in simplicity and godly sincerity, not with fleshly wisdom, but by the grace of God."[2598]

13. The power of our High Priests mediation is held within His name's Holy Ghost, and this power is in reality called grace. It is "the grace of God that bringeth salvation,"[2599] and this salvation "through sanctification of the Spirit, unto obedience and sprinkling of the blood of Jesus."[2600] Because "the Spirit is life,"[2601] when once faith on His name stirs up the heart to search the scriptures for knowledge of His conversation, "the Spirit of grace"[2602] secretes into our conscience "the grace of life"[2603] as it is asked for, that every effort to execute His words may combine with the human will for proper strength and accomplishment. This is why we are counseled, "He that hath the Son hath life."[2604] This is why it says, "These are written, that ye might believe that Jesus is the Christ, the Son of God; and that believing ye might have life through his name."[2605] The believer is to experience the religion of Christ and retain knowledge of His God from the moment their heart is inclined towards Him. This is why it says, "Give me thine heart, and let thine eyes observe my ways,"[2606] and, "Be ye doers of the word, and not hearers only, deceiving your own selves."[2607]

2595 2 Timothy 2:15
2596 1 Corinthians 4:20
2597 1 Corinthians 2:13
2598 2 Corinthians 1:12
2599 Titus 2:11
2600 1 Peter 1:2
2601 Romans 8:10
2602 Hebrews 10:29
2603 1 Peter 3:7
2604 1 John 5:12
2605 John 20:31
2606 Proverbs 23:26
2607 James 1:22

14. Self-deception occurs due to an insatiable appetite. This is why it is counseled, "Put a knife to thy throat, if thou be a man given to appetite."[2608] Self-denial, on all points, is to deprive the heart of its strange delights that there may be a greater inward capacity to comprehend what the current will of the Spirit is. Necessary affliction to the inward man is better understood as mental taxation to arrive at a rightly understanding the LORD's voice. When "comparing spiritual things with spiritual,"[2609] that is, when bringing verse to verse, and when analyzing one of the LORD's statements with others found in His Bible, and until the point is understood, what is received into the spirit will be sealed by His Spirit that it may fuse tightly into the mind. Independent "communion of the Holy Ghost"[2610] will cause the believer to "be filled with the knowledge of his will in all wisdom and spiritual understanding."[2611]

15. Until what is retained is believed on and executed through the power of His Spirit by faith, the heart will know no thing of God. No thing gives life to the decrepit members of the flesh unless that thing comes from the spirit of the mind, and this is why it says, "The spirit giveth life."[2612] The spirit of the mind is to retain every precept of God so that those precepts may be easily carried out in daily life. There is no other way to obtain the acceptable knowledge of the Spirit's religion other than by proving His saying to conform unbelief to belief. Irrational policies and superstitious ordinances are put to death by capturing and gathering together the sure principles of the His Son's Faith.

16. It is written of an old king, "He began to seek after the God of David his father: and in the twelfth year he began to purge Judah and Jerusalem from the high places, and the groves, and the carved images, and the molten images. And they brake down the altars of Ba'alim in his presence; and the images, that were on high above them, he cut down; and the groves, and the carved images, and the molten images,

---

2608 Proverbs 23:2
2609 1 Corinthians 2:13
2610 2 Corinthians 13:14
2611 Colossians 1:9
2612 2 Corinthians 3:6

he brake in pieces, and made dust of them, and strowed it upon the graves of them that had sacrificed unto them. And he burnt the bones of the priests upon their altars, and cleansed Judah and Jerusalem."[2613]

17. This is that fast for "the doers of the work which is in the house of the LORD, to repair the breaches of the house"[2614] of their character. This is that "work of righteousness"[2615] as enumerated within that "word of righteousness,"[2616] teaching, "He that hath no rule over his own spirit is like a city that is broken down, and without walls."[2617] The foul priests of the members of the heart, the homage paid to our certain sun, moon, and star, the altars and the places of worship that have been erected due to a false education and surface understanding, are to be handled from direct contact with the living God's voice.

18. "Why call ye me, Lord, Lord, and do not the things which I say?"[2618] says our High Priest. "Even to your old age I am he; and even to hoar hairs will I carry you: I have made, and I will bear; even I will carry, and will deliver you."[2619] "If ye keep my commandments, ye shall abide in my love; even as I have kept my Father's commandments, and abide in his love. These things have I spoken unto you, that my joy might remain in you, and that your joy might be full."[2620]

19. Do we want the joy of this Christ or the vain prosperity, and the cruel comfort, of religious tradition? Are the charges of this High Priest superior to the nationally prevalent commandments of men? No thing of man can secure a right heaven-accepted religion. The fast that the Spirit calls for is one ordained to have the doer of it written in Life's Book. The current discomfort will spring scars eternally appreciated for entrance into His presence for ever. This current work of learning right by an abstemious diet will be the life of every conscience within the new earth, even as it is now at this time. This work will be the primary

---

2613 2 Chronicles 34:3-5
2614 2 Kings 22:5
2615 Isaiah 32:17
2616 Hebrews 5:13
2617 Proverbs 25:28
2618 Luke 6:46
2619 Isaiah 46:4
2620 John 15:10,11

occupation for the new earth's inhabitants. If it cannot be appreciated now, and if there is an unwillingness to learn of God from tilling the ground of the heart in His presence, if tangible and corrupt knowledge is not given the opportunity to be corrected through a "spirit of wisdom and revelation in the knowledge of him,"[2621] we will get passed over due to our continual rejection of His name and course.

20. Our current year is a year of atonement, one wherein the heart is made to fast in order to encounter that "fellowship of the Spirit"[2622] for knowledge to regenerate, and then regulate, the dead members of our conversation. This is why it says, "If ye live after the flesh, ye shall die: but if ye through the Spirit do mortify the deeds of the body, ye shall live."[2623] Every reform, and every victory to overcome in what needs reforming, is accomplished through the power of the Spirit's higher learning. A flesh-born heritage is but a dead religious practice, but a soul that retains the Word's heritage from communing with Him, and is "a doer of the work, this man shall be blessed in his deed."[2624]

21. It is time to know that the LORD is in fact a living Spirit, and it time to prove the voice of His love. The soul suffers when separated from what it is accustomed to, but our Father will supply a blessing seven times stronger than normal for the grief endured. The time in which we live is one wherein the will of God is finishing. He is writing every law of His throne within every willing and obedient spirit, and today is our opportunity to quit rejecting His voice to personally know Him.

22. This is the year of the LORD's Faith pertaining to our rationalizing the validity and the certainty of our atonement to His Spirit. This is the hour where taking knowledge of His Son, with our own hands and eyes and feet, will birth living and joyful faith. Now is the time to prove the sacrifice of Christ by removing self from the pattern of existence to achieve a new mind for a new belly. It is time to know His name before religious distress becomes magnified beyond tolerance. Thus "(as the Holy Ghost saith, To day if ye will hear his voice, harden

---

2621 Ephesians 1:17
2622 Philippians 2:1
2623 Romans 8:13
2624 James 1:25

not your hearts, as in the provocation, in the day of temptation in the wilderness: when your fathers tempted me, proved me, and saw my works forty years. Wherefore I was grieved with that generation, and said, They do alway err in their heart; and they have not known my ways. So I sware in my wrath, They shall not enter into my rest.) Take heed, brethren, lest there be in any of you an evil heart of unbelief, in departing from the living God."[2625]

2625 Hebrews 3:7-12

32

The Memorial Of Dietary Victory

1. When we read, "Jesus returned in the power of the Spirit into Galilee,"[2626] in reality we are reading of that point of reference concerning the beginning of the Spirit's new dispensation: His actions are announcing the beginning of heaven's new covenant will. This is fair to say because after He had exited that trial in the wilderness, He "came into Galilee, preaching the gospel of the kingdom of God."[2627]

2. Christ could not work for mankind, He could not begin His ministry, without first returning to where man failed in the beginning, and continually had failed since then. Man lost his position with His LORD by placing his appetite above faith and reason, and the time that Christ spent in the wilderness was to secure to Himself not only a knowledge of the plight of the human nature when pressed to hunger, but to also secure within Himself, after He had endured, power to overcome every cruel and unhealthy indulgence attached to that hard nature. Christ suffered such a lengthy fast for any one who should care to exchange their nature for His. His victory in the wilderness means

---

2626 Luke 4:14
2627 Mark 1:14

a sure victory over hurtful indulgences for every one who believes on the certainty of His person. Thus, an intemperate spirit will now find silence while under the wings of His mediation. There is now power to fight self, and to re-write self, and this power Christ secured through the Spirit of His God for us. From applying our heart to engage in the reform of our conversation through His name, He will supply for us the same power concealed within that same Spirit as we grow in "patience and comfort of the scriptures."[2628]

3. Having gained victory over self, having experienced self-reclamation through the power of God, the Christ of God set Himself to begin His public ministry. What was one of the first things that He did after He returned from the wilderness? What is recorded? He entered into the synagogues on many occasions to teach, and upon quitting His time with temptation, "as his custom was, he went into the synagogue on the Sabbath day, and stood up for to read."[2629] A synagogue a religious congregation, and by analogy, now that this Christ has entered into it, it is an assembly for His LORD's new covenant Faith. For proper context, Christ should be viewed no longer as Christ the man, but rather as it says, "The messenger of the covenant."[2630] Because He is the messenger of the Spirit's new covenant, it is not that Christ came to Galilee, but rather God's own living "faith came"[2631] into the presence of the people.

4. How often have we heard the saying, "Guilty by association"? If three individuals are charged with theft, and only one commits the crime, the charge is not only given to that one who stole, but to all three who had every intention to steal and to assist in the theft. The same saying applies for the seventh-day Sabbath and the Church that LORD established by this Christ. Christ's presence within this Jewish synagogue on the seventh day is Him advocating the seventh day that the Word of His discourse ordained in the beginning of the world. Bear in mind that although He was born to Jewish lineage, this Man, above all men, had no lineage, unless it be found in Eden and at creation.

2628 Romans 15:4
2629 Luke 4:16
2630 Malachi 3:1
2631 Galatians 3:23

This is that Man "whose goings forth have been from of old, from everlasting."[2632] This is that Man who said to His own flesh, "Woman, what have I to do with thee?"[2633] And again He said, "I proceeded forth and came from God."[2634] Thus, when as a baby, and taken into Egypt, His God and Father said, "Out of Egypt have I called my son."[2635]

5. This Christ is the Minister of the living God, therefore as a child does not care to disrespect their parent, so this Christ will not overrule His Father. His Sabbath law He will honor, for it was written of Him concerning every law of His Father, "He will magnify the law, and make it honourable."[2636] Again, if the United States government had to erect a religious symbol on a land devoted to the government, that would equate to the government sanctioning and placing favor on the religion which that symbol is drawn from. The government would be establishing a regard for that preferred religion by them entertaining the symbols surrounding that religion. A reasonable mind would deem the government supporting a religion, and the cause behind that religion. When we see the Christ of God holding fast a Sabbath that did not even begin with Judaism, but rather began in Eden by His Father's own voice, He is in fact placing favor on that Sabbath simply by His presence on that day in an assembly. When we see the Head of the LORD's Church keeping His seventh-day Sabbath, that Church is therefore making a statement that this Christ supports, and encourages the keeping of, the seventh-day Sabbath.

6. Scripture further states, on this subject of recognizing the seventh-day Sabbath, and its place in His Christ's doctrine: "It came to pass on the second Sabbath, after the first."[2637]

7. The Bible has given us a new way to explain the new times. Why should Luke dissect the times in this manner? Why did Luke write in this complicated fashion? Why didn't He simply say, "On the next Sabbath," or, "Again on the Sabbath"? Why did he take the time to

---

2632 Micah 5:2
2633 John 2:4
2634 John 8:42
2635 Matthew 2:15
2636 Isaiah 42:21
2637 Luke 6:1

carve out sections of Sabbath's movement? The second Sabbath is in reality the second seventh day Sabbath of the gospel dispensation that His Christ partook of. And he wrote, "After the first," because this in fact means the Sabbath after the first seventh-day Sabbath of the gospel dispensation that Christ partook of. A break in the history of the religious world took place when Christ was born, and then was anointed as Messiah. This is why Paul writes, "Wherefore when he cometh into the world."[2638] The world is better understood as meaning the religious age. Christ turned the Jewish age upside down, and "the beginning of the gospel of Jesus Christ, the Son of God,"[2639] marked out the living God's new spiritual world, which world did not separate itself from the Sabbath of the Creator.

8. "The beginning of the gospel"[2640] announces "the acceptable year of the Lord."[2641] From this point forward, all things are under "the dispensation of the fulness of times,"[2642] and these times pointing to "the time of reformation"[2643] through a proper digestion of "the word of reconciliation."[2644] A new divine economy to the Word commenced within the first world's economy through His Christ, and this is why Luke's language is so specific. The goal is to recognize the ordinance with the One by whom that ordinance is associated. At the commencement of the acceptable year of the LORD's Faith, that same Faith sealed to the flock of His sheep the acceptable Sabbath of "the dispensation of the grace of God."[2645]

9. The doctrine of Christ is absolutely joined to His LORD's seventh-day Sabbath, and this is why Luke recorded what Christ said with His own mouth: "The Son of man is Lord also of the Sabbath."[2646] Christ could have been born to any race of people on the earth, but He

---

2638 Hebrews 10:5
2639 Mark 1:1
2640 Philippians 4:15
2641 Luke 4:19
2642 Ephesians 1:10
2643 Hebrews 9:10
2644 2 Corinthians 5:19
2645 Ephesians 3:2
2646 Luke 6:5

was born to Jews because His LORD knew "salvation is of the Jews."[2647] He knew that the God above all gods, and that the only KING and LORD in existence, His Father and the Majesty of the heavens, dwelt only among this people, for His Father chose them. Christ wasn't ignorant of the fact, nor did He forget, that it was His Word that gave the Jews their heritage by Abraham; who at the first concealed His Faith in Shem, who then taught Abraham. The people and religious tribes of the earth do not know the living God; this is nothing new. Gentiles have a religious preference that resonates with their lifestyle; this is no thing new. But the LORD's servant longs for His Spirit, and because this is the case, he or she will reverence the things of His voice. God sectioned out the Hebrew denomination to disclose the knowledge of Himself for all on the earth, and for us, we "who sometimes were far off are made nigh by the blood of Christ."[2648]

10. Paul did not write the book of Hebrews just for his own literal denomination, but rather for the Hebrews who should be born to his LORD through the spirit of their mind by His Spirit. The Word dwelt within the spirit of His Christ's conversation, and by His sacrifice on the tree, that same Word and conversation is shared with us all for taking knowledge of, even as by error of the first Adam religious negligence passed to all. To reject His seventh-day Memorial for another of personal preference, and to yet announce *His name* over that preference, is to confess that Christ is not in fact that Christ of all flesh. To such individuals, Christ says, "Why call ye me, Lord, Lord, and do not the things which I say?"[2649] To speak is not actually to speak, but rather to fulfill the word, "He that walketh uprightly, and worketh righteousness, and speaketh the truth in his heart."[2650] To speak is in reality to do, to work, which is why Paul wrote, "Those things, which ye have both learned, and received, and heard, and seen in me, do."[2651] Christ spoke by His actions when He found Himself in church on the Hebrew

2647 John 4:22
2648 Ephesians 2:13
2649 Luke 6:46
2650 Psalm 15:2
2651 Philippians 4:9

Sabbath day, and what He says through His actions is, "I am that Lord and High Priest of the blessed and hallowed seventh-day Sabbath."

11. Every human being who comes to feel for this Christ is in fact joined to His name, and should not every spirit speak all things as He spoke? Must it continue to be forgotten, "He that saith he abideth in him ought himself also so to walk, even as he walked"?[2652] Compelling the heart to fear investigating the voice of Christ will draw that heart away from the true Christ to embrace that false *Christ* of the people. To ignore the blatant commandments associated to His Faith's dispensation, and to yet say, "I know Christ and love Him," is to call God a liar, His Christ a fraud, His sacrifice valueless, every bit of knowledge relating to Him as corrupt, and to confess ourselves as stubborn and rebellious haters of God and lovers of self. Thus, "many deceivers are entered into the world, who confess not that Jesus Christ is come in the flesh. This is a deceiver and an an'tichrist."[2653] May none of us ever join into this acknowledged category of persons in the books of heaven, wherein the Church of the living God, and the Christ and Minister of His Spirit, do also reside.

12. This current year of the creation demands consent to one prerequisite in order to know God, and that is a reform on diet. The new reign of His Son's name did not publicly know the Sabbath until a battle over appetite had taken place; neither will the new creature of God flourish in that newness to joy in the seventh day of Christ until a war against the members of the heart begins. If the mental constitution is unsound, the organs of the body will fail. If the organs are suffering disease, or if they are being overworked, analytic processing will decline, for the powers to think are being sent to handle the troubles of the organs. If the intestines are constantly being filled with material, and if that material is not given the chance to work out and degrade what is in them, but is continually slammed with more substances on top of what it is trying to compress, the energy of the body will die in that one location. Because there is no ease to the organ, other organs will give their energy to that struggling organ for the completion of its

---

2652 1 John 2:6
2653 2 John 1:7

duty. The ability to properly rationalize the things of God cannot occur without full mental power.

13. With the organs continually used, and with other organs lending their hand to help one another because of the abuse we put on them, eventually greater nerve power from the brain is gong to have to be given to the entire body of organs. With the organs now stealing power from the brain, the brain is itself in a weakened condition. What we perceive to be a headache when we want to actually think on some thing given us by the Spirit, or as we begin to feel lightheaded when there is a moment to settle down and study His words, this is actually due to the organs working out the stress put on them. The body cannot lend power to both the organs and systems of the frame while also exercising power to think. Every thing within us needs time for recovery that it may properly function. Due to such a feverish condition of the mind when other members are overworked, the mind will find itself easily aggravated, the heart will find itself uneasy, and the flesh will find itself restless. The primary center for defense against "lasciviousness, lusts, excess of wine, revelings, banquetings, and abominable idolatries,"[2654] finds itself in a deplorable state due to intemperate eating, drinking, sleeping, seeing, thinking, and hearing. This is why compromise with sin and known error occurs. The powers of the mind to combat the natural inclinations of the heart are vanquished.

14. Thus, if our uncontrollable diet rules our life and is willingly allowed to conquer our sensibilities, and if we are individuals caring to learn some thing from the LORD, whenever there is then a desire to hear any thing from Him, this is the condition that we meet His Son in. The power to communicate with Him is spent taking care of our worn out organs, and even worse, when we open up the Bible we are yet still eating! And not only eating, slumped in manners to cut of a proper circulating blood flow to the brain. Due to such a poverty stricken condition, our time with His Son is short, our mind is aggravated that we cannot understand what we are reading, the body is restless because now the exercise is pointless, our person becomes disinterested and a flurry of worthless distracting thoughts consume the being, and instead

---

2654 1 Peter 4:3

of spending time with His Spirit, the time is spent hearing a man or a woman, like as we hear a news report or a movie. We cannot hear Him, to speak as Him, in this condition. The organs do consume a great amount of energy for mental activity, which is why a lighter and more beneficial diet, and a higher regard for the state of the constitution, is the first work for the lover of Christ and of God.

15. A greater knowledge and respect for our own bodies will deliver a great boon to chase knowledge for respecting His Word. It should not be avoided that the entire religion of Christ is fashioned around temperance. His faith began and ended with self-restraint, and if our faith is to be that of God's, and not of the religious world or of self, real and genuine religion must also begin and end with self-sacrifice. If this were not true, Christ Himself would not have said, "If any man will come after me, let him deny himself, and take up his cross daily, and follow me."[2655] This is exactly what the year of reformation means for the reformer. The conscience, who has within himself or herself a fondness for His Son's name and course, is to learn how to properly regulate their conversation according to the knowledge of His mediation. Heaven's will is founded upon the promise of a personal interaction with God alone, and the greatest way to maintain that interaction is to put in check every familiar habit and tendency by the divine resources given us. This is why the Spirit counsels, "Look unto Abraham your father,"[2656] and, "I called him alone, and blessed him, and increased him."[2657]

16. Today is the season to obtain, and perfect, the mind of the faith of Abraham within our conversation. "The steps of that faith of our father Abraham"[2658] educate the members of the heart and mind to exist in that "righteousness which is by faith."[2659] When once the reformer accepts His Christ's name as their personal Savior over the dead member of their inward person, and is then linked to His righteousness by their faith in His ability to help them conquer self, His

---

2655 Luke 9:23
2656 Isaiah 51:2
2657 Isaiah 51:2
2658 Romans 4:12
2659 Hebrews 11:7

power will be given to overcome the base and nether regions of their human being. With appetite now receiving an education by the Spirit, the believer says, "I can do all things through Christ which strengtheneth me."[2660] And being strengthened by the power of the Spirit of God, this same person will confess the new strength wherein they are strengthened with, saying, "Wisdom strengtheneth."[2661] Experiencing the hardship of a famished appetite has delivered intelligence to their understanding of the Word's commandments. This is why "wisdom giveth life to them that have it,"[2662] for it is written of every digested word of God, "They are life unto those that find them, and health to all their flesh."[2663]

17. With the limbs of the body made still by the LORD's breath, and with the voice of the organs quiet by His Spirit, the mind now has the ability to digest the things of God that it may properly instruct that mind within the flesh. When once the spirit is made to embrace an education by the Spirit, it will be fulfilled, "The spirit giveth life."[2664] When once the spirit is blessed by His Word, and consents to accept that blessing, then it will be understood, in regard to every word of God, "The law is spiritual."[2665] The voice of God cannot be understood by the flesh's labor, but rather only by and through the spirit of the mind. This is why we hear, "Be renewed in the spirit of your mind,"[2666] and, "Worship God in the spirit."[2667] When once the mind is allowed the stillness it needs, from a simple and patient execution respecting a reform on diet, then the great things of God will be appreciated. His blessed seventh-day Sabbath will no longer be neglected, but will find open and public acceptance by the love established through self-denial.

18. Thus, concerning what is joined to a right reform on diet, the Spirit counsels: "If thou turn away thy foot from the Sabbath, from

---

2660 Philippians 4:13
2661 Ecclesiastes 7:19
2662 Ecclesiastes 7:12
2663 Proverbs 4:22
2664 2 Corinthians 3:6
2665 Romans 7:15
2666 Ephesians 4:23
2667 Philippians 3:3

doing thy pleasure on my holy day; and call the Sabbath a delight, the holy of the LORD, honourable; and shalt honour him, not doing thine own ways, nor finding thine own pleasure, nor speaking thine own words: then shalt thou delight thyself in the LORD."[2668]

19. The seventh-day Sabbath is "trodden under foot of men."[2669] But if the foot is removed from off of His Sabbath, if ministers honored the living God and gave the Sabbath a chance to add to their joy His name, it is promised that a higher knowledge of His will would be given. It is this higher understanding that causes one to reverently delight in the living God. The Spirit saying, "The mouth of the LORD hath spoken it,"[2670] seals this promise to every obedient soul. One cannot uphold a right diet to the LORD, nor perfect their faith in His Son, if that health promised of His Spirit for His Sabbath day is not received. God has in fact called His Sabbath, "My holy day,"[2671] and, "The honourable of the Lord,"[2672] and His Christ says, "The Son of man is Lord also of the Sabbath,"[2673] therefore to keep the soul from entering the day blessed and sanctified by this LORD's Word is to actually cause the soul to further perish in its confusion.

20. Our diet, along with our faith, plays a major role in our ability to retain a personal knowing of the Godhead's science. A lack of respect for the Word's blessed seventh day will fill our efforts to know His LORD and High Priest with pain, and every proper requirement of God will become a complete burden to our heart. There should be no lethargic demeanor on this matter of a reform on diet. The LORD has not shut Himself out from us. There is in fact a new door hope, and His Christ is in the Most Holy Room of that door in heaven. "I have set before thee an open door," says the Spirit, "and no man can shut it."[2674] The only one who can shut us out of any thing concerning God is our own self. This is why self needs to be re-educated. Because that

2668 Isaiah 58:13,14
2669 Matthew 5:13
2670 Isaiah 58:14
2671 Isaiah 58:13
2672 Isaiah 58:13
2673 Mark 2:28
2674 Revelation 3:8

re-education is a purification wherein the spirit is daily aggravated, and the heart pressed by revelation, self also needs the balm of His Son's Spirit for such an experience, and that sanctifying balm is found within and greatly magnified on His blessed and holy seventh-day Sabbath.

33

Binding Commandments For A Proper Atonement

1. It is true that the LORD would have no one ignorant as to where He is, or where they are supposed to meet Him for communion. The LORD is very particular on this subject because it is possible to render service to a perception of Him without actually carrying living knowledge of Him. It is actually possible to hang our devotion on an image of what devotion is, and on an image of what our devotion is to, without actually having within us pure and rational devotion to any thing. Intimate and personal intercourse between the conversation's spirit and His Spirit will benefit the personal religion. Because the LORD knows this, the one who would receive any benefit from the mediation of His Christ needs to be where He is.

2. Hear what the LORD said of old on this matter: "This is the thing which the LORD hath commanded, saying, What man soever there be of the house of Israel, that killeth an ox, or lamb, or goat, in the camp, or that killeth it out of the camp, and bringeth it not unto the door of the tabernacle of the congregation, to offer an offering unto the LORD before the tabernacle of the LORD; blood shall be imputed unto that man; he hath shed blood; and that man shall be cut off from among his people: to the end that the children of Israel may

bring their sacrifices, which they offer in the open field, even that they may bring them unto the LORD, unto the door of the tabernacle of the congregation, unto the priest, and offer them for peace offerings unto the LORD."[2675] The LORD then sealed this commandment by saying, "This shall be a statute for ever unto them throughout their generations."[2676]

3. The generations of Israel are no longer literal. Concerning the throne and priesthood of Israel, the LORD promised, "David shall never want a man to sit upon the throne of the house of Israel; neither shall the priests the Levites want a man before me to offer burnt offerings, and to kindle meat offerings, and to do sacrifice continually."[2677] A Man of God was to be born, and this Man was to fulfill the prophecy, "A king shall reign in righteousness"[2678] "and a man shall be as an hiding place from the wind."[2679] The LORD said, concerning this Man, "The isles shall wait for his law,"[2680] and, "I will preserve thee, and give thee for a covenant of the people."[2681] Who is this that the Spirit is speaking of? It is written, "He shall build the temple of the LORD; and he shall bear the glory, and shall sit and rule upon his throne; and he shall be a priest upon his throne."[2682]

4. This individual, in whom the generations of Israel were to continue through, is One who sits both as a king and priest in His spiritual office. There is but one figure that we may liken Him to, and he is that man who once presented Abraham with gifts after a victorious battle. It is written, "Melchiz'edek king of Sa'lem brought forth bread and wine: and he was the priest of the most high God."[2683]

5. This Melchiz'edek is both king and high priest of Sa'lem, and this is why Paul says of the Christ of God, "Jesus, made an high priest for ever

---

2675 Leviticus 17:2-5
2676 Leviticus 17:7
2677 Jeremiah 33:17,18
2678 Isaiah 32:1
2679 Isaiah 32:2
2680 Isaiah 42:4
2681 Isaiah 49:8
2682 Zechariah 6:13
2683 Genesis 14:18

after the order of Melchis'edec."[2684] The generations of God continue in His Christ, and this is why it says, "In the dispensation of the fulness of times he might gather together in one all things in Christ, both which are in heaven, and which are on earth; even in him."[2685] The fulness of times began to appear when Christ said, "The time is fulfilled."[2686] Thus, when it should be fulfilled, "The Son of man came"[2687] "to give his life a ransom for many,"[2688] all things would remove from the earth and be translated to heaven. The Spirit's course, along with His host, would cease this physical realm and enter into the spiritual after He should be brought up to His LORD and Father.

6. From the moment Christ resurrected from the grave and ascended up to the Father, God the Father pressed the refresh button on His religious heritage. Instead of a man receiving praise for communicating with God, instead of flesh picking up the role as intercessor between Him and flesh, instead of an earthy temple, instead of carnal practices and commandments that did absolutely no full right thing for carnal human beings, when Christ stood before the Father it was then acknowledged, "Worthy is the Lamb that was slain to receive power, and riches, and wisdom, and strength, and honour, and glory, and blessing."[2689] The lineage of God turned over to better hands. All things relating to God are given to His Christ. "Now hath he obtained a more excellent ministry, by how much also he is the mediator of a better covenant, which was established upon better promises."[2690]

7. "Verily the first covenant had also ordinances of divine service, and a worldly sanctuary,"[2691] and the second and new covenant also has its own divine service and its own heavenly Sanctuary. If one desires to subscribe to this Temple's Faith, then it cannot be ignored that they are subscribing to be members of the living Tribe and Church of the Word

---

2684 Hebrews 6:20
2685 Ephesians 1:10
2686 Mark 1:15
2687 Mark 10:45
2688 Mark 10:45
2689 Revelation 5:12
2690 Hebrews 8:6
2691 Hebrews 9:1

through His Christ in heaven. There is no thing of God on the earth, for all things have been translated by the Word to its rightful Place through "Jesus the author and finisher of our faith."[2692] The last person to sit on the throne in the presence of God was Zedeki'ah. Because he failed, the LORD promised, "Remove the diadem, and take off the crown."[2693] "I will overturn, overturn, overturn, it: and it shall be no more, until he come whose right it is; and I will give it him."[2694] When the Jews were taken captive by Babylon, the kingdom was first overturned. When ruled by the Medes and the Persians, it was overturned the second time. When ruled by Greece, the third. Then after three times of overturning, He who should eternally rule the Spirit's throne of creation would come to claim it. Christ fulfilled the vision, and would later confess, "My kingdom is not of this world."[2695]

8. All things stood before God "till the seed should come to whom the promise was made."[2696] Christ was that seed. The word that said, "My name shall be great among the heathen,"[2697] was fulfilled in Christ, who confessed, the moment He was anointed the High Priest of God, "Thou hast made me the head of the heathen: a people whom I have not known shall serve me."[2698] Because "the Lamb which is in the midst of the throne"[2699] is better understood to be the Faith in the midst of the ten immutable laws of the LORD's throne, and because this Christ's name is the object of all affection, that affection in reality extends to LORD His God. Is this not what Christ taught? Hear Him: "He that believeth on me, believeth not on me, but on him that sent me."[2700] Christ would not claim Himself to be independent from His Father, nor would He compel worship away from His Father. "I have not spoken of myself; but the Father which sent me, he gave me a commandment,

2692 Hebrews 12:2
2693 Ezekiel 21:26
2694 Ezekiel 21:27
2695 John 18:36
2696 Galatians 3:19
2697 Malachi 1:11
2698 Psalm 18:43
2699 Revelation 7:17
2700 John 12:44

what I should say, and what I should speak,"[2701] He says. He is the Messenger and Priest of the dispensation of the Spirit's new covenant promise, and if joined to Him, then communion to God does not end with Him, but rather begins to draw the mind to His LORD.

9. With it established that He who suffered the tree is yet alive and is High Priest over the heavenly economy of His God, it can now be understood that the things of old are for the current Faith of His God. Christ is that High Priest concerning all things relating to the services and duties of the House of God, therefore no one claiming to be a lover of Christ should be ignorant as to what the Temple of God is, where it is, where His Christ is, and what their acceptable and reasonable service to the LORD of that Temple, and to its Priest, is. The generations of Israel are no longer literally made up of a bloodline, but are rather spiritually produced by God Himself. In every willing and obedient soul who hears, and follows after the report of soul reconciliation and regeneration for their conversation's reformation, the LORD has provide the means for every active believer to bear the name of the lovely character of what Israel represents. Them that confess to His Spirit, "I will not let thee go, except thou bless me,"[2702] these are them created of God to be His new creature. "This people have I formed for myself,"[2703] says the LORD.

10. Every one, male or female, may now become a son or a daughter of God through "the adoption of children by Jesus Christ."[2704] Every soul who takes confidence on the fact that the sacrifice of Christ has renewed their position before God to approach Him through His High Priest, is immediately adopted into the fold of God simply by their faith on what they had heard and accepted concerning His Son. Being now members of the Family of God by adoption, it is not simply Christ who we turn to if Christ is the means for our adoption, but now that He has sealed our adoption to His God, from accepting His voice, we are to turn directly to the living God Himself. This is why it says, "Unto the adoption of children by Jesus Christ to himself (to God the Father),

2701 John 12:49
2702 Genesis 32:26
2703 Isaiah 43:21
2704 Ephesians 1:5

according to the good pleasure of his (God the Father's) will."[2705] It is not the will of Christ that Christ is accomplishing, nor is Christ bringing His adopted seed to Himself, but rather the will is of God the Father that every believing spirit may be brought to Him through His Christ's name and learning. This is why it says, "Having made peace through the blood of his cross, by him (by His Christ) to reconcile all things unto himself (God the Father); by him (by His Christ), I say, whether they be things in earth, or things in heaven."[2706]

11. The religious experience does not stop at an acceptance of whatever is first accepted concerning Christ. An earnest and sincere belief will advance to perfect what is presumed, and will prove what is believed to be unquestionably valuable. Because "Christ also hath once suffered for sins, the just for the unjust, that he might bring us to God,"[2707] it is a fact that "we draw nigh unto God."[2708] Because Christ is High Priest over the House of God, it is right to know that in this Place occur all services of health and education. Would the LORD leave His children ignorant of that Temple to commune with? Would He leave His host without telling them where their Priest is? If He was so strict on where an earthy service met, and where earthy sacrifices should have been offered and accepted, has His strictness lessened? If any one was found offering any thing outside of the place where it was required, that soul was cut off from the congregation. How much worse is it for us to be ignorant on this matter, we who are to be brought directly to God by His Son's intercession, who "is not entered into the holy places made with hands, which are the figures of the true; but into heaven itself, now to appear in the presence of God for us"![2709]

12. The eye of faith is to vacate the earth and is to find itself within the heavenly Sanctuary. Why must the religion find itself so elevated? "This is the sum: We have such an high priest, who is set on the right hand of the throne of the Majesty in the heavens; a minister of the sanctuary, and of the true tabernacle, which the Lord pitched, and not

---

2705 Ephesians 1:5
2706 Colossians 1:20
2707 1 Peter 3:18
2708 Hebrews 7:19
2709 Hebrews 9:24

man."[2710] Within the Temple of God there are two rooms, the first called the Sanctuary, and the second is called the True Tabernacle. Said in another way, the first and second rooms are called "the holy place and the most holy."[2711] The eye of our faith is to commune with the living God from within this Place. This is why Paul counsels, "Ye are come unto mount Si'on, and unto the city of the living God, the heavenly Jerusalem, and to an innumerable company of angels, to the general assembly and church of the firstborn, which are written in heaven." "And to Jesus the mediator of the new covenant."[2712]

13. This is why the Spirit counsels, "Look unto me, and be ye saved,"[2713] and, "Look upon Zion, the city of our solemnities: thine eyes shall see Jerusalem a quiet habitation, a tabernacle that shall not be taken down."[2714] This is that Temple wherein the living Christ of God ministers over the things of the Spirit for all who come to His LORD through His name. Every thing within these two Apartments tells of the unbreakable love that God has for us. This is what Scripture means when saying, "In his temple doth every one speak of his glory."[2715] Every instrument within the House of God, every surface, every wall, every substance, every charge, speaks of the Word's revealed glory in gathering and recovering the conscience to His will and wisdom. Every thing we need for a right and heaven-accepted education rests in these two Rooms, and this is why the Psalmist wrote, "Thy way, O God, is in the sanctuary."[2716]

14. Notice the LORD's language: "My people shall dwell in a peaceable habitation, and in sure dwellings, and in quiet resting places."[2717] The LORD has given His people resting places, plural, and sure dwellings, plural. The "dwellings" and the "places" are synonymous with what Paul writes: "Blessed be the God and Father of our

---

2710 Hebrews 8:1,2
2711 Exodus 26:33
2712 Hebrews 12:22-24
2713 Isaiah 45:22
2714 Isaiah 33:20
2715 Psalm 28:9
2716 Psalm 77:13
2717 Isaiah 32:18

Lord Jesus Christ, who hath blessed us with all spiritual blessings in heavenly places in Christ."[2718] The heavenly places are the same sure dwelling places, and these places are the Holy Place and the Most Holy Place. Christ receiving of God the office of the priesthood of Aaron means that He too works under the same phases of Aaron. When Christ ascended up to God from the grave, as it was customary for the priest to render service first in the Holy Place, so Christ accomplished the service of God within the Holy Place of that Temple in heaven. But the order of the first ministration of Aaron within the holy place did not last forever. Every high priest knew that he had "to make an atonement for the children of Israel for all their sins once a year."[2719] This is why Paul wrote, "In those sacrifices there is a remembrance again made of sins every year."[2720]

15. The time for a change in priestly ministration marked what was called, "The Day of Atonement." It was the only day out of the 360-day calendar where sins were actually removed from God's presence. Sins were not actually "removed" from God's knowledge when an individual brought their sacrifice for sin, but rather the sin, figuratively, was held up in the air, it was kept in suspense until the time of its handling; it was but pardoned and not acknowledged until a specific time. Sin was not acknowledged by God to be held to the individual because their sin, instead of being found on the sinner, was transferred to the Sanctuary. The Temple became the place of transfer between the sin and the sinner. As our bank account holds our money as we put funds into it, so the temple stored up the sin of every sinner within the congregation.

16. This is why John said of God's Man, "Behold the Lamb of God, which taketh away the sin of the world."[2721] The correct rendering of the phrase, "taketh away," is that He "beareth away" our sin. Christ is for us what the Sanctuary of old represented. This is why it says, "He was bruised for our iniquities: the chastisement of our peace was upon him; and with his stripes we are healed."[2722] Through His passing,

---

2718 Ephesians 1:3
2719 Leviticus 16:34
2720 Hebrews 10:3
2721 John 1:29
2722 Isaiah 53:5

regenerating, and priestly anointing, we have pardon with God, just as pardon existed between the sinner and the Sanctuary. Our errors yet fall on, and received health by, the One who died for our religious errors and suffered for their remedy. He died so that we could for ever have a sure Friend and a Physician to bless our conversation before His God. This is why it is important, when the heart is pressed of God to ask for repentance, to not only repent with a full confession, but to also pick up self confidently, knowing that we are in fact forgiven and blessed to go on in new strength from our experience. We are for ever pure to the eyes of God so long as we do not lose active confidence on His Christ's name and learning. "Being justified by faith, we have peace with God through our Lord"[2723] to revive and reform our heart and mind by His voice.

17. 31A.D. marks the time when Christ began His high priestly ministration in the first Apartment of the Temple in heaven. For many years Christ would officiate in this Room, but as there was a change in the earthy office, so too would the priesthood of Christ need to enter into its second phase. Sin built up on the Sanctuary throughout the days of the year. The earthy temple was utterly gross with blood, thus a time was set apart by God for the high priest to handle the sins of the people. On this day, the high priest was to accomplish "reconciling the holy place, and the tabernacle of the congregation, and the altar."[2724] Every thing within the temple, along with the people of the temple, was to be purified to the LORD God by His high priest. Therefore, for us in relation to the heavenly Temple, the prophet once inquired when the House of God in heaven should find itself embracing this season of atonement. He was told, "Unto two thousand and three hundred days; then shall the sanctuary be cleansed."[2725]

18. The twenty three hundred days, or years, begin when the commandment to restore Jerusalem was given, 457B.C. Daniel chapter 8 and 9 are one vision. When Daniel says, in chapter 9, that his angel returned to him from "the vision at the beginning"[2726] to explain

2723 Romans 5:1
2724 Leviticus 16:20
2725 Daniel 8:14
2726 Daniel 9:21

that vision, the vision spoken of is "the vision of the evening and the morning,"[2727] or the vision concerning days, even the two thousand and three hundred days. The seventy weeks of years mark the beginning of this prophecy, which beginning is the same beginning of the commandment to restore and to build Jerusalem.

16. The days thus end in the year 1843A.D., at a time when the Spirit promised His then anxious host, "Blessed is he that waiteth."[2728] The disciples who were alive at this time better understood the numbering involved with the prophecy, and the date for the new movements of Christ were correctly placed at 1844A.D. At this time, the saying was fulfilled, "The Lord, whom ye seek, shall suddenly come to his temple."[2729] Them that waited for the appearing of the LORD's Son were blessed to know that "the temple of the tabernacle of the testimony in heaven was opened."[2730] Christ had left the holy place and entered into the Most Holy, and those alive at the time had this to report: "The temple of God was opened in heaven, and there was seen in his temple the ark of his testament."[2731]

19. Both Christ and God are currently in the Most Holy Place of the heavenly Temple. Christ no longer officiates in the Holy Place, for He has moved, and the same counsel of old that He gave still stands: "My sheep hear my voice, and I know them, and they follow me."[2732] It is time to follow this Christ into this Room. Active faith was the means for every believer of old to enter into the first Apartment of the Temple in heaven, and nothing has changed. Every thing that we would render to the LORD should be with His Temple and position in mind. The LORD of old desired every one to know where His name rested so that proper service and blessing could be given and received. The counsel of the LORD's Spirit has not changed, for it is marked by a statute for ever to the one who should continue in Him as the chief governor of His religion. This is why He says, "I am the LORD, I (My Name and

---

2727 Daniel 8:26
2728 Daniel 12:12
2729 Malachi 3:1
2730 Revelation 15:5
2731 Revelation 11:19
2732 John 10:27

My Character) change not."[2733] This is how we know that "the word of our God shall stand for ever,"[2734] and that it is our duty to place that word in its proper context.

20. This is the living word of God, and it is His everlasting statute that every one who would be joined to Him should reverence His Temple and order themselves after the ordinances of that Temple. Because this is a fact, hear the LORD Himself: "Ye shall keep my Sabbaths, and reverence my Sanctuary: I am the LORD."[2735] If the eye of faith is to find itself, by a statute of God for ever to His generations, within the Place of God, then that same eye cannot neglect the seventh-day Sabbath of that same God. Hear Him speak by His own mouth: "My Sabbaths ye shall keep: for it is a sign between me and you throughout your generations; that ye may know that I am the LORD that doth sanctify you."[2736] "Wherefore the children of Israel shall keep the Sabbath, to observe the Sabbath throughout their generations, for a perpetual covenant. It is a sign between me and the children of Israel for ever: for in six days the LORD made heaven and earth, and on the seventh day he rested, and was refreshed."[2737] Herein is a perpetual covenant for the same generations of God through His Christ.

21. This Jesus is the Son and Minister of the LORD's Faith, and all who are joined to Him are not to be without that same Faith. Being "an high priest over the house of God,"[2738] and fully knowing that this was His lot after He should resurrect from the earth, He said, "The Son of man is Lord also of the Sabbath."[2739] Because He knew that "the word of God, which liveth and abideth for ever,"[2740] is but "the thoughts of his heart to all generations,"[2741] and because He taught the people, "Neither in this mountain, nor yet at Jerusalem, worship the

---

2733 Malachi 3:6
2734 Isaiah 40:8
2735 Leviticus 19:30
2736 Exodus 31:13
2737 Exodus 31:16,17
2738 Hebrews 10:21
2739 Mark 2:28
2740 1 Peter 1:23
2741 Psalm 33:11

Father,"[2742] He knew that in Him both the word and the generation of God would continue to find magnification. He is "the Apostle and High Priest of our profession."[2743] "Him hath God exalted with his right hand to be a Prince and a Saviour, for to give repentance to Israel, and forgiveness of sins."[2744]

22. The religion of God is to be closely and personally examined by every one who is drawn to God by the voice of His Son. There is a binding statute of the Word to not only observe and reverence His Place and Minister, and to not only observe the immutable seventh-day Sabbath of that same of God and Minister of that same Sanctuary, but the day of atonement is also bound by a continual statute through Christ. It says, "This shall be a statute for ever unto you":[2745] "ye shall afflict your souls, and do no work at all, whether it be one of your own country, or a stranger that sojourneth among you: for on that day shall the priest make an atonement for you, to cleanse you, that ye may be clean from all your sins before the LORD."[2746] "This shall be an everlasting statute unto you, to make an atonement for the children of Israel."[2747]

23. The season of this commandment is best understood by how it is said, "Ye shall do no manner of work: it shall be a statute for ever throughout your generations in all your dwellings. It shall be unto you a Sabbath of rest, and ye shall afflict your souls."[2748] The labor of the soul is to be that labor to purify the inward parts, and such a labor occurs only by soul affliction and mental taxation. One who endures such a labor will confess, "For peace I had great bitterness: but thou hast in love to my soul delivered it from the pit of corruption: for thou hast cast all my sins behind thy back."[2749] The mind is to undergo "salvation through sanctification of the Spirit and belief of the truth,"[2750] and

---

2742 John 4:21
2743 Hebrews 3:1
2744 Acts 5:31
2745 Leviticus 16:29
2746 Leviticus 16:29,20
2747 Leviticus 16:34
2748 Leviticus 23:31,32
2749 Isaiah 38:17
2750 2 Thessalonians 2:13

a right knowledge of creation's Word is to be sealed within the soul temple for properly functioning members of the conversation.

24. It is to be remembered that since Christ is High Priest, it is His name that furthers our atonement to His God. Knowledge obtained "through the righteousness of faith"[2751] is to purify the soul. It is the accepted righteousness of His doctrine that opens the door for every precious gift and promise of God to be received, and by active and experimental faith, knowledge of the surety of His person is to further recover the person for complete reformation. The rule of the hour is, "God imputeth righteousness without works."[2752] The believer is to commune with God, in all things, through the righteousness of Christ their High Priest, and this is why it says of this service of atonement, "He shall put the incense upon the fire before the LORD, that the cloud of the incense may cover the mercy seat that is upon the testimony."[2753]

25. The goal for the priest during the Day of Atonement was to reconcile the members of the congregation to the LORD's throne. The incense is a symbol of the righteousness of Christ, and that incense covers the ark of God, wherein are the laws that the congregation is to be reconciled to. This is in fact a blessed revelation. Only by the righteousness of Christ may any thing of God be transferred to the spirit of the reformer. By learning how to cease eating flesh meats, the spirit will receive an education that will serve to uplift the mind away from an emotional or superstitious practice of policies, to a reasonable religion based upon learned principles by faith through the Spirit. With the mind retaining the wisdom of God concerning His will for the dead portions of the heart, the reformer will submit to the commandment, "Through the Spirit wait for the hope of righteousness by faith."[2754] With the education given by the Spirit, it will be better understood, "Live according to God in the spirit,"[2755] and, "Worship the Father in spirit and in truth: for the Father seeketh such to worship him."[2756]

2751 Romans 4:13
2752 Romans 4:6
2753 Leviticus 16:13
2754 Galatians 5:5
2755 1 Peter 4:6
2756 John 4:23

26. There is a duty for the congregation of our Aaron, the Christ of God, therefore "bless the LORD, O house of Israel: bless the LORD, O house of Aaron."[2757] Every soul of heaven's will and commandment, who has love for His Son's name and office, no matter how much or how little, is to let that love grow and flourish from finding and experiencing His love. This law of the Spirit's love is not found in any institution on earth, it is not received through "blood, nor of the will of the flesh, nor of the will of man, but of God."[2758] Only a living experience by faith in the sayings of Christ through the Spirit of His God may perfect the love that the heart longs for, and this is that work assigned to every reformer on this current Day of Atonement. An understanding of the science of the gospel is to be sealed within the soul temple that right living may commence. A care for the spirit will birth an ever-growing love for our faith's body that we "may be holy both in body and in spirit."[2759] Therefore, "O house of Aaron, trust in the LORD."[2760]

2757 Psalm 135:19
2758 John 1:13
2759 1 Corinthians 7:34
2760 Psalm 115:10

34

The Work Of Atonement

1. Our current Day of Atonement should be viewed as an appointed season to take knowledge of the work accomplished by Christ on that tree, to the end that what was accomplished should become established within the inward person. This day is that feast and solemn assembly of the congregation of God ordained for proving the fact behind the atonement wrought on the tree to the sensibilities. The appointed time to let the heart and mind encounter the revelation of God that true repentance may birth right conversion, and that a right knowledge of the operation of the Spirit's will should properly convince the mind to cooperate with God in that operation, is now. When this season of true education began, it was revealed, "He shall sit as a refiner and purifier of silver."[2761] This is the year of the LORD's Faith when His doctrine is refining and purifying a special people to fulfill the character, "The law of truth was in his mouth, and iniquity was not found in his lips."[2762]

2. If "the truth is in Jesus,"[2763] and if it says, "Thy law is the truth,"[2764] then in reality the Spirit's law is "in the doctrine of Christ."[2765] That

2761 Malachi 3:3
2762 Malachi 2:6
2763 Ephesians 4:21
2764 Psalm 119:142
2765 2 John 1:9

law within the law of the Ten Commandments of God is "the law of Christ."[2766] That law of truth is the law of heaven's Faith magnifying the righteousness of the LORD's ten laws. This is that law wherein purification is centered, which is why "the law of the Spirit of life"[2767] is ordained to reconcile us to the LORD's Word. This is why it is said that health is obtained "through sanctification of the Spirit and belief of the truth."[2768] The Spirit's Faith is to become a living substance within the veins of the spirit of the mind. The word of reconciliation is to cease being simply a word, and is to become a natural diet.

3. The Faith of Jesus is to be accomplished within the believing soul from personal and active acceptance. This living confidence working within the inward parts is to educate the character on how to "speak the mystery of Christ."[2769] The self-sacrificing nature of the Spirit's Son within the soul temple is the aim of the Word's purpose, and this character is not to find itself within the conscience without applying to the work assigned for its establishment. "Casting down imaginations, and every high thing that exalteth itself against the knowledge of God, and bringing into captivity every thought to the obedience of Christ; and having in a readiness to revenge all disobedience, when your obedience is fulfilled,"[2770] is the work for the reformer. All things that take away from an opportunity to retain knowledge of God are to be expelled from the person, for it is "sin" to heaven's new covenant will. Atonement revolves around the work of purging filth to substitute it for some better and good thing. That soul consecrated to this work of atonement says: "Help us, O God of our salvation."[2771] "Deliver us, and purge away our sins, for thy name's sake."[2772]

4. To say, "For thy name's sake,"[2773] is better understood to as saying, "For thy name's cause, zeal, intent, or purpose." The frailty

---

2766 Galatians 6:2
2767 Romans 8:2
2768 2 Thessalonians 2:13
2769 Colossians 4:3
2770 2 Corinthians 10:5,6
2771 Psalm 79:9
2772 Psalm 79:9
2773 Psalm 79:9

of the believer is to be healed by the power of the His Son's life and conversation, and they are to be delivered from that blemish only by purging that defect by "his name through faith in his name."[2774] This type of purging cannot find completion unless it is regulated by examination, and this why it is counseled, "Examine yourselves, whether ye be in the faith; prove your own selves."[2775] This current season is one wherein self is to be examined and faith is to be proven. Knowledge on how to exercise faith in the sayings of Christ is to gather into the spirit an understanding of the proof of God. Christ "gave himself for our sins, that he might deliver us from this present evil world, according to the will of God and our Father."[2776] Christ gave Himself for us according to the will of His God, and our deliverance from strange thoughts and feelings, and from cruel and damaging tendencies and habits, is to also commence according to the charge of that same Spirit. His commandment is: "Hear the voice of the Son of God: and they that hear shall live."[2777]

5. When any thing is naturally heard, it enters into the ear, touches every auditory organ within it, and the sound is then filtered to the auditory portions of the brain, only to be delivered to the reasoning portions of the brain for proper analysis regarding right reactions based upon the stimulus received. When the spirit hears any thing of God, this same process is not to be neglected. The mind that digests the word of God says, "We have heard,"[2778] "we have seen with our eyes,"[2779] "we have looked upon, and our hands have handled."[2780] To "hear" is better understood as to meditate and to take knowledge of. This why it says, "His delight is in the law of the LORD; and in his law doth he meditate day and night."[2781] To meditate is to ponder and to converse with. "Rightly dividing the word of truth,"[2782] and then applying in the

2774 Acts 3:16
2775 2 Corinthians 13:5
2776 Galatians 1:4
2777 John 5:25
2778 1 John 1:1
2779 1 John 1:1
2780 1 John 1:1
2781 Psalm 1:2
2782 2 Timothy 2:15

life that "which the Holy Ghost teacheth,"[2783] as mentally taxing as this course may be, every faithful individual will pick up the report, "By these things men live, and in all these things is the life of my spirit: so wilt thou recover me, and make me to live."[2784]

6. The only course for personal recovery, and to properly speak the dialect of the love of the Spirit's government, is soul aggravation through mental and physical exercise. Without exercising the limbs of the body of our faith, no thing concerning the LORD and His Christ will be retained in purity and in honesty. Self is to be rejuvenated into a new creature and mind, the conversation is to have its mental and moral powers combine to form a proper person, and the scars acquired from obeying the testimony of Christ will remain as emblems of principal remembrances. By these things men and woman are to live unto God as faithful commandment keepers. From allowing the heart to experience the sayings of Christ, faith will receive great strength, and love for God will be both purified and educated. Thus, the reformer says, "The life which I now live in the flesh I live by the faith of the Son of God,"[2785] and because the conversation is not chained to flesh, to tradition, to superstition, or to policy, the personal religion has the opportunity to think and to reason for itself, and is able to fully delight in the LORD.

7. The experience held within the Spirit's tidings is to be made known at this time. Personal communion with the Spirit of the LORD is to deliver life and power for the accomplishment of what is learned, and it is the execution of what is heard that is to fulfill the Spirit's will within the mind of the active believer. The LORD says, "I will put my laws into their hearts, and in their minds will I write them,"[2786] and He says laws, plural, because the Law of His commandments and the law of His Faith are to be written within the obedient. These things are sealed to the spirit by a process of self-correction through divine resources, even as the angel once told Daniel, "Thou didst set thine heart to understand, and to chasten thyself before thy God."[2787]

2783 1 Corinthians 2:13
2784 Isaiah 38:16
2785 Galatians 2:20
2786 Hebrews 10:16
2787 Daniel 10:12

8. The chastening is a self-evaluation by the mirror of His Son's likeness, and the affliction of self is not literal. Daniel records: "In those days I Daniel was mourning."[2788] "I ate no pleasant bread, neither came flesh nor wine in my mouth, neither did I anoint myself at all."[2789] Daniel has revealed to us the diet required for rightly perceiving heavenly things. Seasoned and familiar delights are exchanged for a plain diet to obtain understanding. His experience is better pronounced as: "He is chastened also with pain upon his bed, and the multitude of his bones with strong pain: so that his life abhorreth bread, and his soul dainty meat. His flesh is consumed away, that it cannot be seen; and his bones that were not seen stick out. Yea, his soul draweth near unto the grave, and his life to the destroyers."[2790]

9. The heart is to receive correction so that every foul substance within it may perish. The mind within the members of the conversation is to be held back from its habitual delights and sensual pleasures. An abstemious diet against the heart's various religious inclinations and dispositions is to be waged by the reformer through the power of God combined with their own will. To retain any good thing, a re-construction of the diet is to be had that right knowledge may not only be secured to the memory of the spirit, but that those principles of righteousness may never be removed. For this cause, the Spirit says, "Understand the words that I speak unto thee, and stand upright,"[2791] for it is that "when wisdom entereth into thine heart, and knowledge is pleasant unto thy soul; discretion shall preserve thee, understanding shall keep thee."[2792] Understanding is the only means whereby the heart can properly face the LORD to continually approach Him. Digesting and applying the learned wisdom of His Spirit is the means whereby one may perfectly, and acceptably, love Him, "and this is love, that we walk after his commandments."[2793]

2788 Daniel 10:2
2789 Daniel 10:3
2790 Job 33:19-22
2791 Daniel 10:11
2792 Proverbs 2:10,11
2793 2 John 1:6

10. "Because the love of God is shed abroad in our hearts by the Holy Ghost,"[2794] the education obtained by "communion of the Holy Ghost"[2795] will further strengthen every effort to reform the conversation for respecting His throne's religion. "Having received the word in much affliction, with joy of the Holy Ghost,"[2796] it will be fulfilled in us, "His flesh shall be fresher than a child's: he shall return to the days of his youth: he shall pray unto God, and he will be favourable unto him: and he shall see his face with joy: for he will render unto man his righteousness."[2797]

11. This labor of soul affliction is "the work of righteous-ness"[2798] for "the effect of righteousness."[2799] The effort to cultivate a temperate spirit through the righteousness of Christ cannot escape the supervision of the Spirit, for it is the Word's Spirit who is the primary educator of this current dispensation of His LORD. What begins, as a cruel force against the flesh, will be turned into a joyful experience if there is a preserving spirit. This is why it says concerning Abraham, "After he had patiently endured, he obtained the promise."[2800] This is written for us to hear "that we might receive the promise of the Spirit through faith."[2801] Active faith leads one into the hand of the Spirit for blessings of health through correction. It is the Holy Spirit that convicts the heart of its falsehood, and it is this same Holy Spirit that supplies "the grace of life"[2802] for our "washing of regeneration, and renewing."[2803] As faith is exercised above fear, and as the appetite is controlled, the spirit will be strengthened by the Spirit to order the limbs of the body.

12. Because the word "day" is synonymous with the light, and because "God is light,"[2804] the day of our atonement is better under-

---

2794 Romans 5:5
2795 2 Corinthians 13:14
2796 1 Thessalonians 1:6
2797 Job 33:25,26
2798 Isaiah 32:17
2799 Isaiah 32:17
2800 Hebrews 6:15
2801 Galatians 3:14
2802 1 Peter 3:7
2803 Titus 3:5
2804 1 John 1:5

stood as the season to embrace the light of the Word of our atonement. Because "God is a Spirit,"[2805] it is therefore the duty of the believer to study after the surrendering of the soul temple to the LORD's Spirit of creation. The soul drawn out to His Word is to cooperate with His will for their conversation's growth and preservation, and for this cause the counsel is applicable: "To him that worketh not, but believeth on him that justifieth the ungodly, his faith is counted for righteousness."[2806] A commandment for this hour says, "Ye shall do no manner of work: it shall be a statute for ever throughout your generations."[2807] Self-righteousness is to be re-educated. The work forbidden of God is that effort to give off the appearance of righteousness, when in reality the heart is in the darkness of that nailed to the tree. It is the privilege of every believer to commune with the Spirit to obtain the righteousness of Christ for a mind that is liberated through active self-examination to receive divine nutrition.

13. The eye of our faith is to see the face of His Son, and the hand of our faith is to be given to His name. The only way to embrace such a powerful experience without resistance is to quit ignoring the influence of God's Spirit over the heart. Honest conversion occurs when once there is personal cooperation with "the power of the Spirit of God."[2808] When the voice of Christ is heard and the influence of His words are allowed to be felt, He will say to the soul, "To day I must abide at thy house."[2809] Our Priest does not say, "I should abide with you," or, "I may abide," or, "I would," but rather, when we accept Him, He says, "I must."[2810] Our advancement in heavenly things, whether they concern knowledge of "the world, or life, or death, or things present, or things to come,"[2811] depends largely up our willingness to cooperate with the divine influence of His Spirit. When the heart and mind both agree to accept His law and doctrine as a personal Savior, it is then that His

---

2805 John 4:24
2806 Romans 4:5
2807 Leviticus 23:31
2808 Romans 15:19
2809 Luke 19:5
2810 Luke 19:5
2811 1 Corinthians 3:22

name and Spirit will rush to the aid of the soul, and will not vacate its temple until it is clean.

14. He promises, "I will not leave thee, until I have done that which I have spoken to thee of."[2812] What is the hope that He has placed upon the soul? "Ye shall know that I am the LORD, when I have opened your graves, O my people, and brought you up out of your graves, and shall put my spirit in you, and ye shall live,"[2813] He says. The atonement of the human being to God accomplished on the tree is the means whereby reconciliation without hindrance became official. There is now no thing ordained, nor any thing framed, to separate the willing and obedient soul from knowing the living God, and from retaining health for the decrepit portions of their conversation; not even sin. The LORD has promised to bring up our spirit out of our graves, and concerning a grave we read: "The grave is mine house: I have made my bed."[2814] The grave is a "house," and this house of our bed is better understood as: "I will not come into the tabernacle of my house, nor go up into my bed."[2815]

15. A tabernacle is a church, and the tabernacle of my house is the church of my heart. The chain on the human being is the church and priesthood of the bed of the heart, and it is this foul bed that heaven's Faith longs to recovery the conscience from. This is why Christ charges, "Rise, take up thy bed, and walk."[2816] We are to confront our bed through His wisdom to recover our conversation. The spirit is to receive strength to its limbs from obeying the voice of Christ, and this is why He says, "Hear the voice of the Son of God: and they that hear shall live."[2817] The promise is, "A new heart also will I give you, and a new spirit will I put within you: and I will take away the stony heart out of your flesh, and I will give you an heart of flesh. And I will put my spirit within you."[2818] No thing from the mouth of God fails, and this

---

2812 Genesis 28:15
2813 Ezekiel 37:13,14
2814 Job 17:13
2815 Psalm 132:3
2816 John 5:8
2817 John 5:25
2818 Ezekiel 36:26,27

promise is the will of God revolving around His new covenant between Him and His child. But a promise is not a promise unless it is first received and then believed on. This promise will not find fulfillment in any one if it is not acted upon. "The heart of the wise teacheth his mouth, and addeth learning to his lips,"[2819] leading the LORD to say of him or her, "The law of truth was in his mouth."[2820]

16. The law of the revelation of the name and character of God is to be exchanged for "the law of sin and death."[2821] The spirit of the reformer is to receive the very same mind of their High Priest. The atonement wrought on the tree is to become a living fact as that reconciliation is examined through "fellowship of the Spirit."[2822] And why only through the Spirit? Communion with His Son's name and conversation will bring one to confess, "The law of the Spirit of life in Christ Jesus hath made me free from the law of sin and death."[2823] It is a law of the Word that the Spirit is the only educator and agent of this experience. The law of the truth is on the tongue because the finger of the Spirit has engraved it there. The Spirit has received consent to work on the heart because the believer has heard, and has followed after the commandment, "Let thine heart retain my words: keep my commandments, and live."[2824]

17. Learning is to be added only from personally searching through the scriptures with the Spirit of the LORD by faith. Why is it written, "The lips of knowledge are a precious jewel"?[2825] Because is it known that "through knowledge shall the just be delivered."[2826] When the LORD said of old, "A law shall proceed from me,"[2827] it was that "the LORD giveth wisdom,"[2828] and this wisdom revealed in the One who

---

2819 Proverbs 16:23
2820 Malachi 2:6
2821 Romans 8:2
2822 Philippians 2:1
2823 Romans 8:2
2824 Proverbs 4:4
2825 Proverbs 20:15
2826 Proverbs 11:9
2827 Isaiah 51:4
2828 Proverbs 2:6

confirmed, "I proceeded forth and came from God."[2829] This day of our atonement is that season to "give ear unto the law of our God"[2830] as it is revealed to our conscience through "the law of Christ."[2831] A personal knowing of "the power of God unto salvation to every one that believeth"[2832] is the divine appointment of this hour. God Himself may have ordained a course to free the mind from religious corruption, and His Son and Spirit may govern deliverance, but true deliverance, which is reformation from spiritual falsehood to right principles of existence, is through obtained knowledge.

18. "It is the spirit that quickeneth"[2833] the mind of the flesh from the understanding it retains by the Spirit, and it is the application of that knowledge, and by faith, that renders one just, and their recovery certain. The believer is to know the certainty of the promise of God. They are to prove His intentions. Love for God will not put on hold the desire to search for Him. Whether in confusion, or distress, or anxiety, or perplexity, or sorrow, or joy; in ignorance, in death, in exhaustion, in hunger, in thirst, in nakedness; "by pureness, by knowledge, by longsuffering, by kindness, by the Holy Ghost, by love unfeigned";[2834] for every particle of honest and sincere love, we are honored to be "always bearing about in the body the dying of the Lord Jesus, that the life also of Jesus might be made manifest in our body."[2835] The life and mind of Christ is to be transferred into the believer that they may "speak the mystery of Christ"[2836] through "the work of faith with power."[2837]

19. Because "the Spirit is life,"[2838] "he that hath the Son hath life."[2839] The soul temple is to undergo a cleansing "by the washing of

---

2829 John 8:42
2830 Isaiah 1:10
2831 Galatians 6:2
2832 Romans 1:16
2833 John 6:63
2834 2 Corinthians 6:6
2835 2 Corinthians 4:10
2836 Colossians 4:3
2837 2 Thessalonians 1:11
2838 Romans 8:10
2839 1 John 5:12

regeneration, and renewing of the Holy Ghost."[2840] The atonement to God is to become a living reality only through the Spirit of God by our active faith in the precepts of His Son's name. The work of faith is currently the only acceptable work of righteousness. The soul is to be drawn out to the LORD's Word; the heart is to embrace open surgery for repentance and conversion by the operation of the Word personally. The present call is a movement to grow fond of "weeping, and to mourning, and to baldness, and to girding with sackcloth,"[2841] for it is written, "Because thine heart was tender, and thou didst humble thyself before God, when thou heardest his words against this place, and against the inhabitants thereof, and humbledst thyself before me, and didst rend thy clothes, and weep before me; I have even heard thee also, saith the LORD."[2842]

20. The time approaches when it will be that "the wrath of God is revealed from heaven against all ungodliness and unrighteousness of men, who hold the truth in unrighteousness."[2843] Because "we are all as an unclean thing, and all our righteousnesses are as filthy rags,"[2844] our current profession of heaven's Faith without His Son's mind amounts to the same thing. The conversation is to be corrected. To hold the law of the truth in unrighteousness is to fail to represent both God and Christ in our dress, in our speech, in our diet, in our business transactions, in our temper, in our affections, in our rationality, and so forth. This is why it is not just the law of the truth that is to become apart of the diet, but also the truth that the law of Christ magnifies. Self is properly managed in full by a regard for every one of the LORD's Ten Commandments. His Faith sprung out of these ten precepts, and to these precepts the His faith returns. "Unto the place from whence the rivers come, thither they return again,"[2845] and if there is a subscription to His Son's knowledge, then there is to be a return to the Place from where that subscription not only fell out from, but commenced.

2840 Titus 3:5
2841 Isaiah 22:12
2842 2 Chronicles 34:27
2843 Romans 1:18
2844 Isaiah 64:6
2845 Ecclesiastes 1:7

21. Since the Spirit of God is the primary educator of His Faith, it cannot be forgotten that this is that same "Spirit of truth, which proceedeth from the Father."[2846] Both the law of the Faith of Christ and the law of the Spirit of life come out from their LORD as the Physicians of soul recovery to obtain His moral image. It is the Father that issued every precious gift and promise to know Him, and by these same resources He says, "Be ye reconciled to God."[2847] The soul temple, when once that reconciliation is given active power to live, is to become "an habitation of God through the Spirit."[2848] A new tabernacle is to be reared up within the spirit of the mind, and the brain of the spirit is to hold, and is to rightly provoke for execution, every law of commandment from the living God's mouth. Welcoming the Spirit to educate the spirit to govern the members of the body will lead that Spirit to engrave the principles of His LORD within the mind. "That eternal life, which was with the Father, and was manifested unto us"[2849] in the person of His Christ, is ordained to do for us as it still does for Him. The will of God is to continually repeat the saying in every believer: "The Word was made flesh."[2850]

22. When there is an apparent effort to quit wrongfully afflicting the soul from hurting, and overworking the stomach, then the right work and effect of righteousness may envelop the experience. The same Spirit and Faith that came out from God are ordained to bring to God. A regard for health is strengthened when repentance has consumed the being, and a willingness to quench the imaginative spirit of the heart, along with every hurtful indulgence, is born through a regard for the character of God, and from experiencing the magnificence of His name. Heaven's benevolent will is the revealed image of God, and an honest conversation in that confidence will eventually allow the eyes to be confronted with the commandments that they have broken. A faithful continuance to know the LORD has allowed the process of sanctification to transform the moral faculties to match His. The will of

---

2846 John 15:26
2847 2 Corinthians 5:20
2848 Ephesians 2:22
2849 1 John 1:2
2850 1 John 1:14

this LORD is the sanctification of the spirit of our mind, which sanctification is the process of inward recovery to find harmony with every one of His commandments. This is that work of atonement to assure our hearts before Him.

35

The Work To Combat Forces

1. "And I beheld another beast coming up out of the earth."[2851]

2. Viewing this statement in a most natural understanding, it is understood that John saw a second beast coming up out of the earth. In a most plain understanding, to come up out of the earth would mean to come up out of some depth of the earth. It is therefore fair to say that this second beast ascends from some pit, for to say that it has come up from the earth means to say that it has come up from under the earth, to then arise above it. It is again reasonable to assume that if this second beast has arisen from the earth, then it has a brother who also has achieved this same lot, for John saw "another," a second beast coming up out of the earth, the first justifiably accomplishing this feat before it. These notions are affirmed from how it is said: "I shall bring thee down with them that descend into the pit, with the people of old time, and shall set thee in the low parts of the earth."[2852]

3. The only way to come up from the earth is to first have descended into some lower portion of it. When once descended into the earth, to come up out of the earth is to arise out of those same lower portions to break the ground of the earth, to stand upon the ground of the earth.

2851 Revelation 13:11
2852 Ezekiel 26:20

To again confirm these things, we view an event of old: "If the LORD make a new thing, and the earth open her mouth, and swallow them up, with all that appertain unto them, and they go down quick into the pit; then ye shall understand that these men have provoked the LORD."[2853] "They, and all that appertained to them, went down alive into the pit, and the earth closed upon them: and they perished from among the congregation."[2854] Whatever is in this pit within the earth, it is there because the earth has swallowed it up. It is therefore fair to say that when John saw this other beast, he saw this second beast coming up not simply out of the earth, but out of the bottomless pit of the earth.

4. The first beast that came up from the pit of the earth must be understood in order to ascertain the work and mind of the second. This second beast of the earth that John saw causes every one on the earth to worship the first beast before it. The first beast, that leopard beast before this new republic of the earth, came from out of the sea and not the earth, so this kingdom cannot be the first kingdom to have arisen out the earth per se. Concerning this leopard beast, John writes, "I stood upon the sand of the sea, and saw a beast rise up out of the sea."[2855] This beast does not concern us, but if we should follow the tone of the vision given to John, we will arrive at our desired entity. We read: "When they shall have finished their testimony, the beast that ascendeth out of the bottomless pit shall make war against them, and shall overcome them, and kill them."[2856]

5. This portion of the vision is speaking on the "thousand two hundred and threescore days,"[2857] or, the "forty and two months"[2858] given to the leopard beast before the history of the new earth beast should commence. John records of this leopard beast, "There was given unto him a mouth speaking great things and blasphemies; and power was given unto him to continue forty and two months."[2859] This power

2853 Numbers 16:30
2854 Numbers 16:33
2855 Revelation 13:1
2856 Revelation 11:7
2857 Revelation 11:3
2858 Revelation 11:2
2859 Revelation 13:5

"cast down the truth to the ground; and it practised, and prospered."[2860] The record of this beast's history began when it was fulfilled, "They shall pollute the sanctuary of strength, and shall take away the daily sacrifice, and they shall place the abomination that maketh desolate."[2861] This leopard beast is that abomination that maketh desolate, and it is by this power that the two witnesses of the living God on the earth were to be "tread under foot forty and two months."[2862]

6. Those two witnesses of God "have power to shut heaven"[2863] "and to smite the earth with all plagues."[2864] He that rules heaven fulfills the saying, "Eli'as"[2865] "prayed earnestly that it might not rain."[2866] "He prayed again, and the heaven gave rain."[2867] He who governs all plagues fulfills the word, "I will send thee into Egypt."[2868] "This is that Moses"[2869] whom the LORD instructed to tell Pharaoh, "I will at this time send all my plagues upon thine heart, and upon thy servants, and upon thy people; that thou mayest know that there is none like me in all the earth."[2870] The two witnesses of God fulfill the character of the two representative men of God, for they represent Moses, a symbol of the Law of God, and Elijah, a symbol of the spirit of prophecy, as both are found within the old and the new testaments of the Bible. "If any man will hurt them, fire proceedeth out of their mouth, and devoureth their enemies,"[2871] and because the leopard beast cast these witnesses of the Spirit to the ground, and also destroyed those that honored them, it says of this beast, "He that killeth with the sword must be killed with the sword."[2872]

2860 Daniel 8:12
2861 Daniel 11:31
2862 Revelation 11:2
2863 Revelation 11:6
2864 Revelation 11:6
2865 James 5:17
2866 James 5:17
2867 James 5:18
2868 Acts 7:34
2869 Acts 7:27
2870 Exodus 9:14
2871 Revelation 11:5
2872 Revelation 13:10

7. The leopard beast is that institution "who opposeth and exalteth himself above all that is called God, or that is worshipped; so that he as God sitteth in the temple of God, shewing himself that he is God,"[2873] but it was through that beast "which spiritually is called Sodom and Egypt, where also our Lord was crucified,"[2874] that the leopard beast accomplished its work. It is important to know that the leopard beast is in fact Rome under its Papal phase, for under Papal Rome the word of God was "clothed in sackcloth."[2875] Nevertheless, when the two witnesses of the Word were to have finished their mission, a cruel force was to war against them as oppressors separate from their Papal head.

8. A spiritual rendition of some thing is not a literal rendition, but is rather the image of the literal form. Spiritually this cruel beast is recognized as being Egypt, for it has within it the mind that says, "Who is the LORD, that I should obey his voice"?[2876] This is an atheistic disposition fulfilling the character, "The wicked, through the pride of his countenance, will not seek after God: God is not in all his thoughts."[2877] The natural heart of this beast utters the sentiment, "Who is the LORD?"[2878]

9. Again, this beast is spiritually characterized as Sodom. Concerning Sodom we read: "This was the iniquity of thy sister Sodom, pride, fulness of bread, and abundance of idleness was in her and in her daughters."[2879] This beast would know only itself and its appetite, and would base its existence off of the *knowledge* derived from its natural senses. Should we travel back in time, we would find ourselves "among winebibbers; among riotous eaters of flesh."[2880] Because of their disposition to entertain the natural portions of the human being, Scripture says that "the men of Sodom were wicked and sinners before the LORD exceedingly."[2881] This is said of them because it was known that "Sodom and Gomor'rha, and the cities about them in like manner,

---

2873 2 Thessalonians 2:4
2874 Revelation 11:8
2875 Revelation 11:3
2876 Exodus 5:2
2877 Psalm 10:4
2878 Proverbs 30:9
2879 Ezekiel 16:49
2880 Proverbs 23:20
2881 Genesis 13:13

giving themselves over to fornication, and going after strange flesh,"[2882] were but "natural brute beasts"[2883] "that walk after the flesh in the lust of uncleanness, and despise government."[2884]

10. The first beast that came up out of this pit is an atheistic and idolatrously flesh-based people, and about the year 1793, the French fulfilled the vision in the midst of their revolution. Joined to the French, before their revolution began, the Catholic Church further enflamed herself against supposed heretics to her doctrine. Scripture doesn't simply say that this beast is spiritually Egypt and Sodom, but it is the place "where also our Lord was crucified."[2885] Besides the body of the doctrine of Christ crucified by the Catholic Church, the body of the believers of Christ also suffered. The Inquisition to silence, and to combat all suspected heretics of the Catholic persuasion, began in France about the twelfth century. Christ was crucified in the person of His faithful believers, for many "were slain for the word of God, and for the testimony which they held."[2886] It was said, "These shall make war with the Lamb,"[2887] but them that suffered "overcame him by the blood of the Lamb, and by the word of their testimony; and they loved not their lives unto the death."[2888]

11. If the first beast that came up out of the earth served to cause such devastation "against God, to blaspheme his name, and his tabernacle, and them that dwell in heaven,"[2889] should the second beast to come up out of the earth be any different? Joined to the first beast of the pit, the Catholic church was to fulfill the word, "He shall speak great words against the most High, and shall wear out the saints of the most High, and think to change times and laws,"[2890] and should not the same thing be expected under the reign of that new republic to arise? Howbeit, while the Papacy accomplished its work against the LORD's

---

2882 Jude 1:7
2883 1 Peter 2:12
2884 2 Peter 2:10
2885 Revelation 11:8
2886 Revelation 6:9
2887 Revelation 17:14
2888 Revelation 12:11
2889 Revelation 13:6
2890 Daniel 7:25

Faith in every way, she was to face an end similar to that which she had inflicted. The ones who gave her power, "these shall hate the whore, and shall make her desolate and naked,"[2891] it was prophesied. While God used the first beast that came out of the earth to fulfill His will against Himself; for it was "put in their hearts to fulfill his will";[2892] they were at the same time the helping hand of His Word. This is why it says, "The earth helped the woman."[2893]

12. The events of the French Revolution fulfilled the word, "And the same hour was there a great earthquake."[2894] To better explain the meaning behind an earthquake, it is written, "There was a great earthquake, so that the foundations of the prison were shaken."[2895] An earthquake is a symbol of an overthrowing. The foundations of the leopard beast were overthrown, and "his power, and his seat, and great authority,"[2896] was stripped away. At this time it was fulfilled, "I saw one of his heads as it were wounded to death."[2897] The Revolution "swallowed up the flood which the dragon cast out of his mouth,"[2898] for "the earth helped the woman, and the earth opened her mouth."[2899] Because these events of liberty were taking place, the tremors from such a quaking against Papal authority, even before the time of the end of the leopard beast, were being felt across the entire world. That woman of God, who had suffered for "a thousand two hundred and threescore days,"[2900] or rather years, under Papal rule, was finally able to openly escape into her own place, to live in peace. Them that saw the fulfillment of the LORD's word "were affrighted, and gave glory to the God of heaven."[2901]

2891 Revelation 17:16
2892 Revelation 17:17
2893 Revelation 12:16
2894 Revelation 11:13
2895 Acts 16:26
2896 Revelation 13:2
2897 Revelation 13:3
2898 Revelation 12:16
2899 Revelation 12:16
2900 Revelation 11:13
2901 Revelation 11:13

13. To this woman, a new land was given that fulfilled the word, "Behold, I create new heavens and a new earth: and the former shall not be remembered, nor come into mind."[2902] Concerning the definition of the earth, we read: "Shall the earth be made to bring forth in one day? or shall a nation be born at once?"[2903] The earth is a figurative representation of a nation, for a new nation was to be founded on the earth. And concerning the heavens, we read: "God made two great lights; the greater light to rule the day, and the lesser light to rule the night: he made the stars also."[2904] The sun and the moon and the stars represent a hierarchy of government. They represent "the king, and his counsellors, and his lords,"[2905] and in a fashion best observed from how it is written: "It pleased Dari'us to set over the kingdom an hundred and twenty princes, which should be over the whole kingdom; and over these three presidents; of whom Daniel was first: that the princes might give accounts unto them, and the king should have no damage."[2906]

14. This new land was to abide by the principle, "Nation (denomination) shall not lift up a sword against nation, neither shall they learn war any more. But they shall sit every man under his vine and under his fig tree; and none shall make them afraid."[2907] To further support this devotion to liberty of religious conscience, and of religion, for the perpetually safe pursuit of happiness without government interference, this new land was to be governed by an Executive, a President; a legislative power called Congress; and a judicial power called the Supreme Court. Each power was to exist separately, yet under a most perfect union, to destroy every chance to return to that former tyrannical reign of terror experienced by the fathers of the old world. Because of the catastrophic events that took place in Europe, the earth was given a new kingdom inspired by the mind of the Spirit's doctrine, that is, freedom of conscience without unnecessary government encroachment. The United States thus quickly blossomed into a superpower to fill up and

---

2902 Isaiah 65:17
2903 Isaiah 66:8
2904 Genesis 1:16
2905 Ezra 8:25
2906 Daniel 6:1,2
2907 Micah 4:3,4

conquer the entire earth, but this blessed land will not forever maintain its founding principles. Out of it, out of the earth, a new republic contrary to it will arise contrary.

15. The place where Christ was crucified was found under the reign of the first beast that came up out of the earth, where also the spirit of the people was both spiritually Sodom and Egypt. Nothing less should be expected for this other beast coming up out of the earth, but rather every thing possibly worse. The question then arises from the Spirit to every soul currently professing His name: "When thou art spoiled, what wilt thou do? Though thou clothest thyself with crimson, though thou deckest thee with ornaments of gold, though thou rentest thy face with painting, in vain shalt thou make thyself fair; thy lovers will despise thee, they will seek thy life."[2908] "Can thine heart endure, or can thine hands be strong, in the days that I shall deal with thee? I the LORD have spoken it, and will do it."[2909]

16. The LORD has told us the mission of this new republic, how that "he exerciseth all the power of the first beast before him"[2910] to eventually have "the earth and them which dwell therein to worship the first beast."[2911] The leopard beast is that beast before this new republic, "and power was given him,"[2912] the leopard beast, "over all kindreds, and tongues, and nations."[2913] According to the word of the LORD, the Land of Liberty will forsake the principles of its Constitution to pick up a new mind. If in fact it will exercise all the power of the first beast before it, then it will abuse its civil authority, as did the leopard beast, and will also compel that civil authority to control the conscience of the people under its power, and most certainly to demand homage to the religion of its preference. This is what the first beast before it did, and the result was that man sought to become *God*, and by force demanded other men to honor the perception of his thoughts, which resulted in an exhibition of what human nature may become when the foul mind

---

2908 Jeremiah 4:30
2909 Ezekiel 22:14
2910 Revelation 13:12
2911 Revelation 13:12
2912 Revelation 13:7
2913 Revelation 13:7

behind it is enflamed without the LORD and His High Priest. Thus the word was fulfilled against the Spirit's host, and against His name, and His Sanctuary, by the craft behind this power: "The beast that ascendeth out of the bottomless pit shall make war against them, and shall overcome them, and kill them."[2914]

17. This is the only end that this new republic serves to accomplish, and should we be alive under its formation, the only means to keep ourselves sober will be to reproduce this same spirit of old: "They overcame him by the blood of the Lamb, and by the word of their testimony; and they loved not their lives unto the death."[2915] Before she who received her deadly wound is returned to full strength, the faithful of God have to first overcome that which prepares her way. This new republic, and the mind centered within it, is the first great test for the Spirit's assembly. Spiritual Sodom and Egypt will have a new name to abide by, and the body of our High Priest's knowledge will again be openly crucified. Herein the LORD asks, "Can your heart endure these times when I should sanction them?" As we currently are, we who profess to be servants of both the Word and His Christ name, the answer is no, which is why these times have not yet arrived. God Himself is in fact holding back these events from happening that He may have a purified host to represent His name to a very strange age. Therefore, "Hurt not the earth, neither the sea, nor the trees, till we have sealed the servants of our God in their foreheads,"[2916] says the LORD.

18. The current season is one of personal and active atonement, and the current counsel is, "Be thou faithful unto death, and I will give thee a crown of life."[2917] The death, at this time, is not literal, but rather serves to fulfill the word, "My heart is sore pained within me."[2918] The counsel is, "Ye shall afflict your souls,"[2919] and this soul affliction is heart agitation, it is mental taxation from diligently reviewing the voice

---

2914 Revelation 11:7
2915 Revelation 12:11
2916 Revelation 7:3
2917 Revelation 2:10
2918 Psalm 55:4
2919 Leviticus 23:27

of God, it is a fasting from self to prove the will of His Spirit. That crown of life given for striving after understanding the fact behind the voice and commandment of His Word fulfills the saying, "Blessed is the man that endureth temptation: for when he is tried, he shall receive the crown of life, which the Lord hath promised to them that love him."[2920]

19. Because "the Spirit is life,"[2921] the crown of life is the crown of the Spirit, and because this same Spirit is "the Spirit of grace,"[2922] the one who willingly presses themselves by His Son's Faith, and in the presence of His face, will receive into their spirit "the grace of life"[2923] to further combat personal all sin against His LORD's name, and to receive understanding to continue reforming from that error. This is why it says, "Where sin abounded, grace did much more abound."[2924] Because sin fully consumes the entire conversation, the power of the grace of God, when accepted and applied to, will consume the entire conversation even more than sin. It is "the grace of God that bringeth salvation,"[2925] and this salvation of God being the regeneration of the inward person to retain the same heart and mind of that regenerating Spirit. Herein is why it is counseled, "Be renewed in the spirit of your mind."[2926] When once the mind is drawn out to His Son, to learn of, and to do His charge, the mind will retain both the power and the precepts of the Spirit to keep the body properly regulated. The retained knowledge of God will be "be an ornament of grace unto thy head, and chains about thy neck."[2927] "Then shalt thou walk in thy way safely, and thy foot shall not stumble."[2928]

20. In order to overcome a physical enemy by the law and the doctrine of His Son's blood, the enemy within the human being, self, must be first defeated by the same law beforehand. Man cannot defeat self by himself. No matter what mankind independently applies him or

---

2920 James 1:12
2921 Romans 8:10
2922 Hebrews 10:29
2923 1 Peter 3:7
2924 Romans 5:20
2925 Titus 2:11
2926 Ephesians 4:23
2927 Proverbs 1:9
2928 Proverbs 3:23

herself to, while regulated solely according to the familial spirit within them, they will only achieve all that flesh can achieve, which is no achievement at all. "There is no man that hath power over the spirit to retain the spirit."[2929] "For what man knoweth the things of a man, save the spirit of man which is in him? even so the things of God knoweth no man, but the Spirit of God."[2930] Flesh is trash; "verily every man at his best state is altogether vanity";[2931] but a man consensually joined to the Spirit of the living God, who can speak against that man? The saying is therefore true for the one who longs after reform: "Without me ye can do nothing."[2932] "Salvation through sanctification of the Spirit and belief of the truth"[2933] is the only way "to obtain salvation by our Lord Jesus Christ."[2934]

21. The salvation of the LORD is framed around death to self for the reward of divine assistance to advance in the divine nature. This season of atonement is so important that the LORD says, "He that overcometh shall not be hurt of the second death."[2935] Our eternal destiny begins with our decision to embrace the process of a reform on diet. Our eternal hope hangs in the balance, and is further called into question, the more we refuse to hear, "I keep under my body, and bring it into subjection."[2936] "If Christ be in you, the body is dead because of sin,"[2937] and Paul can say this because it is written, "He that hath the Son hath life."[2938] Complete surrender to Christ means an experience where the mind of the flesh will no longer seat itself upon the throne of the conscience. The power of God to overcome every irrational and hurtful indulgence is through that divine "abundance of grace,"[2939]

2929 Ecclesiastes 8:8
2930 1 Corinthians 2:11
2931 Psalm 39:5
2932 John 15:5
2933 2 Thessalonians 2:13
2934 1 Thessalonians 5:9
2935 Revelation 2:11
2936 1 Corinthians 9:27
2937 Romans 8:10
2938 1 John 5:12
2939 Romans 5:17

which grace is "the gift of righteousness."[2940] Righteousness is sealed and maintained by the "by the power of the Spirit of God,"[2941] and the experience obtained from adhering to the process of perfecting righteousness in the virtue of Christ is that experience necessary to not only quit self, but to also protect the mind against open environmental oppressors whenever and however they should arise.

22. By the blood of our salvation's Captain; by the experience contained within the law of our High Priest's Faith; and by our testimony; "the testimony of our conscience"[2942] "in demonstration of the Spirit and of power";[2943] "I can do all things through Christ which strengtheneth me,"[2944] says His reformer. The retained and exercised precepts of justification by faith on His Son's name will fulfill the saying in the obedient soul, "He that is begotten of God keepeth himself, and that wicked one toucheth him not."[2945] Suffering the heart to endure temptation, withdrawing the flesh from its delicacies to obtain a right comprehension of the voice of Christ, and achieving active success by faith in the power of the Spirit of God to procure health to the conscience, even as them "that have hazarded their lives for the name of our Lord,"[2946] will in fact lead to a blessed quietness. The time to grow familiar with the effect of righteousness is now, for the obtained experience of purification will be the only voice to quell the agony of the heart under a newly sanctioned reign of terror.

2940 Romans 5:17
2941 Romans 15:19
2942 2 Corinthians 1:12
2943 1 Corinthians 2:4
2944 Philippians 4:13
2945 1 John 5:18
2946 Acts 15:26

36

The Security Behind A Refined Diet

1. "Joseph was brought down to Egypt; and Pot'iphar, an officer of Pharaoh, captain of the guard, an Egyptian, bought him."[2947] "And Joseph found grace in his sight, and he served him: and he made him overseer over his house, and all that he had he put into his hand."[2948]

2. "And it came to pass after these things, that his master's wife cast her eyes upon Joseph; and she said, Lie with me. But he refused, and said unto his master's wife, Behold, my master wotteth not what is with me in the house, and he hath committed all that he hath to my hand; there is none greater in this house than I; neither hath he kept back any thing from me but thee, because thou art his wife: how then can I do this great wickedness, and sin against God?"[2949] "And she caught him by his garment, saying, Lie with me: and he left his garment in her hand, and fled, and got him out."[2950]

3. These things should not be viewed in their natural sense, for then the full lesson would not be understood. A "woman" or a "wife"

2947 Genesis 39:1
2948 Genesis 39:4
2949 Genesis 39:7-9
2950 Genesis 39:12

is figurative language denoting a church. This is understood from how it is written, "Love your wives, even as Christ also loved the church."[2951] Pot'iphar's wife is in reality a figurative representation of his church and religious assembly. Pot'iphar, on the other hand, seeing as how he is a man that is an officer, even captain of the Egyptian guard, he is a man with a profound position in the Egyptian State; he is a military governor of high rank. This man is in reality a representative of the government of Egypt. Joseph is also not Joseph, but he is a representative of the living religion of the living God.

4. What we have before us is the image of an institution of God; Joseph; bound under a State that has a national religion, honoring the State of which he is bound to without, at first, any conflict against his conscience. This servant of the Spirit freely honors the State of Egypt while remaining faithful to his God. His character set a seal on the uprightness of not only the land, but of also the other high-ranking individuals around him. He served his God in peace while the Egyptians served their *God*. There was no controversy between liberty of self and freedom of religion, for the LORD Himself prospered His Joseph, which is proof that the LORD approved of the situation that His Joseph found himself in with the Egyptian State. "The LORD blessed the Egyptian's house for Joseph's sake,"[2952] and as long as there was a structural division between the church bearing the name of God and the governmental policies of Egypt, that prosperity, whether economical, educational, political, or cultural, would not end. But eventually something shook the foundation of the earth. A particular institution of the Egyptian State, Pot'iphar's wife, wanted the institution of God, Joseph.

5. The State of Egypt sought to court the institution of God. "She said, Lie with me. But he refused."[2953] "In this the children of God are manifest, and the children of the devil."[2954] The pure institution of the Spirit's heritage will for ever say, when courted by a State, "How then

---

2951 Ephesians 5:25
2952 Genesis 39:5
2953 Genesis 39:7,8
2954 1 John 3:10

can I do this great wickedness, and sin against God?"[2955] God Himself is teaching a lesson on any thing relating to religion on this earth in a political atmosphere, and especially one that bears His name. Religion and politics should not mix, especially in an unlawful manner.

6. There was in fact an institution that claimed *His name* as their own, which also desired political favor to accomplish their vain ambitions. The result of its amalgamation with the Roman State is written for us: "They worshipped the dragon which gave power unto the beast."[2956] The dragon was worshipped under an apostate Christian garb, and the tragedy that developed was called the Papacy. The policies of the dragon were maintained by a supposedly pure institution of *God*, and by accepting the call of the Roman State for favor, civil power was then given to this institution. "The dragon gave him his power, and his seat, and great authority,"[2957] and "power was given him over all kindreds, and tongues, and nations."[2958] The liberty that Rome had known up until the formation of this abomination had vanished away. With the civil and legislative authority of the State at her feet, the Catholic Church announced: "Whosoever therefore resisteth the power, resisteth the ordinance of God: and they that resist shall receive to themselves damnation."[2959] A period of gross darkness thus commenced.

7. Joseph, being brought up under Israel, knew the mind of God on the matters of separation between law and religion. When approached by the woman, he received her advances as an abnormal gesture. "How can I do this great wickedness?" he thought, for he knew how it was written, "Neither shall any woman stand before a beast to lie down thereto: it is confusion."[2960] A dragon is a beast, as it says, "I saw a woman sit upon a scarlet coloured beast."[2961] Herein is the image of confusion, a woman, or a church, supported and seated upon a beast,

2955 Genesis 39:9
2956 Revelation 13:4
2957 Revelation 13:2
2958 Revelation 13:7
2959 Revelation 13:2
2960 Leviticus 18:23
2961 Revelation 17:3

a dragon, a State. This image is an image of confusion, and "God is not the author of confusion."[2962] The author of this madness says: "I will exalt my throne above the stars of God: I will sit also upon the mount of the congregation."[2963] A throne is symbol of State power. A congregation is that of ecclesiastical. The conviction that is born in and encouraged by Lucifer[2964] is the union of them both; of religion and government; for it is his open ambition to join a State and a particular church together. He found his institution in the Papacy. After he beguiled the Catholic Church, he said, "Let 'that Wicked be revealed.'"[2965]

8. But Joseph would not surrender to her. Joseph was victorious over the spurious advances of his State, and of even his own inward nature. He has set the standard of excellence for any one calling themselves lovers of both the Word and His Son. The sons and daughters of the living God will not lower themselves to the image of any man or woman. It is inevitable that these events will in fact reoccur on the earth against the servants of the LORD and His name, for His Spirit has spoken it by that vision given to John. When the time is set, when the dragon is again openly manifested, a "certain of the sect of the Pharisees,"[2966] "false brethren unawares brought in,"[2967] "who were before of old ordained to this condemnation, ungodly men, turning the grace of our God into lasciviousness, and denying the only Lord God, and our Lord Jesus Christ,"[2968] will apply themselves to obtain political favor with the new republic of the earth. They will eventually get their wish. They will join themselves to the State, and by them, the State will be transformed. Nevertheless, the people of the living God will not fold. The LORD's inheritance will suffer terrible hardship, but they will not draw back from Him, because they know Him.

2962 1 Corinthians 14:33
2963 Isaiah 14:13
2964 Isaiah 14:12
2965 2 Thessalonians 2:8
2966 Acts 15:5
2967 Galatians 2:4
2968 Jude 1:4

9. When the people of God begin to resist the woman of this new State, it will be said, "He spake as a dragon."[2969] "Love is strong as death; jealousy is cruel as the grave: the coals thereof are coals of fire, which hath a most vehement flame."[2970] Pot'iphar will defend his wife. What happened to Joseph? Pot'iphar's "wrath was kindled. And Joseph's master took him, and put him into the prison."[2971] Herein the word is fulfilled, "The dragon was wroth with the woman, and went to make war with the remnant of her seed, which keep the commandments of God, and have the testimony of Jesus Christ."[2972] The inheritance of God will be foully handled. Because the dragon is a symbol of a State, the only way that he can make war with the house of God is through his voice of legislation. Laws and amendments will be erected to defend the beauty of the mistress of the land, and any one who should disrespect her in any way will suffer. But the distress procured from refusing her voice did not faze Joseph. "Whether it be right in the sight of God to hearken unto you more than unto God, judge ye. For we cannot but speak the things which we have seen and heard,"[2973] says this lovely institution of the Spirit's Word.

10. These things announce to us the current counsel: "If any man worship the beast and his image, and receive his mark in his forehead, or in his hand, the same shall drink of the wine of the wrath of God."[2974] As Joseph did not bow down to this sensual woman of Egypt, so the seed of God is instructed to forsake any image of any woman seated upon any beast at any time. It is important to know the religion and the Faith that comes out only from His Son's mediation "because many false prophets are gone out into the world,"[2975] and if you do not know His LORD personally, "through covetousness shall they with feigned words make merchandise of you."[2976] Intimate communion with His

---

2969 Revelation 13:11
2970 Song of Solomon 8:5
2971 Genesis 39:20
2972 Revelation 12:17
2973 Acts 4:19,29
2974 Revelation 14:9,10
2975 1 John 4:1
2976 2 Peter 2:3

Son's name will keep the heart and conscience free from error, and this is why He counsels, "Keep my commandments, and live; and my law as the apple of thine eye. Bind them upon thy fingers, write them upon the table of thine heart. Say unto wisdom, Thou art my sister; and call understanding thy kinswoman: that they may keep thee from the strange woman, from the stranger which flattereth with her words."[2977]

11. There is a work to accomplish before our current age is turned upside down. Joseph endured in the LORD's name from embracing every divine principle to remain "temperate in all things"[2978] beforehand. A temperate culture will fasten every precept of the LORD's Spirit within the heart. As one studies with His Spirit, what is retained from the Spirit is to be executed by the limbs of the body that the spirit of the mind may retain new principles of government. To keep and live any thing of God is to do and apply to every thing of God. The heart should not be kept from acting out the love that it has to Him, and the spirit should not be refused the knowledge obtained from experiencing His religion from an experimental faith. The LORD's Order is to be written on our heart from our own cooperation with His voice. When faith and obedience give birth to a diligent examination of the sayings of Christ and of God, the work will be perfected by God Himself, for His Spirit will work over, and further engrave within the walls of our soul temple, that which we have retained from remaining faithful to His wisdom and science.

12. The shield that protected Joseph from Pot'iphar's wife was the security behind a refined diet, coupled with "the helmet of salvation, and the sword of the Spirit, which is the word of God."[2979] This period of our atonement is one wherein the believer is to grow familiar with their armor. A religious test is coming for individuals who claim to be members of the body of Christ. As members of the LORD's heavenly Church, it should be known that as He was crucified, so too will we also suffer the same fate. A decree will be issued that says, "Fall down and worship the golden image."[2980] Who will stand for the living God, to

---

2977 Proverbs 7:2-5
2978 1 Corinthians 9:25
2979 Ephesians 6:17
2980 Daniel 3:5

not pierce themselves through to honor a false image of government? When the people of God refuse to have their conscience compromised, the then king will be "full of fury,"[2981] and it will be known, "The form of his visage was changed."[2982] Who will stand before his face? Only them have "yielded their bodies, that they might not serve nor worship any god, except their own God."[2983] Only them that have lowered the credibility of self to remain "sober, just, holy, temperate."[2984]

13. The flames ordained for the disobedient did not hurt the sons of His Spirit. The lesson is again reinforced that a civil power has no justified authority over and between religious matters. The LORD expressly charged, "The nation and kingdom which will not serve the same Nebuchadnez'zar the king of Babylon, and that will not put their neck under the yoke of the king of Babylon, that nation will I punish."[2985] The Hebrews blatantly disobeyed God and were not punished. The lesson is to educate His student that He will protect and honor them that long to honor and serve Him, despite what is conceived by any one, even our own State. The Word and His Son are above them all. All who honor His name, and grow up in Him to become a habitation for His Spirit, will never be separated from His throne. Integrity is what preserved Joseph and those three Hebrew ministers, and that integrity was not gained in the time of their trial, but rather in the quiet seasons leading up to that test.

14. A new age is quaking to situate itself upon the earth. The John writes, "I beheld another beast coming up out of the earth; and he had two horns like a lamb."[2986] A new religious republic will be born from out of the confusion of an earthquake, and it will have policies to convince all people that it is deserving of reverence. It has two horns, or powers, as a lamb. Its force will be, on the surface, pure, but his heart is set to overthrow many by those horns. The word will be fulfilled, "With

---

2981 Daniel 3:19
2982 Daniel 3:19
2983 Daniel 3:28
2984 Titus 1:8
2985 Jeremiah 27:8
2986 Revelation 13:11

them he shall push the people together to the ends of the earth."[2987] It voice longs to spread the message, "I have said, Ye are gods; and all of you are children of the most High."[2988] It will perpetuate the state of religion by saying, "All the congregation are holy, every one of them, and the LORD is among them."[2989] These are lies, and the men by whom these things are preached are robbers of the living God.

15. Through his voice, Pot'iphar will please his wife, and she will take joy in robbing the house of God of its garment. The time in which these things will occur will be a time of gross spiritual and moral poverty, wretchedness, nakedness, blindness, and misery. For this reason the Spirit currently counsels, "Before the decree bring forth,"[2990] "seek ye the LORD, all ye meek of the earth, which have wrought his judgment."[2991] The call of the LORD is for His House to accomplish a specific work within their conversation's conscience before certain laws are enacted to honor the image of an ecclesiastical government; to serve the voice of a State bound to a woman. To have wrought the judgments of the Spirit is to have pursued or slaved after obeying His voice. It is to have moved self to carry out a behavior that is proper to receive a benefit from establishing that word from directing and subduing self. For this reason we are counseled, "Be in behaviour as becometh holiness,"[2992] and, "Let your conversation be as it becometh the gospel of Christ."[2993]

16. Knowledge of the work of God within the heart from obeying His doctrine is to be obtained to regulate the organs of both the mind and the conversation. Our behavior is our conversation, and our conversation is our personal religion, and our personal religion is to be purified from "obeying the truth through the Spirit."[2994] The many statutes or decisions concerning justification by faith are to be

---

2987 Deuteronomy 33:17
2988 Psalm 83:6
2989 Numbers 16:3
2990 Zephaniah 2:2
2991 Zephaniah 2:3
2992 Titus 2:3
2993 Philippians 1:27
2994 1 Peter 1:22

retained through "fellowship of the Spirit,"[2995] and what is retained is to gravitate toward the counsel, "Work out your own salvation with fear and trembling."[2996]

17. The current standard is for every believing reformer to be "created in righteousness and true holiness."[2997] Willingly surrendering to the experience contained within the Word's will and commandment begins with a decision to search after "the acknowledging of the truth which is after godliness."[2998] A new creature is to be born to the Spirit when once he or she applies to the work of atonement, and it is this work that will seal the soul and spirit to the living God that it may not betray Him, no matter what force is against them.

2995 Philippians 2:1
2996 Philippians 2:12
2997 Ephesians 4:24
2998 Titus 1:1

37

Reform's Estate Under The Second Adam

1. It is written, "God blessed the seventh day."[2999] If God blessed the seventh day of the week, then it is that the day, in and of itself, would be nothing special if it were not for the blessing constrained to it. The fact that God Himself blessed the last day of the week, and with His own voice, is enough to testify, to the sincere and obedient soul, that He has passed a law for His assembly. And the fact that God Himself passed this law not simply by His voice, but by His own actions to acknowledge this day and its blessing, to have rested on it Himself, is enough to compel the pure in heart that where the living God is, there too they must also be. "On the seventh day God ended his work which he had made; and he rested on the seventh day from all his work which he had made,"[3000] Scripture records. It is from His actions to join Himself to this period of time that there is a conclusion made that God blessed and hallowed this day for His Adam. Let it then be remembered how it is said, "As in Adam all die, even so in Christ shall all be made alive."[3001]

2999 Genesis 2:3
3000 Genesis 2:2
3001 1 Corinthians 15:22

2. Adam's disease is death. Adam now knows no thing but death; whether that death is literal or spiritual; concerning his mental and moral faculties. Adam is a figurative representative of the species of mankind, and from what we learn about the nature of the human being through him, it is fair to conclude that Adam is low, hypocritical, is full of blood in his face and without life in his mind, and is altogether common. There is no thing fully desirable in the natural human being. There is no mind or heart to elevate self; according to the things of God and by the voice of God; in the natural human being. The intellect of Adam's conversation goes no deeper than his flesh, and the faith of Adam, and his care for right things according to the charge of the living God, goes no higher than the clouds above his head. In his face is blood, and "the life of the flesh is in the blood,"[3002] therefore all Adam knows, and is most likely to prefer, are natural categories of existence most common to his senses. His face, due to that blood, should he remain without God, will never consider "the knowledge of the glory of God in the face of Jesus Christ."[3003]

3. The conflict for the human being is to remain settled under the knowledge of the glory of the face of Adam, or to personally embrace the influence of the Spirit over the heart to obtain the light of the knowledge of the glory of the Word in the face of His Christ. If all Adam knows is death, then all Adam is will be death, and a consistent existence in that depression becomes a retardant to regeneration. But if the heart is willing to embrace an experience with the Christ of God from obeying the law of His Faith, then all who do so will be made alive. Scripture says that the one obedient to embrace an education in the presence of God will be made alive, created alive, which means that as we naturally stand, and as we are naturally born, we are in fact no thing at all. Thus, the saying is true, "In Christ shall all be made alive."[3004] Adam cannot change any thing within himself, and by himself. He is death, or rather, we are all currently dead and are confined to every aspect of spiritual death. Nevertheless, both God and His Christ took

3002 Leviticus 17:11
3003 2 Corinthians 4:6
3004 1 Corinthians 15:22

pity on us. "God sent his only begotten Son into the world, that we might live through him."[3005]

4. Right life is now attainable for the spirit of the mind. Adam is now no longer held to that death nailed to the tree. If he or she cares to abandon their inherited sickness, and if Adam cares to receive both his diagnosis and the remedy for that illness, the door to the Master Physician is open. Because Adam has no life in himself, and because the error in him naturally seduces his heart to refuse to acknowledge a right heritage of life, God Himself took it upon Himself to labor for His creation that every soul who wants life by Him should have "an inheritance, being predestinated according to the purpose of him who worketh all things after the counsel of his own will."[3006] "And so it is written, The first man Adam was made a living soul; the last Adam was made a quickening spirit."[3007] The last and true Adam is that Christ. After this Christ had "given himself for us an offering and a sacrifice to God for a sweetsmelling savour,"[3008] after "he had by himself purged our sins"[3009] and "sat down on the right hand of the Majesty on high,"[3010] faith's claim over the conscience of the human race became official. Anyone who should feel after this Christ, to then move him or herself to know His name, will be "created in righteousness and true holiness."[3011]

5. Herein is the Faith the heavenly Sanctuary: "That the name of our Lord Jesus Christ may be glorified in you, and ye in him, according to the grace of our God and the Lord Jesus Christ."[3012] The name or the character of His Christ is to be engraved within inwards by the grace of God, for it is "the grace of God that bringeth salvation."[3013] This salvation is the perfecting of "wisdom, and righteousness, and

3005 1 John 4:9
3006 Ephesians 1:11
3007 1 Corinthians 15:45
3008 Ephesians 5:2
3009 Hebrews 1:3
3010 Hebrews 1:3
3011 Ephesians 4:24
3012 1 Thessalonians 1:12
3013 Titus 2:11

sanctification, and redemption"[3014] within the mind "by the washing of regeneration, and renewing of the Holy Ghost."[3015] The last Adam was made a spirit quickened, or a negligent conscience regenerated to honor the living God by faith. Christ came "in the likeness of sinful flesh, and for sin, condemned sin in the flesh,"[3016] to open up the fact that through His name and mediation, all forms of death against the heart are abolished. This is a fact. For He fulfilled the saying, "Unto GOD the Lord belong the issues from death."[3017] But freedom from death is not without work. Every one desiring life will say, "I put my life in my hands."[3018] To be made, or to be created, puts forth the notion of a work to be accomplished. The mind inherited from Adam must be expelled from the personal religion, and the Spirit must quicken the heart of the conversation.

6. It is the Holy Ghost that washes the soul from filth, and in exchange for the mind of Adam, will seal within the spirit of the mind that mind of God. How then must Adam quit self to join self to the true Adam of God, His heavenly High Priest? What counsel is given for Adam? Our Priest says, "If any man hear my voice, and open the door, I will come in to him, and will sup with him, and he with me."[3019] Should any one open the door of their heart to Him, His Christ will in fact bring them to His table, and He will eat with them, and they will commune with Him. This is why He says, "If a man love me, he will keep my words: and my Father will love him, and we will come unto him, and make our abode with him."[3020] Christ does not, and will not come alone. He can never come to us alone, simply because His words are not His own, but are in fact the words of the Spirit. "I have not spoken of myself; but the Father which sent me, he gave me a commandment, what I should say, and what I should speak,"[3021] He says.

3014 1 Corinthians 1:30
3015 Titus 3:5
3016 Romans 8:3
3017 Psalm 68:20
3018 Judges 12:3
3019 Revelation 3:20
3020 John 14:23
3021 John 12:49

7. The heart open for surgery must accept both the Father and the Son for a full and progressing recovery. This is why we are counseled, "Truly our fellowship is with the Father, and with his Son Jesus Christ."[3022] The Father and the Son should be properly viewed as the Spirit and the Faith of His name. This is how "your fellowship in the gospel"[3023] is beautified by "your love in the Spirit."[3024] The religion of Christ is not bound by flesh or flesh-based, therefore every reforming soul will announce, "I serve with my spirit in the gospel of his Son."[3025] Because the power of the grace of God is the primary medicine to quit the mind of Adam, it is counseled, "The grace of our Lord Jesus Christ be with your spirit."[3026] The washing of regeneration by the Spirit is perfected by the Spirit's grace as we meditate on His words, which is why it is ordained, which is why He says, "Ye are clean through the word which I have spoken."[3027] When once there is faithful and active belief on the virtue of Christ, it is ordained for the soul to be "sanctified by God the Father,"[3028] that is, "sanctified by the Holy Ghost,"[3029] and this "with the washing of water by the word."[3030] Only the soul and spirit is to be cleansed while in sinful flesh. This is why it says, "That the spirit may be saved in the day of the Lord Jesus."[3031]

8. Sanctification comes by none other means than through the Spirit of God. Purification and re-creation of the inward constitution into the likeness of His Son occurs only by the hand of the living God personally upon the heart of His creation. The means to obtain this benefit is from believing on, and executing, the learned precepts of heaven's Faith as we personally engage our conversation with them. Opening up the heart to retain the voice of God means to consistently, and to perseveringly, sup or commune with His Spirit by reviewing His

3022 1 John 1:3
3023 Philippians 1:5
3024 Colossians 1:8
3025 Romans 1:9
3026 Galatians 6:18
3027 John 15:3
3028 Jude 1:1
3029 Romans 15:16
3030 Ephesians 5:26
3031 1 Corinthians 5:5

words. This is why our Priest says, "If any hear my voice,"[3032] and that hearing He equates to opening up the door of the heart to receive Him.

9. Any action to carry out what is heard and retained from His Spirit will procure blessing to the mind. This blessing will be the continual shower of rain from the cloud of the Spirit over the heart for "wisdom, and righteousness, and sanctification, and redemption."[3033] What then is His voice that must be heard? He says, "The sword of my mouth."[3034] What then is the sword of His mouth? John records, "Out of his mouth went a sharp twoedged sword."[3035] Again, what is this sharp two-edged sword? It says, "The sword of the Spirit, which is the word of God."[3036] This sword is the living words of the LORD, and it has two sharp everlasting points forming one harmonious doctrine. This is that word announcing the Spirit's two judgments, and He says, "Keep the commandments of God, and the faith of Jesus."[3037]

10. The reformer is to study after the accomplishment of this word within the soul temple. From applying self to learn of the Spirit's will through the law and knowledge of His Son's name, to then value that name through the LORD's Word, and to love self from hearing them both, division within the heart will occur, and a cleansing will occur within the conscience to embrace a new diet of existence. Christ said of this sword of His: "Suppose ye that I am come to give peace on earth? I tell you, Nay; but rather division."[3038] The members of the heart will war against themselves when the voice of Christ is given consent to enter into the spirit. This is why "the word of God is quick, and powerful, and sharper than any twoedged sword, piercing even to the dividing asunder of soul and spirit, and of the joints and marrow, and is a discerner of the thoughts and intents of the heart."[3039] By exercising Faith on our Priest's intercession, and intimately fellowshipping with His Spirit to

3032 Revelation 3:20
3033 1 Corinthians 1:30
3034 Revelation 2:16
3035 Revelation 1:16
3036 Ephesians 6:17
3037 Revelation 14:12
3038 Luke 12:51
3039 Hebrews 4:12

retain laws of nature for self-regulation, is the work of faith constrained to this year of atonement.

11. The voice of Christ is the doctrine of Christ, and "whosoever transgresseth, and abideth not in the doctrine of Christ, hath not God. He that abideth in the doctrine of Christ, he hath both the Father and the Son."[3040] Having both the Father and the Son, the believer has the full Godhead to watch over the operation of their development. In the presence of the LORD and His Son, the reformer may confidently say, "Create in me a clean heart, O God; and renew a right spirit within me."[3041] From accepting "salvation through sanctification of the Spirit and belief of the truth,"[3042] it is a fact that every believer will have "received the sign of circumcision, a seal of the righteousness of the faith which he had yet being uncircumcised."[3043] Now that one has received the seal of circumcision; which seal is the branding of that heaven-appointed faith and religion; uncircumcision is no more uncircumcision, for now the heart longs to celebrate the Memorial of his or her Creator. With Adam refined and regulated under the last Adam, he will hear, "God blessed the seventh day, and sanctified it."[3044]

12. Adam, because he is yet natural, does not know the effect and reward of righteousness by faith, nor is it in him or her to experiment therein. Adam's confusion persists because they are never found in the classroom of Christ. They will not properly honor the LORD God or His Christ, for how clearly can one functioning in death discern a right manner and conversation? They will ascribe greatness to self, and will inevitably consent to have "sacrificed unto devils, not to God."[3045] They will therefore see the Christ of God, and will hear Him say, "I am the root and the offspring of David, and the bright and morning star,"[3046] and will hear how it is written of Him, "His going forth is prepared as

---

3040 2 John 1:9
3041 Psalm 51:10
3042 2 Thessalonians 2:13
3043 Romans 4:11
3044 Genesis 2:3
3045 Deuteronomy 32:17
3046 Revelation 22:16

the morning,"[3047] and will in turn honor some *one* of a contrary fold, as it says, "O Lucifer, son of the morning."[3048] Satan recognizes himself as the chief deity of the morning, and because the morning is synonymous with the day, and the day with the sun; as it says, "The sun to rule by day";[3049] Adam will hear how of Christ it says, "His countenance was as the sun,"[3050] and being the natural man that he is, Adam will honor what he will honor on a sun-day, to some thing so falsely portrayed to their imagination. This is "the spirit of error."[3051]

13. "Satan himself is transformed into an angel of light"[3052] to the mind of Adam, and it is him that is honored when the way of *life*, as sanctioned by Adam, is endorsed. Without the right blessing of God bestowed from obedience, Adam will work a pattern of that blessing given of God for himself, and will thus *sanctify* his conversation. Such a work of error leads Adam to section out a day of blessing for Adam. Indeed it will be "like unto the feast that is in Judah,"[3053] which feast is the seventh day Sabbath, but it is not the seventh day Sabbath, but rather a first day sun-worshipping feast to that great counterfeiter, the serpent. This is why it is written, "God blessed the seventh day,"[3054] and it is confirmed, "Thou blessest, O LORD, and it shall be blessed for ever."[3055]

14. The creation of God know the living God, and they know Him because they are blessed and cared for by His Spirit, and by that blessing are given permission to enter into His blessed appointment to further strengthen their knowledge of Him. Adam knows no blessing of God as he naturally stands, so what does it mean that both the creation of God, and His seventh day, is blessed to hold the full blessing of God?

3047 Hosea 6:3
3048 Isaiah 14:12
3049 Psalm 136:8
3050 Revelation 1:16
3051 1 John 4:6
3052 2 Corinthians 11:14
3053 1 Kings 12:32
3054 Genesis 2:3
3055 1 Chronicles 17:27

We read: "And the child grew, and the LORD blessed him. And the Spirit of the LORD began to move him."[3056]

15. God blessing the seventh day means that contained within the hours of this day, from the beginning of this day until its end, the Spirit of God is moving therein. One who has never experienced the movement of the Spirit over their heart cannot appreciate the communion of the Spirit on this day. Therefore "to day if ye will hear his voice, harden not your hearts."[3057] Many clear their day to keep the seventh day according to the commandment, yet have never known the blessing therein for failure of knowing "the fulness of the blessing of the gospel of Christ"[3058] throughout the week. The seventh day is not just the object of the affection for the creature of God, it is the blessed institution therein called the Sabbath. The joy of the Sabbath engraves the day of the Sabbath in the heart to be remembered. The Sabbath makes the seventh day what it is; the blessing therein magnifies the joy of reverencing the last twenty-four hours of the week. This is why God counsels, "Remember the Sabbath day,"[3059] for "the LORD blessed the Sabbath day, and hallowed it."[3060] This day the living God did ordain to be on the seventh day of the week.

16. The fact that God Himself says to remember the Sabbath day is a testament to the joy and love that He has for this institution. He does not need to specify in His commandment that the Sabbath is the seventh day, not only because He immutably set it that way from the beginning of time and it cannot be changed, but because He is speaking to individuals that love Him, and that have suffered themselves to be created by Him. He does not say, "Remember the seventh day," because it is not the seventh day that people will forget. Man will forever "observe days, and months, and times, and years."[3061] Many keep this day as others observe their Sunday or first day, and have never entered into the blessed Sabbath of the seventh day. Seasons that are, and are not of

3056 Judges 13:24,25
3057 Hebrews 3:15
3058 Romans 15:29
3059 Exodus 20:8
3060 Exodus 20:11
3061 Galatians 4:10

God, are kept without humbling the heart to experience the movement of God over the heart throughout the allotted soul-working days of the week. The Sabbath, says God, is to be remembered on its assigned day, because a true refreshing by God, and a right experience of purification, will be forgotten. The LORD knew that it was inevitable that erroneous priests and ministers should forget about His seventh day Sabbath. Adam does not care to surrender self for any good thing of the LORD's Word, or to prove the necessity behind surrendering any thing to Him. But when Adam cares to learn humility from obeying the counsel of soul reconciliation to prove his atonement to this LORD's Spirit, He will not only remember the Sabbath day, but the seventh day will be to him a joy, and no burden at all.

17. Any thing taught of God or Christ without educating on the immutable love contained within His Sabbath is of no value. A voice that never speaks on the sign of His authenticity is contrary to Him, and is but an enemy to heaven-appointed religion. The foundation of salvation's science rests in this institution. It is purchased by the blood of His Son to continue in the hearer and doer of His Faith. The law and commandment confirming the seed of God from that of Satan will for ever exclaim, "God blessed the seventh day, and sanctified it."[3062] Christ suffered the tree that we might function through His conversation, and not according to the mind of Adam, which mind is nailed to the tree. This Christ's Faith passes the eyes of Adam away, leaving it that the new creation of the Spirit "is renewed in knowledge after the image of him that created him."[3063] It is the Word who formed "in himself of twain one new man,"[3064] that His new creature should confess, "The Spirit of God hath made me."[3065] If there is no knowledge of the Father and the Son personally obtained from examining His voice, Adam will remain, and the sacrifice of God will be made of none effect. But as the spirit retains the principles of the Faith of His Son from communing with Him by the Spirit, "then they which be of faith are blessed."[3066]

3062 Genesis 2:3
3063 Colossians 3:10
3064 Ephesians 2:15
3065 Job 33:4
3066 Galatians 3:9

18. This is why our Priest counsels, "Behold my hands and my feet, that it is I myself: handle me, and see,"[3067]and, "Thou shouldest take knowledge of me."[3068] To properly live through His name, to know that He is that Christ and High Priest of the living God, involves the effort of taking knowledge of Him. The work of faith in the presence of God is to prove the certainty of the will of God, and that proving cannot commence until one is so bold to confess to Him, "I will not let thee go, except thou bless me,"[3069] and, "Whither thou goest, I will go; and where thou lodgest, I will lodge: thy people shall be my people, and thy God my God: where thou diest, will I die, and there will I be buried: the LORD do so to me, and more also, if ought but death part thee and me."[3070] Until the conversation is willing to confess, "I die daily,"[3071] no thing of this Christ will be given to the heart that it may recover its conversation. Honest faith in His name will lead one to gradually decline from former religious habits and tendencies. A right attitude to embrace a change in diet will move the heart to pray, "Blessed be he that did take knowledge of thee."[3072]

19. This current Day of Atonement is one wherein the Spirit's assembly is taking knowledge of His operation, and is exercising self to learn reform from what is retained. Where Christ is, and where He has gone to in the heavenly Temple, there also the spirit of the mind of His believer must be. Where He has died, there also must the heart die, so that the spirit "shall be also in the likeness of his resurrection."[3073] The eye of faith must commune with the conscience to say, "Who shall separate us from the love of Christ? shall tribulation, or distress, or persecution, or famine, or nakedness, or peril, or sword?"[3074] "Nay, in all these things we are more than conquerors through him that loved us."[3075]

3067 Luke 24:39
3068 Ruth 2:10
3069 Genesis 32:26
3070 Ruth 1:16,17
3071 1 Corinthians 15:31
3072 Ruth 2:19
3073 Romans 6:5
3074 Romans 8:35
3075 Romans 8:37

20. Hope and confidence in this Christ's Faith as a personal Savior is at this time to be perfected. The new constitution is to be put on from a continual renewing of the mind concerning the person of its Intercessor. Accomplishing the works of His mediation is to be that diet for the personal religion that the fruit of the Spirit may have a chance to spring up and blossom within us. Obeying the commandment, "My son, give me thine heart, and let thine eyes observe my ways,"[3076] is the only means wherein one may be "sanctified by God the Father, and preserved in Jesus Christ."[3077] With the eye considering no thing but "Jesus Christ, and him crucified,"[3078] and with the soul willing to "suffer persecution for the cross of Christ,"[3079] the spirit will consider "the Lamb which is in the midst of the throne"[3080] of the Father, and when viewing Christ through a right lens to see Him not separated from the Father, but ultimately joined to the throne of His LORD, and "made an high priest for ever after the order of Melchis'edec,"[3081] there will be great joy in acknowledging the charge that He declared with His own mouth, "The Son of man is Lord also of the Sabbath."[3082]

21. The LORD's religion is complete in the law of the Faith of His Son, which is why we are counseled, "Ye are complete in him."[3083] With His name's reformer complete in His confidence, He says, "Thou followedst not young men, whether poor or rich."[3084] Our High Priest is the only source of knowledge on the living God. The heart has abandoned self with all of its strange vanities and inclinations for intimate communion with His Spirit, and from giving the Spirit of the LORD a fair opportunity to place life into the being, loyalty to Him is no longer based off of crude policies of a tradition, but is rather framed by the laws and judgments of the Spirit etched onto the heart by His own finger. To take knowledge of God is to diligently examine His person

---

3076 Proverbs 23:26
3077 Jude 1:1
3078 1 Corinthians 2:2
3079 Galatians 6:12
3080 Revelation 7:17
3081 Hebrews 6:20
3082 Luke 6:5
3083 Colossians 2:10
3084 Ruth 3:10

that there may be a shedding of hard thoughts and irrational imaginations, even as a snake sheds its skin. He who should behold the Christ of God, and desire to obtain the heart and mind of that Christ, and is not careful for fear or for what apparent loss should occur within their conversation, will receive to themselves the full heritage of the living God, and a place in His kingdom of glory.

22. The current work of atonement is to make perfect the gift to be given to God at that time when His Spirit finally appears to gather His host together, and to fail in letting the heart know the blessing earned from obedience is to prepare self for death. Every word that comes out from the mouth of God is for the benefit of the receiver. Concerning His words, it is said, "They are life unto those that find them, and health to all their flesh."[3085] The law of the doctrine of Christ is not within any educational or ecclesiastical institution on this earth. It is not gained in the presence of men nor obtained from flesh. As the man of the LORD says, the knowledge of the Faith of the Father and the Son is found in His presence, and when found and properly exercised by faith, it will add health to the governing mind behind the members of the flesh. This is why it should be remembered, "Blessed be he that did take knowledge of thee."[3086]

3085 Proverbs 4:22
3086 Ruth 2:19

38

The Pillar Supporting Every Successful Reform

1. What is observed under a first day sacredness? Because no thing related to the living God is found in any of His scriptures confessing any relevant duty to this day, nor any special precedence of it above any other day, when ignorant tradition is stripped away from a first day preference, and when superstition is allowed to pass away, what in reality is one honoring? If the foundation is not known to the LORD God, and neither blessed by Him through His blessing, and is therefore is not of God, what is the mind behind the tradition? What is the statement being made when one honors this strange thing?

2. It is known what took place on the seventh day, and why God Himself should have set it apart from any other day. "God blessed the seventh day, and sanctified it."[3087] Herein the Memorial of His creative power deserves due reverence and respect for what that power had accomplished the previous six days. If this fact of creation should be left at this level of understanding, a reason to acknowledge His seventh-day Sabbath would be as much of a tradition as that of the first day. Says this LORD's Spirit, "Remember the former things of old: for I

3087 Genesis 2:3

am God, and there is none else; I am God, and there is none like me, declaring the end from the beginning, and from ancient times the things that are not yet done, saying, My counsel shall stand, and I will do all my pleasure."[3088]

3. The creation of old is but an example of the creation that His Spirit had in mind for Adam in his sinless nature. The science of creation is founded upon the creative power of the voice of His Spirit. "God, who quickeneth the dead, and calleth those things which be not as though they were,"[3089] with His own mouth turned the earth into a green plain from whence it was first "without form, and void."[3090] This was the condition of Adam, both mentally and morally, when the LORD constructed him. Adam, internally, although unfamiliar with apostasy, was no different than us. The methods of the living God concerning health and knowledge do not change, therefore it is proper to conclude that Adam, upon his birth, was just as ignorant on heavenly things as any one now is when born on the earth. The Spirit's higher education is never born into any one, nor is any one bestowed with any thing above any one else. In all generations and with all people, the LORD's counsel is, "All the words of my mouth are in righteousness; there is nothing froward or perverse in them. They are all plain to him that understandeth, and right to them that find knowledge."[3091]

4. Adam, the LORD's first thinking and feeling creature after the earth's woe, was to find the knowledge of his LORD's Word. He was not born with any special knowing, although his intellect; untainted by sin to gravitate towards a natural inclination to magnify distractions through the baser portions of his heart; was at the height of its superiority. With this mind that had every engine of its members fully functional to a maximum degree, Adam was to strictly examine his environment to retain a right notion of the God of that environment. While communing with his world, he would in turn develop confidence not only to approach the God of that world, but also to intellectually communicate his heart to that God to receive any remedy for any issue that ever came up within

3088 Isaiah 46:9,10
3089 Romans 4:17
3090 Genesis 1:2
3091 Proverbs 8:8,9

him. And when Adam picked up this work, it should not be forgotten that he was alone. It was simply he and his God. Face to face communion with God's Spirit was a natural occurrence. Adam spoke alone to the face of God, and the LORD was content, for he loved Adam.

5. How special is a child's call to a parent? Adam may have had power to understand all things, he may have had a heart that knew absolutely no thing contrary to the LORD His God, but he was in reality a little infant in that same mind. When we read, "They heard the voice of the LORD God walking in the garden in the cool of the day,"[3092] what we are hearing about is God Himself joining Himself to His assembly. The way that the language is constructed, it tells of the fact that this communion was routinely expected. God literally was there with His Adam, and He literally communicated with Him at certain times in the day. When Adam was born, he called out to God not only because He only saw God, but because of the innocent simplicity with which his heart was constructed, his eyes cared to know no other thing than His operation, even as our eyes, when an infant, do not care to know any thing else besides our parents. Yet God is a superior Parent. For "God left him, to try him, that he might know all that was in his heart."[3093]

6. The creation isn't just about Adam, but it is also about right manners to raise children. When the LORD created Adam, He didn't lord over Adam. Adam was not a slave to God, but rather Adam had his own identity within the mind of God. The fact that He gave Adam a commission to dress and to keep the garden proves that God did not intend for Himself to be constantly over Adam, nor for Adam to be for ever under Him. God let Adam be, and He let him exist as his own individual to cultivate his own person by the counsels he received of His Spirit, for this is exactly what Adam's commission was, and the LORD needed Adam to understand this for himself. Thus, as Adam exercised the powers of his heart and mind on creation's science, not only would his faith and love increase, but when he saw, from his examinations of the Sprit's work, his natural limitations as a human being, how that he actually needed his Creator for more than his mind could explain, every

3092 Genesis 3:8
3093 2 Chronicles 32:31

personal experience, governed by his faithful and simple diligence, pulled him to further cry out to His LORD for help.

7. When we hear Moses saying to the congregation of Israel, "God led thee these forty years in the wilderness, to humble thee, and to prove thee, to know what was in thine heart, whether thou wouldest keep his commandments, or no,"[3094] we see the everlasting law of the living God's educational ministration. From the time of Adam until now, retaining the knowledge of God has been better understood as experimenting and proving the voice of God to own His wisdom as a substance for soul nutrition. The fact of the LORD's name cannot be bought. No man can obtain any thing of God in its precise manner from consuming the foul wisdom of men or the imaginative thoughts of the heart. I will have better luck beating the wind than to come upon any right thing of God from my flesh. "The LORD God took the man, and put him into the garden of Eden to dress it and to keep it,"[3095] and this charge given to Adam is best relayed through the counsel, "My son, attend unto my wisdom, and bow thine ear to my understanding: that thou mayest regard discretion, and that thy lips may keep knowledge."[3096]

8. As God's child, who can imagine the height of greatness that this Father had for His son? "Who is sufficient for these things?"[3097] Every parent desires the best for their child, how much more God for Adam! As much as God may have wanted to dominate his heart, and to involve Himself with every portion of his conversation's character and ambition, God would not commit Himself to such a trial. He would be breaking the very laws that He Himself had established for the general upbringing of the human conscience. He may have wanted Adam to be this way, and he may have wanted to shelter Adam from that thing, He knew what was wrong according to what contained falsehood, and he may have wanted Adam to know what falsehood was, but a blatant charge of what any way was, and a non-consensual shelter erected, and a perception of falsehood given him, would not have helped Adam, but would have been creating an ethic that was without genuine faith and love. For this

---

3094 Deuteronomy 8:2
3095 Genesis 2:15
3096 Proverbs 5:1,2
3097 2 Corinthians 2:16

reason God said in His heart, "Not for that we have dominion over your faith, but are helpers of your joy: for by faith ye stand."[3098]

9. In order for Adam to be the best creation that he could be, and also, in order for God to be the best Father and Physician that He should be, he taught Adam, "saying, Not by might, nor by power, but by my spirit, saith the LORD of hosts."[3099] With the creation set as an example for the nature within him, and how the core spirit of his conversation was to be transformed and educated, God instructed Adam on his duty not only to his Creator, but also to himself. To do this, God counseled Adam on the science behind His voice. He instructed Adam on the diet needed to acknowledge that voice, to the end that what that science contained, it would inhabit and imprison His voice within his own self, thus fostering an unspeakable joy retained from obeying His confidence through the willpower that he himself contained.

10. When Christ was on earth, He once taught a large group of people. An individual near Him said to Him, "From whence can a man satisfy these men with bread here in the wilderness? And he asked them, How many loaves have ye? And they said, Seven. And he commanded the people to sit down on the ground: and he took the seven loaves, and gave thanks, and brake, and gave to his disciples to set before them; and they did set them before the people."[3100] "They that had eaten were about four thousand."[3101] How did Christ feed four thousand people with so little food? The answer is in the phrase, "He commanded." This is that same Word who sat with Adam in the garden, whom God "hath appointed heir of all things, by whom also he made the worlds."[3102] This is that same Word "who is the image of the invisible God, the firstborn of every creature: for by him were all things created, that are in heaven, and that are in earth, visible and invisible, whether they be thrones, or dominions, or principalities, or powers: all things were created by him, and for him: and he is before all things, and by him all things consist."[3103]

3098 2 Corinthians 1:24
3099 Zechariah 4:6
3100 Mark 8:4-6
3101 Mark 8:9
3102 Hebrews 1:2
3103 Colossians 1:14-17

11. It was "God, who created all things by Jesus,"[3104] therefore it was this same Word who, in the beginning, "spake, and it was done; he commanded, and it stood fast."[3105] This is how His Christ could have fed that host with such little resources. Because His speech and conversation was blessed of the Word without measure, and because there is none other than that Word, what is little is in reality of no weight, and what is much, by the creative power held within His voice, can either increase or decrease. Christ, as a human being, housed within His spirit the science of His LORD from first learning of that science by faith in the voice of His Spirit. It is the voice of the LORD's Spirit that brought about and still keeps all things in their proper realm, and it is this lesson within the creation of the earth that convinced both Adam and Christ to confess, "Thou hast delivered my soul from death: wilt not thou deliver my feet from falling, that I may walk before God in the light of the living?"[3106]

12. The creation was to Adam an example of how obedience procures divine aid. As he analyzed the mind of God, he began to notice the mind working within creation, and thought, "Consider the ravens: for they neither sow nor reap; which neither have storehouse nor barn, and God feedeth them."[3107] "Consider the lilies of the field, how they grow; they toil not, neither do they spin."[3108] "Who hath put wisdom in the inward parts? or who hath given understanding to the heart? Who can number the clouds in wisdom? or who can stay the bottles of heaven, when the dust groweth into hardness, and the clods cleave fast together? Wilt thou hunt the prey for the lion? or fill the appetite of the young lions, when they couch in their dens, and abide in the covert to lie in wait? Who provideth for the raven his food? when his young ones cry unto God, they wander for lack of meat."[3109]

13. Adam began to notice a pattern. He began to observe the thoughtlessness that nature partook of due to her confidence in her

---

3104 Ephesians 3:9
3105 Psalm 33:9
3106 Psalm 56:13
3107 Luke 12:24
3108 Matthew 6:28
3109 Job 38:36-41

Creator to provide for her. Adam saw that all things not only exude an essence of faith, but that as nature worked in whatever category she worked in, somehow, and in some way, nature remained always sufficient. Adam then took his discoveries to God. "How much more are ye better than the fowls?"[3110] He said to Adam. "Take no thought, saying, What shall we eat? or, What shall we drink? or, Wherewithal shall we be clothed?"[3111] "Look unto the heavens, and see; and behold the clouds which are higher than thou."[3112] Adam obeyed. Adam put God's counsels to the test, and in return he received God's righteousness with a mind thoughtful towards His intention for the development of his mental and moral faculties. We know that both Adam and Eve did this work in an acceptable manner from how it is written, "They were both naked, the man and his wife, and were not ashamed."[3113]

14. It was to commemorate, and to let rejuvenate within the conscience, the victory wrought in the benumbed portions of Adam from his obedience, that God instituted the blessing pronounced on the seventh day. It would be utterly foolish to believe that the intention of God in creating any thing ended at creation. We would do God an injustice to celebrate the natural world without comprehending the fact that He has no thing natural in Him, for "God is a Spirit."[3114] We would violate every law of nature if only looking upon nature as the height of the power of this LORD. An observation of nature is not enough to compel the heart to worship the Creator as a Creator, for what is He Creator of if creation has ended? God created the earth, and so what? Must I now look at nature and only find the God of nature only confined to that nature? What then was the point of Him creating any thing at all? What was the point of His Son's passing and regenerating? Must I now worship God from the nature He has created? On the contrary: I must now look beyond the natural to know a God that is not flesh, but rather Spirit.

3110 Luke 12:24
3111 Matthew 6:31
3112 Job 35:5
3113 Genesis 2:25
3114 John 4:24

15. Obedient nature is but an example of what an obedient heart would become. Again, "God is a Spirit,"[3115] therefore the LORD's religion has never been natural, but rather mental and spiritual. This is why He says, "As the heavens are higher than the earth, so are my ways higher than your ways, and my thoughts than your thoughts."[3116] Nature is left, for our observation and study, to bring our heart to shame and right contemplation. The earth and the sky were not too proud to obey the voice of God, yet for a man or a woman to humble their conversation's conscience before God, it is unheard of. Throughout creation, God did not have any thing in mind other than His thinking and feeling human being. In the exact manner that health sprung up on a sick surface of the earth, God Himself sought the same for the inward portions of the members of Adam's heart and mind.

16. Herein is the tremendous ambition that God had for His child, and now hopes to accomplish through His more perfect Adam, which Adam is that Christ who He anointed as that High Priest over the will of His throne. Adam had been born with every thing in a perfect manner, and now it was Adam who had to continue a work of creation that God would not touch, but would only join into with him unless by a pure and open consent. Adam consented to the work of soul regeneration, and daily the LORD experienced a joy that filled Him tremendously. God says of Himself, "I make all things new,"[3117] therefore we can know that the LORD's joy overflowed as His new creation willingly came to Him to learn how to further exist in that newness. In every meeting and with every interaction, the LORD always told Adam, "Put me in remembrance: let us plead together: declare thou, that thou mayest be justified."[3118]

17. In this we can understand that the LORD is in fact a parent with the heart and intention of a parent, therefore His message is also for parents. Parents are but children, and their parents were once children also, therefore a parent can understand the joy of a child constantly squeezing information from them. A parent knows the joy of caring for

3115 John 4:24
3116 Isaiah 55:9
3117 Isaiah 43:26
3118 Revelation 21:5

a child, of laughing with a child, of bathing a child, clothing a child, protecting a child, feeding a child, quenching the fears of their son or daughter, and showering that child in a love that only they know best how to give. A parent also understands the pain, yet the respectable and desired result, of instructing their child in matters of right and wrong, of industry and sobriety, of cleanliness, of self-defense, and of tender regard for others different than themselves. For this reason, no parent should confine himself or herself away from the education of the living God. If we should magnify the responsibility of a natural parent seven times, we would arrive at the concern of God for us. "If ye then, being evil, know how to give good gifts unto your children: how much more shall your heavenly Father give the Holy Spirit to them that ask him?"[3119]

18. "The ordinances of heaven"[3120] are to become the new diet of the reformer, even that regimen centered on "the ordinances of justice."[3121] It is this diet that God designed Adam to rigorously maintain by an ever advancing faith in His commandments, and in the creative power of His voice to continually elevate the inward portions of his being to match that of His. As God saw the earth in its original deplorable state, only He knew and understood the depth of the conformity of a decrepit earth into a habitable land. Seeing what He saw, and embracing all that He had to embrace concerning the invisible materials of life combining to form visible patterns of equitable substances, and understanding what He did not create in man, but what man had to embrace and practice within himself through faith in His name, our LORD and Father knew what awaited the human heart when it should apply to His voice. He knew that from such a work, the heart needed a moment of rest.

19. Six days man should work the garden of his heart and add more materials to the house of his character, and when God observed what He had observed from the earth and the atmosphere working to do what He thought it should, He knew that His obedient son and daughter, who also sought to daily die to self that they may learn of His heavenly will, needed to quit for a little season that He may then refresh, and further

3119 Luke 11:13
3120 Job 38:33
3121 Isaiah 58:2

recover, the energies of their soul and mind. This is why it says, "On the seventh day God ended his work which he had made; and he rested on the seventh day from all his work which he had made. And God blessed the seventh day, and sanctified it: because that in it he had rested from all his work which God created and made."[3122] Being a partaker of creation, it is not that God did not learn any thing about creation. He gained knowledge of the hard experience of soul conversion for the new species of being that He should create, and He learned much of the trial that man should endure in relation to his inward members. This is why He says, "Put me in remembrance and come to me. 'Why are ye fearful, O ye of little faith?'"[3123]

20. The seventh-day Sabbath is a Memorial concerning the height of the power of the LORD's Word, and the blessing pronounced to the obedient and willing soul who will cooperate with that counsel for creation. His Sabbath is a testimony to the Spirit's goal within "the word of righteousness"[3124] "whereof ye heard before in the word of the truth of the gospel."[3125] Individuals who are obedient to this Faith will receive entrance into the Sabbath of the living God. All can keep free the seventh day of the week, yet it should be considered that the seventh day would be no day at all if not for the Institution held to it. One can keep the seventh day and never know the blessing contained therein. Keep not the traditions of men, but "remember the Sabbath day, to keep it holy."[3126]

21. Tradition will water down the seventh day to be kept without teaching an understanding as to why, while throughout the week, the work to receive the reward of the Sabbath is not once touched. The seventh day holds the Sabbath institution of the only LORD God. To remember the Sabbath, one needs to remember the operation of His hands. When that operation is considered, and is even faithfully and carefully experimented with, then the seventh day will be no tradition at all, but it will be the highlight of the activities of the week and a

---

3122 Genesis 2:2,3
3123 Matthew 8:26
3124 Hebrews 5:13
3125 Colossians 1:5
3126 Exodus 20:8

new breath to the personal experience. It will no longer be that, every seventh day I quit all things that I perceive to be ungodly according to the memory I have of my mother and father, but rather it will be that every Sabbath day, that blessed seventh and final day of the week, I will spend time with the God who has been fashioning my mind and person into His Son's likeness these past six days. Six days have I sought to watch self, to educate self, to remain in communion with God and not with my self, to cultivate a culture of learning, of self-denial, of moral development and of intellectual enlargement through heavenly communications, and now on the seventh day I quit all labor. I rest in the bond of the blessing of my God to keep my spirit, and to heal my understanding, in a way more sufficient than any other day. Blessed, in fact, is the seventh day!

22. No other day serves the purpose of God, nor does any other day reflect the intention of God concerning the regeneration of sinful man to Himself. There is foolishness in following tradition, whether it is right or wrong, without investigating the fact of the activity. When one inclines themselves to reverence the first day of the week for any thing, they are making a basic statement that God did not properly finish creation, that His thoughts and intentions are irrelevant, that He is no Creator at all, and that His creation is better served creating itself. It is to confess that there is more knowledge in self than there is in God, for what is the subject of the first day? "God said, Let there be light: and there was light."[3127] "And the evening and the morning were the first day."[3128] To celebrate the first day as any thing is to celebrate "light." And this worship reaching deep into "the depths of Satan."[3129]

23. The mind of Satan is after the saying, "Hath God said, Ye shall not eat of every tree of the garden?"[3130] This is the "light" of the one "transformed into an angel of light."[3131] When speaking of "light," it is better understood as the "light" of *knowledge*, or rather, as "science

---

3127 Genesis 1:3
3128 Genesis 1:5
3129 Revelation 2:24
3130 Genesis 3:1
3131 2 Corinthians 11:14

falsely so called,"[3132] "where the light is as darkness."[3133] Thus, the foundation of this heritage teaches to undermine the authority of the LORD's Word, to trust in self to know all *things*, and to retain a knowing that satisfies to the pleasure of the mind of the flesh, never counting that what is retained is actually destroying the force of life within the being. The premise for taking on such a practice is, as he says, "Your eyes shall be opened, and ye shall be as gods."[3134] When speaking of eyes, it is better understood as "the eyes of your understanding."[3135] This is the religion of Satan, and the first day *memorial* of such a practice is based upon "the lust of the flesh, and the lust of the eyes, and the pride of life,"[3136] eroding from the inwards a good faith and conscience.

24. "All that is in the world, the lust of the flesh, and the lust of the eyes, and the pride of life, is not of the Father, but is of the world. And the world passeth away, and the lust thereof: but he that doeth the will of God abideth for ever."[3137] The will of God endures just as long as His seventh-day Sabbath endures, for the two are wound tightly together. The will, and the new promise of God concerning reconciliation and sanctification, cannot be accomplished outside of the standards that He has erected. The practices of that false angel teach otherwise. Any willing disobedience is in fact disobedience, and there is open disobedience against the everlasting laws of the LORD's Spirit. A first day sacredness is in fact as imaginary as Satan's power over the conscience blessed by heaven's will and doctrine. Satan is a dead and defeated enemy that exists in death; so are all things proceeding from him, which is why it is well to remember how it says, "T sting of death is sin; and the strength of sin is the law."[3138] A first day tradition falls under the category of a legal religious law and handwritten ordinance, and is therefore blatant "sin" against heaven's Faith. We need to know that "the prince

3132 1 Timothy 6:20
3133 Job 10:22
3134 Genesis 3:5
3135 Ephesians 1:18
3136 1 John 2:16)
3137 1 John 2:16,17
3138 1 Corinthians 15:56

of this world is judged,"[3139] his sentence is death, and if we do not know that we serve "death," we may understand that we do by the *sabbath* of his sentence. "Never shalt thou be any more,"[3140] says the LORD of the serpent's philosophy by the passing flesh of His Christ on the tree; we need to know this.

25. The plan for the disobedient angels, and for their captain, is a loss of conscious existence for ever. This is the direct end that the first rebel spirit against the LORD's name wants for every one joined to it. And because Satan has never openly announced any of this, but rather works through human instruments, what is the end of the institution that devotes their practice to him? The Spirit says, "They shall defile thy brightness."[3141] Who will destroy this institution in full? Who defiles the glory of Satan's craft? It is written, "The Lord cometh with ten thousands of his saints, to execute judgment upon all, and to convince all that are ungodly among them of all their ungodly deeds which they have ungodly committed, and of all their hard speeches which ungodly sinners have spoken against him."[3142] At this later hour, the Spirit's vengeance for His name "shall be revealed from heaven with his mighty angels, in flaming fire taking vengeance on them that know not God, and that obey not the gospel of our Lord Jesus Christ: who shall be punished with everlasting destruction from the presence of the Lord, and from the glory of his power."[3143]

26. Notice that these individuals suffering this wrath fail on two points: they know not the living God, neither have they obeyed the Word's will and course. These are them who have spoken against His name, and if against His name, then against His voice. If they speak against His voice then they speak against the credibility of His authority to be reverence. If they see no thing valuable in Him to be reverenced, this means that to them He is no God at all, and they in fact see themselves as gods. If they see themselves as gods then they are partakers of the various practices of liars, are but rebellious towards the name

---

3139 John 16:11
3140 Ezekiel 28:19
3141 Ezekiel 28:7
3142 Jude 1:14,15
3143 2 Thessalonians 1:7-9

and honor of God, and the operation of His hands. And if this is so, then classed among them that "might be damned who believed not the truth, but had pleasure in unrighteousness,"[3144] are them that upheld and preached the keeping of the day of unrighteousness, even a first day superstition. These do not know God in spirit and in truth, they know not the sanctifying and refreshing commandments of God, nor have they surrendered themselves to allow the Spirit of God to write those commandments within their inward parts, which is the root of the foundation of salvation's science. This is why they will suffer the same fate as that spirit of error and its followers.

27. Because this prophecy has not yet occurred, the time is ever before us to know and to keep both the commandments of God and the Faith of His Son. "See then that ye walk circumspectly, not as fools, but as wise, redeeming the time, because the days are evil. Wherefore be ye not unwise, but understanding what the will of the Lord is."[3145] God blessed and sanctified the seventh day for a reason, and that reason was to commemorate a celebration for the conversion continued every week in Him. This is the Memorial of the living God who in heaven said, "I AM THAT I AM,"[3146] and who on earth said, "Before Abraham was, I am."[3147] This is that day celebrating the fact that it was God who carried us throughout the week of our toiling with self, and not ourselves. This is that day of joy concerning a stronger relationship with both the Father and the Son born from the events of the week within the heart. This is that day confessing, "Know ye that the LORD he is God: it is he that hath made us, and not we ourselves; we are his people, and the sheep of his pasture."[3148]

3144 2 Thessalonians 2:12
3145 Ephesians 5:15-17
3146 Exodus 3:14
3147 John 8:58
3148 Psalm 100:3

39

Refrain From Working

1. Christ's entrance into "the temple of the tabernacle of the testimony in heaven"[3149] in the year 1844A.D. signaled a change in His ministry. "The judgment was set, and the books were opened"[3150] against them that willingly followed Him into that new Room, even as His reformers of old had to follow Him into the first Room of the Temple by their faith. What separates this current Apartment from the first is that, today, every soul joined to the heavenly congregation of the Spirit's High Priest is under an investigative judgment. So what may be one thing the LORD His Father is judging among individuals who profess loyalty to the Faith of His Son? The commandment states: "Ye shall do no manner of work: it shall be a statute for ever throughout your generations in all your dwellings."[3151]

2. What is interesting to note is that, even though the earthly priesthood under the Mosaic dispensation has ended, this is a perpetual statute of the Spirit for the Church of His High Priest. This means that whoever is the LORD's high priest, wherever his congregation currently is, this statute is ever applicable, seeing as how being servants

---

3149 Revelation 15:5
3150 Daniel 7:10
3151 Leviticus 23:31

of this same very LORD God of ancient Israel, every charge from His voice is sustainable throughout any and every one of His generations. Who then is His Faith's current high priest? It is written, "Christ glorified not himself to be made an high priest; but he that said unto him, Thou art my Son, to day have I begotten thee,"[3152] and, "Christ being come an high priest."[3153] If in fact we profess love for the Faith of this LORD's Spirit, then we cannot profess love to His name without honoring the name of His Temple and Priest. If we love the Priest and Son of the Father, then there should be no refusing to acknowledge the LORD and Father that priesthood serves. The Father, not His Son, has issued a perpetual statute to be respected for His generation through the blood of His Son, and for the congregation under His High Priest, to regard.

3. Concerning the duty of His Christ, the Father confessed to the tribe of Judah, "Out of thee shall come a Governor, that shall rule my people Israel."[3154] Thus, when the Father raised His Christ from the grave, what was confined to the earth received a new structure, and what was but a pattern of perfection was translated to our LORD's heavenly Temple to complete the image from which that pattern derived its essence. A shift occurred in both the priesthood and in the institution of the living God when this Christ "sat down on the right hand of the Majesty on high."[3155] This is why Paul says, "For the priesthood being changed, there is made of necessity a change also of the law (the law of the priesthood). For he of whom these things are spoken (for "they that are of the sons of Levi...receive the office of the priesthood"[3156]) pertaineth to another tribe, of which no man gave attendance at the altar. For it is evident that our Lord sprang out of Juda; of which tribe Moses spake nothing concerning priesthood. And it is yet far more evident: for that after the similitude of Melchis'edec

3152 Hebrews 5:5
3153 Hebrews 9:11
3154 Matthew 2:6
3155 Hebrews 1:3
3156 Hebrews 7:5

there ariseth another priest, who is made, not after the law of a carnal commandment, but after the power of an endless life."[3157]

4. It was the Father's intention to "gather together in one all things in Christ, both which are in heaven, and which are on earth,"[3158] and this He did "when he raised him from the dead, and set him at his own right hand in the heavenly places."[3159] These "places," plural, signify the Place where His Christ ascended to, along with the Order that He was to pick up. The Father anointed Christ to "be a merciful and faithful high priest in things pertaining to God, to make reconciliation for the sins of the people."[3160] This Christ is the only High Priest of the Spirit's Faith over the only Temple of the living God, and His priesthood is, as Paul says, for the sins of the people; what people? If God has literally ended all things on the earth, what people are currently receiving the benefit of His heavenly priesthood? If the LORD has brought up His Christ to His throne, but our mind is yet on the earth, who then may be joined to His heavenly Church? Hear the blessed revelation given to us by the apostle: "The Father, which hath made us meet to be partakers of the inheritance of the saints in light: who hath delivered us from the power of darkness, and hath translated us into the kingdom of his dear Son."[3161]

5. Just as the Father translated His Christ to Himself, so too by our faith on the virtue of Christ's sacrifice, the Father will translate us "unto the adoption of children by Jesus Christ to himself, according to the good pleasure of his will."[3162] The apostle tells us that by our faith on the certainty of our atonement to His Spirit by the blood of His Son, we are adopted into His Royal Family to begin creation's course. There is therefore no excuse in stopping the ear from hearing any one of God's commandments, for our faith has allowed us entrance into the bloodline of Israel, and because of Christ the saying is fulfilled, "The number of the children of Israel shall be as the sand of the sea, which

---

3157 Hebrews 7:12-16
3158 Ephesians 1:10
3159 Ephesians 1:20
3160 Hebrews 2:17
3161 Colossians 1:12,13
3162 Ephesians 1:5

cannot be measured nor numbered; and it shall come to pass, that in the place where it was said unto them, Ye are not my people, there it shall be said unto them, Ye are the sons of the living God."[3163] Let us then, if we profess the LORD's Christ, cease stubborn ignorance to acknowledge a faith that moves the limbs of the body by love to purify the soul. Every law uttered by the mouth of God is literally and officially mandated for obedience by every faithful soul resting on the blessed hope purchased for them by Christ.

6. With it now understood, without any debate, that the Spirit's heritage is secured to Him by His Christ, thus binding every current perpetual covenant and law ratified by the mouth of His LORD to every soul born to Him, it is yet not answered as to who the people of His congregation are. By adoption, the believing reformer is translated into the reign of His Christ's mediation mediation, but who are these adopted individuals? Should they not even be as their Captain is? It is written, "He took on him the seed of Abraham."[3164] Christ took on Him Abraham's seed, and Abraham; in proper context of language; is not Abraham. Abraham was no member of any of the tribes of Israel, and to simply say that Christ was born of the line of Abraham takes away the apostle's point. Abraham is a symbol representing a mind, a disposition, and his seed is representative of a doctrine or understanding. Christ honored the Father "through the righteousness of faith,"[3165] that is, through the "faith of Abraham."[3166] It was His faith that allowed the Father to dwell within the spirit of His conversation; it was His faith in the Father while in the grave that allowed the Father to resurrect and to glorify Him; and by our faith in the Father, His Spirit will do the same for us. He will translate our conversation's conscience into the reign of His Son's name as we prove the will of that name.

7. This is why the apostle counsels, "Believe on him that raised up Jesus our Lord from the dead,"[3167] and why Christ Himself teaches, "He that heareth my word, and believeth on him that sent me, hath

---

3163 Hosea 1:10
3164 Hebrews 2:16
3165 Romans 4:13
3166 Romans 4:16
3167 Romans 4:24

everlasting life."[3168] Obedience to the sayings of Christ is the means for the human being to fall into the hand of the One that resurrected Him from the dead. Scripture confirms concerning Christ, "Being put to death in the flesh, but quickened by the Spirit,"[3169] and, "God raised him from the dead."[3170] To say that God raised Christ from the dead is better understood to mean that it was the Spirit of the LORD His Father that raised Him from the dead. Thus, the apostle confirms: "The Spirit of him that raised up Jesus from the dead."[3171] It is this same Spirit of the Father who translates our inward person, or rather, recovers the spirit of our mind "by the washing of regeneration, and renewing of the Holy Ghost,"[3172] to dwell within His heavenly House by faith on the voice of His Son. There is no such thing as calling Christ God without acknowledging the Father, and there is no such thing as calling the Father God while refusing to acknowledge "salvation through sanctification of the Spirit and belief of the truth."[3173]

8. This is exactly why, in this season of judgment, the Spirit Himself has issued a statute that says: "Ye shall do no manner of work: it shall be a statute for ever throughout your generations in all your dwellings."[3174] What is the work that He speaks of? This "work" is better understood from a question asked by the Preacher: "What profit hath he that worketh in that wherein he laboureth?"[3175] Work is labor. Working is placing self in a position where there is a performance of manual labor. To work is to physically carry on operations, whether severe or moderate, within any business that one may be engaged or employed in. To work is to toil, to strain, to mold or to manufacture by action, labor, or by violence, and because the commandment is not literal and dwells on no temporal matter, "the law is spiritual."[3176] To be terribly clear, what is utterly forbidden at this time, and what warrants imme-

---

3168 John 5:24
3169 1 Peter 3:18
3170 Acts 13:30
3171 Romans 8:11
3172 Titus 3:5
3173 2 Thessalonians 2:13
3174 Leviticus 23:31
3175 Ecclesiastes 3:9
3176 Romans 7:14

diate death to the eyes; as the Spirit says, "Whatsoever soul it be that doeth any work in that same day, the same soul will I destroy from among his people";[3177] is found in the counsel, "To him that worketh not, but believeth on him that justifieth the ungodly, his faith is counted for righteousness."[3178]

9. The Spirit counsels against individuals establishing devotion to Him through "the works of their hands."[3179] The work that is spoken of is a labor to obtain righteousness by either "the commandments and doctrines of men,"[3180] or by "the imagination of the thoughts of the heart."[3181] Any thing that may make the heart believe its devotion is pure from some tradition, whether cultivated or inherited, goes against the principle the apostle tried to get the Christian elders to understand, namely, that "God imputeth righteousness without works."[3182] The personal religion is to be regulated by no outward form, but is to learn sobriety from exercising faith on the Spirit's power and wisdom. This is what the current season of atonement is. The spirit is to retain the Spirit's wisdom from a living experience to prove the validity of the sacrifice of His Christ, for, by proving the certainty of His name, the sensibilities will retain knowledge concerning the full will of His Father. It is God's intention to sanctify the soul and spirit by His Spirit when once there is a willingness to apply every mental, moral, and physical limb to the sayings of His Christ. To accomplish this sanctification by means outside of the prerequisite experience is the definition of "work."

10. This is why He says, "Ye shall do no manner of work."[3183] Concerning that word "manner," to get a better understanding of it, we read, "One law and one manner shall be for you."[3184] A manner is a religious law, and the Spirit specifically counsels against reverencing any law establishing righteousness. It is therefore time to quit any manner

---

3177 Leviticus 23:30
3178 Romans 4:5
3179 Revelation 9:20
3180 Colossians 2:22
3181 1 Chronicles 29:18
3182 Romans 4:6
3183 Leviticus 23:31
3184 Numbers 15:16

surrounding "days, and months, and times, and years"[3185] contrary to the voice of the living God. For example, the world honors a pagan feast attributed to some thing on the first day of every week, and even while it is yet confessed, "God blessed the seventh day, and sanctified it."[3186] Sunday sacredness is a law establishing righteousness, for its observance was appointed by unsanctified and unconverted men under a spirit of self-righteousness to further public favor. Being appointed by men, there is no righteousness in it. There is righteousness in no thing not pronounced of the LORD's voice, which is why it says, "All thy commandments are righteousness."[3187] Who will find the commandment of God to be unrighteous but them that love to work righteousness? "I hate every false way,"[3188] say them that have surrendered their religion to Christ's righteousness, for in His name is no thing contrary to the LORD His Father. Thus, "Great peace have they which love thy law: and nothing shall offend them,"[3189] writes the Psalmist.

11. It is time quit honoring falsehood, and to begin examining self to know, and to overcome, personal and devotional error. The Spirit's heritage continues through, and is perfected under, the supervision of His High Priest. When once the Spirit of God is allowed to fully operate within the heart, as opposed to the heart operating itself, the religion of God will be known. The day blessed and sanctified by this LORD; His seventh day; will be known to them who are blessed and sanctified by the same Spirit that sanctifies this day. For, Scripture says of these that know Him, "Them that are sanctified by God the Father."[3190] Who may continue to claim His Christ while rejecting that appointment, established by His own voice after creation, that testifies to an honest conversation with His Spirit? This is even that Sabbath that He Himself partook of to know the blessing held to it for His Adam, for it says, "The LORD made heaven and earth, and on the seventh day he

3185 Galatians 4:10
3186 Genesis 2:3
3187 Psalm 119:172
3188 Psalm 119:104
3189 Psalm 119:165
3190 Jude 1:1

rested."[3191] There is no thing in the LORD's Bible that testifies to any perfection found in falsehood, but rather it is strictly advised against. God Himself is examining His Household, and He will know who will be willing to learn how to unlearn violence to confidently say, "I may know him, and the power of his resurrection,"[3192] and, "With the mind I myself serve the law of God."[3193]

12. "Days, and months, and times, and years"[3194] that leave one "subject to ordinances,"[3195] is proof of this fact: "The carnal mind is enmity against God: for it is not subject to the law of God, neither indeed can be."[3196] The Spirit reports, "They have done violence to the law,"[3197] for there is a strange adherence to "bondage under the elements of the world."[3198] His laws are forgotten because bondage is accepted. Did not Christ offer Himself that every soul may quit the foolishness of the religious age to know the living God personally? Is it not written that He sought to "deliver them who through fear of death were all their lifetime subject to bondage"?[3199] Christ's sacrifice, when accepted, frees individuals from the useless ordinances of priests and elders, opening up a way for the conversation's conscience to retain His mediation's pure instruction. How then is His sacrifice turned into trash through faithlessness? We, who would honor mother and father, brother and sister, comrade and pastor, above the living experience that is required to enter into the presence of the LORD and His High Priest, are we exempt from the rebuke, "They crucify to themselves the Son of God afresh, and put him to an open shame"?[3200]

13. The longer we refuse to let obedience reign by the fact of the commandment made plain to us, we are but crucifying the Faith that we say is our confidence. Christ's entrance into the second Room of the

---

3191 Exodus 31:17
3192 Philippians 3:10
3193 Romans 7:25
3194 Galatians 4:10
3195 Colossians 2:20
3196 Romans 8:7
3197 Zephaniah 3:4
3198 Galatians 4:3
3199 Hebrews 2:15
3200 Hebrews 6:6

heavenly Temple signifies that this is now the time to learn how to stop crucifying His body of knowledge, and to cease putting His name and faith to shame, by exercising the free and unlimited power of the Spirit given to us. No manner of work is to be accomplished if the Spirit is to correctly recover the spirit of the mind. If no manner of work is to be accomplished, this means that the soul is to be drawn out to the Spirit's course alone. Christ has ratified our atonement to His Father's Spirit, this is true, but the fact of the matter does not end here. This is the time to know the Spirit that we are atoned to. There is now ample provision given to know the light of the knowledge of soul recovery and reformation, and to receive these blessings from acting out the learned precepts of the Faith of His Son. May every soul then know the name of both the Father and the Son, for when the spirit is hidden in the righteousness of His Christ, every law of His Father's mouth will be written on the heart by the finger of His Spirit.

14. There is no need to force a righteousness that is already freely given by faith's course, but rather "seek ye first the kingdom of God, and his righteousness; and all these things shall be added unto you."[3201] If we care to be converted to the Faith of His heavenly Temple, then it must not be forgotten, "The law of the LORD is perfect, converting the soul."[3202] No thing of man, and no thing within self, can administer heaven-appointed and heaven-approved conversion. God by His Spirit personally regulates every godly conversation. Obedience to every one of the Spirit's commandments is the means for a proper conversion, but how is this so? We are counseled, "As many as I love, I rebuke and chasten: be zealous therefore, and repent."[3203] Obedience to any counsel of the Spirit will allow the heart to rightly comprehend the tone of His voice and the binding responsibility behind the commandment. Such a realization will cause the soul to burn in pain, thus compelling the spirit, after being "filled with the knowledge of his will in all wisdom and spiritual understanding,"[3204] to soberly repent for the

---

3201 Matthew 6:33
3202 Psalm 19:7
3203 Revelation 3:19
3204 Colossians 1:9

stubborn mind that was bound to it in ignorance. This is why it says, "The commandment of the LORD is pure, enlightening the eyes."[3205]

15. The Psalmist writes, "The statutes of the LORD are right, rejoicing the heart,"[3206] for it is good and well for our personal faith to learn of and do the judgment of His Son's intercession. There are many obvious manners of "work" established by ministers and by self through customs and ordinances without the mind of the Spirit, yet the manner of the first day tradition is here mentioned as an example of an established religious bill to nurture self-righteousness, thus nurturing every other falsehood within the practice to withdraw the mind from entering into the light of heaven's will and understanding. The Word blessed the seventh day for a perpetual covenant for all who care to learn of Him through His Son's name, but what does it mean that He blessed this day? The angel told Mary, "Blessed art thou,"[3207] and, "Thou has found favour with God."[3208] The seventh day is favored of the LORD's Spirit, and that favor is not removed, and never can it be removed; this is why it says, "Thou blesses, O LORD, and it shall be blessed for ever."[3209] This is why He calls this day, "My holy day,"[3210] and, "The holy of the LORD."[3211] This Sabbath celebrates the LORD's name, for it was His Spirit that blessed the seventh day after He completed creation, even as it says, "The LORD God made the earth and the heavens."[3212] This is that same LORD and Spirit that Moses counseled Israel on when He said, "To morrow is the rest of the holy Sabbath unto the LORD."[3213]

16. This LORD, is He Jesus the Christ? Notice how Scripture says, "LORD God," and now notice how it says, "As I live, saith the Lord GOD,"[3214] and, "Unto GOD the Lord belong the issues from death."[3215]

3205 Psalm 19:8
3206 Psalm 19:8
3207 Luke 1:28
3208 Luke 1:30
3209 1 Chronicles 17:27
3210 Isaiah 58:13
3211 Isaiah 58:13
3212 Genesis 2:4
3213 Exodus 16:23
3214 Ezekiel 18:3
3215 Psalm 68:20

There is obviously more than one God mentioned by Scripture. As opposed to an all capital LORD and a lowercase God, we now have a lowercase Lord, and an all capital GOD. To One; that GOD; all issues from death belong to Him, but also, concerning Him, it is written, "Ah Lord GOD! behold, thou hast made the heaven and the earth by thy great power and stretched out arm, and there is nothing too hard for thee."[3216] Moses in Genesis records the LORD as the Creator, but Jeremiah records the Lord GOD as Creator; is there an error? Returning to Genesis, we read, "And God said, Let us make man in our image."[3217] The LORD God and the Lord GOD were both at the creation of the world, and the phrase, "Let us make in our image," allows us to perceive this fact. Because it was "God, who created all things by Jesus Christ,"[3218] He to whom all death belongs was the Creator, which is why it is well to know how it is written, "In the beginning was the Word, and the Word was with God, and the Word was God."[3219] It is this same Word that accomplished the thoughts of the Father by the name and power of His LORD's voice, allowing us to understand that the seventh day Sabbath is for ever bound to the LORD His God. For, through this same Spirit of the LORD, "All things were made by him; and without him was not any thing made that was made."[3220] Therefore, if we care to lawfully keep creation's feast by the name of His Son, it is well to know that "we which have believed do enter into rest,"[3221] "for he spake in a certain place of the seventh day."[3222]

17. Every soul born to the LORD through His Spirit will know His dialect, and no soul born to Him will reject the joy of reverencing His seventh day's appointment. Did not even Christ counsel, "That which is born of the Spirit is spirit"?[3223] And did not the apostle counsel, "Hereby know we that we dwell in him, and he in us, because he hath

3216 Jeremiah 32:17
3217 Genesis 1:26
3218 Ephesians 3:9
3219 John 1:1
3220 John 1:3
3221 Hebrews 4:3
3222 Hebrews 4:4
3223 John 3:6

given us of his Spirit"?[3224] Note the prerequisite of divine adoption that explains how His Christ's name hides us in the Spirit of His LORD: "The Spirit itself beareth witness with our spirit, that we are the children of God."[3225] For this cause, every law without the Spirit is falsehood. The manners of the religious world do the living God and His living Christ an injustice, for as natural human beings, we will place self as god if not found at the throne of God. Any thing contrary to a law established by the Spirit's Word, and whatever does not bear the seal of the name of the Father, and whatever is not perfected by the virtue of His Christ through the wisdom of His heavenly intercession, is a lie constructed by "them that walk after the flesh in the lust of uncleanness, and despise government. Presumptuous are they, selfwilled."[3226]

18. It will do well for every soul drawn out to the Spirit's Priest to learn a reform on personal diet, and to stay from what destroys the soul. Must we forget, because of fear, or for a vain and presumptuous stance against the living God, how it is written, "In the beginning was the Word, and the Word was with God, and the Word was God. The same was in the beginning with God. All things were made by him; and without him was not any thing made that was made"?[3227] In His Christ, "the Word was made flesh,"[3228] which Word created all things, and even situated a blessing on the seventh day to remember Him by, for without Him there would be no thing. Should we forget how He says, "If I wash thee not, thou hast no part with me"?[3229] Who then is willing to let self be washed by Him? Who is willing to pick up His mind? This is that same Christ who "was come from God, and went to God,"[3230] so must we ignore the work of coming to God by the sayings of this Christ? Must we ignore the fact that His heritage does not begin with Him, but with the LORD His God, who is also our Father through adoption if we

3224 1 John 4:13
3225 Romans 8.16
3226 2 Peter 2:10
3227 John 1:1-3
3228 John 1:14
3229 John 13:8
3230 John 13:3

accept the illustration of Him on the tree? Must we forget how He says, "He that receiveth me receiveth him that sent me"?[3231]

19. "By the washing of regeneration, and renewing of the Holy Ghost,"[3232] we will have our part with His Son's name and course of learning, and we will know both the Father and the Son. Without surrendering to this divine washing, the human being will work some form of this washing; it will then not be so hard to discount the authority of every word of the Spirit over the personal religion. This is why He counsels, "Ye shall do no manner of work: it shall be a statute for ever throughout your generations in all your dwellings,"[3233] and, "If a man love me, he will keep my words: and my Father will love him, and we will come unto him, and make our abode with him."[3234] This language that Christ uses is drawn specifically from creation, in that it was agreed upon in the beginning, "Let us make Adam in our own image."[3235] Cultivating a spirit of self-denial and self-sacrifice to gain "knowledge of salvation"[3236] will result in the accomplishment of the Spirit's will, even the creation of His own creature. The reformer is "to be strengthened with might by his Spirit in the inner man"[3237] that a new conversation devoted to the Word should be born. This is the Spirit's intention by counseling His creatures to refrain from working a religious experience, for that experience should exist in all confidence on His name "through the faith of the operation of God."[3238]

3231 John 13:20
3232 Titus 3:5
3233 Leviticus 23:31
3234 John 14:23
3235 Genesis 1:26
3236 Luke 1:77
3237 Ephesians 3:16
3238 Colossians 2:12